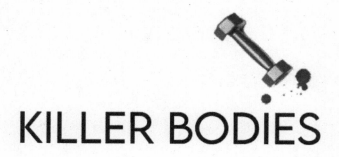

KILLER BODIES

HELEEN KIST

To my favourite Doodle of all

PROLOGUE

The glazed doors to the gym were propped open. From here, on the twelfth-floor landing, you could not yet see the bodies.

Evie counted her breaths and stood motionless, forcing the flow of people to go round, like a boulder in a river.

A woman in a dark blue trouser suit strode towards her, emanating the kind of authority that underscored they knew what they were doing. She frowned and scanned the full length of Evie, oozing the unsettling suspicion of airport security with a glove on.

'I'm Detective Inspector Ansford.' A terse smile. A click of her pen. A flip to a new page in her spiral-bound jotter. Rapid, efficient movements. 'What's your name?'

'I'm Evie Stirling. I'm the receptionist here in the residents' gym.'

Evie caught a glimpse of dark green trousers. How many ambulances would they have sent?

'Do you need a paramedic to look you over?' Ansford asked.

'What? No. I'm fine. I'm just...'

'Miss Stirling, I appreciate you will be in shock after today's events. I'm quite happy to let you go home to recover. You can give your statement at the station tomorrow. But can I ask you one thing?'

'Uhuh.'
'Do you have any idea who killed all these people?'
'No,' Evie lied.
And if pressed, she would lie again.

Two days earlier

CHAPTER ONE

Evie

'So, who will you kill today?' Mrs M asked, reclined on the sofa behind Evie, her voice raspy from the latest coughing fit.

'You'll see when I'm finished, you nosy woman.'

Sat on the floor, Evie felt the sofa shudder against her back as Mrs M chuckled. She smiled and doodled on, a notebook perched against her bent legs, the first few pencil lines already converging into a human shape.

But the shaking didn't stop, and the laughter morphed into a series of dry hacks. Evie's ears pricked. She turned and looked up. Breathless convulsions jerked Mrs M's torso from the armrest as she stifled another cough, bursts of smoke escaping from clenched teeth. Her grey curls leapt like zappy springs.

Evie's pulse quickened, her limbs primed to rise.

Mrs M shook her head and waved as if to stand Evie down. Tears slithered into the creases around her eyes. She patted her chest, releasing a last puff, and managed to reach for the crystal ash tray before the bowed cinders of her roll-up risked burning a hole in the tartan blanket draped over her legs.

'I'm fine,' she croaked. 'I'm fine. Unless you're drawing *my* death, of course.' She winked and stretched out again.

Evie noticed a faint flush linger on Mrs M's cheeks; a pink her pallid skin could do with more—though preferably without the choking. 'Are you sure?' she asked.

'Stop fussing, girl. Draw.'

Evie sighed. It was hardly fussing, but she'd learned through many rolled eyes and helping hands smacked away that Mrs M didn't suffer sympathy well. Besides, Mrs M always said that when she goes, it will be with a bang (cue jazz hands). This would merely count as a whimper and definitely wouldn't do.

When Mrs M started humming, and her feet wriggled to the beat of the music from the radio, Evie relaxed. She grabbed the notebook that slipped off her knees during the commotion and got to work again, taking care to capture the chosen victim's haughty snarl perfectly before she plunged the weapon into her. If only she'd remembered to sharpen the pencil. The tip was too dull to get the blood spatter right.

A few bars into the second tune, Evie recognised *I'm on My Way* by the Proclaimers. It was hard not to, when you're from Edinburgh. Evie swivelled to the floor-length penthouse window and gazed out at the darkness. Like in the song, sitting on top of the world.

A sliver of a crescent moon peeked from under a thick cloud, exposing black shapes with twinkly lights on tall masts bobbing along the vast expanse of the Firth of Forth. On their way, *aha aha ahaa*.

Where to?

Evie wondered where she'd head off first if she ever got the opportunity of real travel—not that there was much chance of that with her pitiful wage.

Mrs M had been everywhere. Evie glanced at the wall opposite the sofa, taking in the mammoth rectangular frame crisscrossed with wooden slats that showcased travellers' keepsakes in little compartments.

Vials of sand in shades from tropical white to mud brown stood interspersed by miniature figurines: heavy-thighed clay women with sagging breasts, a wiry twine man, a small fez, a felt donkey. Enamel jars with scented balms to ward off malicious spirits, a wax-sealed flask said to eradicate evil men. Evie liked the teensy bottles best. Their pointy, speckled corks looked like they could pop up any minute, spilling the water from all the planet's rivers and seas onto the carpeted floor of this apartment in Newhaven.

Sixty-eight trinkets. Endless experiences.

Evie's mind cast to when she first saw them. She'd been heading home at the end of only her third shift. As the lift doors opened onto the lobby, she was met by a giant, wobbling cardboard box that fell to the ground to the sound of 'Shit'. She'd gasped in surprise when she saw who'd said it: an old lady, dressed in a drab beige outfit of twin set and trousers, her oversized earrings the only hint of the colourful character Evie would find inside.

'Who are you?' the woman had asked.

'I'm Evie, from the gym.'

She'd raised a perfectly plucked eyebrow and said, 'Do you work out?' in a tone you'd expect from someone checking you out in a pub.

Thinking the old bird's mind might not be all there, Evie spoke slowly, enunciating as best she could. 'No, I am the receptionist in the residents' gym. In this building. See?' She pointed at the logo on her jacket.

'Good God, girl. I'm not the slow one here. I thought you'd get the hint.' She kicked the box. 'Muscles. I need help with this blasted parcel.'

'Oh.' Evie laughed and bent down to push the package into the lift. She stepped inside. 'What floor?' A confused frown creased Mrs M's brow. Evie tapped a finger on her temple and said, 'Maybe I'm too thick, but my guess is that if you need help going in, you'll need help coming out.'

The old woman's opal-painted lips had curled into a wicked smile. 'Touché.'

Admiring her friend's collectibles now, their exact placement and vivid stories since memorised, Evie couldn't remember when or how it became a habit to come here after work. Hanging out for about an hour. Complaining about the other residents. Eating all the biscuits when they got the munchies. It was nice to be with someone who didn't think you were a freak for a change.

'Come on, let me have a peek.' Mrs M poked Evie in the shoulder with gnarly toes, the seam of her tan tights like a thick rope holding the flakes on the yellowed nails in place. Such a difference to the immaculate fingernails others got to see; the manicured hands of an accomplished businesswoman. Her lungs wheezed as she took another drag of the thin, white joint.

Evie smirked. The woman was incorrigible.

Mrs M bent forward and exhaled a thick cloud of earthy, herbal smoke that practically enveloped Evie's head. 'Want some?'

'Nah. Not today. I'm going out after,' Evie said. She put the finishing touch to her caricature and handed over the notebook. 'Here.'

Mrs M shrieked. 'It's Beatrice! I'd recognise that poufy hair and scraggly neck anywhere. But Jesus, what the hell did she do to you to deserve a pen in the eye?'

'She took my pen.'

'That hardly calls for—'

'No, wait for it. She waltzed in mid-morning, grabbed one of the feedback forms to write God-knows-what petty grievance on, and snatched my pen. Straight from my hand. And then... she put it in *her mouth.*'

'Oh, that's not on. Burn the witch,' Mrs M said, scowling and lifting an arm as if holding a torch. She swivelled round and patted the sofa for Evie to join her. 'She's a horror, that woman. Always walking around like she owns the place.' Mrs M cocked her head, examining the picture intently. 'I don't know what our bossy Beatrice would mind more: that you killed her or what you did to those thighs.'

A fat belly escaped Evie's lips. 'I think she got off lightly, all things considered. Particularly compared to the last one.'

'When she borrowed the tampon?' Mrs M asked, grinning.

'Yes. I mean, who does that? Her apartment is only downstairs. And it wasn't even the first time. Like I'm her personal dispensary.'

'Show me.'

Evie took the notebook and flipped through its pages of motley illustrations. 'Now let's see... When was it?' She tested her memory, navigating past small practice sketches she'd made in minutes snatched between life's demands and the more elaborate manga stories she drew at the weekend. 'There you go, four weeks ago.' She ran her hand over the cool, white paper to press it flat.

Mrs M howled with laughter. 'Look at those entrails flying all over the place. And that surprised face among the flames.'

As she took in the sight before her, it dawned on Evie she might have gone a step too far with this one. An explosive tampon was a gruesome weapon, even by her dark standards. Still, it was only a bit of fun. A way to get rid of inner frustrations from the residents treating her like crap. No harm done.

Mrs M wiped her eye. 'If I didn't know you had a lovely boyfriend, I'd worry about your fixation on crotches.'

Evie stiffened. 'What do you mean?'

'Don't you remember? Stephen. On the exercise bike. You drew a big knife coming out of the saddle. Split him in half.'

A flush invaded Evie's cheeks. 'Oh God. I did, didn't I? I completely forgot about that.' She nodded at Mrs M's joint and quipped, 'Perhaps I need to lay off that stuff for a while.'

Mrs M took a demonstratively long drag and exhaled. 'Ah. By all means. More for me.' She pulled her legs up and slunk them behind Evie on the sofa. She laid her head back on the armrest, eyes on the ceiling. 'Just please don't stop bringing it.'

Evie scooched aside and placed the blanket over Mrs M's thighs. How vulnerable she looked. Evie wondered how long she had left. Years, surely? She was only seventy-something. Then again, it was only months ago that she'd been full of beans, hips swaying, legs kicking to the sound of a swing orchestra. Evie smiled as she remembered tripping over her two left feet, Mrs M intent on teaching her a complicated Lindy Hop she would never need. Mrs M was so vivacious that to this day Evie wasn't completely sure whether her story of needing weed for pain relief, but the doctor refusing to give it, wasn't an elaborate con to get her hands on drugs without risking her reputation.

'Remind me,' Mrs M said. 'What was Stephen's heinous crime to deserve such a punishment?'

'He's too sweaty. He never cleans the gym equipment after working out. It's gross.'

Mrs M's nose wrinkled. 'My husband was a sweaty man. I certainly don't miss that.' She sighed and closed her eyes. Evie got up and stuffed the notebook in her satchel. Mrs M grabbed her wrist. 'I'll have a word with the building manager to get a tampon dispenser put into the gym. I'm not happy with the garden maintenance. I arranged to speak with him anyway.'

'Lucky you.' Evie pulled a face and swung the bag over her shoulder. 'He's ordered me to stay late tomorrow to help with some meeting.'

'Sorry. That's my fault. It's an owners' association meeting, and I figured since we need people to actually attend this time, we should have a bar, serve drinks. I don't think it will take very long.'

'That's fine. I could do with the extra cash. I wish Arsehole Alan would have asked nicely instead of slotting me in through the app without even checking my schedule.'

Mrs M lifted her head and gave Evie a hard stare. 'Do you want me to take care of him?' she said, in a mobster's Italian American accent.

'Ha ha. No thanks. I'll manage. No need for a horse's head in the bed quite yet.' Evie checked her watch. 'I'd better go.'

She took hold of the knob at the same time as the front door opened, forcing her to take two steps back. Mrs M's daughter marched in, her white blouse crisp under a navy suit jacket. 'Oh, hi.'

'I was leaving,' Evie said.

Anna sniffed the air and rolled her eyes. She strode past Evie to the living area shouting, 'Mum, you can't keep doing this. You're a terrible influence on that girl.'

As Evie pulled the door to a close behind her, she heard Mrs M cackle and say, 'I can assure you, darling, it's quite the opposite.'

Cheeky cow.

CHAPTER TWO

Evie

Evie's smile faded when she waved a wrist in front of the lift's call panel and it didn't respond. She sighed. What was the point of having all these super high-tech features in the building if they didn't work half the time? Okay, she conceded as the lift doors opened, 'half the time' might be a tad unfair, but it did feel like all the sensors were slower to respond to the bracelet lately. Perhaps her device was running out of battery? Alan had never explained that part.

She shuddered at the memory of that first day: the building manager's stale coffee smell as he leaned in to help set up the app on her phone. His dry, calloused hands holding her wrist to slip the sensor bracelet on. The way he'd spoken too close to her ear, his breath moist on her neck. 'It opens everything you're authorised to open.' He let his eyes drop to her chest with a leering grin. 'It can *lock* doors, too.' She'd made a point of never visiting his office again.

Less than a minute later, the doors parted on the ground floor. Evie rearranged her bag and took a deep breath. Her eyes adjusted to the sharp lights of the large, minimalist lobby, casting the almost blue shade of white that reminded her of the toilets in clubs.

She walked past the wall of copper-fronted lockers that let the postie deliver parcels while people were out. A pile of Amazon boxes lay on the ground by number 8's locker.

Must be full. There were always parcels lying about. Where she lived, they'd be nicked in no time. No chance here, she thought, gazing up at the green light on one of a zillion wall-mounted cameras. It's easy to trust each other when there is security everywhere.

The tall, glazed automatic doors opened inward as she approached, exposing her to a blast of November air. She raised her collar and braced herself, head lowered, to face the chill. As she stepped outside and veered right, she stopped short of colliding with a dark blob, low down.

She jumped back and saw it was someone in a trench coat, bent over awkwardly, jerking sideways. A homeless person? Nerves tingled in her neck. Long dark hair flapped in the wind. Who was this? A woman. Evie swerved around her.

'It's not over yet, I'm telling you.' The woman's face sprung up, wincing, a phone to her ear. She hopped on one leg. The free hand was tugging at her shoe, its heel caught in the cobbles. She spotted Evie and made an exaggerated eye roll, tongue out.

Evie chuckled; remembered her. She'd come in for her induction in the gym only a few weeks earlier. Sam? Suzy? No. An Asian name. Suki, that was it.

Evie pointed at the shoe and to herself, offering Suki a questioning look. Suki beamed and nodded. Evie bent forward and nearly toppled over as Suki leaned on her back—without asking—while she tried to dislodge the stiletto, careful to not damage its red sole. One more tug. Success.

Suki slipped her foot back in. She straightened, gave Evie a big smile and a thumbs up, then turned to the building entrance, screaming into the phone, 'If you don't get this done, I swear to God, I will kill you.'

Evie was glad she wasn't on the other end of that line.

She walked on, hands in her pockets. It wasn't even seven o'clock, but the darkness and the isolation of this water-front block of high-rises gave her the heebie-jeebies. Platinum Peak. Black hole, more like. No one in sight and a half-mile walk to the bus stop.

A gust of wind slapped her sideways as she strode past the gigantic courtyard. She steadied herself on the iron fence. The barren branches of the single tree in the middle quaked and twisted in the whistling vortex moulded by the three buildings surrounding it.

Further up, the muted lights from the arched windows of the Loch Fyne restaurant offered a welcome reassurance she was nearing civilisation.

She quickened her step. At the corner, she heard the diesel rumble of the double-decker bus approaching and sprinted to the stop. She couldn't miss this one. She was already too late to change clothes before meeting Kaif.

Taking her usual seat near the rear, she fished the note-book from her satchel, a pencil wedged between its pages. She sketched the courtyard tree, its branches elongated and curved into menacing claws, a small child on the ground, staring up in horror.

'Daddy.' A girl's voice. Evie looked up.

Two seats ahead, on the other side of the aisle, she saw a pink bobble hat. 'Daddy, look.' Evie leaned forward. The girl must have been six or so. In her tiny hands, a notepad. Her blue polka-dotted wellies pressed against the seat in front, her legs functioning as an easel. On the page a multi-coloured animal that was probably meant to be a magical unicorn. The father's bowed head suggested he was engrossed in his mobile phone. 'Uhuh, that's great,' Evie heard him say, his head never moving. Her heart sank. For all their shortcomings—and there were many—at least her parents had paid attention.

Flipping the page, Evie began a new drawing, hoping she'd finish before the pair got off.

Soon after, the blue sign of the chippie flashed into view, heralding her destination. She quickly added the last touch to her sketch: a large bow on top of the girl's head. She admired her handiwork and smiled. Not bad for something so different from her usual themes.

The museum setting was obvious, achieved with only a few strokes indicating a wall of paintings. She'd drawn the little girl stood in front of an assembled crowd, pride shining on her face. In her palm a thick, tasselled cord that was attached to a curtain, pulled aside to reveal the girl's wonky unicorn inside an opulent frame. Her masterpiece.

Evie ripped the page out and got up. 'Here, for you,' she said, using her good hand to give the drawing to the budding artist. She didn't wait for a reaction, but her stomach fluttered at the girl's small gasp on the way out.

The warmth of the pub was a welcome relief, even if it did come with a heavy dose of body odour. Evie took off her beanie hat and scrunched her hair. She spotted Kaif and his friend from college, Martina, at a table close to the bar, a set of empty glasses next to their full pints. A packet of crisps split open for sharing. Served her right for being late.

'There she is,' Martina said, her ridiculously blue eyes shining behind a candle. 'The almost birthday girl.'

'Hey babe.' Kaif pulled out the chair beside him and puckered his lips.

'Hey,' Evie said after a quick smooch. 'What's going on?' Did she see a flicker of panic in Kaif's eyes? Or was it the candle?

'I will get you a drink,' Martina offered, a hint of a Polish accent peeping through in the R. 'The usual?'

'Yes, thanks,' Evie said. 'My round next time.'

Martina waved her away. 'It's fine.'

Evie bristled. Everything was always fine with Martina. She never had a mood, never had a bad day. Always laughed at your jokes. Kaif's jokes, in particular. Generous to a fault. Probably her only fault, Evie reckoned. Was it any wonder Kaif liked to hang out with her, still?

Kaif took Evie's hand. 'You're cold.' He cupped it and blew. 'How was work?'

'Nothing exciting. They've brought in some new fruity health water for the residents to trial. All exotic flavours. They even had lychee.'

Kaif pulled a face. 'Ugh. Lychees are snot balls.'

'One guy gave me a hard time when I was unpacking. Moaning there was only one mango and that, because of allergies, it's the only one he can drink. I mean really, like I'm responsible for deliveries.' She paused. 'By the way, any post today?'

'Sorry, I didn't check.'

Another day made it another week, no, another month of no news. She rubbed the tight, scarred skin on her left hand. The insurance pay-out would make such a difference to their plans. They'd be able to leave their tiny studio apartment.

'Here's your Dead Pony,' Martina said, sitting down. 'I thought I'd try a Nanny State. It's alcohol-free. I've got more code to write tonight.'

Evie took a slug of her ale. 'Mrs M says thank you for your help, by the way.'

'Oh, it was nothing.' Martina flicked her long brown hair over her shoulder before taking a sip of fake beer. 'A simple issue of channels interfering with each other on the Wi-Fi.

Plus, she had some nasty malware on her computer. She was very annoyed because she got it from one of her businesses and expected they would be better with security. She is a funny old lady. You should have seen her eyes pop when I explained about the dark web.' Martina raised her glass. 'She also paid me way too much. So, cheers.'

'She can afford it,' Evie said, raising her own. 'Actually, Kaif, she wants another *delivery*.'

He nodded.

'Speaking of money, my team leader got shouted at today by the big boss,' Martina said. 'Maybe I will get a promotion next.'

Her cold stare took Evie aback. Not all sunshine and light, after all. 'What happened? Was it bad?'

Martina pulled a face. 'Who knows? Did you fight with anybody at work today, Evie?'

Kaif gave her a stern look.

'Wh-what?' Evie said.

'Kaif told me about your drawings of the residents in your building. I would love to see them.'

Heat rose along Evie's neck. Kaif averted his gaze. How could he? 'I don't have my notebook with me,' Evie lied.

'Some other time maybe.' Martina's face was bright with hope. 'I'm sorry I won't be able to congratulate you on Saturday itself.' Her eyes darted to Kaif. 'I have work.'

Evie's senses prickled.

'But I got this for you. For inspiration.' Martina bent over and pulled a present from underneath the table. It was wrapped in gold paper, with a small, glittery blue tag on it.

'I'm... Wow... Okay. Thank you,' Evie said, accepting the package. Her hands dropped with the weight of it. She put it on the table and read the tag.

To Evie, the artist. From your friend Martina.

Evie sensed a blush forming on her cheeks. 'Thank you, but I'm hardly an artist.'

'Don't say that. I have seen the tattoos you have designed on your arms. They are scary, but very... how do you say? Evocative. You have a talent, and you should use it.'

'Yeah well, doodling doesn't pay the rent.'

Kaif nudged Evie's shoulder. 'Open it.'

Feeling all eyes on her, Evie gently tore off the wrapping. Her heart jumped. She flipped over the hard cover of the graphic novel to double check... It couldn't be. 'The collector's edition Uzumaki. I can't believe it. How did you—'

Martina clasped her hands together. 'Oh, I am very happy you like it. I wasn't sure, but Kaif explained what you liked was called manga. The darker the better.'

Kaif swung his arm around Evie and kissed her on the forehead. 'My little ray of horror.'

CHAPTER THREE
Suki

Suki pressed the button marked *12* in the lift and took off her coat, raindrops dripping on the metal floor. She'd need to be careful not to slip; her ankle remained sore from when she got stuck in the pavement the day before. It didn't help that she'd had to rush from her city-centre office for this meeting. Five-thirty? Really? Did these people not work?

She was in the middle of a huge corporate finance transaction and could do without this hassle. But the message in the building's app had said attendance at the owners' association meeting was mandatory. It had better be worth it. Having had to hobble for the bus, it was a miracle she was only five minutes late.

When she stepped out, the gym's frosted glass doors were closed, completing the glazed wall's serene image of a field of sunflowers. Nothing like a bit of faux nature in a high-rise to make you feel zen. Noise rose from inside. She waved her armband in front of the sensor and decapitated two flowers as the panels parted.

'Shoes off.' The male voice startled her as she entered. The building manager rushed over, his brown shirt stretched over a sizable belly.

'What?' she asked.

'No heels on the gym flooring.'

She looked down at her shoes and the imprint she'd left behind her on the spongy green mat. 'Fine,' she said through gritted teeth. She spun away. No way would she give him the satisfaction of seeing she'd end up eye-to-Adam's-apple when the heels were gone.

'No chair?' he barked.

'No manners?' she replied, with a fierce stare.

He retreated a step. 'Sorry. You're meant to bring a chair.' He cocked his head to the main area of the gym and raised his hand, holding a stack of brown plastic circles.

She followed his gaze. The reception desk was covered in white towels and functioned as a makeshift bar. Plastic cups in hand, people milled around five wide rows of chairs. Brown disks placed under all the legs. How ludicrous. Wouldn't it have been easier if someone had hosted this meeting in their apartment? Not that hers could fit this number; it was merely a two bedroom. But the penthouse or perhaps other ones that wrapped around three sides of the building.

'Next time, put that in the message.' She scowled.

'Hey, don't look at me. Anyone can post.'

Oh joy. Just what she needed: the prospect of people's inane domestic issues cluttering her phone. Come to think of it, hadn't there been a notification of a missing parcel earlier?

'Gather around everybody.' A forty-something woman with poufy hair and a ruffled red dress waved to the chairs. 'We're going to start.' She walked to a table at the front and, to Suki's horror, erected a flip chart with the help of a man in a suit.

Suki waited as the residents took their places. She'd need to slot in somewhere. She recognised a politician, not by name—that wasn't her world—but from TV, remembering his ruddy cheeks and outraged spittle. She wondered what size apartment a Scottish parliamentarian's salary would stretch to.

As they sat, Suki spotted a yellow Swiss ball. She rolled it over and perched her bum on it, next to a muscular man at the end of the middle row, whose extended leg had obstructed her moving further forward. Suki tsked internally. Take all the room you need, why don't you? At least he smelled nice. Cotton fresh.

He noticed her and shifted his bum a smidge. 'Apologies, I'd give you my seat but—'

'It's your chair.' Suki shrugged.

He looked her over like they always did: all the way down, most of the way up, pause, then face. 'I'm Dave. Dave Barr. Apartment 8A,' he said, holding out his hand.

She took it. 'Suki Aksornpan.'

'New?'

'Uhuh.'

'Welcome to the house of fun,' he said, nodding to the flip chart.

Suki smiled. She knew he was being sarcastic, but the truth was she couldn't believe her luck. She'd be the last one to credit 'the universe' with anything, but it had been like a sign when the apartment became available at the same time she'd received a big fee from selling her friend's start-up. This cutting-edge development had been in her sights for ages.

Suki admired the Louboutins resting on her lap. With the seller in a huge rush to move elsewhere, she'd even managed to achieve a great price, leaving money to spare. Sucker. The woman's hapless solicitor had been no match for Suki's negotiation tactics. Long live a Stanford MBA.

She chit-chatted with Dave for a while, who made a groan-worthy superstitious joke about the building having thirteen floors. Red dress up front clapped her hands. 'Can we get some quiet please?'

Dave whispered, 'That's Beatrice. 11A. Best avoided.'

Beatrice remained on her feet. The hubbub subsided. 'Thank you. I'm glad to see you all here, as the owners' association has an important matter to dis—Oh.' All heads turned to the rear. 'Er... Alan. This is a closed meeting. We'll call you in when it's time to clear up. Thank you. Shall we say an hour?'

A groan ran through the crowd.

The building manager's eyes narrowed. He pressed his lips together, nodded curtly and left, shooing the receptionist-slash-barwoman-slash-shoe-saviour out of the space as well. Suki made a mental note to ask her name next time. It hadn't registered when she got the gym induction.

Beatrice wiped her hands over her dress and laughed nervously. 'Well, that could've gotten awkward with agenda item one. I'm afraid we're continuing—'

She stopped again, this time noticing the suited man sitting by her side. 'We're continuing discussions about the *Alan situation*... But we can move along to item two, which is the development.' She grinned broadly and gestured to the visitor. 'We are joined today by a representative from SMBSLT Property Developments Limited.' She sought his eye. 'Did I get that right?' He nodded.

'That's a bit of a mouthful,' Dave whispered to Suki.

'Bet it stands for Some Mediocre Builder Selling Lame Transformations.'

Dave snorted. A big, loud, probably painful snort that made the couple in front of them turn around and shush.

With that and holding the meeting here, Suki reckoned there was no love lost between the residents. She scanned the room, curious about the dynamics. She'd read up on some of them, but who was who? Her gaze rested on the old lady with the big earrings up front. That one was easy.

'As I was saying...' Beatrice had raised her voice. It must have hurt, as she took a big swig of her wine glass. She cleared her throat. 'We've been asked to consider the proposal to sell part of our courtyard for the construction of a new multi-use property. It's important to say at this point that no decisions will be made today. There would need to be considerably more information before we can take it to a full vote. However, S-M-B... the developer would like us to give them an indication of our appetite for this before they spend too much money on the preparatory work.'

She sat down and the man sprung up, as if on a seesaw. 'Thank you.' He lifted a large architectural drawing from the table and attached it to the flip chart with bulldog clips. 'Don't worry, I don't expect you all to see the detail. It's merely for me to point.' He handed a stack of A4s to the front row and introduced himself as the sheets were passed around.

Suki didn't need to listen to his presentation to understand the ramifications of their proposal. People with windows on the courtyard side of the building would end up with an obstructed view. While the apartments on the first four floors would suffer most—basically peering directly into the neighbour's windows—those higher up would be looking down on a roof. And no amount of rooftop AstroTurf would make up for losing real grass and the lovely courtyard tree.

On the other hand, anyone with a smidge of real estate nous would know that the addition of a café and retail space on the ground floor was going to have a very positive effect on the whole estate's desirability—and therefore value. View versus money, which would it be? Easy choice for those with windows facing the other directions.

She examined the handout. They'd drawn the remaining garden with optimistic, blooming flowers. Pretty in spring, yet it didn't take away from the fact the residents would be left with only a slip of outdoor space. It wasn't as though she ever got time to use it, but the idea of a garden was nice. And you had to have outdoor space for a child—if she ever found a wife to have one with.

Her mother's gleeful voice popped into her head, calling her name, '*Sukhon*.' Next, Mum's face, tinted pink by the reflection of the lanterns dotted around the Fragrant Orchid, shining with delight at whichever date or friend Suki brought in for her to fuss over. Suki groaned internally, picturing her cackles and winks, the dreadful, unsubtle signals she hoped this guest would be the one to bear her the greatest gift of all: grandchildren. If it was up to her mum, Suki would've been shacked up years ago. Then again, if it were all up to her, Suki would be managing the family restaurant, not on track to make a killing.

A rustle of paper made her pay attention again. The man was unclipping his poster. 'In conclusion, we hope that you will consider the proposal in a positive light. We at SMBSLT firmly believe this is a great opportunity for us all, and I will happily take any questions.'

'Interesting.' Dave said to her when the last question had been answered.

Suki checked out the others' postures for signs. She figured most people would've immediately decided. So had she, of course.

Beatrice took the floor again. 'All right everybody, settle down. What we're going to do next is vote *in principle* to accept or reject the proposal. Remember, this is informal, and you can always change your mind later once they submit the full plans and we hold the official vote. As a reminder, the association's articles state we need seventy-five percent.'

She picked up a notebook and a pen. 'Does anybody object to doing this by show of hands?... No? Good. One vote per apartment. What?' A murmur at the front. 'No Fiona, the size is irrelevant.' She sighed deeply. 'Show of hands in favour...'

Heads turned and murmurs grew among the group. Beatrice scribbled the count down. '... and against?' She took a note, frowned, then turned to the man. 'Well, I'm not sure we've got everybody, but I believe you've got enough buy-in to proceed.'

'I didn't see you vote,' Dave said to Suki. 'Jury still out?'

'Something like that.'

As people got up and battled with tangled chair legs, Suki's stomach stirred in excitement. She'd now seen all her targets' faces.

Chapter Four

Evie

Evie's bum felt numb on the stone step. Her neck was stiff from resting her head against the wall in the stairwell, waiting. Her back ached from being hunched over. She untangled the elaborate knots she'd made in the laces of her trainers and started over. Criss-cross, loopedy-loop. So, so bored.

Bloody Alan had chased her out of the gym without giving her a chance to snatch her bag or phone. At least he buggered off straight away. Thank heavens for small mercies—even though she was left to tidy up alone when the meeting was over. She yawned. If it would ever be over.

A cacophony of voices gave her hope. The gym doors parted, and the first lot spilled out. She stood up. The polyester uniform trousers crackled on her thighs. Mrs M waved and headed up the one flight to her penthouse.

The other residents started lining up in front of the lift, chairs in hand. Trust them all to happily spend an hour sweating in the gym but not to dream of setting foot on the stairs. Even Dave, Mr Body Builder himself, the size of a house and with the kind of thick, veiny neck that often made her wonder if he was on steroids.

Evie pressed herself flat against the wall to let Charles and Fiona pass. They didn't acknowledge her. No change there. She took pleasure from the fact they might not care to know anything about her, but she knew all their in-securities. The things you pick up from watching people exercise... Charles, in particular, appeared desperate to win the battle against the middle-aged spread. Hundreds of sit-ups to keep his abs with a semblance of firmness. Fiona got away with less, blessed with better genes. Better teeth, too. Almost American. One of those huge, straight, white smiles—not that Evie had been on the receiving end of many.

'I'll take Pebbles out. It's raining,' she heard Charles say.

'Thank you, darling. I'm tired,' Fiona replied. Typical. Never the one to take actual responsibility for their pam-pered 'Baby-boo.' She often saddled Evie with the tiny white pooch, like it was the most normal thing in the world. Not only was it not Evie's job, but who brings a dog to the gym?

Pebbles sat cradled in Charles's arms, an oversized tartan bow on his head like the bone on his Flintstones namesake. A bone would frankly have made more sense.

Evie bet the pup hated that bow. She'd be willing to bet he wasn't too keen on Fiona, either, using him as a prop and perpetually foisting him onto others. Like her.

Evie suppressed a grin as she remembered her first mur-der. After a morning in which Pebbles had been a real nui-sance, darting in between her legs all the time when she had stuff to do, she'd drawn Fiona in the floatation tank, dark protective goggles on, oblivious to Pebble's paws about to press down on her shoulders to drown her.

Since then, the doggie had grown on Evie. She'd folded two yoga mats into a makeshift bed, and he generally lay quietly by her ankles—as long as she tickled him on the belly occasionally.

Evie slunk along the queue to return to the room. 'Excuse me... Hi... Sorry... Hi... Have a good night... Sorry.'

Inside, she surveyed the damage. Not too bad. Beatrice was continuing to talk to the developer man up front. Evie started by tidying her desk, placing empty bottles and cups in a bin bag. A towel lay on the ground; someone's half-arsed attempt at cleaning up a spill, judging from the gluey glister on the mat.

A high-pitched screech made Evie jump. She saw the suited man, startled, holding an unsteady Beatrice by the elbow, while straining to balance the flip chart in his other hand.

Beatrice's eyes bulged. 'Evie, will you take these sodding protective disks off the floor, please? I nearly broke my neck.'

'Yes, sorry.'

Left alone, Evie was able to get on with her tasks. It was late, and she wanted to go home. At least she was off the next day. She pictured a nice birthday lie-in, breakfast in bed, the works... which included a naked Kaif. Her cheeks warmed. She wondered what he'd bought her; hoped he hadn't spent too much. Maybe they could go grab a movie in the afternoon?

She cleared the last of the stuff away and whipped under the desk to get her bag. She frowned. It had been knocked over. And what was that parcel lying by the wall? Her belly fluttered. Could it be an early present from Mrs M? She knew Evie wouldn't be in tomorrow.

Her excitement wilted like a shrivelled balloon as she grabbed the box and saw it was addressed to Stephen in 2A. He must have forgotten it. The purple logo of a showy brand of sportswear was plastered on the side. Made sense. He always had the nicest kit. It only ever shone brightly, too, as if he had a magic washing machine to soak up his excessive sweat. She spotted the sleeves of her own jacket, the original white dulled to off grey, the green stripe furry like a caterpillar wriggling down her arm.

When she could finally leave, she stepped onto the landing feeling every inch a bag lady: her hair greasy, armpits icky, her satchel on one shoulder, the bin bag at her feet and Stephen's box tucked under an arm. She locked the gym doors with the app, turned to a brushed metal square on the opposite wall and waved her armband. The door to the rubbish chute popped open, and she threw the black bag in. Of all the cool gizmos in the building, this was the best. She didn't know where the waste went and didn't care.

She took the lift down and walked along the elegant corridor until she reached 2A. She knocked on the door; didn't like the way the bell was connected to a camera. She looked like crap.

Stephen opened, his forehead raised in surprise—to the extent the Botox allowed it. 'Evie?' His top two shirt buttons were undone, a sheen on his skin reflected the overhead spotlight.

'Sorry to disturb you. I found this.'

He eyed the box. 'Ah, I've been looking for that. It was marked as delivered yesterday.' As he reached out to take the box, Pebbles scuttled into view, barking. Stephen froze.

Another male voice rose from the rear. 'Pebbles, come here baby, we need to—' Charles, who'd been fidgeting with his belt as he entered the lounge, dropped his hands and stood still at the sight of Evie. 'Oh.'

Pebbles sniffed at Evie's trainers, tail wagging, happy as Larry. An urge to run away overcame Evie, but she worried the dog would follow. And then what? A white heat flushed the back of her neck.

Stephen scooped the dog up. He and Charles exchanged anxious glances. He bit his lip as he searched Evie's face. 'Could you...?'

'I-I. Um. It's fine,' Evie said, retreating. 'I wasn't here... Pretend I don't exist.'

She fled down the corridor, to the sound of her phone's ring tone emanating from her bag.

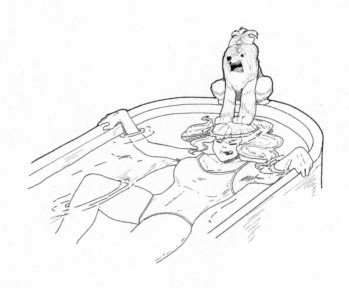

CHAPTER FIVE

Evie

'Happy birthday to you. Happy birthday to you,' Kaif sang softly into Evie's ear.

She pulled the pillow over her head and groaned. 'Too early.'

'You have to get up, love. It's seven.'

Evie curled deeper into the duvet. What she'd give for a few more minutes...

Kaif stroked her head. 'Come on. Get showered and I'll have your birthday breakfast ready for you.'

Thoughts of his sweet, syrupy pancakes washed away the residual resentment of having been ordered into work after all. There had been no arguing with Alan when he called the night before. The other receptionist was sick. It was up to her.

She stretched and discharged a tentative bare foot into the cold room.

When she later came out of the shower, the fresh smell of apple shampoo mingled with the buttery scent of baking. Her mouth watered. She flung on a clean polo shirt and trousers while watching Kaif scoop the pancakes onto a plate.

He slapped the worktop, and she sat down on one of the stools. She reached over and unplugged her phone from where it had been charging overnight. Kaif flipped the switch on the wall socket. Ever since her accident, he'd become a stickler for fire safety. Charging cords couldn't be left dangling with the socket on and he'd nagged her more than once about keeping the phone plugged in while they slept. A single spark could ignite the whole studio, he'd said. Evie felt a tad bad. She kept forgetting. He'd even made the point that it wreaked havoc on the battery life, but that was something she'd already learned the hard way. It didn't really matter; she kept the phone off inside her locker at work, anyway. After some anonymous complaints of tinny music escaping from people's earphones and aggravating fellow exercisers, the owners' association had decreed no phones were allowed in the gym, not even for staff.

Kaif sprinkled a handful of blueberries onto the pile of yumminess. 'Ta-dah.'

Evie's chest filled with warmth. He'd gone to such an effort. How lucky was she to have a boyfriend who cooked? She had his mum to thank for that, passing down the family's Pakistani recipes, turning him into a completely self-sufficient man so that, as Kaif told it with an exaggerated accent, '*he would choose a capable, educated girl, not one who would only cook and clean up after him*'. Evie hoped that when the time came to meet his family, she'd be good enough.

'Thanks, babe,' she said and tucked in. Her phoned pinged. As she chewed, she read a birthday message from her sister. Out of habit, she switched to the building app. 'What the...?'

'What's up?' Kaif asked.

'The Platinum Peak app has the gym marked as closed. But there's no notification to explain. I will kill Alan if he made me get up for nothing.' She swiped her fingers across the keyboard, composing a text message.

Hey Alan. Am I to come in today?

A reply came within seconds.

FFS it's early. Yes.

Evie sighed. 'Well, that clears things up—not.' She slipped the device in the front pocket of her bag.

'What time will you be done?' Kaif asked.

'I'm not sure. It's probably another glitch in the app. So, the usual, I guess.'

'But you'll keep me posted? Can you text me by lunchtime?' he asked, to Evie's mind looking a bit cagey.

'Yes... But what are you up to?' Evie grinned.

He blinked a few too many times. 'Nothing. Only... Your present isn't here yet.'

Burying her face in her orange juice, Evie tried very hard to hide her disappointment. 'That's okay. This breakfast is great.' She saw his lips curl slightly, a dimple forming in his chin. The rat. 'You *are* planning something, aren't you?'

He broke into a broad grin. 'That would be telling.' He leaned over the countertop and kissed her on the sticky lips. 'You're going to have the most amazing day ever. I promise.'

CHAPTER SIX
Evie

Evie folded the letter up and slipped the thick paper back in the envelope. The bus's vibrations rumbled through her as she rested her head against the window. Tears bubbled up. She should never have checked the post on her way out. She should never have opened it. Not on her birthday.

All that waiting... For nothing.

She scrunched the letter into the pocket of her work jacket. Bastards. She sniffed. Of course they were going to win. Of course they wouldn't compensate her for the burn she suffered in her last job. Of course the insurance company was going to go along with her past employer's lies. Had she truly expected anything different? People like her didn't get justice. Or a break.

Much as she hated the gym job, it had been the only one she found. People didn't want someone with an ugly, deformed hand helping them, handing them goods or money—let alone food. Not that she'd ever choose to work in fast food again. She massaged the unnaturally smooth skin on her hand, the memory of the burning oil ingrained in every scarred line.

If only she'd gone to college like Kaif. But she wasn't smart enough. No, she was destined to spend her days in uneventful stagnation in the sweaty confines of an airless gym. Birthday after birthday—until how old?

Condensation clouded the glass in ever-expanding swirls as she breathed. Her head ached from the sobs she made herself hold in. No need to make a public scene.

At her stop, the bus shuddered to a halt.

'Thanks,' she said to the driver, testing whether she could speak to another human without the floodgates opening. The answer was no.

The winter cold slapped her face as she got off, her cheeks stinging where the tears froze in their tracks. She took in a large gulp of seaside air. Beside her, the grey water lapped at the harbour walls. Dark ripples on a dreary morning.

So much for *'most amazing day ever'*.

As she neared the entrance to her building, she heard a child's cries. The doors swung open, and a harassed-looking woman stepped outside, pushing an overloaded pram, bags hanging off every side. Inside, a toddler bundled up like the Michelin man. He kicked and arched his back, wrestling against the restraints, small fists raised in infant insurgence.

She locked eyes with him, the kid startled mute by her presence. But soon the fury erupted again, howls and screeches of outrage—the outward manifestation of all Evie felt inside.

In the lobby, she spotted what was behind the tantrum: a half-eaten cereal bar on the floor, its crumbs dispersed like an abandoned trail. She picked the rubbish up and placed it in her pocket, then kicked the crumbs to the side wall.

As she rode up the lift, she was faced with her reflection on the metal surfaces. A right state. She licked her finger and wiped the mascara from under her eye. She primped her hair, her straight fringe sweeping across her forehead. She thought of today's letter. The worst had happened. The only way was up.

Kaif:
Hey. She's gone. Are you ready for later?

Martina:
Not quite. I have some coding to get done
Don't worry. Everything will go to plan

CHAPTER SEVEN

Evie

The gym lights came on instantly when she waved her wrist in front of the sensor pad, and the doors parted. Last night's stale smell of alcohol made her stomach turn. She couldn't even open a window. An entire wall of floor-to-ceiling glass overlooked the water, but no way to bring in air.

She dropped her stuff on the desk. The crumpled letter fell to the floor, and she placed it in the drawer. Didn't want to see that again—not today. She'd share it with Kaif tomorrow. No point ruining whatever he had planned with the dream-shattering news.

At the lockers, she lifted her satchel and held the flap under her chin as she searched for her notebook. It wasn't there. How very odd. Evie couldn't remember when she'd seen it last; her attention had been diverted to Martina's gift.

She grabbed the heavy graphic novel and swiped her armband to lock her belongings away before getting to work.

As she pulled out the chair from behind her desk, she found a blue-striped plastic bag. Where did that come from? She'd been the last one out the door after the meeting.

It held a box of tampons. Alan must've caved into Mrs M's demands. She chuckled, imagining his reaction at having to deal with 'women's stuff'.

She rummaged through her drawers for the ceramic bowl she knew was in there somewhere, then displayed the goods by the sink in the women's bathroom, like she'd seen done at the library. She looked forward to telling grabby Beatrice to sod off next time.

On her return, she saw Charles come in, Fiona by his side, Pebbles trotting at their feet. Fiona wore a loose-fitting T-shirt and jogging trousers, a far cry from last night's pashmina. Evie sighed. No sign of a dog lead in their hands.

Charles mumbled, 'Hello, Evie,' his eyes downcast.

'Good morning,' she replied cheerily, trying to send a comforting signal. He'd probably been bricking it all night, wondering what she'd do, who she might tell. He needn't have worried. It wasn't her business. They'd always made it quite clear she was merely part of the furniture.

Watching his wife march to reception, leaving him in her wake, Evie wondered if sometimes he felt part of the furniture too.

'I've got the floatation tank booked for 11 a.m.,' Fiona said, 'but if the gym is going to close, then I'd like to have my soak now.'

'What do you mean, close?' Evie asked.

'Didn't you see?' Fiona pulled out her phone and showed a notification from the building app.

Gym will close at 10.30 a.m. due to plumbing and electrical works. Residents will have a limited window in which to make use of the facilities.

'No, I didn't get that. But it explains a lot.' Evie went to her desk and shook the mouse to wake the screen. 'Give me a minute. I'll check.'

While waiting for the calendar to load up, Fiona rearranged the business cards, leaflets and feedback forms on the raised, see-through part of the desk, next to the promotional display of cosmetic products. Impatience oozed from every pore.

'You know what?' Evie said. 'I'm sure it will be fine. On you go.'

'Good,' Fiona said, then tapped a finger on the glass.

'Oh, yes, sorry. A towel.' Evie swivelled towards the cupboard. There was only one towel in there and the packet of ear plugs she handed Fiona was also the last. Her stomach sank at the thought of having to talk to Alan for supplies. But at least it looked as though she'd be able to go home earlier than expected. A weight lifted. Perhaps it was all in her mind, but it seemed like the skies outside had lightened, too.

'Thank you.' Fiona took the things and pointed at the base of the table. 'Pebbles, sit,' she said. Just like that, without even asking.

Evie clenched her jaw. 'Oh Fiona? Remember to lock the door this time. We wouldn't want a repeat of last month.' She suppressed a smirk watching Fiona's flustered face before the selfish woman turned into the left corridor leading to the dedicated massage and floatation rooms.

Evie returned to her post and stroked Pebbles, subtly guiding him into a comfy corner under her desk. 'There you go. You be good and stay here.'

When she stood up, Beatrice had slipped past reception. She was headed for the bathroom at the far end on the right, holding a towel that looked distinctly like those belonging to the gym. Evie reckoned she'd go straight for a steam bath or sauna.

Charles had climbed onto the second bike of the row that occupied the middle of the large gym area. Deep in concentration, selecting a programme on the dashboard. Evie noticed he glanced at the clock on the wall more than once.

Pebbles snuck out and nudged her ankle. Evie scratched the thick tuft of hair between his eyes. His bubble-gum-pink tongue darted over his black nose, but she felt in no mood to entertain him. She lifted him up and walked to Charles.

'There. Why don't you stay with your daddy?' she said. Charles looked up in surprise. Emboldened by the palpable shift in power following the last night's discovery, she put the dog down and hurried away.

'Fine, Evie... Yeah... Thanks,' he said, panting.

A female voice rose from the entrance. 'I don't care if it makes you uncomfortable. Suck it up.'

Evie turned to see Suki, in a tight shirt and leggings, her long black hair tied back, two white pods sticking out of her ears. Suki clutched a phone and shouted, facing the screen, at someone whose shoes Evie wouldn't want to be in. Funny to see a small woman behave so big.

Suki strode to the water dispenser next to Evie's desk. Evie gave chase, certain she could feel her thighs chafe more than normal. She was such an elephant in comparison.

'Hey,' Evie tapped her on the shoulder. 'No phone.'

'Wait a second,' she said to the person on the other end, then to Evie, 'I've got an important deal. I won't be long.' She multi-tasked, filling a water bottle and issuing instructions in a garble of big words.

When Suki caught her eye, Evie winced. 'Sorry. No exceptions.'

'Gotta go, dude. Sort it.' Suki took the pods out of her ears and gave the screen a quick glance. 'Wait, why does this say the gym's closed?' she asked, looking around the obviously not-closed place.

'Yeah, must be a glitch. You should've received a notification to say it's closing at 10.30. Others did. Plumbing works, apparently.'

'Good thing I never check it.' Suki laughed.

'Phone?' Evie called after her as Suki walked on.

'Yes, yes. I'll take it to the locker.'

Confident everyone was duly occupied, Evie picked up Uzumaki and flipped it over, the need to read Japanese comics from back to front second nature. She found where she'd left off: the appearance of the snail with a man's face, his eyes at the end of the two stalks. A classic image that had inspired one of her tattoos.

After a few pages lost in her reading, she sensed the doors slide open once more.

Stephen cocked his head in first before striding in, more confident. A door at the rear of the gym clunked shut. He stopped in his tracks but exhaled in relief when it was Suki who came out.

Suki leaned on a bike's handlebar to flick something from her trainers, nodded at Stephen and made a beeline for the rowing machine.

Stephen gave Evie a sheepish grin. 'Good morning,' he said, pretending he hadn't already clocked Charles cycling.

Evie smiled. 'Hi. Nice shorts.' The brand of last night's delivery was emblazoned in a gigantic purple font along his thigh.

'Thanks.' He part-laughed, part-coughed. 'Um. I forgot my water bottle. Have you got a spare by any chance?'

Remembering the collection of junk in her drawers from her earlier search, she bent over and produced an army-green flask. 'I know this one's clean.' She turned to the dispenser and waited as the sound of the water trickling in changed from a tinkle to a glug. 'Here you go. Enjoy.'

'Thanks.' He didn't leave straight away. 'I have something for you. To... erm... thank you.' He slid an envelope across to her and practically ran off.

Watching him go, Evie sniggered at the awkward padding by his bum. It looked like he'd pooped himself. Or like those jellied inserts she'd seen advertised online to give you a Brazilian bum lift. He also shaved his legs as if he were a cycling pro; they looked smoother than hers.

The white envelope had *our little secret* written on it. She turned it over. It was glued shut. She took her ring with the miniature dagger off her middle finger and used it to slice the note open, her curiosity amplified with every tear.

A folded fifty-pound note. Fifty whole pounds. Or were there two? She checked. Only the one. Still. Nice. But as she stuck the envelope in a drawer, she felt a growing unease. Should she feel happy... or insulted? He should've known she'd keep his and Charles's secret, regardless. No need to buy her off. Typical of Mr Flash-the-cash thinking money solved all problems.

Further up, Stephen adjusted the saddle and pedals of the bike next to Charles and hopped on without giving Evie a second glance. She watched them from the corner of her eye. They murmured, smiled. Charles shook his head and jutted his chin towards the corridor, where his wife would be lying in perfect quietude. Floating on salty water inside a peaceful pod. Perfectly in the dark—in more ways than one.

CHAPTER EIGHT
Evie

Evie consulted the maintenance log. She'd memorised her own recurring tasks, after all these months, but wasn't familiar with the Saturday routine and didn't want to leave her colleague in the lurch. Two entries only: oil the mechanisms on the cable pull machines and check the belt on the treadmill.

Another swoosh of the doors and Dave came in. She hoped that would be the lot of them. It wasn't normally this busy. The tasks would have to wait.

Dave ambled past her with that swaying strut of his, Popeye arms bowed at his sides. She didn't know what he did for a living—or what anyone did for that matter—but his bulk, combined with a number two haircut and the inexplicable sensation he was hiding something, gave her the impression his line of work would be iffy. The building's developers had evidently been happy to take anyone's money, with no consideration of where it came from.

She spotted Stephen and Charles position themselves a little bit more distant, a little bit more... straight.

Evie checked the schedule for the next week on the computer. She counted her allocated hours while Dave grunted at the weights. He was always a noisy one. Invasive, somehow. Not only because he stood rigidly, towering over her when he needed something, but the way he acted like the whole place was his, going where he wasn't meant to.

She added up the blocks in the diary. Seventeen... twent y-three... twenty-nine... thirty-five. Plus, a short day today. All accounted for. Wouldn't put it past Alan to cheat her, though.

Suki's rowing machine purred rhythmically. The very upright cyclists panted in unison. Pebbles had given up trying to jump onto Charles's rotating legs and snored at her feet again. Evie switched to the Internet browser and typed in *Gmail*. She wondered who might have remembered her birthday.

A flurry of messages covered the screen, names old and new. Even her former art teacher, wishing her well, asking how she was. Evie didn't know how to reply, already sensing his disappointment. He likely regretted the free lessons he'd given her when she'd lost the previous job. '*Your success will be my reward*,' he'd said. How could she tell him she still hadn't dared submit her portfolio to the Art College? Or anywhere else. Having spent a taster day among the students, she quickly got the sense manga wasn't considered a 'proper' art form.

Evie's ears pricked when Stephen sputtered, coughed, then sputtered again. She looked over. He'd stopped pedalling and was tugging at his top, wheezing. Charles stepped off his bike and stroked his arm, eyes wide. 'Stephen, what's wrong?'

The rowing sound stopped. Evie tensed up. Stephen's head lolled to the side, and he slid to the floor, one leg stuck across the bike frame.

'Help.' Charles sank to his knees beside him. Poking, pulling.

What was he doing? Why was he lifting Stephen's arms? Oh God, Stephen wasn't moving.

'Stop.' Evie raced over. The blood had drained from Stephen's face. Recovery position? Sit him up? Her first aid training flashed through her mind in useless fragments of mangled instructions as she checked his pulse and ducked to listen for a breath.

'What's going on?' Dave asked, coming near.

'Do something,' Charles pleaded. 'Is he having a heart attack? What's wrong? Stephen?'

'Shut up.' Sweat sprung from Evie's temples. He was unconscious. Think. Think. Mouth to mouth. Compressions. She remembered *ha, ha, ha, ha, staying alive, staying alive.* The rhythm for compressions. Her count was messed up by a disquieting chorus of 'He's not breathing' from the men, huddled around too close.

'You. Call 999,' Suki's voice sounded from the rear. 'You. Give the girl some space, for Christ's sake.'

Free from their oppressive presence, Evie's mind cleared. 'Suki, get the defibrillator. It's on the wall behind my desk.' Her heart was thumping in her throat, forcing a tremble into her rescue breaths. One, two. Nothing. She pushed and pushed, her armpits clammy, wrists sore. *Staying alive, staying alive.*

Suki handed her the device. 'Pull up his shirt,' Evie said as she opened the box and the automated voice started up. She peeled off the sticky pads and placed them on Stephen's baby-smooth chest.

'How does this phone work?' Charles shouted. 'I'm not getting a line... Evie?'

'Be quiet, you ass,' Suki said. 'Can't you see she's busy?' She left Evie to it. 'You probably need to dial a nine first or something... Move over. Let me.'

'I'll get my mobile,' Dave said, running to the men's changing room.

'Everybody shut up.' Evie sat on her knees, focused on the display. Come on, come on.

Press the shock button. Do not touch the patient.

Evie pulled her hands to her side. Behind her, Charles sobbed and Suki cursed. Dave's voice rose in alarm in the distance. All that noise. The room swirled around her. Stop. Must concentrate. Breaths, compressions.

Press the shock button. Do not touch the patient.

Another jolt, another nothing.

It was no use.

'Stephen's dead.'

CHAPTER NINE
Suki

Stephen's lifeless body lay on the gym floor. Suki held the silent receiver in her hand. Disbelief crackled through the air.

'He can't be... he...' The man whose name Suki didn't know raced to Evie's side. Started pawing at Stephen, wailing, 'Nooo.' A white, fluffy dog darted past Suki's legs. She yelped, nerves on edge. Where had that come from? The dog bounded to where the collapsed man was stretched out. It nudged his limp elbow, whining, its black nails leaving pitted indents in the mat.

As she leaned over to hang the phone up, a flurry of papers slid off the desk. The rustling sound triggered a memory: a rapid flash of her father slumping across the overflowing desk in his tiny office behind the kitchen. Her pulse quickened. She squeezed her eyes shut, trying to block out her dad's heart attack. An echo of her own voice rattled through her head, calling out to him, asking what's wrong. '*Pôr, bpen à-rai ká?*' She exhaled slowly, skilled in blowing the visions away by now. A year on and the guilt gripped her as tightly, like a vice on her throat.

She could still hear the wail of the ambulance. Green-clad paramedics ordering her aside. They'd arrived in an instant; whisked him away.

Focus, Suki.

'Dave, did you call 999?' she asked. The dumb lump stood, mouth agape, in the middle of the room. 'Dave?'

'No, I told you, I can't open the locker,' he replied, waving his wrist with the access bracelet on it.

'Then try the doors. Get help, for crying out loud.' Suki sighed. All brawn, no brains, that one. 'Receptionist. You... Yes, you. Are you sure he's dead?' The young woman blinked, nodded. Poor lass. She looked shell-shocked. No wonder. She'd jumped straight in. Not a single second's hesitation. Suki had to give her props for that... even if it hadn't helped. She hoped the girl wouldn't be too hard on herself. Suki had learned from one of her healthcare clients that amateur CPR rarely worked—not that they'd say that publicly; they had devices to sell.

Thank God her dad had lived.

Dave banged against the glazed doors. 'They won't open.' He patted the edges of the frames looking for a switch or mechanism but appeared to come up empty.

Suki's stomach stirred. Phone? Check. Doors? Check. She scanned the desk. 'You. Come here. Sorry, name?'

The receptionist walked over like a zombie. 'Evie.'

'Good. Evie. Your email is open on the screen. See if you can contact someone. Or Skype the police? No wait, that doesn't do emergency calls.' Suki sprinted away. 'Do *something*. I'll try the emergency exit.'

'Go upstairs,' Evie said.

'What?'

'Upstairs, to Mrs M. She'll be in.'

Who the hell was Mrs M? Suki rattled the metal bar, shoved her shoulders against the solid door. 'It won't open.'

A loud bang came from the front. Dave was pummelling the sunflower doors with his fists.

'Stop it,' Evie cried. 'It might break.'

Dave aimed again. 'That's the whole point.'

Suki felt adrenaline course through her body. 'What the hell is going on in this place?'

Dave gave the doors another beating so strong the windows on the other end of the gym quivered.

'Careful, please. I'll get in trouble,' Evie begged. 'You'll hurt yourself. Or lock us in even more.'

'She's got a point, Dave. Let's take a moment and think.' Suki put two fingers to her temple. 'That means you too,' she said to the other chap, who was lying in a snivelling heap.

'There's no Internet.' Evie plonked into her seat, defeated. 'It's like everything is down.'

The weeper by the body lifted his head. 'If it's an electrical failure, why aren't the lights out?'

Dave walked over to Suki, rubbing his wrist. 'Have you tried the emergency exit?'

'I tried that one. It's stuck,' Suki replied. 'Is there another?'

Evie shook her head.

'Why do people always block fire escapes? Goddammit.' Dave's eyes bulged in rage. 'The number of times I've had to move a misplaced keg...'

'It's hardly going to be a bloody keg on the twelfth floor of an apartment building, is it?' Suki snapped.

'Maybe it's an unfortunate glitch,' Evie said. 'It wouldn't be the first time. I remember one day—'

'Maybe it's the workmen,' the other man mumbled, in a daze.

Dave pointed at him, a light coming on inside that thick skull. 'That would make sense. There's work due to be done. Someone is bound to show up any second.'

'Not until 10.30,' Evie said.

Dave raised his shoulders. 'Maybe they're early.'

'Either way, sounds like they'll be here soon.' Suki said. Her eyes were drawn to Stephen, his neck at an awkward angle, a blueish tinge to his features. His oddly hairless calves were flopped apart. A wet patch had grown from his crotch. She pressed her lips as bile rose in her throat. She'd never been good with body fluids. 'What do we do with him?'

The Charles guy stroked Stephen's head in a surprisingly intimate move for what she'd assumed was a neighbour. 'We should cover him up.'

'We can put him on the yoga mats.' Evie pointed to the pile by the window. 'He'll be more comfortable.'

Was she stupid? He was dead. Comfort was the least of his worries.

'Good idea.' Charles motioned for Dave to help lift the body up.

Suki watched them struggle with how to get a hold of him. His upper body lopped forward as they each clasped one of his arms around their neck. Charles couldn't get up. He fell sideways. Stephen slumped to the ground. The dog barked and jumped on them, thinking this was a game. It licked Stephen's face. Charles shooed it away. Suki felt ill but couldn't stop watching the car crash. Evie cried quietly behind her.

Trying a different approach, Charles helped Dave hoist the dead man up in a firefighter's carry. A dribble of drool escaped upside-down Stephen's mouth and splattered into the soppy puddle of sweat staining the mat. The dog pounced on the glob. Suki pressed her fingers to her mouth and ran to the bathroom, her gut churning.

She stormed through the door, the bright overhead lights assaulting her senses. As she headed for the toilet, she collided with Beatrice, who'd come out of the changing area, scrunching her wet hair.

The woman smirked, like she'd done more than once at the meeting the night before. 'Are you all right?' Her voice a singsong of false concern.

CHAPTER TEN

Evie

The clock on the wall showed it was only nine-thirty. None of this made sense. If the workers had switched off—or somehow damaged—all the access controls, why weren't they here yet? Trust Alan to let it all go to pot. He'd probably hired some dodgy mates of his.

Evie tried the phone again. Still dead. She clicked on her mouse. Still nothing. Perhaps she should check her locker? Then again, Suki had run to the bathroom. She was sure to grab her phone once she... Would she really have vomited? It's what it looked like, the way she'd clasped her mouth and ran. Talk about a weak stomach. There wasn't even any blood.

Evie stared at the dark green patch where Stephen had lain. So sweaty. She remembered laughing about it with Mrs M only the other night and now... dead. Plus, in a sick twist of fate, he died on the bicycle—like she'd drawn.

A thump rocked her from her thoughts. Dave had let go of Stephen on the tower of mats. Charles straightened his lover's arms along his side. Poor man. The colour had drained from him, his ash grey complexion made even more sickly by his orange top. He tried to pull a mat from underneath, but it failed to dislodge. He looked at Evie. 'Have you got a towel? Something to cover him up with?'

She stepped nearer to where the men were, feeling she should do something. But what? She'd never been in the presence of a dead body before. She'd drawn plenty of them, but in the flesh—chalky and limp as it was—no. 'I'm sorry. None left.'

'Never mind.' Charles took off his top. He placed the shirt gently over Stephen's face, unsuccessfully hiding a caress of the dead man's cheek. He wrapped his arms around his bare chest, a clutch of grey hairs between the brown. His shoulders quaked as he let out a sob.

Tears welled in Evie's eyes. 'Wait.' She unzipped her work jacket and took it off. 'Put your shirt back on. Use this.' Charles's eyes grew wide at the sight of her inked arms. She grinned awkwardly and flapped her top in front of him to get him to focus. 'Here.'

She didn't want to be forced to go into the whole conversation the tattoos always kick-started. Yes, they're Japanese style. Yes, they're eerie. Yes, she designed them herself. No, she wouldn't regret them later. No, she wasn't an axe-wielding murderer.

He took the jacket and slunk into his top before replacing the shroud over Stephen's face. Evie sat on the floor, cross-legged.

Dave exhaled loudly. He leaned against the weights rack, facing the sea, his arm resting on the thirty-pounders. 'I didn't know him. But he was too young. Could've been any of us. You can be in the best shape of your life and in an instant...' He snapped his fingers.

Evie wondered who he'd lost; he seemed to speak from experience.

The bathroom door swung open. Beatrice's hair hung wet and listless around her face as she strode into the gym. Her tight-fitting T-shirt revealed a pot belly Evie was surprised she'd let show.

'Our new neighbour had one too many drinks last—' Her confusion was clear as she took in the scene. And no wonder, with Charles kneeling by a horizontal Stephen on top of a mound of yoga mats like some sort of monk. 'W hat's...?'

'He had a heart attack,' Evie said. 'I tried to save him.'

'She did,' Charles said. Evie thanked him with a small smile. It was kind of him to make that point. Everyone knew how much power Beatrice wielded over the building's staff matters.

She recalled catching Beatrice and Alan in discussion once. Evie had come out of the massage room where she'd rearranged the table and overheard her hissing at Alan—about how he'd 'be sorry' and something 'disgusting'.

That Alan had done something disgusting didn't surprise Evie. She wasn't thrilled with his behaviour at the best of times. But beggars can't be choosers and when it came to jobs, Evie was definitely in the beggar camp. Employers tended to take one look at her scars and find some bullshit excuse.

Beatrice was naturally intimidating, but now her eyes were wide, their pupils freakishly dilated as if two beetles wanted out. She brought her hand to her bosom and took a strangely long breath in.

Deep creases formed on Beatrice's forehead. Her face contorted as though she'd chomped on rancid meat. She wheezed, then gulped. Evie wondered if she was going to be sick too. But Beatrice started beating on her chest, gasping. Panic spread across her face. Her sports bottle fell to the ground. Its built-in straw dribbled water onto the floor.

Evie's heart thumped. What was happening to the woman?

Dave turned around.

Charles got up. 'Beatrice? Beatrice? What's wrong?'

Beatrice stumbled forward, her tongue hanging from her mouth, as though too swollen to fit. Her pleading eyes fell on Evie, conveying a fear that stunned her cold.

'It's an anaphylactic shock,' Charles said. 'We need to get an EpiPen.'

'Are you sure?' Dave asked.

Beatrice sank through her knees. Charles caught her before she hit the ground. 'Yes, I'm sure. I'm allergic to nuts. This is what it looks like.' He lay Beatrice on her side and turned to Evie. 'Grab the first aid kit. Quick.'

He was right. There was an EpiPen in there. Charles had asked her to check, once, so he wouldn't need to carry his with him. His countless allergies were the reason no food was permitted in the gym.

Evie ran to the green box on the wall, her throat constricting. She tried to think back to Beatrice's induction, to the health questionnaire she made everyone fill in. Each of the tick boxes to go through: diabetes, heart disease, respiratory conditions, allergies—she couldn't remember what she'd put down—musculoskeletal problems, pregnancy... Her stomach lurched. Could Beatrice be pregnant? At her age? She lived alone. But what did Evie know about her life outside the gym? She tried to picture Beatrice with a man but could only see her clumsily clinging on to the developer chap the night before. No. Besides, pregnant women didn't swell up and choke. At least, she didn't think they did.

'Shit,' she heard Dave say.

Shit what? Evie wanted to look, but she needed to get those damned clips undone. She pulled hard, grabbed the kit, and ran to Charles's side. She opened the box up and threw all its contents onto the floor. A yellow tube rolled across the mat. Charles snatched it and jiggled the device from its case. Pebbles sniffed at the pickings and walked off, having sunk his teeth in a thick roll of gauze.

Beatrice lay on the floor, shallows breaths raising her chest, her lips darkening.

Dave crossed the gym and started beating down the door again. 'Help.'

'Here goes.' Charles stuck the pen against Beatrice's thigh and clicked.

Evie's mouth was dry. She waited on her knees, next to Charles, for Beatrice to recover, searching for any sign of life, trying to block out Dave losing his shit by the glass doors. Bang. Bang. Bang.

'It's not working. Why is it not working?' Evie cried.

'I don't know.' Charles felt for Beatrice's pulse and stuck his cheek in front of her nose. 'She's not breathing. I don't understand...'

'Maybe we're wrong. Maybe it's something else.'

Evie pushed him aside, a reawakened CPR muscle memory taking control of her body. Confident she knew what to do this time. But would a defibrillator even work twice? Would they have enough pads? She put one hand over the other and pressed... and pressed... wishing, praying, that this one would stay alive.

CHAPTER ELEVEN

Evie

'You can stop, Evie.' Two firm hands tugged at her shoulders. She shrugged free and blew another gust of air into Beatrice's mouth. One more round. A tear snaked down her nose and landed on Beatrice's cheek. Where it wouldn't be felt. She knew that now.

Evie fell back, panting. Spread-eagled on the floor. Spent. The room was thrust in gloom as, outside, thick, rolling clouds gathered around the pearly winter sun.

'You did everything you could. More than we did,' Dave said.

Suki let the bathroom door fall to a close behind her. 'What's happened?' She'd sleeked her hair into a tight plait that highlighted her gauntness.

'Beatrice came out,' Charles explained. 'Next thing, she's swelling up, not breathing.'

'At first, we thought she was just shocked, you know? Because of Stephen,' Dave said.

Charles continued, 'But I realised she was having an anaphylactic shock. I have severe food allergies. I thought I recognised it. But we stuck the EpiPen in and she didn't respond.'

Evie covered her face with her hands, slowing her breath. Keeping the light out. Keeping all the horror out. She wished they'd all be quiet so she could mentally escape. This wasn't happening...

'Holy shit,' Suki said. 'And the phone's not working? The lockers? Let me check mine.' She turned. The door clunked. A sullen silence fell, the three wordlessly resigned to their failure to keep Beatrice alive. Or Stephen. Both men staring down, as though their feet held the answer.

A scrunching sound came from underneath the desk. And a whine. Evie dropped sideways onto the floor to peek. Pebbles had gnawed the wrapping from the roll of gauze and found himself with a lengthy white beard as his canines had pierced through the holey material. Evie crawled to his side and picked the gauze from his teeth, rewarded by a dry lick on the hand.

Suki returned, looking harassed. 'No luck. Can't get it to open. Let me try the emergency door again.'

Evie heard the rattle of the metal bar, three hard slaps on the door. A 'fuck'. Her shoulders slumped.

'No point trying the main doors either,' Charles said. 'Dave's even thrown the chair against it. Solid as a rock.'

'Building regulations. Toughened. We'll have to stay put until someone comes.' Dave's voice sounded distant and muffled. He was standing by the window again, gazing out, resting his forehead against the glass.

Evie thought how nice and cool that must feel. He was only a few feet from where Stephen lay on what looked, with the backdrop of the rippling stretch of sea, like one of those Indian funeral pyres. She imagined his body spitting orange embers, like she'd seen on photos. Mourners draped in colourful fabrics, struggling in the sweltering heat. Low moans of sorrow. Would it be similar in Pakistan? She made a mental note to ask Kaif when she saw him again. She sighed. He'd be waiting for her call at some point.

Evie binned the gauze, gave Pebbles a belly rub and sat down in the middle of the room. Though these people weren't her friends, she didn't want to be alone.

Suki hunched by her side. 'Evie, are you okay?'

What could she say? Two people had died. She'd touched them. Felt their lips on hers. 'I-I don't—'

Beatrice's body was beside them, eyes cast towards the horizon in a blank stare, her sallow skin accentuating her every wrinkle. She would've hated that. Always coiffed to perfection, faultlessly presented—though come to think of it, Evie had noticed an occasional dishevelled state lately, a duller expression on her, skipping her work out for a mini spa experience in the sauna. Not bothering to blow dry her hair. Could she have been ill?

Guilt gripped Evie's chest. Maybe Beatrice's bitchy behaviour had been down to her being sick. Evie, too, could get crabby when she wasn't feeling well. Perhaps she should've been less quick to be offended, not rushing to draw her spiteful vengeance. Not make Beatrice explode from inside, or strangle her with a skipping rope, or stab her in the eye.

Oh God, the things she did to this woman... Evie sighed, for the first time detecting a faint medicinal aroma in among the soap and cream that perfumed Beatrice's body.

Evie picked at her nails. She listened out for more Pebbles mischief but only picked up the odd tiny snort. What a gift to be oblivious. She'd swap places in an instant—though only until they got out. Being Fiona's lap dog was something she'd already experienced and had no further interest in. That and having to wear a silly bow.

'Why is she blue?' Suki asked.

'Huh?' Charles came nearer.

Suki pointed. 'The tips of her fingers are blue, see?'

'I noticed her tongue was a bit blueish earlier,' Evie said.

'Really?' Suki leaned forward. 'What gives someone blue fingers?' She asked it like Evie should know.

Jesus, Evie only had first aid training. She wasn't a sodding doctor. She was only a receptionist. Weren't *they* supposed to be the smart ones, these rich people? Evie shook her head, stress sparking shoots of pain in her skull. 'How should I—'

'Don't touch her,' Dave's outburst caused them to instinctively lift their hands up, far from Beatrice, as if she were a live electrical wire. Dave was crouched next to Stephen, holding the dead man's forearm. 'He's got blue fingers too... This doesn't feel right. Don't touch anything. I think this may be a crime scene.'

A chill ran through Evie. The sombre clouds behind Dave had become ominous, sinister, seeming to suck the air from the space along with the light. 'You mean someone killed them?'

Suki scoffed. 'That's insane—'

Charles gasped and jumped up. 'Fiona. Oh my God. She's in the floatation tank.'

Chapter Twelve

Evie

'Stop.'

In a flash, Dave blocked Charles' path to the rear corridor with his bulk, arms spread, ready to catch. A menacing enough—or confusing enough?—sight to stop Charles mid-sprint.

'What?'

'Nobody should go anywhere alone until we know what's going on,' Dave said, seizing him by the shoulders. 'I'll come with you.'

'He's not going to kill his wife,' Suki said.

'How do you know?'

Suki wriggled her fingers like a spooky ghost. 'Oo. What if *you're* the killer?'

Dave's eyes narrowed. 'Ha ha. Fine. We all go.'

Evie scrambled up, her mind swirling. It was all happening too fast. Why were two people dead—maybe a third? It was crazy to think there could be a killer hidden somewhere. Surely, that couldn't be true. There had to be a rational explanation. You heard of people having heart attacks in gyms all the time. But two...?

'Let me go. It's my wife,' Charles whimpered as he tried to escape Dave's forceful clutch.

'Okay, we all go,' Suki said.

The group squeezed through the archway to the rear corridor, almost as one. A rippling sense of dread travelled through Evie's stomach. What would they find? Were the two deaths related? Who would do this? Why?

'I told her to lock the door because of last time. I walked in. It was awkward,' she said. 'I truly hope she locked it.'

They stood by the room, huddled together. Charles pounded on the door 'Fiona? Fiona? Are you there?'

Dave reached in front of him and pushed the door handle. 'The light's green,' he said, nodding to the sensor. His face twitched; a subtle wince. 'It's unlocked.'

Charles slapped Dave's hand away and took the handle, seemingly reasserting his rights. His wife, his door. Then, an instant of hesitation. Not a breath from anyone.

A springy click breached the silence. 'Fiona, can you hear me?'

They spilled into the room. Fiona's clothes lay discarded over the chair. Her earrings were on the small side table that held the floatation tank's instructions.

The large white pod sat unnaturally in the middle of the space, a blue glow coming from tiny LEDs dotted along the bottom of its case. The tank had always reminded Evie of those slime eggs, with a foetus-like alien inside. The kind she'd tortured her younger sister with, squishing the alien until the gunk oozed out from between her fingers, making guttural, otherworldly noises to creep her out.

No noise here, only a hum from the water heater. She pictured Fiona, curled up, with tiny fists and protruding eyes. Blue? Evie shook her head. No. She was fine. She had to be fine.

'Fi, darling?' Charles held the others back with one hand and gripped the metal bar on the lid of the tank. Evie noticed a slight tremble in him as he pulled up. 'Fiona?'

The first thing Evie saw was Fiona's feet. Veiny. Flaked, black nail varnish on her toes. Heels floating on the murky water. She stepped forward, along with the others, as Charles leaned into the dimly lit container and touched Fiona's shoulder.

Fiona's shriek pierced the air. They jumped back. She thrashed around like a captured fish, until she was on all fours, water halfway up her forearms, staring at the others in disbelief. 'What are you doing?'

'Oh, thank God.' Relief infused Charles's voice. He slid his hands down her arms but struggled to find a suitable hold, bent as he was halfway into the tank. He patted her instead, as though wanting to confirm it was her in the flesh, that she was real. 'You're okay...'

Fiona sloshed out of the tank, water sliding off her onto the floor. She pulled the swimmer's earphones from her ears and let them hang around her neck. 'Why are you here? Why are *they* here? What's going on?'

As she looked round in confusion, her gaze lingered on Evie's arms. She frowned. Evie hugged herself, feeling exposed—maybe even more than Fiona did, standing there, her toned body wrapped in a shimmering purple bathing suit.

Suki offered Fiona the towel from the table and retreated, pulling Dave and Evie along by their sleeves. 'Show's over.'

But was it? Was Fiona safe? Had she ever been in danger? Were they? Evie let herself be led. It all felt utterly unbelievable.

Charles grabbed Fiona in his arms and held her, cocooned in the towel. 'Our neighbours Stephen and Beatrice... they're dead.' He stroked her hair as she remained motionless. 'We were worried you—'

Her questioning eyes darted from person to person. 'Dead? Here?'

Charles kissed her cheeks, her forehead, her eyes. She dodged him while searching Dave's face. 'What happened?'

'I was lifting weights when I heard the man, Stephen, coughing on the bike, right by your husband. Next thing I know, he's on the floor. Gurning.'

Suki and Evie watched from the corridor as Dave filled Fiona in, her skin tone gradually dropping until she was beige, her mouth forming a silent O. Evie couldn't take her eyes off Fiona's earphones. Something pulled her to them. The strap connecting them coiled around her neck, black with a yellow stripe—like a snake.

'We can't leave you in here,' Dave said as Charles tried to get Fiona to sit down next to the pod. 'It may not be safe.'

Suki sighed. 'Oh come on, don't you think you're taking this too far, Dave? Who's even to say those two were killed? It could all be a big coincidence.'

Dave sneered. 'Sure. And it's a coincidence we can't get out or call anyone. Wake up.'

Evie saw the ire burn in Suki's eyes.

'Dave's right. Come,' Charles smuggled Fiona out into the hall. 'It's not safe.'

'What's not safe?' Fiona asked just as her wet feet slipped on the linoleum floor. She stumbled and hit her ankle against the wall. 'Ouch.'

Suki said, 'Can we not let her get dressed at least?'

'Yes, I'll only be a minute. I'm soaking wet.' Fiona turned to the door and pressed the handle. 'Dammit.' She waved her wristband in front of the sensor, but the red light stayed on. She gave Evie an accusatory stare. 'It's locked.'

'I... Don't look at me,' Evie said. 'All the doors are locked.'

'But it was unlocked before. You all managed to barge in. Even though I locked it. I'm sure of it.' Fiona tugged at the door. 'I can't stay like this. I want my clothes.'

'I don't know what to say.' Evie shrugged. 'It's like every-thing is back to front.'

'That must be it,' Suki said. 'The system's knackered. Back to front. All the doors that were open switched to closed—and vice versa.' She glanced at the row of warm-toned spotlights in the ceiling. 'Thank God the lights are still on.'

'To think anyone could have walked in and...' Charles said, tears pooling in his eyes. He escorted her away. 'I have to warn you. What you're going to see is very distressing.' That last word was swallowed inside a big sob.

Evie's heart broke for him. With his wife around, he'd have to keep his grief for Stephen in check. Although... Maybe she knew of the affair? Evie fixed her gaze on Fiona as they entered the main gym area. How would she react?

CHAPTER THIRTEEN
Suki

So that was a floatation tank. Suki had heard of them, but never seen one in real life. It was huge. She wondered how they'd ever brought it in. And what did people do in there, anyway?

It didn't sound like her idea of fun at all, floating on salt water—with the germs of who knows how many other people swishing in the water. Yuck. She wasn't good at relaxing. Never had been. All this mindfulness stuff everyone was on about was lost on her. Why avoid stress? Stress was what got shit done.

She peeked into the tank from the doorway. Why would you choose to be in the dark, inside a plastic bubble? Isolated. Vulnerable. Lying there all quiet... She shuddered. What happened if you moved, anyway? Did you sink?

As Suki pondered the physics of the question, she followed Fiona, who was being led into the main gym by her sapless husband.

An eerie silence cloaked the space. The girl, Evie, was hovering around her desk, trying the phone and computer again. Didn't seem to be having much luck. Dave paced the room, his broad shape casting a cold shadow over Suki as he passed in front of the already thin ray of sun gracing them.

Fiona stood over Beatrice, drips from her wet hair landing at the body's feet. When Suki saw her brush her eyes with the tip of her towel, her first thought was tears. But given the cold stare on Fiona's face, it was more likely to be the stinging of the tank's salty water. That or she was a crap actress. There was clearly no love lost there.

'What do we do?' Charles asked, holding onto Fiona's towel like a toddler its mother's skirt.

'We stay put. Someone's bound to show up,' Suki said.

Fiona snapped round, face crumpled as though there was a bad smell. 'Who are you?'

The woman's condescending tone scraped down Suki's spine like nails on a chalkboard. Suki took three steps forward and squared up to her. 'Who are *you*?' She knew damn well who Fiona was, but it was always smart to even the field of respect—it helped when the counter party looked like a drowned cat rather than cloaked in the usual power and prestige of the Selkie's Lair, the exclusive member's club she ran.

Fiona pressed her lips into a tight smile. 'I'm Fiona King. 11A,' she said, the accent very much on the 'A', the water-facing side of the building. The expensive side.

'Suki Aksornpan, I'm new. Across the hall,' Suki said, cocking her head to the gym's exit. Definitely not mentioning her B.

'Sorry, where are my manners?' Charles said, extending his hand. 'Welcome to Platinum Peak. I'm Charles. Fiona's husband. Not King though, Evans. Fiona likes to use her maiden name. A big feminist, our Fiona.'

Suki stifled a laugh as she anchored herself to his firm grip. It was all surreal. The man introducing himself politely, too much detail, a half-naked feminist by his side and two dead bodies on the floor. And it wasn't even ten o'clock.

'You're babbling, darling,' Fiona said, pushing her husband's arm down. His red-rimmed eyes stared back at her.

Suki's heart sank as she realised he must've been clinging to etiquette as a means of coping. What was his relationship to the dead man? It was close, that was for sure.

In the corner of her eye, Dave rocked his hips, seemingly never able to stay fixed. 'We need to find out how the killer is killing them,' he said. 'Any one of us could be next.'

Evie frowned. 'Do you really think someone is after us? Are they here?'

Suki held up her hands. 'Hey. Let's all take a step back here and not get carried away. Let's think. What do we have? Two people who are dead.' She saw Evie hug herself. 'Despite best efforts to save them.' Evie thanked her with a meek smile. Poor girl. This would stay with her forever. 'We don't know what happened to them, but they suddenly became critically unwell.'

'People don't drop down dead like that. Definitely not two people. And the doors are locked,' Dave said. 'There's something very sinister going on.'

Suki sighed. 'Come on, we know there was work due to be done. It could all be an unfortunate coincidence. I accept the probabilities are one in a gazillion, but it is possible.'

Dave scoffed. 'You would say that.'

Suki's shoulders tightened. 'What do you mean?'

The veins in Dave's neck sprang up like thick ropes as he clenched his jaws. 'If you're the killer, that's what you'd say. To keep us here. And then bam.'

Suki jumped as he pounded his fist into his other hand. She felt everyone's stunned gaze on her. 'That's ridiculous. Why would I want to kill anyone? I just got here.'

'It's always the stranger,' Fiona said.

'What?' Suki asked.

Evie nodded. 'It's true. In comics, films...'

Encircled, Suki spluttered, 'No it's n—'

Charles appeared to grow in stature. 'And you were in the bathroom with Beatrice before she came out. What did you do to her?'

Suki waved her arms in the air. 'Stop, stop, you guys are insane. It wasn't me. Why would I do this?' She sighed. 'Look. Before we start arguing about vaccines and 5G conspiracy nonsense, let me remind you that these is no evidence at all these two were even killed. Like, how did they die?'

'What about the blue fingers?' Charles said, looking forlornly at where Stephen lay near the window.

Suki had to admit the idea that there had been a convergence of unrelated, improbable events was almost ludicrously incredible. But she was a firm believer that the simplest answer was usually the correct one. The fewer assumptions you needed to make, the better. And she'd seen enough corporate finance clients completely mess up their negotiations to know confirmation bias was a real thing. They'd believe any bit of data was pointing with a big fat arrow towards that which they dearly wanted to be true—but wasn't.

She scanned the room, suspicious faces on her. A chill ran over her arms. She needed to give them a reasonable explanation, or they'd not let up. 'I don't know. I'm not a doctor. Maybe blue fingers and lips are normal when someone dies. I've not seen a dead person before, have any of you?' From their shrugging and shuffling of feet, she could tell Evie, Fiona and Charles hadn't. But a dark veil came over Dave's expression. 'Dave?'

'I don't know about the blue,' he said, coolly.

Suki wasn't tricked by the deflection. No answer to whether he'd witnessed death. She'd have to watch him.

Chapter Fourteen
Evie

Evie wanted to go home. She was convinced the ceiling had dropped, and that the walls were inching in. Even the air held an oppressive whiff of neoprene she'd never noticed before. The scent of boats and damp loch-side changing rooms.

She didn't care what had happened to the two residents, how they died, or who did it. She only wanted out. Away from the dead bodies.

At least Stephen was covered up, tucked away in the corner. Evie kept being drawn to the leaning tower of yoga mats beneath him, expecting it to topple, the many layers slipping from each other like a croupier's rapid card deal.

But Beatrice remained where she'd fallen. Bang in the middle of the room, inescapable. Evie couldn't watch the woman's splayed shape without her heart rate jumping, her mind sparking with images of the terror in Beatrice's eyes, the sound of the EpiPen clicking, Beatrice's gurgled response. She couldn't get near without feeling her frantic gasps burning in her throat as she'd sought her very best breath to save the woman, without being slammed by the memory of the immense ache as she'd surrendered to her failure and sensed a second soul slip away.

Why were the others so preoccupied with theories and accusations? What was the point? There was no way of knowing what caused the attacks, not until the doctors came. Stephen had been on the bike. Beatrice had showered. Next thing, they were dead. None of it made sense. Suki was probably right. This was all a clusterfuck of epic proportions.

And Evie wanted out.

As the others piled onto Suki, Evie tried the phone again. No dial tone. She shoogled the mouse on the computer. Refresh. Refresh. Refresh. The screen remained static. The connection to the outside world cut.

She waved at the sensors for the big, opaque doors. Tried to reach higher. Jumping jacks of desperation. When they stayed stubbornly shut, she pressed her palms against the crisp glass and tried to peek through the thin slit where the doors met. 'Hello?... Help?...' Tears pooled in her eyes, chilled by a slight breeze through the crack. The smell of stone walls, like home. 'Mum?'

Mum would know what to do. She always did. To the infuriating point of intrusion. How many times had her mother told her where to go, what to do, what to choose? Forcing her go to college, when Evie was obviously not cut out for that and was the one who'd had to suffer the shame of dropping out. Shitting on any idea Evie had ever had about her art because '*They're called starving artists for a reason*'. Telling her not to move in with a boy she'd only met a few months before—a Muslim, no less.

Yet Evie would give anything to have her here because Mum stepped in. Mum had stepped in when school had objected to Evie's blue hair, despite Mum hating the manga style herself. She'd taken care of Susie-the-bully and her nasty mother in high school. She'd called the lawyers when Evie got burned, not letting her take the employer's first offer. Evie pictured her mother in battle mode—all fiery five-foot-three of her—and felt a firm tug at her heart. What if she were to die in here like the others? What if she never saw her mum again? Or Kaif?

The ruckus behind her was quieting down. She turned and peered straight into four sets of eyes on her. A cold sense of dread spread through her veins. 'What?'

'I'm telling you, she was at the computer,' Fiona shrieked, pointing. 'She's the one who locked the doors.'

'Wh-what? No.'

Fiona advanced on Evie, her fists white from clutching her towel tightly. 'You know how all this technology works. You're always letting people in or out. You must have the admin-or-whatever access... Who's behind this? What do you want?'

Charles tried to grab his wife's shoulder but missed. 'Fiona. Don't.'

Evie bristled. The closed doors loomed large behind her. Nowhere to run. What was happening? When had the accusations turned to her? She searched Suki, Dave, Charles, hoping to catch an understanding eye, but they glowered—not only at her, but at each other. Recriminations had clearly flown high. What did she miss?

'I didn't do anything,' Evie pleaded. 'I don't know how this stuff works any more than you do.'

'I don't believe you,' Fiona said. She gestured at the others. 'She's a freak. Check out her arms. Who has tattoos like that? It's sick. *You're* sick.'

Evie brought in her shoulders and crossed her arms. The inked human snail's head pressed against the fur of the opposite forearm's demonic, hundred-eyed cat.

'Yeah, what's with the tattoos?' Dave asked, as he also stepped forward. 'What do you want with us?'

Evie retreated; skirted the doors, her nerves on high alert. 'Nothing. They're drawings. Like in graphic novels. They don't mean anything.'

'From comics? They don't look very funny to me,' Charles said, crowding Evie from the right.

Suki remained standing with her arms crossed, divorced from the others. Did she think Evie was to blame too?

Fiona's pointy finger was mere feet from Evie's nose. 'You told me *specifically* to make sure I locked the door to the floatation tank room this morning. Why? Because *you knew* what would happen. You needed me there... like a sitting duck.'

'I didn't. No. I swear,' Evie stammered.

'Listen, if someone's made you lock us in, is somehow forcing you, tell us,' Charles said gently. 'We can help you. We won't be mad.'

Dave snorted. 'Yes, we will.'

Tears flowed down Evie's cheeks. She slunk into a ball and crossed her arms over her head. 'Please. It's not me. I don't know anything.' She sobbed.

'That's enough.' Suki's outburst startled Evie. She peered up to see Suki peeling the others away. Wondrously fearless, her small hand pulling at Dave's big bicep. 'Can't you see the girl is terrified?' Suki grabbed Evie's elbow and guided her up. 'Come on. You're okay.'

Evie tuned out the accusers' background grumbles and focused on Suki, her sleek black hair, her delicate nose, the steely don't-mess-with-me gaze she gave the others. Her light. Evie let herself be pulled along as she struggled to find oxygen in the rapid, shallow breaths that had overtaken her. 'It's not me,' Evie croaked. She was shaken by a violent hiccough. Tears spurted out. 'It's not me. You have to believe me. Why would I do this? It's my birthday.'

A collective gasp filled the room. Suki threw her head back as she broke into a raucous laugh.

Evie smiled nervously at the three others, each stunned silent.

'Bloody hell. You can't make this shit up.' Suki chuckled. 'See? It can't be her. Only a psychopath would murder people on their birthday.' She jutted her chin at Charles. 'Do you think she's a psychopath?'

The atmosphere shifted; a skittish energy took hold.

'Um. No,' he replied.

'So what do you say?' Suki pressed.

He winced. 'Sorry?'

'No, you fool. Happy birthday. Come on. You too,' she said, waving at Fiona. Suki began singing. '*Happy birthday to you*... Come on...'

Fiona and Charles shot each other a look. It seemed... it seemed like they were afraid. Why would they be afraid of Suki? They sang. '*Happy birthday*...' An awkward pause. Charles, firmly, '*dear Evie.*'

Dave didn't join in, pursing his lips in defiance. His wary gaze made Evie's skin crawl. If anyone looked like a murderer...

As the last '*happy birthday*' sounded, Evie wished she'd paid attention to what they'd all been shouting before, when she'd put all her efforts on getting out rather than understanding the potential enemy inside. If they feared Suki, should she?

CHAPTER FIFTEEN
Suki

'Now leave her alone. Shoo,' Suki said, creating a safe space for the birthday girl who still looked a tad disoriented, eyes wide open and the wisps of hair that framed her face spiking upright with static electricity from the tacky polyester uniform.

Suki had endured her share of terrible birthday experiences. More than once, she'd been stuck in the office solving yet another last-minute glitch before a deal deadline, late for her own parties—one she never made it to at all, leading to her sexy-as-hell last girlfriend dumping her. But being stuck in a smelly room with a couple of dead bodies really took the cake. Ha. Birthday. Cake. Suki snickered. She remained wired from her performance saving Evie from the wolves.

It had been a gamble, a snap decision to take the nut-case approach. One of many tactics she used to unsettle her opponents during negotiations: throw something random into the mix, the more absurd the better, and watch them flounder. A sleight of hand to distract from whatever didn't serve her cause. While the other side would try to figure out what the hell had happened, Suki would be making her next move.

Only, this time, she had to decide what her next move would be, seeing as her plans had been thoroughly derailed.

She scanned the room. Dave sat perched against the reception desk, fists balled, legs rigid. That he hadn't been taken in by her show didn't surprise her. He looked like the kind of man who had *seen things*. Not one to be easily shaken, that's for sure.

There was a darkness in his eyes she'd noticed when they met at the homeowners' meeting. An unnerving intensity to his stare she hadn't been able to put her finger on until she'd reminded herself, later, who he was. He'd definitely been around trouble before today. And judging by this morning's behaviour, he was no stranger to death.

Unlike Charles and Fiona, huddled together by the magazine rack. A rainbow of Benetton brightness. She watched them whisper, holding hands. The soft hands of the privileged. The type who didn't get embroiled in messes—or more likely had someone else clean them up. Whose closest brush with death was probably an expiring Roomba. Suki smirked. Part of her was delighted she'd spooked them with her act. Those startled faces. What a hoot. Though she could do without them thinking she was a killer. That would mess up everything.

Maybe she should've let them accuse Evie and not jumped in. But it was crazy that anyone could think the girl capable of murder. Look at her, crouched down by the glass doors. In her green top, white trousers, she did an excellent impersonation of a pot plant.

'What's funny?' Charles asked.

'Oh. Nothing,' Suki answered. More solemnly, she added, 'Nothing about any of this is remotely funny. Two people have died. And Evie did her utmost to save them. You saw it. That isn't something you can fake. It's not fair to have a go at her. I mean, what did you do to help? Hmm?'

Charles cleared his throat, let go of his wife and wrung his hands. He cast a mournful glance at Stephen's body. What was it with those two?

'I wasn't even here,' Fiona said. 'I was floating.'

Suki sighed. 'My point is, none of us is a killer. What happened this morning is bound to be a series of extremely unfortunate events. It's only normal to be upset, but we must stop getting carried away.'

Charles gave a sheepish smile and rubbed Fiona's shoulder, who nodded.

'Well, you would say that,' Dave's voice boomed.

'Huh?' Suki asked.

He pushed himself up from the desk and he approached, walking slowly, assuredly, with a distinctive gait. His biceps seemed to flex when Suki blinked. 'Sure. Play dumb. But if you were the killer, that's exactly what you'd say.'

Heat flushed Suki's neck. He was a big man, and he was coming close. That didn't tend to end well for her. 'Seriously? We're doing this?'

Dave put on a high-pitched voice and flapped his hands, like a cartoon girly-girl. 'No, there's no killer here. Look away, look away.' His eyes narrowed. 'And boom,' he said, punching his hand, 'You've got us smack where you want us.'

The prickling on Suki's skin became unbearable. She could almost hear it crackle in the room's menacing silence. 'You need to get a grip. I have nothing to do with this.'

'Don't you?' Dave snarled. 'Because you were asking me an *awful* lot of questions about everybody at the owners' meeting yesterday.'

Fiona jumped in. 'And you are a stranger.'

'You wanted to know all about Beatrice,' Dave said. He began counting on his fingers. 'Which apartment she stayed in, whether she lived alone, if she went out much. Now she's dead.'

He performed for the others as if he were an attorney in court, listing the evidence with which he'd want the jury to convict. Suki understood why her questions would make him jump to conclusions. She thought about the night before. Finally seeing Beatrice Quinn in the flesh. A conflict of big hair, subtle make-up, loud dress, bad shoes. The woman had been more obnoxious than she'd expected. Giant ego. Pretending after the property presentation to care about getting a good outcome for everyone. But who was she kidding? She only cared about herself. She'd proven that with what she did to Suki's dad.

Suki's mind rattled through her options. It was time to give them an explanation or she might lose them even before she'd snared them—and all would have been in vain.

CHAPTER SIXTEEN

Evie

It wasn't odd to want to know your neighbours. Evie'd known neighbours on all sides all her life. Still today, in the studio. But even she thought the depth of questions Dave suggested Suki had asked were a bit much. Either way, better having them focus on Suki than on her.

She was quite happy sitting here, with nobody paying attention to her. That is, until Pebbles came to sniff her fingers. He had a stealthy knack for showing up out of nowhere. You'd expect to spot a white, bouncy dog with a bobbing tartan bow a mile away. It helped that the spongy mat muffled his steps.

She saw Suki raise her hands in surrender. 'Okay. Fine. I'll come clean. There is a reason I was—I am—interested in who is who in the building. I'm a corporate financier. At Madainn Finance.'

Judging from the others' faces, Evie wasn't the only one to be confused. But Fiona perked up. 'You work with Angus?'

'Yes.' Suki smiled. 'And I wanted to learn more about Beatrice because she's a valuable person to get close to.'

'Why? What does she do?' Charles asked. A troubled expression crossed his face. 'Um. Did. What did she do?'

'Beatrice is at NatClyde Bank, darling,' Fiona answered. 'Remember that charity event you hated?'

In the corner of Evie's eye, Dave's face turned sour.

'That's right,' Suki said. 'The head of corporate banking for Scotland. She's got tonnes of clients she'd be able to introduce me to and tonnes of capital she could deploy as loans in my deals.' She pointed to Beatrice's body. 'She was the embodiment of the Golden Goose for me professionally. Why would I want to kill her?'

All this talk of finance and business went straight over Evie's head. Numbers had never been her thing. Not much had been her thing, academically speaking. Otherwise, she wouldn't be here. She might be in an office somewhere, nice and safe, with doors that opened and people who breathed.

Instead, she was witnessing a social one-upmanship she couldn't participate in, even if she wanted to. She concentrated on what was being said. You never knew what you'd pick up. The police might need it. She, like Suki, didn't think they were here because of some sick killer getting his kicks, but something felt off that she couldn't put her finger on.

'She did know *everybody*. Well, anybody who matters.' Fiona smoothed her hair. 'Of course, all my members had access. The rear booth in the lounge was practically Beatrice's second office.'

Suki put her finger on her nose and pointed at Fiona as though they'd been playing charades and she'd guessed the movie title. 'And that's why I wanted to meet you too, Fiona. Angus would've given me a strong reference to join the Selkie's Lair, but I need two recommenders to join your private club and I figured if we were neighbours...'

'Wait. You're trying to tell us you moved into the building for business?' Dave bellowed, and Evie braced herself for another one of his outbursts.

Suki pre-empted it with an enthusiastic smile. 'I did. Honest. Which is why I wouldn't murder anyone. I don't

know how well you know your neighbours professionally, Dave, but I've done my research. This place is full
of people I can do business with. I've even got a lucrative
opportunity for you.'

He cocked his head and frowned. 'Oh?'

'Barr Security. The bouncer agency. That's yours, no?'
Suki asked.

He nodded.

'It was a bad year for you last year, financially. I
thought—'

'I wouldn't say that.' If Dave had feathers, they'd be
ruffled, the way he reacted. 'Where did you get that?'

Suki grinned apologetically. 'Companies House
doesn't lie, I'm afraid. The losses are there in your filed
accounts, in black and white, if you read between the
lines of a balance sheet. Anyway, what I tried to say is
that I've got a great idea for a merger.'

'A merger? Who with? Iron Guard? Because if you
think I'm going to let that—'

Suki rolled her eyes. 'God no. Nothing as uninspired
as merging with a competitor. The real value lies in
diversification. I'm thinking a pest control company.'

Dave's eyes narrowed. 'Which one?'

'If I told you, I'd have to kill you,' Suki quipped.
Evie's heart jumped, and she heard Charles gasp. Terror
crossed Suki's face as Dave recoiled. 'I mean. Shit. No.
Argh.' Suki shook her head violently. 'That's just an
expression. I meant if I tell you, you'll bypass me, and
I won't get a fee. Not that I'd... you know... actually *kill*
you.'

As Evie's momentary shock subsided, she reckoned,
even with her limited knowledge of business, that it was
actually a clever idea. Not that she'd say so. She was
happy to stay on the side with Pebbles.

Didn't they say you were never more than 10 feet from a rat in Edinburgh? If she pictured all the dingy, sticky-floored clubs and pubs she'd gone to, she could totally see why it would make sense to combine pest control and door security. After all, both were ways of keeping out the undesirables.

Thinking about it some more, she suspected she even knew which company Suki was alluding to, which gave her a secret thrill.

Her mind sprung to the cluttered windowsill in Mrs M's kitchen. On one of Evie's first visits, she'd gone to fetch Mrs M a glass of water for her tablets and found herself staring at a stuffed white mouse on skis behind the tap, tiny red gloves round miniature poles, pink ears poking out from under a helmet made from half a hazelnut shell.

There was never a shortage of eccentric things to uncover in her apartment, but this had been her first inclination that Mrs M had the kind of warped taste that would make them firm friends. Evie smiled to herself. She remembered returning to the lounge, a crystal tumbler in hand. 'What's with the taxidermy?' she'd asked.

Mrs M had snickered. 'I gather you met Olle.' She lingered on the Ls as though there were five of them.

Scandinavian, Evie guessed. It figured, what with the skis. 'Is that the mouse's name?'

'He was given to me by a supplier in Sweden when I launched my first business, the pest control one,' Mrs M said. 'I was only twenty-three and there weren't many women in the industry. I believe he did it to test my stomach. Not only did I pass, but I proceeded to drink him under the table that night.' She winked and raised her glass in a toast.

'I suppose it's an unusual line of work to be in—for anyone. A bit gruesome,' Evie said.

'Ach.' Mrs M shrugged. 'Not when you're the daughter of a funeral director.'

And that had explained a lot.

Evie scratched Pebble's chin. His wagging tail brushed her bare arm. She looked up, wondering what Mrs M was up to, above them, wondering if there was any way to get her attention. Her friend would normally have been down for a chat already, but Evie wasn't meant to be on shift today. Mrs M had even made a big deal of not wanting to give her a birthday present early—apparently that was bad luck—and Evie having to wait until Monday.

If only Evie could get her to come down somehow. Her mind whirred.

The ceiling was made up of those speckled-beige, square tiles held in place by a criss-cross of metal frames that people in the movies were forever lifting up to stash their bags of cash. The tiles looked too flimsy to hold her weight. Where would the space even lead? This was real life. There wouldn't be roomy cavities connected to ludicrously convenient air vents that took the squished-but-somehow-fitting-precisely, sweaty hero straight to the villain's secret labs. But maybe if she found a way to climb up there, she could pound on Mrs M's floor and shout loud enough to get a message through.

An angry male voice snatched Evie from her daydream. She jumped. Pebbles ran off.

'What the hell is that supposed to mean?' It was Dave, who seemed to be growing a foot as he strode towards Charles, chest puffed up. What had she missed?

'Look. I'm sorry,' Charles said, pushing Fiona behind him in a surprisingly manly protective move. 'But you can't blame me for thinking that.'

'What? Because I run a bouncer agency, I'm some sort of criminal?' Dave's nostrils flared. Evie worried this would escalate. Charles would be no match. In fact, squeezed between the giant Dave and his own fairly tall wife, he was like withered sandwich filling.

He said, calmly, 'All I suggested is that, out of all of us, you might have a better insight into the mind of a murderer.'

Dave roared in frustration. 'Absolutely standard twattery from an entitled, judgemental boarding school boy.'

Charles sputtered. 'I don't understand what my schooling has to do... and how did you know?'

Dave made a show of waving his hands up and down to showcase all of Charles. 'Are you serious? Have you met yourself?'

'That's enough,' Fiona said, stepping forward. 'I'm sorry you took offence, but it stands to reason that in your line of work you'll have more experience dealing with crime, police and such matters than we do.'

'Ha.' Suki laughed. 'That's only because you don't get caught.'

'I beg your pardon?' Fiona asked.

'Oh come on. First of all, Dave is the owner of the business. Not the one standing at the club door.' Suki nodded to Dave, seemingly initiating a truce. 'And secondly, let me guess... You're a stockbroker or fund manager,' she said to Charles.

Charles crossed his arms. 'So?'

'Biggest crooks of all, in absolute monetary terms,' Suki said. 'Billions tainted by white collar crime. Fraud, money laundering, insider dealing, you name it. So you can get off your high horse.' Charles's face looked like thunder, but Suki exhaled slowly. Perhaps controlling her temper? This whole situation had everyone stirred up. And no wonder.

Suki adopted a calm tone. 'Now let's all cool down and start treating each other with a little respect. Okay? Nobody here is a criminal.' She raised her finger at Dave, who'd opened his mouth. 'No. I don't want to hear your warped theories. We're going to all sit down, right here, in the middle of the reception area and wait for the workers to release us.'

Evie checked the clock. Shortly before ten. Oodles of time to go, stuck in this blasted place. Was she imagining it, or was it getting cold? She strained her ears to pick up the hum of the air conditioning that accompanied her days. It was off. She rubbed her arms and wished she'd kept her jacket on. Still, it had been appropriate to cover Stephen up.

Not that anyone had followed her lead with Beatrice. But then she didn't have a lover here. As Evie snuck a peek at the uncovered body, she saw movement. Her stomach dropped.

'Guys, guys...' she mumbled.

CHAPTER SEVENTEEN

Evie

Were they deaf? Evie's owns ears were ringing, adrenaline spiking through her. 'GUYS.'

All heads turned to her.

'Look. Pebbles. He was sniffing at Beatrice's water bottle. I thought he'd lap the spillage up. But he retreated, as if it stinks.'

'I suspect it's Beatrice, Evie,' Suki said. 'Her body will start to reek.'

'No, I remember now,' Evie said, rising. 'There was a medical smell around her. I clocked it before. I think... I think there's something wrong with her water.'

'What?' Charles shot up and took the first steps towards the body. Evie followed, noticing Dave had an awkward way of getting to his feet. Fiona pulled her towel tighter as she reached Evie's side.

Suki bent over the body, hand outstretched.

'Don't touch it,' Charles said. 'If Evie's right, we shouldn't touch anything. Evidence.'

'Yes,' Dave said. 'We can't give you an excuse for your fingerprints to be on the bottle, Suki. In case they're already there.'

Suki sighed. 'Bloody hell, this again? I've got nothing to do with this.'

'You'd say that, wouldn't you?'

'Fuck off, Dave.'

Evie wished those two would stop bickering. Dave's base-less and smug aspersions were getting on her nerves. For all she knew, he could be putting on an act to throw the scent off himself. Wouldn't that be cunning?

She closed her eyes and drew in a measured breath. She couldn't let his paranoia infect her. But the stale, foam-scented air wasn't helping. They were trapped and if they weren't careful, they'd all turn on each other. The truth was any of them could be a killer. Or none of them.

At Beatrice's side, Charles got on all fours and leaned in, his nose close to the wet patch.

'Be careful, darling,' Fiona said.

He sniffed hesitantly, frowned, and sniffed more deeply. 'Alcohol. Vodka, if I were to hazard a guess.'

'But it's morning,' Fiona said. The shock on her face morphed into a snarl. 'Of course, I wouldn't be entirely surprised if she's a raging alcoholic. She can fair knock them back at the Lair.'

'Fiona, let the woman be. For once,' Charles said. His admonishment stunned her, and an awkward silence de-scended on the group.

'What if it's poison?' Dave said.

'Oh God, here we go,' Suki said, exasperation seeping from every pore. 'Sorry if the truth is too boring. But let me propose a much more rational explanation. She keeled over from sitting in the steam room drunk as a skunk.'

'Hmm. Poison or booze.' Fiona sneered. 'I know where I'd put my money.'

Evie pictured the blue plaque with white-lettered in-structions by the door to the steam room. Impossible to miss.

Do not use if:
- you are pregnant,

- you have a heart condition,
- you have low blood pressure,
- you are under the influence of alcohol or drugs.

A long list of restrictions—yet Beatrice was precisely the kind of person who would think the rules didn't apply to her.

Dave gave the group a pleading look. 'Bear with me. Please. There's got to be more to it. There are two dead people. Two. That doesn't just happen. What if the dog picked up something else? On top of the alcohol.' He strode towards the trio of bikes in the middle of the exercise area. 'Because it hit me. Stephen had a water bottle too. It's here, in the bike's holder. He'll have drunk some before he collapsed. What if there's something in both their waters?' His gaze drifted to the water cooler by the reception desk. 'What if there's something in there?'

A chill ran up Evie's spine. She'd filled a bottle for Stephen when he arrived that morning. Had she poisoned him? Had anyone seen her? Would she be to blame—even if she didn't know? With two bodies, each with a water bottle, the poison story was starting to feel plausible.

Even Suki's objections appeared to be waning. She slumped and rubbed her face. 'I don't know. Okay? I don't know. I admit two deaths is statistically improbable. But the alternative... Really? A murderer? Somehow striking invisibly while his victims are surrounded by people? I mean, they dropped dead. Like that.' She snapped her fingers. She sighed and sat down. Stared at her feet. 'I genuinely haven't a clue. But let's wait and leave the police to do their thing. They'll figure out what happened. There will be clues, physical signs...'

'Like blue fingers,' Charles said. He cleared his throat, a faint flush on his cheeks as he realised he'd captured everyone's attention. 'That's a sign of poison, isn't it?'

'Where on earth would you get that from?' his wife asked.

Charles shrunk noticeably. 'TV? I'm sure I watched something with poisoned monks and blue fingers.'

'Old, poisoned manuscripts,' Suki said. 'They licked their fingers when turning the pages and died. I know that film. It's got Sean Connery in it. That's not the same at all. Those fingers were blue—actually, black—because they touched the poison. Their tongues, too. But here you're talking about ingestion. Imagine how much poison you'd have to put into a whole water cooler.'

'Are we even sure that Stephen and Beatrice used it?' Fiona asked.

'We can find out,' Dave said. He pointed to above the main doors. 'There's CCTV.' He spun around slowly. 'There's only one, but given its position, it should cover the entrance and this entire area.'

'Wow. You're right,' Charles said. 'We could rewind and see what happened.'

Tension screamed across Evie's limbs. Should she tell them about Stephen before they saw the tape? Not only did she hand him the water, but he slipped her that money. What would they think? A lump formed in her throat. She struggled to swallow. Relax. Whatever they wanted to make of that, she hadn't touched Beatrice. Didn't even remember seeing her come in, as she'd been under her desk sorting out Pebbles.

She looked at the camera. The green dot that was normally on wasn't there. Nobody else had noticed.

'People,' Suki called. 'If you truly suspect foul play, do you seriously think you should mess with evidence before the police come? I wouldn't touch the video if I were you.' After a second's pause, she rolled her eyes and raised her hands like a robber whose time was up. 'And yes, Dave. I would say that if I were the killer.'

CHAPTER EIGHTEEN
Suki

Morons, the lot of them. Suki watched as Charles slapped Dave on the back.

They walked to the reception desk like newly anointed partners with freshly earned detective badges. Who did they think they were? And what on earth did they expect to find? Any self-respecting killer wouldn't let themselves be captured on film.

But she was done fighting. Since they were aware of why she'd moved in, at least she could talk shop with them. If she ever got the chance.

It irked her how pally-pally those two were, all of a sudden. How come she was the one under suspicion, not any of the others? In typical style, the men bonded with no questions asked.

Fiona sashayed after them. The way that woman kept rearranging her towel, opening wide to cross over her chest again, was beginning to get on Suki's tits. And if Fiona put her mind to it, she could find something to wear. No need to flash that body all the time. If Fiona enjoyed being the centre of attention, more power to her. Suki didn't care. But who did she feel she was competing with here? The dead people?

The men's murmurs were interspersed with the clicking of the mouse.

'Evie, where do we find the tapes?' Dave asked.

The human pot plant quivered. 'I don't know. I've never had to look.'

'Well, come and help anyway. This is your computer,' Dave said. 'You're bound to have access.'

Evie rose with a sigh. 'I'm not sure we'll find anything. Perhaps the videos go straight to Alan. Besides, I agree with Suki. We shouldn't be messing with anything that could be evidence.'

'Come on,' Charles coaxed.

'The camera is not even on,' Evie grumbled, within earshot of Suki.

Why so reluctant? If Suki didn't know better, she'd think Evie had something to hide. She hoped Evie was wrong about the camera not recording. Because now it got interesting.

'Dave, you must know what we're looking for, given your line of work,' Charles said.

'Not really, mate. We contract that out.'

'Let me,' Fiona said. She did her heron-flap again and nudged herself between the two men.

Click, click. Clickety click.

Evie hovered behind them, summoned yet instantly ignored.

'I think this might be it,' Charles said. 'SecCam.'

Suki craned her neck. From a distance, she saw the computer screen turn grey, a black and white blocked menu along the top. Terrible user interface, whatever that software was.

'Now what?' Fiona said.

Charles turned to Evie. 'Now what?'

'I told you. I don't know. That's not my job.'

Suki wasn't looking forward to sliding between the heaving mass of bodies battling for space at the monitor, but it was clear these *bpan-yaa òn*, these idiots, weren't going to figure it out themselves. 'Hold your horses. I got this.'

Dave eyed her suspiciously. 'How come?'

'Because I like technology. You're looking at the technology practice at Madainn Finance personified.'

'That merely tells me you understand finance,' Dave challenged, arms crossed, guarding the entrance to the hard drive as though it were a nightclub.

'Yes, and guess what? Women can be good at more than one thing.' When he frowned, she added. 'I've got an MBA from Stanford, heart of Silicon Valley. I wouldn't normally mention it on a first encounter—I'm not like Harvard people—but since you ask, I did some coding while there. All the more reason to hire me when we get out of here, right? So, if you'll step aside, please.'

He did. Real quick.

Suki familiarised herself with the blocks of text. She knew not to be misled by the basic interface. Often, the simpler systems looked, the stronger and more specialist they were. And she couldn't imagine the building's developers splurging on smart technology everywhere but not on security. There were four tabs:

Stream
Vault
Settings
About

To what should've been no one's surprise, she discovered the vault was the repository of recordings, a long list of AVI files with a cluster of letters and numbers in their names. Suki made out what appeared to be a date format, though the actual time of day wasn't clear. However, it stood to reason they'd be listed in sequence. 'I've got bad news and good news,' she said. 'The bad news is that the camera isn't recording. The stream is blank.'

'And the good news?' Fiona asked.

'I may have overpromised a bit.' Suki grimaced. 'It's good-ish. Some files appear to have today's date on them, but there's about twenty of them and we won't know when the camera stopped without viewing them.'

Charles placed his hand on her shoulder. 'Well done.' Suki tipped sideways to make it slide off. She didn't need the uninvited touching, thank you very much.

'Where do we start?' Dave asked.

Suki pulled the chair to sit. 'At the end, of course. How else do we know when it stopped?' she settled in. 'Gimme some space.'

Charles and Fiona scattered, but Dave stayed put, looming over her in an unbending stance. He gave her a steely glare and shook his head ever so slightly.

'Seriously?' Suki blew a raspberry. 'And here I was thinking we were becoming friends.'

'We'll be friends when I'm certain you're not deleting any files.' He raised an eyebrow. 'Maybe.'

Suki cursed under her breath. So much for her plan to charm them all.

She selected the last file. The video played. No sound, but full colour and high resolution. It explained why the files were fragmented. They'd otherwise be too big if they needed to be shared. Like with the police.

The white-lettered timer ran through the seconds top right, while the reel showed Evie at her desk, reading a comic book. At the far end, Suki rowing. A posture she'd need to improve.

'This is before the deaths,' Dave said. Charles and Fiona returned, curious faces crowding Suki's, breathing moist air against her cheeks. Ugh.

Suki leaned back a bit and watched them take in the action with morbid fascination.

On screen, a very much alive Stephen cycled steadily, his bottle in the holder, cap hanging off a plastic ring. Beside him, Charles's Lycra-clad thigh bobbing up and down as he pedalled.

After a while, Stephen's upper body shuddered. 'Here we go,' Suki whispered, a flutter in her stomach. But no... He was laughing. And, in a blink-and-you'll miss-it moment, he stroked Charles's knee. Suki glanced sideways at Fiona, who'd clearly not blinked. Her mouth was so puckered she might as well have drunk vinegar.

Suki allowed herself a moment's celebration, vindicated in her sense all along something wasn't quite as expected with those two guys. She focused on the screen again where, this time, Stephen's shuddering ended in his collapse.

'Can we fast forward?' Charles asked.

'I guess... Whatever killed him has already happened,' Suki said.

'What about Beatrice?' Fiona asked. 'She's next.'

'We need to go backward, not forward,' Dave said. 'Remember, we're interested in the water dispenser. We need to see when they came in.'

In that instant, Dave was shown walking into the gym and the screen went dark.

'Ha. The camera doesn't like you much,' Suki teased.

CHAPTER NINETEEN
Suki

Based on the one they watched, Suki guesstimated the length of each of the video files and skipped to what would be earlier that morning. If she was wrong, it didn't matter. None of it mattered. Wherever she landed, whatever sequence they chose, they wouldn't see anything incriminating. Of that, she was certain.

The water bottle theory in particular was a huge wild goose chase. But given any protestation on her part would merely deepen their suspicions of her, it made sense to play along—even if it did mean having them all, literally, breathing down her neck as they huddled in front of the monitor.

'Okay, let's try here.' She clicked. The colours on the screen muted, the outlines of the gym equipment barely visible in the moonlight. The timer read 7.45 a.m.

Dave summoned Evie, who'd been hanging back. 'Hey, what time did you get in?'

She approached. 'Shortly before nine.'

'Perhaps it's this one,' Charles said, as he reached for control of the mouse.

Suki swatted him away. 'It'll be this one.'

After a few minutes of shrouded stillness, the gym was flooded with light. The green mat and bright yellow walls assaulted Suki's eyes. She blinked. On screen, Evie entered, picked up something she'd dropped, put it in her desk and disappeared, heading for the rear.

Evie explained, 'I went to put my bag in a locker. They were working fine, then.' She reappeared and found a small plastic bag on her chair.

'What's that?' Charles asked.

'Tampons,' Evie answered, deadpan.

Charles gave a small cough. 'Oh, um, yes. Good.'

Suki sniggered inside at how grown men could be reduced to bumbling schoolboys by a bit of cotton.

They observed Evie head to the toilets again, bag in hand, and return a short while later.

Fiona leaned forward, her bare shoulder brushing against Suki. 'I think we came in around this moment.'

As if on cue, the couple entered with their dog. There was an exchange. Evie checked the computer. It was hard to keep track of the action as it spread across the room: Charles hopping onto the middle bike, legs starting to circle; dog deserted and tucked under the desk; Fiona walking out of frame as Beatrice entered the gym.

'Ah, pay attention,' Dave said.

Beatrice was wearing a tight-fitting red T-shirt over equally tight leggings. The poufy hair had flattened into a squint bird's nest overnight. She clutched her blue-capped water bottle to her chest, as though it warmed her, while carrying a towel under her other arm. Suki was surprised to see her dishevelled, but on the other hand, it made sense. No point applying hair spray before the gym. And if she was drinking vodka in the morning, chances were she was hungover.

Charles, Dave and Fiona sighed in disappointed unison as Beatrice walked straight past the water cooler.

'Can you rewind it a sec?' Dave asked, and Suki obliged. 'Stop there. Damn. You can see there's liquid in her bottle already.'

'So it was her vodka,' Charles said. 'And she brought it in.'

Fiona humphed. 'Classy.'

Dave pushed himself away from the desk. 'We're no further forward.'

'I hate to say I told you so,' Suki said.

'Do you? Really?' Charles sneered. 'And how come you were sure?'

'Because I drank that water,' Suki replied. 'Look.' She fast forwarded to her entrance, with the painful evidence that the camera truly added ten pounds. Then, they dashed past a sped-up Evie gesturing for her to get rid of the mobile. Suki reverted to normal speed as her figure approached the water cooler, filled up her own bottle, and took a sip.

'Fair enough,' Dave said.

Fiona was pulling at her lips. 'No wait.'

What now? Suki thought, as Fiona pointed at her.

'Suki ran to the toilets to throw up. Later. After Stephen died.'

'So?' Suki said.

'Well maybe there *is* poison in the water and you... you kept it in your mouth and spat it out in the toilets.'

'That's ridiculous.'

Fiona frowned. 'You took a sip so you could pretend to be innocent, when in fact, even that one sip messed with you too. And that's why you threw up.' Fiona's eyes lit up like a crazed being. She might not have drunk the water, but she'd definitely drunk the Kool-Aid.

'You could've put something in the cooler after you filled your own bottle,' Charles said, following his wife's lead.

'Wow, that's wild,' Suki replied. 'I quite like the way you have me down as a criminal mastermind. Sadly, I'm going to have to disappoint you.'

'Not so fast,' Dave said. He nodded at the screen. 'Charles, take over. Let's see what happens with Stephen.'

As Charles nudged Suki aside, Evie said, 'We already know.' She took a deep breath. 'He said he'd forgotten a water bottle and did I have one. I gave him a green metal flask I had lying around in my desk and filled it up for him. And that's it.'

Had Evie not added 'and that's it', it would've sounded completely fine, but Suki sensed something else was going on. Charles pressed play as firmly as Evie pressed her lips together.

There was Stephen, dipping his head into the gym. Suki checked the timer at the top of the screen as he strode in. It was hard to imagine that such a short while had passed, yet so much had happened. This handsome man, in his colourful, branded outfit, full of life...

She spotted a slight tremble in Charles's hand beside her. She looked up. He'd turned away from his wife. The sadness in his eyes tugged at Suki's emotions. A sadness he was having to carry alone, in secret—though Suki expected, from Fiona's earlier expression, that the ship of secrets may already have sailed. She gave him a comforting smile.

All eyes were on the flask in Stephen's hand. Would he drink? But Suki spotted something else.

'What did he give you?' Suki asked Evie. 'In the envelope?'

'Huh? Oh yes, that. He was very nice. He gave me a tip for helping with the drinks at the meeting last night.'

'Gosh, Evie. It didn't even occur to me to do that,' Charles said.

'There was no need.' Evie smiled.

'I should hope not,' Dave grumbled. 'We're already paying enough in service charges for this building.'

'He never drank,' Charles said, as he paused the video at the point of Stephen's collapse. 'It can't have been the water.'

A leaden silence hung in the air. Suki kept shtum. She fought an overwhelming urge to gloat, only because the men's glum faces revealed genuine disappointment. Starsky and Hutch had failed. She did warn them but also felt a bit sorry for them. And given Dave's volatility, she was keen not to antagonise him further.

She wiped her hands on her leggings and started walking away from the group. Hopefully, they'd at last let go of their murder fixation and stop making her out to be a killer. That would be nice.

Dave's voice rose from behind her. 'How did you do it?'

So much for that.

Suki snapped round. 'Are you talking to me?'

'Yeah,' Dave replied.

Dave, Fiona and Charles formed a wall of crossed arms. Evie slid to the other side of the desk. Suki couldn't blame her for wanting to stay out of this. Hell, she wanted out of this.

She sighed. 'This is getting tiresome. I really don't see why you think—'

'You touched the bike,' Fiona said.

'Huh?'

Dave took a step forward. 'If it's not the water that killed Stephen, it's got to be something to do with the bike. And Fiona here rewound to where you lean on that bike when you first come in.'

Suki smiled at them, but her lips twitched involuntarily. 'Look, you guys, I think we all need to take a step back.'

'You were in the toilets with Beatrice,' Fiona added.

'And you're the one who's good with technology,' Charles added. 'You said it yourself. You could've programmed the doors to lock.'

'What? No.'

'How did you do it?' Dave asked again.

Suki's heart pounded in her chest. She'd not accounted for this. This complete lack of logic from what should have been intelligent people.

A flurry of sensible arguments filled her brain. Charles had been next to the bike and could've slipped Stephen anything. Anyone could've touched the bike. Fiona could actually have a motive to kill Stephen. Beatrice had died spontaneously when Suki wasn't even in the room. But mostly, serial killers did not murder people in locked rooms in real life.

The moment she opened her mouth to object, she knew it was pointless. She studied the psychology of influence deeply enough throughout her career to recognise what populist leaders the world over had long traded on: when people are scared or confused, give them a common enemy. To hell with common sense. Point and blame, says the playbook. Set the conspiracy theories loose. And Dave was doing just that.

But why?

CHAPTER TWENTY

Evie

They advanced towards Suki like the three dark holes of a bowling ball. She, tiny. A lone, wobbling pin. She stumbled slightly as she stepped away.

A swirl of anxiety gripped Evie's throat. She was catapulted to high school, to evil Jenna and her bitchy sidekicks sweeping down the hall, taking up all the space, sucking out all the air. Long limbs and swooshing highlights. Slithering snakes stopping only at a nose length from Evie. The smell of sneaky cigarettes and Irn Bru. '*Hey freak.*' The soundtrack to year five.

Rage burned remembering how they'd made her life a misery and for what? For, unlike them, not wanting to wear a skirt that was no more than a belt. '*Freak.*' For her blue hair. '*Freak.*' For her black eye make-up. '*Freak.*' For her artwork. '*Freak.*' For merely having the audacity to be different.

Like Suki, the only non-white person in the room. Someone who'd probably had an unfair share of harassment since the coronavirus hit.

'Stop it, please.' Evie gulped. 'You're scaring me.' She'd planned to say, 'This is crazy' or 'You're out of line,' but she felt her voice quiver and went with the truth.

Dave's face softened. His eyebrows squirmed above glazed eyes. He relaxed his fingers.

Pebbles nuzzled Fiona's leg, seemingly breaking a spell, as she and Charles bent down to pet him.

The gratitude she'd anticipated on Suki's features wasn't there. Instead, a curious stare bored into her. A smirk surfaced, an unsettling reminder she didn't know this woman at all.

Evie blushed as she found herself the object of everyone's expectant attention. She'd not thought this far ahead. What should she say next, that they had it all wrong?

Did they?

She had no idea if Stephen and Beatrice had been murdered or not. It seemed completely implausible. But equally, both of them dying within minutes and them all being locked in with no way to call for help was a surely seven gazillion coincidences too far.

'I'm cold,' she said, hugging herself. 'I'm thirsty, too. But like you, I don't know if the water is safe to drink. I don't know if we're in danger or not. I don't know what gives you blue fingers.' Tears pressed against her eyes. 'I don't know if there's a killer and if so, if they're finished with us. Am I next? Did you do it? I don't know. All I do know is I want to go home... in one piece.' She was met with knowing nods. 'And I think the best way to achieve that is to sit here and do nothing, touch nothing, say nothing. Until someone comes. We can't solve this—whatever there is to solve.'

Her cheeks radiated heat. She ran her thumb along the smooth scar tissue on her arm. Nobody moved. A dark shadow engulfed the others. Behind them, black clouds raced by, lashing the windows with rain like a passing jet ski. A static sea gull flapped valiantly against the wind.

With a hint of hesitation, she lowered herself onto the mat.

'Okeydokey,' Suki said, and parked herself at Evie's side in a puzzling denial of personal space. Suki bumped her shoulder against Evie's. 'Nice speech. Didn't think you had it in you.'

Evie shuffled sideways. 'Thanks... I guess?'

'Sorry. You're usually pretty quiet. I meant it as "good for you" because look. It worked.' Charles and Fiona sat down in an open space beyond the bikes, between Beatrice and Stephen. 'So, thank you. Oh, great leader.'

Whether out of remnant nervous energy or due to the springy in-your-faceness of the woman, a smile pierced through Evie's lips. 'No worries. You'd do the same for me. Oh wait, you already did.'

Suki chuckled. 'This is nuts. I bet it's not how you'd planned to spend your birthday.'

'You can say that again.'

The ambient tension dissipated into wisps of compliant quietude. Only Dave was still on his feet, hands in his pockets, circling the three stationary bikes.

He had the searching air of a bloodhound and no sooner had that image lodged itself into Evie's mind than he bent over and sniffed the handlebars of Stephen's bike from one end all the way to the other.

'What's he doing?' Suki asked.

Dave moved onto the water bottle, his neck outstretched. Eyes closed.

'I have no idea,' Evie said.

'Hey Dave,' Suki yelled. 'If you want me to take a sip of that water, I will. Put your mind at ease once and for all.'

He glowered. 'We shouldn't touch anything.'

Suki shrugged. 'Suit yourself.'

Evie's mouth pruned in distaste. Knowing how infrequently the machines got a deep clean, she wouldn't recommend all that sniffing. Stephen was really sweaty, too.

Beside her, Suki made a gagging sound. 'Gross.'

Dave had his arms behind his back and his nose a smidge above the saddle. He breathed in deeply.

'That's sick,' Suki said. 'And what does he think happened here? You can't kill someone with a saddle.'

Rushing sounds in Evie's ears drowned out Suki's mirth. A tightness gripped her skull, and she became light-headed, plunged into muddled visions of paper and inks. The shape of a sharp, bloody blade coming into focus. Slicing Stephen in two.

You *could* kill someone with a saddle.

She had.

CHAPTER TWENTY-ONE

Evie

Evie wished Suki would stop drumming her fingers on the floor. She needed to think, to settle her nerves. It hadn't struck her at the time that Stephen collapsed right where she'd drawn his death, but now it was the only thing on her mind. That and how?

How in the world could a stationary bicycle kill you?

How could whoever was behind this know Stephen would pick that bike? And precisely this morning?

How could there be no trace of any weapon or compound or whatever?

How? How? How?

As Dave abandoned his sniffing expedition with a scowl, and Evie equally came up empty, she reckoned the only reasonable answer was that Stephen had a heart attack. Nothing more sinister than that. And definitely not a spooky coming to life of her art. That was her imagination running away with itself. That is what you got when you spent all your time immersed in horror manga.

She glanced at the tattoos on her arms. The veiny hand whose fingers ended in octopus-like suckers that latched onto each other if she bent her elbow. The stretched-out man wrapped in bandages, moths flying from under the folds as if he were made of insects. People found it creepy. She liked to think of this one as immortal, a giant cocoon of larvae teeming with a perpetual promise of life. But she also knew it was make-believe, the product of her mind in flights of fantasy.

Stephen died a natural death. And that was that. Nothing more to it. At all. Categorically nothing supernatural. Because that shit wasn't real.

Evie blew out a long breath, but her attempt to calm herself was hampered by Suki's restless wriggling at her side. She inched away. A strange noise reached her. The whispered moan grew into a low hum... with words... Where was it coming from? She swept the room and spotted Charles rocking, arms wound around his knees. Was he... singing?

Her ears adjusted to that possibility and, as his volume grew, she made out the lyrics.

'Snow had fallen, snow on snow,
Snow on snow'

Instinctively, she mouthed, *'In the bleak midwinter, long ago,'* the result of years of religious assemblies in school. Charles raised his head and straightened his torso, his baritone voice louder and more purposeful yet, with a slight croak as his gaze swerved from Beatrice's body to Stephen's.

'Our God, heaven cannot hold Him'

Charles stood up. Fiona turned in all directions, eyes wide, self-conscious, checking for the others' reaction.

He reached out for her hand. She didn't take it until Dave joined in with the song, arms by his side, standing to attention like a soldier lining a procession.

'Heaven and earth shall flee away
When He comes to reign'

Charles pulled Fiona to her feet. She surprised Evie by not only singing along but doing so with full solemnity and the voice of an angel.

'What are you doing?' Suki asked them, gaining her a dirty look from Fiona.

'If we can sing happy birthday for her, we can sing a hymn for them,' she hissed.

Evie's nerves spiked, feeling unfairly shamed for being born this day. She rose. 'Come on,' she said to Suki, who humphed and pushed herself up. Seeing Suki concentrating on her lips, Evie enunciated clearly while Suki warbled softly, constantly a fraction of a second behind.

'Enough for Him, whom Angels
Fall down before'

The mournful voices joined to fill the room with harmonious sorrow. A much needed coming together after the morning's tetchy accusations.

Evie's eyes pricked as the tune brought home the severity of what had happened. The loss of life. How fragile they all were. She hoped this soulful moment would bring peace while they awaited their rescue.

CHAPTER TWENTY-TWO

Suki

The last notes of the hymn lingered in the air like a bad smell. She'd objected, at school, to the forced participation in religious clap-trap—what with her interest in girls summoning no end of disapproving lectures. She really didn't need it in the gym.

What she needed was to get her phone. There would no doubt be a hundred emails and missed calls. If she didn't get the investors aligned on the key terms of the deal today, they'd never be able to complete the acquisition before Christmas.

But she was goddamn stuck here, bloody incommunicado, surrounded by a fucking choir.

Plus two bodies. Hard to forget, but not something she could do anything about, anyway. And since the others suspecting her so quickly had scuppered her plan to convince them she was to be trusted, she should at least be allowed to salvage her career differently.

Suki groaned and flopped down to lie on the ground. She threw her arm across her forehead. 'I can't believe it's past fucking ten o'clock and I've not seen the fucking terms for my multi-multi-fucking-million-pound deal.'

She heard an exaggerated gasp. Now what? Suki took her arm off her face and rolled her head sideways to see.

'Language. Have some respect,' Fiona said, clutching her towel by her offended heart in one hand and pointing at Beatrice's corpse with the other.

Suki smirked. 'Come off it. You're not that upset.'

'How dare you?' Charles wrapped his arm around his wife.

Fiona squirmed. 'I'll have you know that I care about Beatrice very deeply. She and I—'

A guffaw from Dave disrupted her outrage. 'No, please, do tell...' He gestured to indicate the floor was Fiona's. 'Because the last time I saw you two together, you were in a screaming match.'

Suki rose partially to rest on her elbows, feeling the satisfactory strain on her abs from the earlier workout. She was going to need a better view for this.

Evie walked across her vision in the direction of the desk, sulking. What was up with her? She'd ask later. This was about to get good.

'No... I... When was that?' Fiona challenged.

'In the underground parking,' Dave said.

'What do you expect? She rammed into my Beemer with her stupid, unnecessarily enormous SUV.' Fiona nodded towards Beatrice's water bottle. 'She was probably drunk, thinking about it.'

Charles pinched the bridge of his nose. 'All right, darling. That's enough.'

Suki sat up. 'So let me get this straight. You've all been giving me, the suspicious stranger, grief about being a killer, and here you are with actual motives?'

'My wife is hardly going to murder someone over a dented bumper,' Charles said.

'Also, I was in the floatation tank,' Fiona added.

Tickled by delicious revenge, Suki said, 'So you keep saying. But how do we know that's true?'

Charles's face reddened. 'Oh for goodness' sake, Suki. This isn't funny. Fine. Beatrice and Fiona had a fall out. But Fiona dealt with it. Stop suggesting she murdered Beatrice.'

'How? How did she deal with it?'

Fiona tapped her fingers to her lips, as if debating whether to open them. She sighed and steeled herself. 'I killed her plant.'

'What?'

'She had a large pot plant outside her apartment door. A thin leafy thing. Pebbles liked to nibble at it. After the so-called accident and Beatrice's most insincere apology, I fed the plant vinegar. Lots of it. Well, a bit every day... for a few weeks.' She grimaced. 'Until it turned brown.'

Charles looked duly embarrassed.

'See? Motive,' Suki said. And that was only one victim. If she was right, Fiona was probably none too happy with Stephen, either.

'I don't have a motive,' Dave said, finger raised as if Suki were a teacher. 'You said, "here you are with actual motives", and I want to clarify this might apply to Fiona—and even Charles for all I know—but it does not apply to me.'

Fiona's eyes narrowed. 'Does it not?'

Suki's stomach leapt. This was getting better by the minute. 'Go on.'

'Everybody in the building knows about your quarrel with Stephen, Dave.'

He pulled an incredulous face. 'That's about music.' To Suki, he added, 'He lives right above me. Doesn't like my music. Keeps stomping on the floor. He's a twat, but I didn't kill him. Besides, it was over. I bought earphones.'

'Huh.' Suki hadn't pegged Dave as the type to retreat. Maybe his big muscle-man thing was all an act. He probably needed to look the part for his business, the security agency she reminded herself she'd invented a lucrative merger for.

She had his future in her hands. She watched him glow-er. He hadn't liked her knowing about his dreadful fi-nances—if only he knew what else she'd found out.

Suki ticked off in her mind what things she'd tell Dave would need to happen to get him on side: rejig his balance sheet; line up the prospect; build a growth plan; bring the bank in to fund the deal; and cha-ching. Bonus time. So, play nice, Suki, play nice. It wouldn't have to be for long.

CHAPTER TWENTY-THREE

Evie

Evie sat in the reception chair, hunched forward, head in her hands. Any hope of peace had gone out the window—the huge, suffocating window—when accusations bloomed again like mould that would not die.

She felt her trousers stretch across her bum, the square ridge of the folded envelope she'd tucked in her rear pocket. She'd pulled it from the drawer in case her desk got searched. The last thing she needed was someone thinking she had a motive to kill Stephen.

His note—*our little secret*—would raise more question than she was willing to answer.

She'd contemplated throwing it in the bin but deemed it too risky. Her plan was to slip it into her bra at the earliest opportunity.

The fifty-pound tip had been unnecessary. Welcome, but not needed. She would've kept Stephen and Charles's secret, regardless. It wasn't the kind of thing you blabbed about—even though Mrs M would've found the gossip delicious.

Now that Stephen was dead, she believed extra firmly it was her duty to honour his wishes. No one else appeared to have the good grace to respect his memory—or Beatrice's, for that matter—the way they were going on about their pathetic neighbour squabbles.

Good thing nobody asked her opinion, because having observed the residents for months, it was clear there was no love lost between any of them.

On the estate where she grew up, the neighbours were like extended family, stopping by for coffee, helping each other out. But not here. No. Never any chit-chat. Cordial greetings at best.

Even Charles and Stephen had behaved coolly while in the gym; though after she'd caught them together the night before, she did remember hearing Stephen's laughter on occasion while she was doodling.

Poor man. A spectre of remnant guilt clamped her chest. She had nothing to do with his death, with either death. And yet, there was a niggle she struggled to suppress, an eerie sense of déjà vu. Not the kind where you see a scene playing out exactly as it happened, in the flesh, in colour, but swirls of familiarity without a clear shape.

At last, it was quiet.

She didn't dare look up for fear of breaking the fragile, new truce between the others.

Why did Suki needle them like that? Like she was having fun. Didn't she see how serious this all was? From what Evie'd seen of her, she was always doing business on her phone—or trying to. Did she not care about people? The idea clashed with how friendly, too friendly almost, Suki had been with her.

Evie watched her, this peppy woman in a tight sports top and leggings, who couldn't be more than a few years older. Suki's swept-back long hair accentuated a dainty profile. She was smirking. What was her deal?

The group had returned to sitting. Suki on the floor, a distance from Charles and Fiona. All staring into space. Dave sat on a weight bench, legs wide in an epic manspread.

Feeling a tingle, Evie scratched her nose. Its tip was cold, which was saying something given her fingers were already ice blocks. How cold would it get in here with the heating off? It struck her. Would it be off across the building? Was everyone locked in? She'd never considered that possibility.

The others probably hadn't either, fretting only over their own predicament.

A spike of alarm shot through her. Had anyone else died? Was Mrs M okay alone upstairs? She was always covered in blankets as it was. How would she cope in this cold?

She tapped her fingers on the desk to stimulate the circulation. Surely if it had affected everyone, someone on a lower floor would've found a way out? Or alerted a passer-by?

Evie walked to the window and bumped into a wall of frosty air. Fat raindrops slapped the glass like gecko feet. She shuddered. November was the worst.

Outside, dark shapes rippled the sea as clouds drifted along. Bar two gliding gulls, not a soul to be seen. She pressed her forehead against the glass and tried to find the street, squashing her nose in the process. It was no use. they were too high up. She whispered, 'Help, help,' moist condensation fanning out like a silent siren.

'Whatcha doing?'

Evie jumped, banged her head.

'Oh God,' Suki said. 'I'm sorry. I didn't mean to sneak up on you.'

'It's fine.' Evie wiped her chin. She detected a shiver in Suki. 'Cold, isn't it?'

'Uhuh.' Suki rubbed her arms while checking out Evie's bare skin. She cocked her head to where Stephen's raised body lay, his face covered by Evie's jacket. 'That was sweet of you.'

'I wish we could cover Beatrice up, out of resp—'

'Yeah, her stare is creepy as —' A pause, an embarrassed smile followed by a solemn look. 'Yes, out of respect, of course.' Suki looked around. 'Have we got anything?'

'Short of pulling one of the yoga mats from under Stephen, no.'

'No towels?' Suki asked.

Evie shook her head. 'I gave Fiona the only one I had.'

'Hmm.' Suki spun on her heels. 'Hey, Fiona. You were right.'

Fiona was all ears. 'How so?'

'We should be more respectful of the deceased. I feel we should cover Beatrice up, don't you?'

After a moment's reflection, Fiona replied, 'Yes, I think that would be appropriate.' Charles nodded earnestly at her side.

'Great,' Suki said. 'So can we have your towel please?'

She pulled the towel close. 'What? No.'

'I thought you said it was a good idea?' Suki pressed.

'Well, yes, but why me?'

'You've got the only towel,' Evie said.

Suki nodded. 'And unless you want one of us to walk around with our tops off—fun though that could be - it's the only reasonably sized thing we have to cover her with.'

Fiona looked around for support. Charles offered, 'Wouldn't Beatrice have had a towel? She must've showered. Her hair was wet.'

Evie remembered seeing the towel wedged under Beatrice's arm when she came in. 'I suspect she'll have thrown it the laundry chute.'

'Oh,' he said, deflated.

'Besides, you wouldn't want to drape a wet towel over a crime scene.' Suki's eyes sparkled.

Evie sighed. Suki *had* to go there...

She heard a grunt. A muttered 'For heaven's sake.' It came from Dave. He was wriggling on the weight bench, pulling the elastic waist of his gym bottoms down.

'Oh, okay. Good on you, Dave,' Suki said.

He stretched his right leg out and leaned to the side to push himself up on his bent left knee. He frowned as he noticed everyone watching.

To Evie, it seemed a terribly convoluted way to take your trousers off, but as the blue cotton slid to the floor, and a series of quiet gasps filled the room, it all finally made sense.

Chapter Twenty-Four
Evie

It was like something out of Robocop. A large, smooth socket cupped Dave's left thigh. Emblazoned with a Scottish flag, the saltire, it was connected to a space-age grey mechanism where you'd expect a knee and shin, and underneath, a short silver tube dived into his sports shoe.

The air was bathed in stunned stillness. Dave worked hard to avoid people's stares as he stepped out of his trousers and bent over to pick them up, keeping both his good and prosthetic legs straight.

Evie watched him walk to Beatrice in his white shorts, with his signature strut. A heavy mass clunked in her stomach as she realised his gait was not the macho claim to space she'd always ridiculed, but in fact a constant battle for balance.

Flashes of an earlier him flitted through her mind: sitting on a chair or bench—never the floor; working only with weights—never machines; legs always spread wide; towering over her with unnatural stiffness; swanning into the disabled toilets. Oh God, the disabled toilets. Shame burned on Evie's cheeks. All those times...

As he reached Beatrice's body, Evie noticed, from the corner of her eye, the residents seeking each other's gaze out in shared, wordless enquiry. *Did you know?*

Dave stretched his right leg to the side and dropped onto his prosthetic knee, then pulled his other leg into a kneeling position, lowering his bum onto his feet. In a swift move, he flapped his trousers in the air to straighten the fabric out and placed the top over Beatrice's face and the rest along her body—carefully rearranging the cloth legs when they briefly slipped apart at her chest. He frowned. Grabbed the trousers and flipped them around, folding the legs over Beatrice's face. He rubbed his hands, satisfied, and Evie understood why. Beatrice would've preferred that to her nose in his crotch.

He remained static at Beatrice's side, hands on his lap, for some time. The others' discomfort was palpable as they shifted positions, hummed, or cleared throats. Evie was bound not to be the only one to wonder how he'd get back up.

She licked her lips, mentally auditioning different phrases. In the end, she decided the simplest would do. 'I owe you an apology.'

He sighed and as he raised his head, Evie's nerves walked a tight rope. 'Not every disability is visible,' he said, his voice a stabbing icicle.

'I'm very sorry. I should've let you use the disabled toilet whenever you wanted to. I didn't expect... I mean, you loo k...' Evie pressed her fingers to her temples, their throbbing chill welcome. 'It's because, well, I got such a bollocking from Mr Hutchinson one day when someone had gone in, and he tried to open the door, leaning far forward in his wheelchair, and of course it was locked and... Oh God, it was awful. He ended up having an accident. And he was irate. Because the rules do say "only disabled" but he was hardly ever in, and, well, I thought he was the only one, so I didn't see the problem with people using it. But he was livid. And I couldn't blame him.' She knew she was babbling, but it felt safe, this filibustering shield. 'So I guess I became a bit obsessive about guarding that door. Didn't want him to complain to Alan. Because I need this job.' Excuses, all of them. Nothing made it right. She steeled herself for a just reprimand and looked him straight in the eye, the way her dad had taught her to be genuine. 'I'm sorry.'

Dave scratched his neck, rubbed his palm over his bristly hair, and the seconds crawled by. 'It's fine.'

How could he shrug it off that easily? It only amplified her throat-clenching guilt. He didn't know the half of it. Every time they'd snapped at each other over that blasted loo or he'd disgusted her with that noisy, slimy grunt, she'd drawn him. She remembered scratching at the paper, jaws tight and whispering obscenities, furiously depicting at least a dozen Dave-deaths.

Her savage doodles flitted through her head like a slide show on speed. The deadly bite in the ass from a mutant sewer rat leaping from the toilet, its bloodied fangs wedged firmly into his muscular bum-cheek, his face contorted in a violent scream. The close-up one. A swollen, blue tongue dangling from his mouth, veined eyeballs popping from his skull, the red alarm cable coiled tightly around his neck. The one with the pretzel of limbs wound over, through and under the metal hand rest as she'd snapped his back in two. The hunks of flesh plopping from his hands into the sink while pure acid streamed from the tap.

She'd loved those drawings. They'd made her laugh and cleansed her of anger for which they were a perfect, innocent outlet. But after today, they'd forever trigger a nasty taste. She'd rip them out, burn them. As soon as she found her notebook.

'Thank you for your understanding,' she said.

'No worries,' Dave replied with a thin smile. 'Can you fetch me that chair?'

She jumped up—she'd do anything for him at this moment—and rushed in with the seat. He used it to lean on with his forearm as he manoeuvred himself up. He then sat down, with a forgivable open crotch.

'May I ask what happened to you?' Charles asked.

Evie sat down on the floor, cross-legged. She'd inadvertently closed their circle, giving the sensation of being around a campfire. Dave in the hot seat and those on the ground angling for the ghost story he looked reluctant to tell.

And why would he? She hated it when people asked her about her arm. It was intrusive. She ran her thumb along the ridges and smooth valleys of her scar. He didn't owe anyone an explanation any more than she did.

'Afghanistan,' Dave said, gruffly.

Charles eyed Dave's patriotic thigh décor. 'Scots Guards?'

'Royal Marines, Helmand.'

Charles nodded. 'My grandfather fought at the Battle of the Bulge.'

'That must have been very traumatising for you,' Dave sneered.

Following a small twitch of the mouth, Charles practically whispered, 'Was it an IED?'

'You're not very good at getting a hint, are you?' Annoyance dripped from Dave's every syllable.

'Please forgive my clumsy husband,' Fiona interjected, squeezing her fingers on Charles's forearm. 'He's always been fascinated—second world war, mostly. A bit of a closet military buff.'

Evie fought to contain a giggle. He was a closet something, that was for sure.

'So tell me, Mr Marine...' Suki gestured to showcase the room. 'Is there anything you learned out in the desert that could help get us out of here?'

Dave's face darkened. His eyes narrowed as he leaned forward, zeroing in on Suki. 'I learned not to trust *anyone*.'

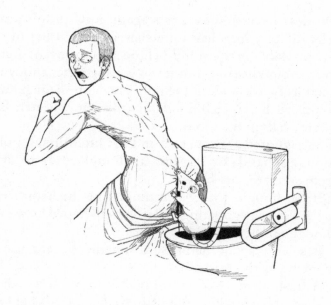

Chapter Twenty-Five
Suki

Oh dear heaven above, this again. Suki didn't know why military-man had immediately singled her out as the plausible mastermind behind an unproven, grand, murderous escapade, but it was getting super annoying. Even if she was indeed the only one with the ingenuity to pull such a thing off, judging from the collective lack of grey cells in the room.

She ignored Dave's stare and his intentional, bulky looming, hands by his sides as though ready to draw from an imaginary holster.

If he thought that was intimidating, he hadn't met her behind a negotiating table. She still hoped he would, though on the same side.

Besides, playing the physical superiority card against women was so... basic. Easy.

A fresh memory of crept into her mind. It was dark, and she'd been taking the pedestrian shortcut between her Rutland Square office and Lothian Road. She hadn't spotted the neds behind the tall, bronze sculpture of a rearing horse, but the click-clack of her heels must've summoned them. Two young men snaked out of their hiding place, their shiny tracksuits swishing over thin legs like a textile hiss.

She remembered the bottle of Buckfast shimmering in the light that leaked from the rear of empty offices. The Burberry baseball caps worn backwards, beige checks over pallid faces. A nasal laugh that echoed in the alley and made the hairs on her neck rise.

'Hey, Joey, fancy a Chinese?'

She'd walked past, head high, eyes forward, but one of them caught hold of her briefcase.

'Not so fast, chow mein.'

No matter if they were pissed or high, there was no way she could outrun them. Blood pulsed in her ears.

Thump thump thump.

Think think think.

'Come on, fortune cookie. Where are you going?'

In if-you-can't-beat-them-join-them-style resignation, she decided to feed the stereotype.

She stopped, swivelled around slowly, shaking her head. 'Oh dear,' she said, yanked her briefcase from the guy's hands and threw it aside. She tutted, narrowing her eyes, and calmly stepped out of her shoes, which she lined up neatly side by side, all the while keeping strong eye contact with both harassers. 'I wish you'd let me pass.' She smiled menacingly, stretched her neck once on each side. 'Let me rephrase that. *You'll* wish you'd let me pass.'

They watched her, bewildered, as she pushed up her blazer sleeves and advanced three steps towards them. A brief hop on stockinged feet and she landed in full kung-fu pose, legs spread, hands poised to strike.

'Now, which one of you little turds wants a chop to the testicles first?'

She'd jumped up again, and before her arms could switch sides on landing, the wee racist scumbags had bolted to the sound of her loud 'Haii-yah.'

She still thanked her lucky stars that particular act had worked. If she said it once, she'd say it a hundred times, there is little man fears more than an overconfident woman. It was wisdom she tired of having to put into practice, but that night proved it was perpetually necessary.

Suki felt a tickle, heard a scrape on the gym mat. That couple's white yapper was nuzzling her, wet nose pressed against her pinkie. She stroked him along his back. His tail wagged in delighted response. She wasn't much of a dog person, but this furry guy was being neglected something rotten by his owners. Why have pets if you don't want to care for them?

At least she didn't kid herself that she'd make time for such things—there was work to do, prospects to seek out. Hell, she hadn't even managed to kit out her new living room yet. The battered old sofa from her previous, smaller flat continued to take centre place.

She looked across to the sunflower doors beyond which lay her apartment. So near and yet so far. And so bare. Anyone else would've decked it out in *hygge* throws and scented candles within a week.

Scented candles. More relaxation nonsense. She read the safety card on one, once. Nothing relaxing there. Keep away from flammable items, which meant pretty much everything. Don't light it for less than three hours, because you need the wax to burn uniformly, but definitely not for more than four. Trim the wick to precisely a fifth of an inch after every use, with special candle wick trimmers, obviously. But first you had to wait for it to cool. Another ten minutes of hanging about. Pfft.

What was wrong with light bulbs? Off-on. Instant lighting. No faff.

Pebbles licked Suki's hand. The slimy strands of saliva made her gag, and she wiped the slabber onto his fur. There was friendly and there was that's-too-much-and-not-okay friendly. Ha. She laughed to herself. It wasn't only dogs that needed to learn that lesson.

Poor chap must be wondering why he was in here, and for so long. Should she give him some water? She checked round for something that could serve as a bowl. She spotted the water cooler, which she couldn't use, else they'd be all over her, claiming she was going to poison the pup.

Had they at least taken him for a walk that morning? Suki didn't really know how often you took a dog out, but *her* bladder was tiny. And now that she'd made the mistake of thinking about it, it became impossible to ignore the stretchy throbbing in her lower belly.

Damn.

She scratched Pebbles between the ears and got up, heading towards the rear.

'Where are you going?' Fiona asked.

'I need to pee.'

'You can't.'

'Excuse me?'

'You can't go alone,' Fiona said, seemingly oblivious to the fact that Suki was a grown woman perfectly capable of wiping her own arse, and whose toilet habits were none of anyone's business.

Dave grumbled, 'She's right.'

Suki sought Evie out and pulled an are-you-hearing-this? face. But the lass merely sat there, stupefied.

'Nobody should go anywhere by themselves,' Dave explained. 'It's safer that way.'

Suki sighed and pasted on a compliant smile. 'Fine. Who wants to come and listen to me tinkle?'

Charles averted his gaze. Fiona hauled herself up. 'I'll come. But I'm not going in there with only you. We don't know how Beatrice died, and you were in there with her last.'

'Oh come on. Seriously? Are we making this a group expedition?'

'Evie,' Fiona said, waving her along. 'You join us, please.'

She did as she was told.

'What about the men?' Suki challenged.

'What?'

'Think about it. If the three of us go into the ladies, that leaves Charles and Dave at each other's mercy. For all we know, one of them could be the killer.'

Fiona frowned. 'Er... I...'

Charles gulped, sporting a suitably aghast expression, a defensive hand to his chest. 'I'm not going to hurt anyone.'

'But I might.' Dave said, his voice a soft growl. 'That's what you're implying, isn't it, Suki?'

Suki shrugged. 'Unlike you, Dave, I'm not accusing anyone of heinous crimes. I'm merely saying, if one's to follow your logic, nobody can be left alone—as they'd be too vulnerable or, dare I propose, they'd be able to set out a new deadly trap. Nor can we have only two people in one place, right? In case one murders the other.' Suki spread out her fingers, palm facing the men. 'By my logic—and I do love logic—there are five of us and basically, there is only one combination that keeps everybody safe. We all go wee-wee together.' She held out her hand to Dave. 'You coming?'

Dave's face threatened thunder. Suki wanted to laugh, but the pressure in her bladder warned her not to.

'You ladies go,' Charles said. 'Dave's a soldier. I'm sure I'll be quite safe.'

CHAPTER TWENTY-SIX

Evie

Evie shuffled behind Fiona and Suki as they strode through to the dressing room.

Suki ducked into the first cubicle with a firm clunk of the lock.

'Evie?' Fiona asked, standing by the only other cubicle, holding open its wood-veneer door.

'No, I'm good, thanks. You go ahead.' Evie hopped onto the marble counter between the two sinks. She sat swinging her legs, kicking the panel below her to drown out the sound of the two women.

'Who would've guessed about Dave's leg, huh?' Suki's voice reverberated in the tiled space.

Trust Suki to be the kind to talk while doing her 'business'. No barriers, that one. It always struck her as odd, to speak at such a private moment. Even more today. After all, it wasn't as though they were girlfriends on a night out, escaping their dates to gossip in the loo. At one point or another that morning, Fiona had accused both Suki and her of murder.

Murder...

It still didn't sound real. Evie wasn't naïve enough to think murder only happened in books and movies. Plenty of killings took place between gangs and criminals in Scotland alone. And yes, sometimes innocent bystanders died at the hands of terrorists too. Awful.

But murder didn't happen to a random bunch of residents in an apartment building. It just didn't. Such bogeyman murder sprees strictly belonged in fiction.

Her stomach lurched at the sudden mental image of Stephen sliding off his bike, leg at an awkward angle. She felt a swirling sickness at the thought she had somehow predicted this. Willed it, even.

But only for an instant.

As a laugh.

Never for real.

She gazed at her forearm, at the inked doll-like girl in a nightdress, holding a manual drill, deep black holes for eyes. Inspired by the stories she read. The stuff of nightmares woven into scary tales to shoo the monotony of life away. Nothing more malicious than that.

She remembered how Kaif had been shocked by her tattoos the first time she'd taken off her top. It hadn't even occurred to her to warn him. Her drawings were such an intrinsic part of her. Plus, they'd talked at length about their interests in the pub where they met. His hockey—which she initially thought was the one on ice. Her manga—which he misheard as liking mango. 'Me too,' he'd said, but when she'd asked, 'which kind?' he'd looked at her quizzically. 'I think I've only ever eaten one kind.' And all became clear.

It still brought a warm rush to her belly when she saw a mango or anything with mango in it. A reminder of his smile, his eyes, his touch. A precious inner moment, like when the new swanky drink samples came in. Mango, lychee and passion fruit 'health water'.

She'd placed them in the small fridge that fronted her desk. It's where residents could help themselves to samples of all sorts of products the building management procured for them, provided they filled in questionnaires. It was clever, given how difficult it must be for companies to get insights from rich, busy people—not like Kaif's student friends who filled in surveys to make money for a paltry thirty pence a pop. She sneered. Alan was no doubt pocketing a tidy sum from the arrangement.

The samples could be anything except food, because of allergies. She'd seen drinks, fancy creams, shampoos, even small gadgets. Evie had quite fancied nicking one of the rotating stick-on thingies that let you sling your mobile phone like a gun. But the proper stuff wasn't meant for her.

Evie played with the tap. 'Health water', what rubbish. How do you make water healthier than water? She twisted on. Off. On, full force. Off. On, a drizzle. Off. The rushing of the running water merged with someone flushing and made her wish she hadn't let Fiona go first.

Fiona, who would've had to wrestle out of her bathing suit. Evie got chills even thinking about standing in this tiled ice cave stark naked. It had tricky crossed halter-top straps, too, which she'd noticed when Fiona climbed out of the floatation tank.

A tightness gripped her chest. Fiona had been where she'd drawn her death. Charles's worried voice stirred in her mind. *'Oh, thank God. You're fine... You're all right.'* He'd been hugely concerned. Why? What did he know?

She shook her head. She was being paranoid. Like Suki said, there was no reason to believe anybody was out to kill them. Or that Evie had some sort of sixth sense for snuff.

No, Stephen dying on the bike was a coincidence.

Beatrice dying was a fluke.

And Fiona, who she'd probably doodle-killed more often than anyone else, was alive. If something otherworldly was going on, why was that witch still standing?

Drops from the tap had sprayed onto Evie's trousers and seeped cold onto her thigh. She leaned over to the paper towel dispenser. The bowl of tampons caught her eye. The neat fan she'd created with the tubes had been disturbed by some thick-fingered person grabbing the one in the middle, ruining the effect. How annoying.

As she rearranged the remaining nineteen tampons, Suki barged out of her cubicle. 'Well, that's a relief. With all that arguing, I thought I was going to *explode*.'

Deep at the base of Evie's skull, a dark, dark thought awoke—and roared. She clutched the edge of the counter as anxiety spiked through her. Tampon. Explode. Oh, God. Beatrice.

CHAPTER TWENTY-SEVEN

Evie

'Evie? Evie? Are you all right?' Suki's voice snaked through the pounding in Evie's head—her pulse, hard, overpowering.

'Evie?' Fiona's voice. Shrill.

Evie winced.

She sat hunched over on the countertop, taking in deep gulps of sickly floral air. The orchid-and-patchouli sensory insult pervaded the gym's bathrooms. Misty spritzes besieged you at every threshold. A luxury scent, the packaging claimed. It claimed nothing about making you gag.

'I'm fine. I'm fine,' Evie said, through thin lips. She straightened and ran the tap beside her; held her wrist under water. The stress dissipated.

Suki lowered herself to Evie's eye line. 'What happened?'

'What's wrong with her?' Fiona said.

Evie smiled meekly. 'I'm fine, really.' She wasn't. She was far from fine. But how could she express the perturbing thoughts that ran through her mind? The growing, queasy suspicion there was something very, very disturbing going on. And that somehow, she was connected to the deaths. Stephen on the bike, and Beatrice with... The idea was too terrible.

'Time of the month?' Suki asked, smirking.

'What?' Evie hadn't realised she clutched one of the tampons in her hand. 'Oh.' Perhaps this was her way in, to test her theory. It had been a strange morning and maybe her imagination was playing tricks on her.

Sure, that had to be it. There had to be a simple explanation. Either one of them could've grabbed one when they came in. But if she didn't check, it would gnaw at her. 'Not me. What about you?' she asked the other two, holding out the yellow wrapper.

'That's awfully personal, don't you think?' Fiona said, appalled.

Suki gestured for Fiona to stay calm. 'What's this about, Evie?'

Evie's tongue felt dry and fuzzy. She was certain this would come out all wrong. It wasn't the sort of thing one talked about in general, and definitely not with strangers. But she needed to check she wasn't losing her marbles.

'Have either of you got your period? Because there were twenty tampons this morning. I know because I put them out in a nice display. And now there are only nineteen.'

Fiona sniffed. 'Not that it's any of your business, but no.'

'What does it matter?' Suki asked.

Evie wished she'd answer the question. She sensed Suki's stare bore into her, a mix of curiosity and concern. She'd been kind, earlier, when the others ganged up on her. And she was super smart, that much was clear. Perhaps she'd understand why Evie felt the way she did. Perhaps she could be trusted.

'Well... if it wasn't me, and it wasn't you two. It stands to reason Beatrice took it.'

The dead woman's name silenced the room. A drop plopped from the tap.

Was that a flicker in Suki's eyes? Did she get it?

Fiona gave her hair a quick zhuzh. 'Really Evie, are you suggesting she died of menstruation? This is silly. Let's go.'

'No.' Suki's sharp tone stopped Fiona in her tracks. She nodded at Evie. 'Go on.'

Evie inhaled, raised her chin. 'What if the poison wasn't in the water but...' She let her gaze rest on her hand.

No caricature she'd ever drawn of Fiona could match the intensity of the shock that spread across her face. The woman gasped through O-shaped lips. 'That's disgusting. How do you even think that? You're sick.' Fiona pulled her towel tight. 'Your tattoos are bad enough but this... I don't know what's wrong with you.'

'She has a point, though,' Suki said. 'You, Dave and your husband have been the ones going on about how there's a murderer in our midst. That these deaths can't have been a coincidence. If that's true—and I'm not seeing it is—then this would've been an extremely clever way of killing someone silently.' She pulled a paper towel from the dispenser, used it to take the tampon from Evie's hand and return it to the bowl. 'And if this is what happened, it tells us one thing.'

If it was clear to Suki, it certainly wasn't to Evie. 'What?'

'No woman would do that to another. Whoever used a tampon as a weapon is one misogynistic fucker.'

An icy shiver doused whatever hot shame Evie had felt in sharing her thoughts, as she realised who the killer could be.

CHAPTER TWENTY-EIGHT
Suki

Fiona left the bathroom first, bumping against Suki as she reached for the door. Suki gave her a dirty look, but if Fiona caught it, she was very good at ignoring things. And people.

She probably thought the others were beneath her, the way she walked tall, nose in the air. A disdainful queen. Cleopatra, with those snake-like earphones wound around her neck. Suki was tempted to take the viper by the ends and pull it tighter.

'Evie has a theory,' Fiona said to the men, who hadn't moved an inch since the trip to the bathroom.

Dave gave the three women the old up-and-down glare. Charles raised his arms to her like a toddler wanting 'up', his relief at seeing his wife unmistakable.

Fiona sat by him. He squeezed her hand. 'And I think I believe her... Even though it's horrible.'

Evie stood cradling herself, white as a sheet. She had quite the imagination, that girl. Suki could see the whirligig of worried thoughts turning behind that startled expression. Given how convinced they all were there was a murder-er among them, she wondered what wild idea Evie might come up with as to how Stephen died.

'Well, um...' Evie began. 'There was a box of tampons on my seat this morning. I thought they were a new thing, you know? For the gym. We've never had a dispenser and I've been asked—' She seemed to correct herself. 'I put them out in the bathroom. In a small bowl I found, nicely fanned out.'

Watching Dave twitch, Suki snickered inside. Let him squirm. It was high time men got comfortable with periods.

Fiona clicked her fingers like an ass summoning a waiter. 'For heaven's sake, Evie. Spit it out.'

'I think Beatrice was murdered by a poisoned tampon.'

It was Charles's turn to take on a pasty complexion. 'You can't be serious. Nobody would—'

'Too distasteful for you, is it?' Suki sneered. 'Have you got a better idea, since we've established it wasn't the water? I mean, given you're hell bent on there being a murderer.'

Dave shook his head. 'We haven't discounted the water.'

'Yes, we have,' Fiona said. 'Beatrice was drinking vodka.'

'That doesn't mean there wasn't *also* poison in there—and in Stephen's bottle.'

Suki issued an exasperated groan. 'There. Is. No. Poison. In. The. Bloody. Water.'

Dave snarled. 'Prove it. Have some. Go on.'

'Hey.' Evie's loud, stern voice caught Suki by surprise, as it visibly did the others. 'Stop it. Do not touch anything. Do not go anywhere. We don't know who or what we're dealing with. We will all sit here and do nothing, touch nothing until somebody comes.' She nodded, as though convincing herself, and plonked her bum demonstratively onto the mat.

'Aye, aye, captain,' Suki murmured. 'Aye, aye.'

The room went still. Dave shifted in his seat, repositioned the crotch of his shorts, and stretched his neck both ways, as if preparing for the long haul. He'd be used to following orders, but Suki hadn't expected him to defer to the gym girl.

Charles and Fiona sat huddled together, immobile, under the spotlights like eggs in an incubator. The whole place, with its glazed walls, stale air and overhead lighting, was beginning to resemble a terrarium. A cold one, though, Suki thought, rubbing her arms. Not like the heated ones at the zoo.

Gosh, she hadn't thought about the zoo in ages. Wouldn't it be weird if they were being watched? She remembered standing by the wide displays for ages, waiting for the spider to come out. Tapping on the glass against strict instructions from her dad.

Then something moved.

As it did now.

Beatrice?

CHAPTER TWENTY-NINE

Evie

Evie was still reeling from her outburst, a lingering inner tremble belying the confidence she'd sought to convey. She couldn't stand to have them bicker anymore.

Didn't they see? They had to concentrate. Listen. Watch.

It had come out, unfiltered, and, frankly, she hadn't expected them to obey. But she knew there was no point in them accusing each other. The culprit wasn't here. The culprit was sick and twisted. Playing a depraved game. Messing with her mind. Her scalp tingled with an acute awareness of being seen. Why her?

'Did she have any children?' Dave asked. His gaze fell on Beatrice. Her nose had pierced through a gap in the crossed trouser legs. Evie imagined her trying to breathe, to snatch thin ribbons of air underneath all that fabric. She closed her eyes, shook her head. She had to stop imagining things.

'No, I don't think so,' Fiona said. 'I've never seen her with kids. She's divorced, but you'd expect them to be with her at least some of the time if she had any.' She turned to Charles. 'Darling?'

He pursed his lips. 'No. Never saw her with a kid. Looked very much married to her career to me.'

Suki tutted in the distance.

'I guess that's a blessing—of sorts,' Dave said. 'My mother died when I was young. I wouldn't wish that on anyone.'

In the solemn silence spawn from Dave's admission, Evie heard Fiona whisper, no louder than the rattle of a dragonfly, 'Still better than losing a child.'

A shroud of sadness engulfed Evie. The room felt even colder. It went to show you never knew what went on in other people's lives. She'd thought them privileged. But this...'You lost a child?'

Fiona's eyes were downcast, her shoulders hunched. Charles squeezed her tight and smiled at Evie as if apologising. 'The baby was...er...never born.'

'Still my child,' Fiona muttered.

'Yes, darling, but maybe now isn't the time.'

She straightened and gave him a defiant look. 'When is it the right time, Charles? Is it ever? Huh? When can we talk about the miscarriage?'

'Shh, sweetheart.'

'No. I will not shush. We could die today. Don't you get that? And I want to remember my baby. Even if you don't.' She crawled away from him. 'You never wanted it, anyway.'

Charles reached out for her. 'Come on, don't say that.'

Dave swivelled away from them. Evie took it as a signal to also turn round. She reckoned it was the closest thing to giving them privacy they could do, under the circumstances.

What was Suki doing? She was ignoring it all and inching towards Beatrice.

A sound came from Charles and Fiona's direction. A small smack. Evie forced herself to focus straight ahead, at a shiny spot on the wall by the door to the rear corridor. The door that led to the floatation tank, frequented almost exclusively by Fiona. Evie shivered, its resemblance to a womb taking on a new meaning. Was that what Fiona thought of when inside?

Poor woman, with her oddly needy and clueless husband. Actually, her heartless, cheating husband. Would Fiona know about Stephen? Evie ran her hand over the envelope in her pocket. She'd already vowed not to spill his secret, but she vowed extra hard again. Fiona didn't need more heartache.

'*We could die today.*' The words bounced around in Evie's mind, like a rabid Tigger. Her lip quivered. What if they...? What if *she* really did die?

How would Mum and Dad cope? A way too vivid flash of her parents and sister howling by an ornate, gothic grave site surfaced and stole her breath. Her pulse jackhammered in her ears, and she felt the room close in.

She had to get out of here. She had to live. For them, for herself. For Kaif. Oh, God Kaif. She loved him. So much. If nothing else came of her life, if it ended today, at least she'd have loved. She'd tell him. As soon as she saw him. She'd jump into his arms and tell him. *If* she saw him again.

'Hey, you okay?' Dave asked.

She wiped a lick of snot from her nose with the back of her hand. 'Not really, but thanks.' She gave a watery smile. 'Worried, you know?'

'Don't be. Nobody is going to get hurt. Not on my watch,' he said, puffing up his chest.

She wanted to believe he was right. She wanted to believe Suki, too, adamant it was all one big crazy coincidence. She wanted more than anything to believe all this was her imagination in overdrive. That she, her drawings, had nothing to do with this. That she'd be safe.

Alan might be a complete cock, but was he really a murderer? It seemed surreal. A man she worked with, lurking in the shadows, plotting, scheming, waiting. Striking.

She pictured his pockmarked face, his overly straight side parting, his sleazy smile with its greying gums. His thick fingers, the chewed fingernails, always an inch too close to you.

Her lips curled in disgust, remembering his beastly smell as he'd snuck up on her one day while she was doodling at her desk and used his fat paws to wrestle the notebook from her. 'Woah. What messed up shit is this?'

Alan had access to the gym. He put the box of tampons on her chair. If anyone was killing them off, it had to be him. Who else? She couldn't conceive of anyone wanting to harm her.

There was something reassuring about the thought, too. if he was going out of his way to frame her for this, using her drawings, wouldn't he need her alive?

Kaif:
Hey - preparations all OK?

Martina:
You worry too much

Kaif:
Can't wait to see her reaction

CHAPTER THIRTY
Evie

Dave sat like a sentinel under the clock, scanning the room in a side-to-side sweep almost in time with the ticking. Evie didn't know what he and Charles had talked about while the women were in the loo, but he seemed to be taking his protective role extremely seriously.

She got up to join him, feeling he might want to hear about her theory. It would be nice to share it with some-one—though she'd have to be careful not to mention her drawings.

He was bound to have ideas about Alan, too. Everyone had been exposed to him and, she suspected from comments in the owners' association meeting, he wasn't popular.

Dave saw her approaching and raised an eyebrow. His head snapped to the opposite side, and he barked, 'What are you doing?'

Evie jumped and looked over in time to see Suki, on her knees, retreat from leaning over Beatrice and close her fist around something.

One trouser leg had slipped, leaving half of Beatrice's face exposed. Her lips shone blue against her pallid skin.

With a grunt, Dave raised himself from his chair and started walking towards them. 'I repeat, Suki. What are you doing?'

'She's got something in her hand,' Evie said.

Charles and Fiona rose, too, and shooed an agitated Pebbles away as he danced around their legs.

Suki wormed away from the body and threw her arms in the air. 'It's not what you think,' she said, wiggling the fingers on her right hand. Against her open palm, held in place by a thumb, was the unmistakable yellow packaging of a tampon.

Dave frowned. 'What's that?'

Evie experienced a sudden sense of betrayal. Was that the missing one? Why had Suki taken it? Why had she lied and let Evie believe she'd sussed things out?

'Can I get up?' Suki asked. 'My arms are getting tired, and this is hardly a weapon.' She clambered up without waiting for approval and strode to Dave, holding the item out between thumb and forefinger, as if ready to drop it.

'Where did that come from?' Fiona asked. 'I thought you didn't have it.'

'What were you doing to Beatrice?' Charles asked, covering the body up, checking for changes.

'I didn't. Nothing,' Suki said. 'I was sitting over there minding my own business while you all started to feel very sorry for yourselves and that's when I saw something move.' She pointed at Beatrice. 'I'm not one to believe in ghost but I'll admit I got a fright. Turns out it was the trouser leg slipping off her. I went to put it back. Only, when I got close, I noticed she had something in the little coin pocket of her leggings, by her hip bone.' Suki handed Dave the tampon. '*Et voilà*. The missing tampon.'

'Why would she put it there?' Fiona asked.

Suki raised her shoulders 'I don't know. Maybe for later?'

'She did that,' Evie said sullenly. 'She was always borrowing things. Well, taking things.'

Evie's shoulders sagged as her prior certainty crumbled to bits. If it wasn't the tampon that killed Beatrice, that meant it wasn't Alan. If it wasn't Alan, who was it?

'So much for that theory,' Charles said. 'In a way, I'm relieved. It was such a horrible idea.'

But for Evie, all it meant was they were back to square one. Sitting ducks, waiting it out. She checked the time. Ten-thirty on the dot. Please let the builders come. Please let us all out of here.

'That's a convenient story,' Dave said, snarling at Suki. 'I mean, you would say that, wouldn't you? You've almost got me believing it, too, with this act. But who's to say you didn't plant this on Beatrice?'

Suki scoffed. 'Why would I do that?'

'I don't know. You seem hell bent on convincing us nothing is going on and that two deaths—not one, two—and us being locked in are purely a coincidence.' He sniffed and pulled a face. 'If it smells like deflection and quacks like deflection...'

'Bloody hell, Dave. Did you protest against the chips in the vaccines too? I'm telling you. I have nothing to do with this. And you know what? It's easy to prove it to you.'

'How?'

'Well, if you're willing to assume I didn't come in here with a sack of spare menstrual products, all you need to do is count the tampons in the pot. There should be nineteen. Plus this one. Equals twenty.' She cocked her head towards Charles. 'Send him. He's the accountant.'

Charles bristled. 'Stockbroker, actually.'

Suki waved him away. 'Whatever.'

CHAPTER THIRTY-ONE

Suki

Suki was winning the staring competition she and Dave appeared to have wordlessly started during their stand-off. What a dickhead.

These residents weren't proving to be the people she'd prepared for. Suki had hoped she might have had some valuable purpose for Dave, what with her merger idea and his company on a financial cliff, but she'd had enough of him.

Charles and Evie returned from the women's bathroom. It had taken a good five minutes' arguing to agree who would go and do the counting. With suspicions still flying high, the rule remained that nobody could venture alone. Dave had insisted on staying to keep an eye on her. Fiona had whined she was too cold. The meek ones gave in.

'And?' Suki asked the two.

'Nineteen, as expected,' Evie said, looking surprisingly morose about it. Suki would've loved to jump into the girl's mind. She was clearly hiding something.

Charles nodded in confirmation. 'Nineteen.'

'I guess I'm free to go.' Suki said, turning away from Dave and his stupid macho-man expression.

'There's nowhere to go.' Evie said.

'Okay. We wait for the builders to come.' Suki lowered herself onto a weight bench. 'What time was that again?'

'Ten-thirty.'

Suki glanced at the clock. 'Ah. They're late.'

'I know,' Evie said.

'Builders are always late,' Fiona said.

Evie shook her head, looking despondent. 'But if they're the ones who locked us in and took everything offline, they'd already be in the building. Surely, they should be here by now?'

Dave paced. 'So much for your coincidences, Suki. Do you still believe there's nothing sinister going on?'

All eyes were on Suki again and she was getting mighty sick of that. She was used to being stared at curiously—all part of everyday racism in whiter-than-white Scotland—but it usually came without an extra portion of murderous accusations.

She recognised a failing strategy when she saw one, and it was time for a different approach.

She rubbed her face and hugged herself, shrinking as best she could to appear vulnerable. 'You're right, Dave. You guys are all right. I guess I didn't want to believe we'd been targeted. But there's no rational explanation for this. I give in.'

Dave cocked his head slightly and narrowed his eyes, as if waiting for the catch. When Suki continued her submissive act, his chest inflated, and he nodded contentedly. Smugness personified.

'So who's caused this?' Fiona asked.

'And how?' Charles asked the sea, as he stood by the window, his pinkie making furtive contact with the pile of mats Stephen lay on.

Evie cleared her throat and wiped her palms on her trousers, as she shuffled beside them. 'I can't explain it, but I think it's Alan.'

Suki had an inkling who Alan was but wanted to make sure. She felt a spark of excitement. It would be hugely helpful if they had someone on the outside they could pin this on, rather than her. 'Alan, the building's maintenance man?'

Evie squirmed. 'Yes.'

'Okay. I am happy to go with Alan.' It certainly fit with the sordid vibe she'd caught off him during the few interactions she'd had. 'But why?'

'I'm not sure,' Evie said, heat spreading on her cheeks. 'But he's the one who's got the most access.'

'Wait,' Fiona said. 'I think I know.' She secured the end of her towel over the top to release her arms and stroked her hair into place. She had the floor and was clearly going to make the most of it. 'Maybe it's to do with Tessa.'

That was a new one on Suki. 'Who the hell is Tessa?'

Charles returned to the fold and stood by his wife. 'Such a shame what happened to her.'

Dave, leaning against the wall, seemed to have a sudden fascination for his cuticles.

'Hellooo, who is Tessa?' Suki pressed.

'A lovely young woman, about twenty-five,' Fiona said. 'Runs a chain of vegan cafés. Actually, I'm not sure if she still does.'

'She owned your apartment before you,' Charles added.

That hit too close to home. Suki's senses went on high alert. 'So what happened and what does it have to do with Alan? What?... Did he kill her?'

'He might as well have,' Charles said.

Fiona rolled her eyes. 'Don't be so dramatic.' She turned to Suki. 'She accused him of *rape*.' Fiona merely mouthed that last word, but to Suki it sounded like a bomb exploding.

'Why is he still here?' Suki asked, incredulous. 'Why isn't he in prison?'

'That's the thing.' Fiona cosied up to her. 'Apparently she waited too long with reporting it for there to be, you know, any evidence.'

Charles winced. 'I heard she was worried about going to the police because she'd been out with a friend and came home drunk. And that's when he supposedly got her.'

'Supposedly?' Suki said. 'Are you shitting me? You don't get to not believe the victim.' Dave's mouth opened, but Suki silenced him with a hiss. 'No. No stupid conspiracy theories from you.'

He looked down, duly chastened. 'I was going to say I believed her.'

'Then you should've done something,' Suki said. 'What else?'

Fiona adopted a frostier tone. 'Alan was put on leave while the investigation ran. Tessa was questioned over and over.'

'We hardly ever saw her, but when I last spotted her slinking into her car, she was like a shell of a human,' Charles said.

Fiona placed both hands on her chest in a show of sympathy that didn't quite convince Suki. 'That poor girl.' She paused, gazing into the middle distance. After a brief moment, she shrugged. 'In the end, the Procurator Fiscal, or whatever they're called, decided there wasn't enough there for a conviction. Nothing got done. Imagine that entire ordeal, for nothing.'

'I heard she went home to Dundee,' Charles said. 'Sold everything she owned.'

A chilling realisation hit Suki: that's why she got the apartment fast and cheap. A bitter taste flooded her mouth. What she believed had been super-cunning negotiating on her part had, in fact, been her taking advantage of another woman who needed to flee. Her stomach heaved with guilt. If only she'd known...

But she was not the guilty one. Alan was. 'So why hasn't he been sacked?'

'The owner's association board has been trying,' Fiona said. 'He comes through a management company. I won't bore you with the details, but it's been complicated because of the way the contracts are set up. And the fact the charges were dropped. Leading to them saying technically there are no grounds for dismissal.'

'I know the owner of the building management company. A real slimy bastard.' Dave said. 'I wouldn't be surprised if he was protecting him.'

Suki gestured for them to stop. 'Rewind. We've established Alan is a rapist who got away, or at the very least, an assaulter. Why would any of this want to make him kill you? Kill us?'

'Because we've been trying to get rid of him. And we finally found a way,' Fiona said, a hint of pride in her upright stance.

Suki thought back to the meeting, to Beatrice urging Alan to leave because of some agenda point they ended up not tackling. She'd referred to the *Alan situation.* Doors had slid shut. That must've been it. 'Did he know?'

'I'm not sure. It was Beatrice who led the work and did the liaising, but she asked everyone for help. I contributed, as did Charles, asking friends for advice and such. Mrs M was spitting mad about the whole thing. Really stood up for Tessa.' Fiona chuckled. 'She said she was ready to knock him over the head herself with her stick if we didn't find an alternative. But we did. I don't know the mechanics of it, but it was a grey area of interpretation in the fine print of the contract that gave us an out.'

Suki tapped her fingers against her lips. 'Hmm, I don't know. It's a bit extreme. People lose their jobs all the time.'

As he paced, Dave punched a fist into the palm of his other hand with what was beginning to be an irritating habit. 'Trust me on this one. Bad reputations linger like a bad smell.' Dave said. 'Edinburgh is small. A city that doesn't forget—or forgive.'

Chapter Thirty-Two
Evie

It was the first time Evie had heard the whole story. There'd been staff gossip of Alan having been in trouble and not actually on holiday, back then. And it having something to do with Tessa, whom she'd only met briefly.

Evie remembered she'd drawn Tessa once, having nearly collided with her, deep in thought, in the lobby. She mentally retraced the image: a bony ghost with cesspool eyes floating out the door to the sea, her stringy hair like whips cracking behind her. She'd caught a despairing sadness in her. Now she knew why.

An angry flame shot up inside like flared gas on an oil rig. How could this all have been kept quiet? How could the building management company, the residents, have let Alan continue to creep around them like that? It was all very well these four standing around commiserating, but had none of them realised young women worked here?

Nothing in their selfish behaviour should surprise her, of course. Four months in this place was training enough to see them blinded by their own privilege.

If she hadn't spoken up about Alan, even though she wasn't sure, this wouldn't have come out. They'd still be at each other's throats, forgetting to look outside this room.

But learning the facts made her believe even more firmly that Alan was behind them being locked up. The swine. He knew it was her birthday. He lured her in here on her day off. Tampon or no tampon, deadly bicycle or no tampered bicycle, she had a disquieting sense of foreknowledge, and her gut told her he orchestrated these deaths. With her in mind.

She raised her hand high, capturing everyone's attention. 'Can I add I thought Alan was acting weird last night. He left me to clean up by myself even though he'd hovered outside the whole time. It's normal for him to be dismissive of me, but there was something very jittery about him, like he had somewhere to go.'

There was no way he'd get away this time. This time, the twisted bastard would pay.

CHAPTER THIRTY-THREE

Suki

Suki felt like a tangled sock in a washing machine. Round and round they went. Debating. Was it Alan? But why? And how? And why me or them? And back to, could he really be a killer?

She groaned and hung her head between her knees, watching the end of her plait sweep the floor between the shiny steel legs of the weight bench.

'But why Stephen? Was he ever involved in Alan's dismissal?' she heard.

Who cares? Wasn't the priority to get the hell out of there?

She was waiting for Dave to take charge. It's what he'd wanted all along. On you go. Because by God, she had no interest in having to lead these numpties. She had enough snot-nosed junior associates at the firm who thought they were oh-so-smart but had proven a paper bag was too much of a challenge without her guiding them by the hand.

Yet it was she that got told off. Go figure. Angus had said, *'If you don't want to burn out, Suki, you'll need to give up this "I'll do it my bloody self then" attitude. Delegate more.'* Easily said for a managing partner who had millions in the bank already.

She closed her eyes and listened in. Nope. Still blethering, debating, as if that was going to do any good. She peeked sideways along her calf. Dave was nodding along to Fiona, who seemed to make even this situation about her.

When it was merely a matter of waiting for the builders, they hadn't tried very hard to solve their problem. But the circumstances had changed.

Suki thrust herself up. She *was* going to have to bloody do it herself again. 'Listen up. Two words.'

The others turned to her, bemused.

'Get out.' Suki held her arms up and swirled around. 'As long as we are in this gym, nothing will change. We could be prey. We could not. I don't want to find out. Why are you lot standing around like green activists arguing whether the climate change target should be one degree or two degrees? Do something.'

'She's right.' Dave finally acted. 'We're not going to solve what killed them. Or who. That's for the police to do. We need to stay safe and that means getting out.'

'We've tried that,' Evie said.

'We try again.' Suki headed to the fire door while issuing instructions. 'You. Jump on the floor. With all your weight.'

Charles stood there like a sack of potatoes. 'What?'

'You're the heaviest after Dave. And he can't jump, so you jump—hard—to attract attention downstairs.'

'I can jump,' Dave objected.

'Oh for heaven's sake, both jump, then. Happy? Evie, check the phone and the computer again. Fiona, go slam the chair against the glass door. You won't break it. It's to make noise.'

Evie did as she was told, but Fiona watched the two men thump against the ground, building momentum by flapping their elbows like bagpipers playing a long note. Pebbles scurried for cover under the desk.

'Fiona, come on.' Suki rattled the metal bar of the fire escape to jiggle the woman out of her thoughts.

'There's no point jumping,' Fiona said. 'Below us is Beatrice's apartment. And she's here.'

Dave hopped to a halt. 'I'll grab the chair.'

'No point either.' Suki let go of the door. 'Thinking about it, the only apartment that's going to hear that is the one across the landing. And that's mine.'

'What about upstairs?' Evie said. 'We could bang on the ceiling. Mrs M might hear?'

'Clever girl,' Charles said.

Suki chewed her lip. 'Right, I'm too short. Let's see... Evie, climb onto Charles's shoulders.'

'Do I have to?'

Suki realised asking her to straddle a stranger after stories of rape might be a bit much.

'No. Fiona, you do it. I'll hand you something to bang with once you're up.'

'Okay.'

Charles grabbed hold of the side post of a gym contraption and got down on his haunches. Fiona hoiked her towel up and, using the handles of the nearby seated press for foot support, she clambered onto her husband.

'Ouch, no, wait,' she said, contorting round his shoulders with all the grace of a gyrating hippo. 'The towel is stuck.'

'Take it off,' Suki said, her arm tired from extending a kettle bell.

Fiona slipped the towel from underneath her and let it float to the ground. Suki watched as the wobbly couple tried to find their balance, Fiona clutching onto Charles's head for dear life, her sparkly purple bathing suit doing nothing to kill off the image of a third-rate circus act.

'The phone line is still dead and there's still no Internet,' Evie reported.

All eyes were on the ceiling-bangers. Fiona held the kettle bell in her right arm behind her, ready to swing. 'Hold on, darling,' she said, nearly choking Charles with the forearm she'd clasped around his chin.

The bell hit the ceiling with a disappointing thud. The beige tile bounced briefly in its metal frame. She tried again. Still no sound, but the tile shifted diagonally, and Suki spotted thick insulation material above it.

'Has anyone seen anything long? To push the insulation away?' Suki asked.

'What about the hose of the hoover?' Evie said. 'There's nothing much in the cleaning cupboard but there's definitely a hoover.'

'That's going to be too bendy,' Suki said.

'Could be worth a try. Where is it, Evie?' Dave asked.

Charles pipped up in a pained voice. 'Will you please hurry? I'm not sure how much longer I can hold.'

Dave came running back, a red Henry hoover trailing behind him. He stretched out his arm as far as he could, but the solid pipe hit Fiona in the shoulder, which won him a death stare.

He bent down and lifted the hoover up to his chest. He tried to aim so Fiona could catch the sucker-head, but the flexible hose drooped limply.

Suki had to contain her laughter and busied herself tucking escaped hairs into her plait, lips pressed hard together. She'd warned them the hose would be too bendy but here was Dave, slinging around a long, flaccid schlong.

'One last try,' Fiona said.

He threw the hose at her, and she caught the black pipe. With both hands she pushed against the ceiling's insulation, then sputtered. 'There's dust in my eyes.'

'Shout,' Evie said. 'She might hear.'

Fiona nudged the tile aside and lifted the cotton-like padding once more. 'Mrs M. Mrs M. Marjorie. Help.'

Everyone kept quiet. Suki strained her ears. 'Any luck?'

'I can't hold this anymore.' Fiona dropped the hose, leaving Dave cradling Henry.

'I can't hold *you* anymore,' Charles said. 'Dave, can you help get her down?'

It took some manoeuvring. Fiona inadvertently pulled Charles's hair as she made her way to the ground. Poor sod roared as if he'd never been hurt before.

'Be quiet,' Suki said, still listening intently. 'Anything?'

CHAPTER THIRTY-FOUR
Suki

Suki couldn't concentrate on upstairs, with Dave's heavy panting. With all those muscles, and a neck that screamed steroids, you'd think he'd be fitter.

'I don't think she heard us,' Evie said ruefully.

'Who is this Mrs M, anyway?' Suki asked.

'It's Marjorie Macaulay. I call her—well, I think everyone calls her Mrs M.' Evie replied.

Suki's shoulders tingled. The woman was as elusive as she was powerful. If the nickname meant the residents were privy to special access, moving here had indeed been one of the smarter things to do.

'She's the old lady that sits outside in the yard most days, talking to herself,' Dave said.

'Well, she is old...' Fiona said.

Evie frowned. 'She's not doolally, if that's what you're thinking. She's talking to her dog Bobby. He died.' A fond smile spread across Evie's face. 'She says he's the only one that doesn't interrupt.'

'Are you saying she buried her dog in our garden?' Charles asked, aghast.

Fiona smacked his shoulder. 'No, silly. Have you never seen the plaque on the bench? The tree was planted in Bobby's honour.'

'That doesn't mean he's not buried there,' Charles muttered. 'Lots of people don't want to pay for a vet.'

Suki snickered. 'I don't think Marjorie Macaulay would look twice at a vet bill. She probably had the best of funerals for him, too. For free.'

'What makes you say that?' Dave asked.

'Don't you know who she is?' Suki's gaze ran along the four blank faces. 'Wow, you people really don't do any due diligence on your neighbours, do you? She's only a massively successful businesswoman with a big portfolio of service companies. Funeral directors, hygiene solutions, pest control.'

Fiona curled a strand of hair behind her ear. 'I knew that.'

Dave's eyes lit up. 'Pest control. You mentioned pest control before. A merger. With her?' He pointed upward.

Suki should've known better than to mention that. If he cut her out of the deal, she'd kill him. She smiled. 'Cat's out of the bag,' she said, and held her finger up in warning. 'But don't you dare circumvent me.'

'All sound like very distasteful sectors to me,' Charles said, pulling a disgusted face.

Dave gave him an icy stare. 'We can't all have the cushy, soft-handed jobs dished out to boarding school boys.'

'This again.' Charles groaned. He rubbed and stretched his neck, no doubt feeling the strain of having his wife ride him. Maybe his throbbing muscles gave him a false sense of strength because Suki was stunned when Charles squared up to Dave in an uncharacteristic display of manliness and said, 'I've had about enough of you.'

CHAPTER THIRTY-FIVE

Evie

Oh great. They were quarrelling again. Evie scratched her forehead and sighed. She'd liked it much better when they worked as a team to escape, confident Alan was to blame. Supporting each other. Focused on getting out.

She was cold, thirsty, and wanted to be home. If only she hadn't taken this damned job. Not that she'd had much choice.

She rolled to and fro on a pink Swiss ball, trying to tune out the others. Dave's sarcastic laugh. Charles's affronted exclamations. To think she'd felt sympathy for him, what with his lover dying. But it had gradually seeped away as it became clear what a self-righteous snob he was.

How could someone have such little regard for hard-working people? Who did he think kept the streets clean, the trains running, his precious concert halls staffed? Sometimes it was dirty work. She hated replacing the hair filter in the floatation tank and wiping the sweat off the bike saddles. But somebody had to do it.

Her eyes were drawn to Stephen's body, laid out by the window. Somebody had to take care of the bodies.

She remembered an old, framed photo she'd admired in Mrs M's apartment. A young boy, trousers too short, a bright, toothy grin beneath a flat cap, holding up a coin. Unmistakeably Leith harbour behind him, bobbing boats and spikey masts a solid black against a sun that glistening white on the grey sea.

'That's my father,' Mrs M had said, coming up behind her. 'His first penny earned.'

'Did his mum take the photo?' Evie asked.

'No, dear. They didn't have that kind of money. The way the story was told to me is that a photographer was passing by and noticed my father, six years old, chasing after a stray cat. He shouted that if he caught it, he'd give him a penny. And my dad ran like the wind.'

'That's adorable.'

'Sadly, he made a habit of running,' Mrs M said bitterly. 'And his debts eventually caught up with him. He died when I was ten.'

'Oh, I'm sorry.' Evie hadn't wanted to press further, but Mrs M took her hand and sat her down on the sofa.

'You know, Evie, sometimes people dying can be the best thing that happens to you. My mother had to work in the steamies to keep the family afloat. The laundry was hard, hard work. She insisted I stay in school but as soon as I was old enough, I went to find work. I took jobs nobody else wanted to do, and therefore paid better. I never stopped, really.' She gestured to showcase the plush living room. 'And I have all this to thank for that.'

Evie'd thought of her many crappy jobs along the way and asked, 'What did you do?'

'I worked as a cleaner at the funeral home and mortuary. Seems I was the only one without silly superstitions.'

'That was brave.'

'Ach, I never feared death,' she'd said. 'Something being scary is all in your mind.'

Evie had agreed with her, then, and had opened up about her love of horror. Unlike most people who thought Evie was weird, Mrs M celebrated her quirks.

In the gym, she looked at the misplaced ceiling tile, wishing they'd managed to contact her. Mrs M may not fear death, but Evie did. Stuck in a room where anything could potentially kill you, given how two people collapsed spontaneously, she was scared stiff.

A huffy Charles passed in front of Evie in the direction of her desk. 'That's it. I want nothing more to do you with you. I'm getting a drink.'

A drink? What drink?

Chapter Thirty-Six

Evie

Charles pulled open the door to the mini fridge under the reception desk and grabbed one of the trial bottles of fancy, fruity health waters.

A flash of orange on the label—a mango—triggered a vivid image in Evie's mind. She gasped and jumped up. 'No. You can't.'

'They're for us, aren't they?' he said.

'Yes. No. That's not it,' she said, flustered. Her cheeks burned. How was she meant to explain the deadly mango?

When Evie had stocked the fridge the other day, she'd noticed there were four bottles each of lychee, dragon fruit and watermelon, but only one mango. And she'd not been the only one to notice. Charles had hovered over her on his way out.

'What's this?' He'd humphed as she placed the drinks in the fridge. 'No good for me. I really do wish you'd take into account my allergies, Evie. Make sure nobody but me gets that mango.'

Evie had closed her eyes and expelled a measured breath before getting up and smiling. 'Of course.' But later, she'd drawn a giant mango, sliced open to reveal Charles's flailing legs in lieu of the pit, his head buried deep within the flesh as though devoured.

That's the picture that sprung to mind and made her wonder. Why was there only one mango? Alan was responsible for the trial products. If Alan needed an easy way to kill Charles, and Charles alone, poisoning this drink could be it.

'I'm thirsty too, but I don't think we should touch anything.' She reached out to take the bottle from him, but thought the better of it, in case it was coated with anything. 'Put it back.'

Charles grumbled and made a big display of straightening the drink on the shelf. The way the light fell made the plastic glow and the yellow liquid sway seductively. 'Happy now?'

'Come on, Charles. Don't be a dick,' Suki said. 'She's right. We all agreed we wouldn't touch anything. If this is a crime scene, you don't want your fingerprints all over it, do you?'

'Close that fridge door,' Fiona said. 'The last thing we need is more cold air in this room.' Fiona stood with her arms wrapped around herself, her fake-tanned hands and feet noticeably paler.

'Why don't you wrap up in your towel?' Suki asked.

'You guys stood on it when I was up there trying to hit the ceiling.'

Evie looked across the room to the machines. The towel lay on a trodden heap on the floor.

'Beatrice's towel must be somewhere,' Dave said, seemingly forgetting it missing was the reason he'd taken his trousers off.

Fiona shivered. 'I'm not touching a dead woman's towel.'

'Come on, darling,' Charles said, stomping towards her. 'Let's go find your clothes.' He grabbed her by the hand. She stumbled alongside him as he beelined to the rack of weights.

'What...?' she asked.

'I'm going to take one of these dumbbells and bang it against the locker until it breaks.'

As Evie watched Charles facing the angled, six-foot-tall tower of weights, a sudden darkness enveloped her. Her throat constricted around a lumpy breath. She remembered wishing him dead, right there. The thick charcoal lines that depicted the rack collapsing onto him. Charles on the floor, flattened by a shower of barbells. A great big cast iron disc crushing his head. The splattered brains.

She grew dizzy.

This wasn't happening... She seemed to be lurching from one of her private illustrations to another. Had Alan seen them all? Had he booby-trapped the whole place? Was *anywhere* safe?

She pulled herself out of her daze and briefly considered the possibility she was being paranoid. But what if she wasn't?

'Don't touch those,' she said, a bit too loudly.

Charles turned, an exasperated expression on his face. Fiona cocked her head, puzzled.

Evie felt her heart rate speeding up. 'We'd agreed we wouldn't touch anything, right Suki?' She urged Suki on with her eyes.

'Yes. Absolutely. And...?' Suki clearly wanted to play along, but unsurprisingly didn't know where Evie was headed.

'Barbells are dangerous,' Evie said. At this point, even Suki's face turned to doubt. 'We also agreed we wouldn't split up. I mean, go anywhere alone or in pairs.' There, that felt like a much more rational explanation for wanting to stop them.

Suki adopted a playful tone as she said, 'Yes, Charles, for all we know you might want to bash your wife's head in.'

'Oh for heaven's sake, you two, stop it. I'm not going to kill her here.'

'Charles!' Fiona let go of his hand.

'I meant to say... If I wanted to kill my wife—which I do not, obviously—I wouldn't need to go through this whole locked-in charade.'

'Oh? Have you come up with an easier way?' Suki snorted with laughter.

'Ha ha, Suki. Very funny. Grow up,' Fiona said, marching toward the diminutive woman, eyes glaring.

Dave, who'd been observing from the side lines, issued an almost animal-like growl. 'Stop. We said we wouldn't split up and that rule stays. Everyone stay here and BEHAVE.'

'But I'm cold,' Fiona whined.

'I've already tried jimmying the lockers and breaking the doors, Fiona,' Dave said as he fished her towel off the floor. 'If I thought we could open them, we'd all be on our mobile phones and out of here. I'm afraid this is all you have to keep you warm.'

Fiona draped the towel over her shoulders.

'Maybe you can cosy up to your darling husband—who is *not at all* planning to kill you,' Suki said. Her cackle was joyous, and Evie couldn't help but laugh along, all tension in her body dissipating.

'Fine. You joke,' Charles said in a huff. 'But in the meantime, we're still stuck. There are still two dead people and who knows what else will happen. There's got to be something we can do. Are you sure there's not a remote or something to open the door? Or a window?' he asked Evie.

'A window?' Suki chuckled. 'Have you seen these bad boys?' She gestured to the wall of glass. 'Besides, we're on the twelfth bloody floor. Were you going to use Fiona's towel as a parachute?'

'All right. You know what I mean,' he said, grumpily.

At Evie's desk, he lifted, rattled, and tipped over the pink cup holding a variety of pens. He swept his hand across the content and, finding nothing, he pulled the top drawer with such a force the desk juddered, and Pebbles shot out from underneath.

He rummaged impatiently, lifting sheets of paper, sighing, clutching handfuls of junk, scattering paperclips, elastic bands and a pencil sharpener all over the table.

Evie approached, feeling protective of her space. It was daft, as she kept her stuff in her locker and this desk was shared with the other receptionist, anyway.

'What's this?' Charles asked, fishing a letter from among the content of the drawer.

'That's mine,' Evie said. That didn't stop him from reading. 'Hey, I said that's mine.'

Charles held out his hand to keep her at bay as he continued to scan the document. 'It's Stephen's.'

'What? No. It's from the insurance.'

He flipped the page around and shoved it in her face. He pointed at the signature, one of those digital scribbles with a printed name nobody ever looks at. 'Yes, Neilson Insurance, but look here. S.J. Watt.'

'That's Stephen?' She'd no idea where he worked. How could this be? Hot prickles ran over her arms like fire ants. She succumbed to an eerie sensation this was too much of a coincidence. Again. Why was everything related to her?

Beads of sweat formed above Charles's snarled lip. His eyes widened. 'Don't pretend you didn't know. Acting all innocent. But it was you. You have a motive.'

The others had slowly congregated around the desk, while Charles became more frantic. His nostrils flared as he shifted feet and pointed at her with an ever-extending arm.

'I promise I had no idea,' Evie said, looking pleadingly at the others for support.

'Charles, calm down,' Fiona said softly. 'What does it matter? What's in the letter?'

Charles refocused on the paper in his hands. 'It's a personal injury case. A response to a complaint.' He frowned. 'It doesn't say much other than they refused a pay-out.' He looked up. 'Forty thousand pounds. And if she doesn't like it, she could begin court proceedings. But that's not what you did, is it?'

Tears squeezed into Evie's eyes. Her head throbbed. How could she be the one in the line of fire again? She'd done nothing wrong. She's the one who got injured, dismissed, given the run around, made to wait for months—almost a year—and then rejected. She couldn't afford to take this to court, however unfair it was, however it sucked and would impact the rest of her life. But that didn't mean she killed anyone. And if not her... who?

CHAPTER THIRTY-SEVEN

Suki

'Give me that letter,' Suki said, snatching it from Charles. She gave it a quick scan. 'Aside from this being Evie's private business, Charles, this is a completely standard letter. And forty K is peanuts. There's no way a director would even have been involved in such a small case.'

Charles seemed to consider this, licking his lips, but his gaze flitted to where Stephen lay and he said, 'Evie doesn't know that.'

Suki spotted Evie was crying, holding her arm, and rubbing that very pronounced scar tissue with her thumb. It looked like a burn. Suki couldn't imagine how sore that must have been. How frightening. The poor girl. She'd been dealt a shitty hand of cards in life as it was, then having to deal with today and all these accusations.

'You're an ass,' Suki said to Charles. 'Leave her alone.'

'She can at least tell us what the letter is about. What was going on. Stephen's dead. She owes us an explanation,' Charles said, getting unnecessarily close to Evie.

Out of nowhere, Dave's arm fell between them like the gate of a railway crossing. He swept Charles away three feet with a single move. 'She owes you nothing.' He looked mournfully at Evie's arms. 'I think we can all guess what this is about. Leave it.'

Shaking and shrunken, with tears streaked down her cheeks, Evie said, 'I got burned.'

Dave said, gently, 'You don't have to—'

'No, it's fine. It's not like I can hide it,' Evie said, with a clumsy smile, followed by a sniff. 'I got burned with oil making fries at McDerry's. While I was in the burns unit, they sent someone who offered me money. I was on painkillers. I agreed.' She shuffled her foot along the floor and kept her eyes down. 'My mum was furious. Insisted it wasn't enough. And it wasn't, really. But when we told them we refused, they made it out to be my fault. That I'd been the negligent one.'

'That's awful,' Fiona said, and might even have meant it.

Evie sniffed once more and raised her head. 'So anyway, I've been fighting them, and they've left it to the insurance.' She shrugged. 'And you know the rest.'

'And Stephen...?' Charles asked.

'I really didn't know,' Evie said.

But Suki saw a flicker of doubt—or fear, even?—in her expression. Her heart skipped like it does when she finds a loophole in a contract. She'd thought it all along, but she was now convinced Evie was hiding something. And while it was clear that girl had nothing to do with these deaths, Suki was set on finding out her secret.

'Hey. It's okay,' Suki said, guiding Evie away by the elbow. She brought her to the corner by the door, where Evie had seemingly felt comfortable before. Pot-plant corner. Fertile ground for digging deeper, she hoped.

They sat side by side, wrists resting on raised knees. Breathing. In-out. In-out. Eventually slowing. Eventually synchronised. They stared at the sky in the distance, where large grey clouds, swollen with rain, gathered to block out the light.

'Thank you,' Evie said.

'No problem.'

As Evie repositioned her bum on the mat, Suki heard a slight crunch. She looked down. A sliver of white stuck out from Evie's pocket. Paper. With a thick edge, like an envelope.

'What's in your pocket?' she asked.

'Huh?'

Suki wasn't buying the dumb act. She swiped the folded envelope with two fingers and presented it to Evie. 'This.'

Evie's eyes widened. A flicker of stress. 'That's nothing. A tip.'

'A tip? Bollocks. I lived in the US and am acutely aware that Scottish people do not tip.' Suki unfolded the paper and read the message. Her heart jumped. 'Shit. From Stephen?' She looked inside while Evie winced. Fifty quid. 'What the fuck, Evie? What is this about a secret?'

'It's not what you think,' Evie said, snatching the money.

'You don't know what I think.'

Evie sighed. 'I promised.'

'Hey,' Suki clicked her finger in front of Evie's face. 'I don't mind having your back while these idiots ride a merry-go-round to nowhere, accusing you and me and anyone of murder. But you have to tell me what's going on. If you have something to do with Stephen...'

'No, no. It's nothing like that. Last night, after the meeting, I found a parcel in the gym with Stephen's name on it. I figured he'd left it behind, so I brought it over. But when he opened his apartment door, Pebbles ran to me.'

'Pebbles, this Pebbles?' Suki asked, cocking her head to the white fluff ball at his mistress's feet. 'You mean Fiona was there?'

Evie shook her head, her lips pressed together. 'Charles,' she whispered.

'Ha.' Suki clapped.

Pebbles's head shot up, ears alert.

'Shush,' Evie hissed, pushing Suki's hands down.

Suki grinned. She liked nothing more than to be vindi-cated. 'I knew it. Just something in the way Charles was acting around the body, and on the video.' She turned to Evie, eyes wide with conspiratorial glee, and asked, 'So what are you going to do?'

'Nothing. I promised to keep quiet. Plus, he's dead. What good would it do to expose them now?'

Suki tutted at her sweet innocence. 'Oh, honey, you have much to learn about leverage.'

'What do you mean?'

'You threaten Charles with disclosure next time he has a go at you,' Suki said. 'Might nicely shift the focus of blame on him for a change.'

'I couldn't. Didn't you see how distraught he was when Stephen died?'

Suki looked her straight in the eye. 'Yes, but I also saw that he was sitting right next to Stephen when he died.'

CHAPTER THIRTY-EIGHT

Evie

Evie blushed at the intensity of Suki's stare. Was she serious? It hadn't even occurred to Evie that Charles could be involved.

He was standing by his wife, fussing, with one hand rested in the small of her back and the other warming her upper arm. They were speaking in hushed tones by the water cooler. Furtive glances across the room. His eyes met Evie's. A cold stare. Her heart jumped.

Why was she feeling guilty? That was ridiculous. She'd done nothing wrong. He had. At minimum, he was a cheater. He had no right to judge her.

But had he killed Stephen?

She squeezed her eyes and lifted her chin in a defiant response. A small frown creased Charles's forehead, and he walked further away, Fiona in tow.

The dutiful husband. A great act. Could the rest of it be an act, too? Could he be behind all of this? But to what end? Had Fiona found out? Were they both in on it?

It seemed unlikely. Stress crept across her shoulders. Why the big elaborate ploy? Why Beatrice? How did they even know how to lock the doors? Why would Charles go for the mango if he knew it would kill him? Why would he reach for the weights?

How would he have known Stephen would choose that bike? Unless they'd agreed to meet...

Why would he want to implicate her?

As her mind whirled with questions, a splotchy image of a male face emerged from the shadows. Saggy jowls and a leery grin. A hand raised as if to grab her. Thick fingers reaching. She gasped. Alan. Alan was still the answer.

'Are you okay?' Suki asked, beside her.

'I'm... Yes, sorry. I'm fine.' She patted Suki's knee. 'But I don't want to play games. This is not fun, nor is it funny. Let's just try to get out of here. And in the meantime, Stephen's secret stays with me.'

'Talk about taking it to the grave,' Suki quipped.

'I mean it. It's not funny,' Evie said and scrambled up. She'd had enough.

But as she stood, she saw something that made her legs quiver. Dave was grabbing the door handle of the disabled toilet. 'Dave, don't,' she shouted.

He yanked open the door and glared at her. 'Evie, we've gone over this.'

'No, you don't understand,' Evie said, heart thumping furiously. 'It's where you die.'

CHAPTER THIRTY-NINE

Evie

Evie felt as though time stood still. Dave faced her open-mouthed. His hand dropped to his side, smacking against his saltire socket.

The room buzzed, and the lights flickered faster than she blinked. Her mouth was parched, yet a cold sweat invaded her shirt.

What had she done? People were looking at her.

But she couldn't *not* warn him. She couldn't let him go in there. Not there, where she'd made him suffer a dozen deaths.

She blew out a long breath. As she fought to steady her pulse, she saw shapes advance towards her: Fiona and Charles backlit by a sharp ray of sun piercing the clouds.

Sound, muffled. Then clear. 'Why did you say that?'

Evie reached for Suki's forearm. Reassurance. Support.

'I've drawn Dave dying. In there. Multiple times. I've drawn all of you dying. Stephen, Beatrice, you, and you.' The wetness on her cheeks felt tight on her skin. 'They were just drawings, I swear. I've got nothing to do with this, but whoever has locked us in—Alan—he's using my drawings for inspiration.' She held her blazing forehead and gulped. 'It's like he's framing me.'

Suki squeezed her hand. 'Evie, I think the stress of this place is getting to you. Come have a seat.' With a nod of the head, she got Dave to fetch a chair.

'Get her some water,' Fiona said. When this was met by an incredulous look all round, she said, 'Not from the cooler, obviously, but can we not get some from the tap?' She stepped in the direction of the bathroom.

'Everybody stays here,' Dave said. 'We stick to the rule. Especially now.'

'You can't be serious,' Charles said. 'You believe this?'

'I'm open to suggestions, yes.' Dave sneered. 'Things are often not what they seem. Do you have a problem with that?'

Charles shrugged. 'Seems terribly convenient, if you ask me. Blame it on Alan and some strange story about her sickening drawings. But all the while she's the one with the motive to take revenge on Stephen.'

'Tell me more about the drawings,' Dave asked Evie.

'I'm sorry. It's boring here, this job. And you people, you're not always very nice to me.' She ran her hand over her tattoos. 'I like manga. Horror comics. I doodle. Graphic death scenes. But it doesn't mean anything.'

'You draw us dead?' Fiona asked.

Evie winced and nodded. It had merely been a fun pastime for her, a way to evolve her art. Practising her submissions to fanzines, which were full of this kind of stuff. This was normal in her circles. She'd never considered how it would reflect on her if regular people saw it, how shocking it could be. 'It was just for fun. A silly, harmless way to get rid of negative feelings. I would never actually hurt you, or anyone.'

She searched Suki's concentrated face. 'You believe me. Don't you?'

'What makes you think it's your drawings?' Suki asked.

'Stephen on the bike. I... He was very sweaty. Never wiped down the handles or moist saddle. So I imagined him being... Oh God.' She put her hands over her face, peeked out through a gap between her fingers at all their condemning faces. She spoke quickly; perhaps it wouldn't sound as bad. 'I drew him sliced in half by a knife in the saddle.'

'Jesus,' Fiona said, her hand clutching her chest, a shocked face at ridiculous odds with her sparkly bathing suit.

Evie looked away and caught a flicker of a smile on Suki's face. A twitch in her lip as she asked. 'So the bike stabbed him?'

'Yes. And another time, his leg got mauled by the chain. And there were others. I apologise. I know this sounds awful.'

Dave paced around the bike, ducked to check underneath the saddle. Never touching it. 'What else?'

'Beatrice. I had a lot of drawings of Beatrice. She could be very demanding. And ungrateful.' Fiona's raised eyebrows signalled agreement, which gave Evie courage to go on. 'The other day she took my pen and sucked on it. God, it sounds stupid, but I was so annoyed. I drew her with a pen jammed in her eye.' Evie's gaze travelled to the body sprawled on the floor. 'And when I saw the missing tampon—and it could only have been her that took it—it reminded me of another day. She was always asking for stuff or snatching it. When she'd borrowed a tampon from me—not for the first time—I imagined it exploding. Inside her.'

'And then she dropped dead, right in front of us,' Dave said, as though new thoughts were dawning.

'But it wasn't the tampon. I found it,' Suki said.

'It doesn't matter,' Dave said. 'It was something. Something we don't yet understand. I definitely sense somethi ng... inexplicable.'

'Well yes,' Charles said. 'We don't have the foggiest how these two died. We can leave that to the police. And I'm sure the police will be very interested in what Evie has to say for herself.'

Dave leaned onto the armrests of Evie's chair, crowding her, his musk snaking its way up her nose. 'Why are you telling us this now?'

'Because I want us all to stay safe,' Evie said. 'And because by telling you, you'll know it's not me.'

He squeezed his eyes as he searched hers. 'How else did Beatrice die?'

'I can't remember,' Evie said, truly wishing she could.

He pushed himself back. 'Let's check. Where do you keep your drawings?'

In that moment, it hit her, the magnitude of her notebook not being in her bag that morning. Somebody must have taken it. She breathed in deeply, but it wouldn't fill her lungs. She bent forward, sucking in thin breaths, as if through a squished cardboard straw. 'In my notebook. My big green one.' She looked up. 'But it's missing.'

'See? Very convenient,' Charles said. He flapped his hands like a girlie stereotype. 'Don't blame me. The bogeyman did it.'

'I'm telling you the truth,' Evie said, rising, quite literally, to her defence.

Suki stood with her arms crossed. 'Who knows about these drawings of yours?'

'Hardly anyone. But Alan's seen them. He's always creeping around. He called me out on them once. Told me I had a twisted mind. So I know he knows. And Mrs M, but she's a friend. And my boyfriend Kaif.' A vision of Kaif and Martina in the pub skipped into her head, triggering a wave of disappointment. Why had he told her? Her art was supposed to be private. What else did he share with her?

'Full disclosure. I've seen you draw weird things,' Dave said.

Evie wasn't sure what to make of that. 'Yes, to be honest, sometimes I wasn't quick enough to close the notebook when people came to the desk. Really, it could be any resident.'

'See? Convenient. Are we meant to believe this supposed confession that is merely a means to blame one of us?'

'Shh, Charles. When did you lose the notebook?' Dave asked. To Evie's relief, he seemed to believe her. Not like Charles, standing there huffing and rolling his eyes. She didn't know what else she could do to convince him.

'It was in my bag last night. Before the meeting. I'd put the bag under the desk. I remember because there was a sticky drink spilt on it. But this morning the notebook was gone. I noticed it when I pulled out my new book to read and put my bag in the locker. You can check... once we get them open again.'

'Could your boyfriend Jeff have taken it?' Suki asked.

'It's Kaif. And no. Well, yes,' she realised, thinking of him cooking her birthday breakfast. 'But why would he?'

'We need to focus on people with motives,' Dave said. 'People with access.' He looked at the large, glazed door, the windows, the fire escape, and up. 'And I know where to look.'

CHAPTER FORTY

Evie

Dave pointed to the CCTV camera, its small light still red. 'If the notebook was in your bag at the meeting, we could see here if anyone took it.'

A frisson of excitement filled the room. Evie felt as though an enormous weight have fallen off her shoulders. A deep breath filled her with much needed oxygen. He believed her. This could be the answer to everything, to knowing who had it in for her.

Fiona, who'd already distanced herself from her husband's sarcasm by perching on a Swiss ball alone, shot up and headed for the desk. 'Great idea.'

'Should we be doing all this? Sleuthing like Scooby-Doo and the gang? Shouldn't we leave that to the police?' Charles said, demonstratively staying put, stroking Pebbles in his arms.

'What are you worried about, Velma?' Suki teased. 'Got a secret to hide?'

Evie gave her a warning look. She'd been forced to tell Suki about the affair, and Suki'd kept it to herself. For the moment. But she wasn't sure how much she could trust her. The woman was a live wire.

'Come on, Suki. You operated this last time,' Dave said, standing, drumming his fingers, by the reception desk.

As the four of them congregated around the monitor and Suki clicked through a series of icons, Evie could feel Fiona lean against her. The skin-to-skin contact left Evie uneasy.

'Did you kill me too?' Fiona asked, a mixture of resentment and curiosity on her face.

Evie recoiled from Fiona's stale breath. 'I'm afraid I did, yes. Sorry.'

'How?' Her eyes shone with what Evie could only describe as an oddly morbid interest.

'Once, strangled by Pebbles's lead. The one you never bring. But mostly drowned in the floatation tank.'

Fiona stroked her very much unharmed throat. A slight sheen covered her cheeks. 'Do you think I was meant to die in the tank today? What did I do?' Fiona waved that question away. 'No, don't answer that. I can guess. My manager at the Lair has told me I can come across as a right bitch to staff.'

Evie was grateful she didn't need to go into it. Her grievances seemed petty now. There were worse problems—something today most definitely showed.

'What about Charles?' Fiona asked, having taken a step away from Evie to peer back at her husband. 'What killed him?'

'A mango,' Evie said, deadpan.

'Will you two be quiet?' Suki snapped. 'I'm trying to concentrate.' She clicked on yet another file and the screen filled with a view of an empty gym, bar Evie throwing towels over her desk.

'Pause that,' Evie said. 'There, see? Underneath the table you can see my bag leaning against the side panel.'

'And you're certain the notebook was in there?' Dave asked.

'Yes.'

'Okay. We keep going.' Suki straightened and rolled her shoulders. 'This could take a while,' she said, fetching the chair. 'If you guys want to sit this out until I've found something, that's fine with me.'

Dave glared at Suki. Evie was half expecting him to say, 'You would say that, wouldn't you?' again, like she was the killer. Even though they seemed to be getting on in this instant, Evie shouldn't underestimate how fragile their truces were.

'All right,' Suki said, clicking the mouse again. 'Let me at least put it in fast forward.'

Along with the others, Evie watched the room fill with a colour-rich medley of people swarming around the drinks, building groups, and separating again, moving towards the chairs.

'There's me,' Dave said, as his distinctive gait gave him away.

'Concentrate on the bag,' Fiona said. 'See if anything is moved.'

'There's Beatrice,' Suki said. The bouffant hair and fig-ure-hugging dress were a dead giveaway. She bent over and grabbed a drink from the mini fridge. Evie shuddered. She still owed Fiona an explanation of how a mango could kill.

Beatrice stood up and though it was hard to tell from the triple-time, seemed to hover by the fridge longer than needed before greeting someone and walking out of sight.

Evie kept her eyes on the bag whenever she could. The view was often obstructed by legs, and it wasn't always clear who was in front of or behind the desk. People had grown impatient that night and helped themselves from wherever they could. She'd been relieved when the meeting started, and she could be alone again.

She blinked and refocused on the scene. 'Hold up.'

'What?' Suki paused the tape.

'Rewind. Slow it down.'

Beatrice returned, greeted the man from the fifth floor in reverse and turned to stand in front of the mini-bar and display above it.

'Never mind,' Evie said. 'I thought I saw someone duck under the table. But it's too hard to tell. And the bag seems unmoved.'

'We were all getting a drink at one point or another. It could be anyone,' Fiona said. 'Or no one.'

'I think we need to keep watching. A notebook doesn't go missing by itself,' Dave said.

They zipped through another few minutes of nothing discernibly wrong happening. Suddenly, tension crept along Evie's skin. On the screen, Alan had grabbed hold of her shoulder and leaned in to say something, way too close to her ear. She remembered wanting to smack the hand off her, but he'd not held her long and left to stand with his back against the wall.

What she hadn't noticed then, but could see now, is that he kept his eyes firmly on her, moving them up and down. She hugged herself, feeling vicariously violated.

'What did he say to you?' Suki asked.

'He said I should go fetch some of the empty cups from the room. Oh.' Maybe he hadn't been checking her legs out. Maybe he'd been looking at her bag. Had he been waiting for her to go to look inside? 'This could be it.'

Evie walked away from the bar. Rather than duck under the table, Alan swerved along the tall end and was seen, from behind, getting down on his haunches, one hand clutching the shelf above. When he rose, he fiddled with his jacket.

Suki pointed at his movement. 'What's he doing?'

He had the air of someone who didn't want to be caught. But as he turned away, it became clear that his only crime had been to snatch a bottle of the residents' health water.

'The bag's still there,' Evie said with a deep sigh, unable to hide her glumness. If not him, who? There was still hope of catching somebody in the act.

'Here's the meeting. Can we speed things up more?' Dave asked.

They watched Alan leave. 'Beatrice booted him out, remember?' Fiona said.

'Okay, it wasn't him,' Suki said, stifling a yawn. She stretched her arms high.

'Keep it running,' Dave said. 'There's still time.'

'Alan stayed,' Evie said. 'I remember seeing his silhouette through the doors for a while as I did a first tidy. I stepped outside, too, when I could no longer see him. Figured he'd gone home. I remember being really annoyed about that, because that hadn't been the deal when I agreed to help out.'

The monitor displayed a big commotion as the meeting broke up. A bottleneck formed at the sliding doors as people said their goodbyes. The backed-up residents obstructed the table and there seemed to be some pushing going on at the front.

'This is pointless,' Suki said, stopping the tape. 'We can't see the bag at all with people coming in and out like that.'

'Keep going.'

Dave's shout made Evie jump.

'Jeez, Dave. Take a chill pill,' Suki said, hands up in defence. 'We're not in the army here.'

Thick veins protruded from his neck as he clenched his jaw. Evie retreated a little, wanting to get out of the blast zone of Dave's short fuse. She'd heard about military men struggling to readjust back home. Whatever made him lose his leg must've been horrible.

'It's moved.' Fiona pointed at the bag under the desk. 'Someone moved the bag.'

The dark rectangle had fallen onto its side, straps no longer tucked in, but extended along the floor. Evie buzzed. Fiona was right.

'Well, I'll be damned.' Suki said. She scrolled back and forth through the video a few times, but the precise moment when the bag was tampered with wasn't clear—nor the precise person doing it.

Evie's shoulders slumped as her excitement waned. She might have been right about her notebook, but Alan had left earlier. Then again, watching the feed whiz by for the umpteenth time, the jam of people wanting to leave could've been caused by Alan wanting *in*.

Charles had suddenly appeared by their side. 'Didn't you say there'd been a spill, Evie?'

'Yes, so?'

'Someone could've moved the bag to clean it up,' he said. 'Perhaps it means nothing.'

Dave looked Charles straight in the eye. 'Or it means everything.'

'Only one way to find out,' Suki said.

CHAPTER FORTY-ONE
Suki

People's doubt whether or not there was a killer on the loose was getting old. Suki's eyes were straining, and her stomach rumbled. She would normally have had her mid-morning muffin by now. But mostly, she disliked uncertainty. Uncertainty meant no control. A divided team meant no control.

And she wasn't about to let herself be led by any of these losers.

The answer was easy. She would take Evie's hypothesis of a notebook-copying killer to its natural conclusion. 'If we believe there is a killer, and this is all premeditated, then the killer must've planned Stephen and Beatrice's death.'

'And who knows who else's,' Fiona added.

'Quite.'

'But we don't have a clue how they died,' Evie said.

'Indeed. But what we do know is that sometime between this moment, with the bag, and the first death, the killer would have had to set things up. So we watch.'

'What? The whole night?' Dave asked.

'On fast forward, yeah.'

'Fine, count me in,' Dave said, fetching a ball to sit on.

'You can leave us to it,' Suki said to the others.

Charles scoffed. 'You would say that, wouldn't you?'

Suki groaned inside. Great. First Dave, now him. And it wasn't nearly as clever in a second voice.

She clicked on the *X* in the top right corner of the screen and reached the folder with video files. A quick calculation showed there would be eight to view before they got back to the one from that morning they'd already watched. The one with people arriving.

As the first file zipped along, showing Evie throwing cups and empty bottled into a bin bag, Suki sensed the other residents' tension, and it made her neck ache. She turned to Evie and pointed at the mess on the video. 'You missed a spot.'

'Shh,' Dave and Fiona shushed in unison.

So much for a little light relief.

On screen, Evie came in and out of shot, but the sliding doors stayed infuriatingly shut. They raced through two more files of nothing: the gym with the lights off, its various shapes identifiable only by the glint of the moon.

A video file further and the static image became engrained in Suki's mind. Her eyelids grew heavy. The screen went abruptly black. She jolted upright. Here we go.

'What happened?' Dave asked.

'It's off. The feed is off.' Suki said, moving the cursor to pinpoint the exact moment the moon was shut down. Two fifty-one. Middle of the night.

'That means it's true,' Charles said, somewhat dazed. 'This was planned.'

A heavy silence fell. Suki sat back, letting the meaning of the invisible time sink in.

After a while that felt like forever, Dave said, 'Check how long the feed is stopped for. We know it recorded again this morning.'

The blackness straddled two files, but at three twenty-four, the reception popped into view again.

'About half an hour,' Fiona said. 'Is that long enough to set up deadly traps?'

Dave nodded, his thoughts seeming elsewhere. Somewhere not nice. 'It's an eternity.'

CHAPTER FORTY-TWO

Evie

Evie trembled. It wasn't as exciting now the cold, hard truth was becoming clear. They were at the mercy of someone who'd had ample time to execute a sick plan.

The windows, the doors, the ceiling closed in on her. She lifted her hands from the forbidding surface of the desk, accidentally smacking a hair care sample off the shelf. As she watched it thud to the ground, her subconscious screamed.

'Is there any way to zoom in?' she asked Suki.

'I don't think so. Why?'

'Can we jump to the morning? When it's light again. There's something I need to see,' Evie said.

Suki obliged, the apparent ease with which she selected the right file unnerving Evie.

Evie raised her hand to her hair. 'Oh my God. It's the shampoo. Quick. Find the moment Beatrice arrives.'

'What's going on, Evie?' Fiona asked.

Evie used her T-shirt to pick the serum off the floor. 'There were three tubes like this.' She gestured to the glass shelf covered in postcards and samples. 'Now only two. The shampoo is missing.'

With a series of clicks, Suki called up the moment the gym opened to residents. A mix of outdoor and overhead lights bringing a colourful, contoured identity to the previously dark shapes. 'You're right, there are three tubes.'

'But it's all wrong,' Evie said. 'When I put them out last week, I made sure to display them in the logical order you'd use them. Shampoo, conditioner, serum.'

Fiona leaned in. 'The purple is the serum. I know, I have it at home. And it's in the middle...'

Evie danced in place, uncertain what to do with the conditioner she was holding. Bin it? Put it back? The police would want to test it. Thank goodness she'd picked it up with her T-shirt. She wouldn't have wanted her fingerprints on that.

A clump formed in her stomach. Of course, her prints would already be on there. She'd touched it. She'd touched everything in this gym at one time or another. And that's how Alan would frame her.

'You think Beatrice took it?' Dave asked.

'I told you. She helped herself to everything,' Evie said. Then whispered to herself, more convinced than ever, 'Completely predictable.'

'Here she comes,' Suki said, leaning back to give everyone a good view.

Evie averted her eyes. Much as she wanted—needed—to know, she couldn't face watching Beatrice unwittingly thieving her way to her death.

'Well blow me down.'

Suki's statement was enough to tell Evie she'd been right. And this time, it didn't feel too good.

'Blow me down indeed,' Charles said.

Dave scrambled up and began walking to the rear. 'I'm going to check the showers.'

'Wait, I'll come with you,' Charles said.

Dave shook his head. 'Piss off, Charles.'

'What about the rule?' Fiona yelled after him.

'Screw the rule. This is war.'

They all stayed in place as he disappeared, though Pebbles nearly got caught in the closing door as he'd trotted behind Dave.

'Is this one of the ways you killed her?' Charles asked.

Evie shrugged. 'I don't think so. But the... er... weapon was always something she'd nicked.'

He scratched behind his ear. 'How did you murder me?'

'A mango,' Fiona replied.

'What?'

'A pen, the juice, the weights. It doesn't matter,' Evie said. 'What matters is that I drew everyone. Now that we know what happened to Beatrice, all of you are at risk.'

Suki raised a finger. 'When you say everyone...?'

'Well, yes, pretty much everyone who came into the gym will have annoyed me at some point or another.' Heat rose along Evie's neck. 'I'm sorry. It was just a silly pastime. Nothing personal.'

Fiona pulled a disbelieving face.

Evie crossed her arms. 'Fine, maybe a little personal.'

'But if you drew everyone,' Suki said, 'why is it only us here?'

CHAPTER FORTY-THREE
Suki

Charles's mouth fell open. The penny had dropped. 'You mean we were *chosen*?'

Dave's voice rose from the back of the room. The door slammed shut behind him. 'Chosen for what?'

'Did you find the shampoo?' Fiona asked, skipping towards him.

'Yes. It was in the left shower cubicle. Lying in the soap dish, with the screw cap off. Seems Beatrice did use it. I thought it best to leave it there.'

'Good shout,' Fiona said.

Dave swerved around her to reach the others. 'What's this about being chosen?'

Charles replied first. 'Suki made the point that if Evie had drawn murder scenes for all the residents—'

'All the residents that came to the gym.' Evie corrected. 'That's not everybody.'

'Point is, if she's drawn all our deaths, why is it only us...' He counted heads—and bodies. '...four, five, six in here?'

'And me,' Evie said.

Charles dismissed her with a tut. 'But you think you're being framed. Ergo, you don't count.'

'That's a bit harsh, Charles. Let Evie die like the rest of us,' Suki said, suppressing a laugh.

Dave huffed and punched himself in the hand. In a low grumble resembling the beginnings of the earthquake Suki had experienced in California. He said, 'If you think this is a good time for jokes, you're as twisted as her.' He pointed to Evie. 'And the killer.'

'At least you've moved on from thinking I'm the killer. I call that a win,' she quipped. She couldn't help it. She had a big funny bone and liked to wield it around at times of tension. It worked wonders in negotiations, got her opponents to take their eyes off the ball briefly, giving her an in.

'Argh.' Dave growled in frustration, his fingers bent like claws about to grab her.

'All right, all right. I'll be quiet. Pretend I'm not here. In fact, I wasn't supposed to be here this morning. My meeting—'

'Neither was I,' Fiona interrupted. 'My tank appointment was for later, but the app bleeped to say the gym would close early. I thought we shouldn't miss our chance and phoned Charles to return from walking Pebbles.'

Evie's brow wrinkled. 'I wasn't supposed to be here either. I don't work Saturdays. That, and my birthday. But Alan insisted I had to be here.'

'I had that notification too,' Dave said. 'Could it have been a way to lure us here? To get the people he wanted in the gym at the same time?'

'It's possible. I received the notification also,' Charles said. His gaze drifted to Stephen. 'I wish we could check their phones.'

'By that reasoning, I shouldn't be here,' Suki said. 'My app claimed the gym would be closed all day.'

'You would say—' Dave started.

Suki put her hand up. 'No, I wouldn't. If I were the killer, I'd pretend to be one of you.' She tapped her temple with her finger to illustrate her smarts. 'Why would I admit to being different?'

'You could be lying,' Charles said.

Evie chewed her lips. 'She's not. I saw it. We were both confused. Because I'd had the same message it was closed and texted Alan to confirm. And that's what's weird.'

'I don't think it has anything to do with the app,' Dave said. 'It must be a red herring.'

'How so?' Charles asked.

'If we're to believe Alan lured us here with the app, to kill us all and frame Evie for it, why would he send her a notification the gym was closed?'

Suki couldn't fault his logic. But he had made an awful lot of assumptions in the process. And the old saying came to mind, *'If you assume, you make an ass out of U and ME.'* Still, she was in no mood to nit-pick. He was annoyed enough with her as it was.

'Maybe it was a glitch in the app,' Evie said. 'There's always techie stuff not working in this place.'

'You'd think with the massive service fees they charge us, they'd get it right,' Charles said. 'It's damaging the resale value of our property.'

Dave slapped him on the back. 'Mate, two people have died here. I don't think anyone's going to want to buy these flats any time soon.'

All of Suki's senses exploded. 'Bingo.'

CHAPTER FORTY-FOUR

Suki

It was time for a new chapter, a new perspective. Suki's nerves were alive with the promise of guiding the group closer to the truth. She made a show of pacing in the middle of the room.

'I think we've hit on something,' she said. 'The building. That could be the motive. Against all of you.'

'What do you mean?' Charles asked.

'You, you, you and them,' she pointed at the living and dead in turn. 'You all voted in favour of the SMB-whatever development. Putting that new building up in our garden. What if somebody felt strongly that it should not go ahead?'

'That's extreme,' Fiona said.

Dave rubbed his chin. 'I don't know. It could have a big financial impact. Maybe somebody needed the money?'

'I suspect you're wrong there,' Charles said, which yielded him a dirty look from Dave. 'First there'd be the cash for the land, which admittedly would be shared between everyone and not amount to much. Plus, in my view—and I've asked a property investor colleague of mine to confirm—having the cachet of the exclusive architecture and the retail premises nearby would improve our value.'

'Unless you're facing it,' Evie offered. 'The lower flats must have a lovely green view of the courtyard. The big tree, flowers in spring. People like views.'

'True. They could end up staring straight into the neighbour's bedrooms, with all that glass they've planned,' Fiona said. 'I guess that wasn't much of a consideration for us, being on the sea-view side.'

Suki balled her fists. Fiona couldn't have been snobbier with her haughty dismissal of the B-side dwellers if she'd commanded to let them eat cake.

'Would you kill for a view, though?' Charles asked. 'Even if it did add value to the property.'

A dark shadow enswathed Dave's face. 'People have killed for less.'

Evie sported a troubled expression. 'What would Alan stand to gain from stopping the development?'

Dave put his hand on her shoulder. 'I think we've moved on from Alan, Evie.'

'But he's still the one with access. The know-how to mess with all the systems. Who else could do this?'

Suki felt for Evie. She seemed distraught at the idea her big bad culprit could be innocent. It sat uneasily with Suki, too. She'd love nothing more than to be able to pin it all on him, for what he'd done to the woman who owned her apartment before her.

'I think we should keep him as a live suspect,' Suki said. 'He may not live here, but there's nothing stopping him from returning at two in the morning. And Evie's right, you'd need knowledge of the systems, or a decent hacker. Besides, we still have the issue of him getting the sack. Plus, perhaps the building management contract would come up for renegotiation, with the new building next door.'

'I don't know. It feels like there are too many people in the frame. I can't get my head around it.' Fiona said, subtly adjusting her boobs with her arms. Suki pretended not to notice. Bathing suits could be a bitch.

'Evie, have you got any sticky tape or blue tack in your drawers?' Suki asked.

'Yes, why?'

Suki strode to the desk, Evie following. 'Grab some paper off the printer.' She flipped various pens from the pot. 'Ah good, a sharpie.'

Evie handed her a stack of A4 paper and a small, colourful piece of cardboard. 'There are a few squares of blue tack in here.'

'What are you doing?' Dave asked.

'We're going to approach this systematically. Here,' Suki said, pulling a stretching of blue tack from its row. 'Paste the paper together to form a big writing area. We'll put it on the wall.'

'Please don't,' Evie said. 'The sharpie will bleed through and make a mark. I don't want to get in trouble.'

Suki snickered gently. 'Aren't you sweet for worrying about that? I doubt this is going to be on the forefront of anyone's mind when we get released.' She waved at Dave. 'But okay, we'll do it on the sliding doors.'

As Suki gathered her tools, three pens rolled from the desk onto the floor, falling next to what looked like an opened cereal bar. Her stomach rumbled, but she wasn't yet desperate enough to pick up someone else's half-eaten snack.

After a few minutes of pleasantly calming crafts, under the circumstances, they had created a big, cobbled-together canvas, four sheets wide and three sheets tall.

Dave and Fiona carried it like a flopping albatross to the sliding doors. As they began pushing the gluey bits onto the glass, Suki said, 'No, the other way around. Portrait style. We're going to be drawing the building.'

They flipped the sheet over. Dave pressed the blue dots into place as Fiona reached up on her tiptoes beside him, looking like a magician's assistant in a gaudy leotard and terrycloth cape.

'Thank you,' Suki said. 'Now, everyone gather round.' She drew a tall rectangle and sliced it horizontally into fourteen equal parts, with another long line down the middle. As she numbered each floor, starting with the ground one, she asked, 'Can anyone remember how tall the new development would be?'

'Seven floors, no?' Charles said.

Suki drew another rectangle that reached up that high next to their building. She drew crossed through the ground floor and all the apartments on the side of sea-view side of the building. 'We can ignore all these because they are unaffected by the new development.'

'It's not a fully accurate representation, Suki, because the penthouse takes up the whole top floor,' Charles said.

Suki clenched her jaw. Fastidious fucker. 'True,' she said, scribbling out the line dividing floor thirteen, 'but Mrs M's view isn't hindered as she's up top. In fact, the gym and anyone on floor eight and above can be discounted too.'

'What if they have another motive?' Dave asked.

'Let's not confuse things. We're examining this particular hypothesis first.' Suki was in her favourite place—in charge—and she wasn't going to let anybody mess with that. She could also see a real advantage in going through this systematically, though she had to admit if it was crazy to be standing here by a makeshift whiteboard among dead bodies. But it would help make sense of it all, gain their trust.

The drawing wasn't half bad. A bit squint maybe, but that didn't matter. 'We're looking for someone who cared so much about this development not going ahead that they chose to get rid of enough people in favour, leading to the formal vote next month going their way.'

Fiona fiddled the ends of the earphones at her neck nervously. 'How many would that be?'

'I'm not sure,' Suki said.

'And yet you knew we voted in favour,' Charles said, gesturing to everyone in the room.

Suki sighed. 'Well yes, I paid attention to the people I was interested in.'

Charles's eyes narrowed. 'And here we all are.'

'Yes. Why were you so interested in us?' Fiona asked.

'I told you,' Suki said, firmly clicking the cap onto the sharpie. 'It's business. I wanted to meet you, Fiona, because I'd like to be a member of the Selkie's Lair. I wanted to meet Dave because I have a merger in mind for his firm that could bring in fees. I wanted to meet Beatrice because she's one of the most influential bankers in the country.'

'What a coincidence all the people you wanted to meet were here,' Dave said cynically.

Suki sent him a venomous look. 'There are a few more meaningful people I can mention, but they're not here. They voted against. After that, I don't know. There's a lot of you. I have no interest in the random people in apartment 5B or 2A or whatever,' she said, waving her hand over the illustration of the building.

'Stephen lived in 2A,' Evie said innocently enough, but Suki wasn't certain if she'd meant something more by it. There was something jittery about her. Like the sous-chef at her parents' restaurant, perpetually on edge. Though she couldn't blame him, having been at the receiving end of her father's temper more than once.

An image of her father slipped into her mind, holding his ladle up in the air in a jokey threat to his staff, a big grin on his face. He was a shouter, for sure, but he'd never hurt a fly.

Even less after the heart attack. Keeping his blood pressure in check was a priority and Mum developed a sixth sense for it, swooping in to diffuse disagreements before they escalated. He'd complained to Suki that it made him look weak. 'I'd rather have you weak than dead,' she'd replied.

'I was making a general point,' Suki said, testily. 'Okay, I did want to meet Stephen. Insurers can be great referrers of clients, if you can get them to slip your name to their high-net-worth clients with seven-figure life insurance.'

Dave pointed at a crossed-out square on the sketch, the apartment opposite them. 'It's very convenient of you to rule yourself out. Particularly as I remember you not voting.'

'Oh for crying out loud. Fine.' She put an asterisk next to her apartment, wrote *Suki*. She added a big un-smiley face next to it. 'Happy?' When no response came and his face was still set like a rock, she added an exclamation market for good measure. And an extra thick arrow.

'Why didn't you vote?' Dave pressed.

Suki slid her hand over the rounded contours of her plait to maintain her calm. She twisted it into a curl while shaking her head. 'Because you gotta know when to hold'em, as the song goes. Don't show your cards unless you have to. This was only a pretend vote.'

'With very real consequences if your hypothesis is correct,' Fiona said.

'It's time you told us,' Charles said. 'Now's not the time to keep anything from us.'

Suki grinned mischievously at him. 'But we all have secrets, don't we?'

CHAPTER FORTY-FIVE

Evie

No, no, no, no, no. Evie felt like sweat oozing from her temples. Surely Suki wouldn't mention Charles's affair right in front of his wife? That would be evil.

She watched Suki's eyes shine with devilry and held her breath.

After an excruciating minute of heavy silence in which Charles's face turned purple, Suki laughed.

She said, 'If you must know, I was planning to vote against. Even though I think the development would be good financially in the long term, I can't stomach the idea of all the noisy disruption for what will be at least a year. I need my sleep. And what if we all need to work from home again?' She looked down and fidgeted with the rim of her T-shirt. 'Plus, it would be a waste of the lovely garden. I've watched a young family play there happily and, well, it's something I'd like for me and a future wife.'

'You're gay?'

Charles had asked what Evie had wanted to, but never would. Evie ran her thumb over her scar as she wondered if that's where Suki's fearlessness came from. Having to grow a thick skin while people judged you.

'Not that it's any of your business, but yes. Out and proud. No secret closet for me,' Suki answered with a slight curtsy and a teasing tone Evie supposed only she and Charles would recognise as menace.

Dave laughed. 'I'm frankly more surprised you want a child.'

Suki glowered. 'You're hardly one to be bouncing a toddler on your knee either.' A collective intake of breath wiped the spite off her face. 'I'm sorry,' she said, waving at his prosthetic leg, 'you know what I mean.'

Having endured enough stressful moments that morning to last a lifetime, Evie stepped in. 'Are we still going to go over the other residents?'

'Thank you, Evie. I think we should,' Suki said, returning to the makeshift whiteboard. 'Let's start from the bottom. Who is in 1B?'

'That's Eylard Wurpel. He's moving out soon,' Dave said.

'How do you know?' Charles asked.

'He told me. Thinks the UK is a complete shitshow since Brexit and is returning to Holland.'

Suki struck the pen across that square. 'Next.'

'2B is Mr & Mrs Hutchinson,' Fiona said, drawing blanks from the others. 'The chap in the wheelchair and the large, frowzy woman in paisley prints.'

'Don't sound like killer material to me,' Suki said, starting to strike them out.

'You'd think that,' Fiona said. 'But Beatrice told me once how she, as owner's association president, had to step in when they had an almighty row with one of the other residents. Seems they were driven to distraction by his many parcels piled high and obstructing the lobby and corridors.'

'Could that be Stephen?' Evie said. 'He's 2A. I delivered a misplaced parcel for him yesterday.' She turned away from Charles to signal she would say nothing further.

But it hit her she'd have to tell the police when they started investigating. Couldn't they charge you with obstruction of justice or something if you withheld information?

She considered Charles as she watched him hoist up his waistband. The way he always stared at his feet, the way he was super affectionate with Fiona. If she told the investigation about the affair, they'd probably suspect him of Stephen's murder. The lover. If it wasn't the stranger, it was usually the lover. In fact, weren't the most murders committed by the partner?

She remembered his opened collar, the pink on his cheeks, the surprise on his face as he spotted her at Stephen's door. His relief when she'd agreed to keep shtum.

Her stomach stirred. Maybe that was what he was banking on. Maybe he was counting on her to testify they seemed in love to *avoid* suspicion. Her whirling mind stumbled on a cold realisation. Could it all have been deliberate? The parcel being left behind for her to bring?

Suki had reminded her earlier that Charles was cycling next to Stephen when he died. Evie hadn't wanted to believe he was involved, convinced that Alan was the culprit, but now...

An oozy, stifling sensation overtook her, as if slimed from above. She felt used. And powerless. Whether it was Alan or Charles or somebody else, she'd been placed in the game like a pawn. The lowly piece sacrificed as part of a grander plan. And it wasn't fair.

Charles's posh boarding school accent grated as he named and described the people in apartment 6B. Evie wouldn't put it past this privileged white male with his faux Hugh-Grant-like bumbling to actually be behind everything—and to get away with it, as they always do.

He had the same round head as her former boss at McDerry's, the same flat ear lobes, the same small curls of hair by his temples. The bastard's image popped into her head. The way he'd stood in the kitchen doorway, his hands tucked deeply in both pockets of his khaki trousers, upper body leaning backwards, as her colleague held Evie's arm under the cold running tap. He stood there, immobile, eyes calculating, as the heat of the oil spill ate into her flesh, and she screamed like a wounded fox. What kind of vermin doesn't act at the scene of an accident to avoid possible responsibility by touching the injury? Because that's what she learned later had held him back.

Her fault, they'd made it out to be. His hands clean. Moving on. Nothing to see here. But the screams never left . here. They clung to her long after they'd removed the film that covered her wound. These screams were sowed within every live skin cell of her forearm and burgeoned at night, haunting her dreams.

'I'd be wary of any man who drives an Alpha,' Charles said, referring to the occupier of the next flat.

Was it a way to deflect attention off himself? Sprinkle suspicion around like fairy dust.

She pressed her lips together and watched him, looking for those calculating eyes. Did he have her notebook? Did her bringing the box to Stephen mean anything? Her fingerprints would be on it. Her fingerprints were on Stephen's water bottle, too. And on Beatrice's shampoo.

What else had she touched? Her heart pounded as she scanned the gym. Everything. She'd touched everything at one point or another: her desk, the doors, the light switches, the first aid kit, the water cooler, all the machines, the floatation tank, the toilet, the sink, even the freaking tampon in Beatrice's pocket.

Evie waggled her hands out in an anxious attempt to rid herself of any guilt. She'd shake off her fingerprints if she could. She covered her face and closed her eyes, needing to blank out the surrounding conversation, the ongoing fishing expedition for another killer in the building.

Think. Murdering your lover is one thing, but why would Charles kill Beatrice?

CHAPTER FORTY-SIX

Evie

Suki pointed at the next apartment on the drawing. 'What about this one?'

'Alice couldn't harm a fly,' Fiona said. 'She's in the arts, for heaven's sake. Writes about Scottish Colourists.' She grabbed the sharpie off Suki.

Suki was having none of it and snatched it again. She underlined the Alice in question's name in a petty act of defiance. Evie exchanged fed-up glances with Dave and blew out a long sigh. It must be exhausting to want to be right all the time.

Yet there was something intriguing about the women's bullheadedness. Maybe, unlike what she'd learned by observing the queen bees at school, leadership didn't require you to be a bitch—part of the reason she'd never aspired to it. Maybe you just had to stand your ground no matter what.

Charles crossed his arms and advanced to the almost illegible panel of crosses, arrows and scribbles. 'I'm with Suki on this one, darling. I don't think we can fully exclude Alice because she likes paintings with flowers.'

The words Evie'd heard all morning as accusations flew tumbled through her mind. *You would say that, wouldn't you?* It would be in Charles's interest to keep more names on the board, to distract from his own.

His remark had triggered a very frosty reaction from Fiona when he sought her hand.

Suki admired her handiwork. 'All right. Step one of testing our hypothesis completed. We've narrowed it down to four possible suspects. Three we know, and one unknown. There's something very intriguing about an unseen resident living among us, don't you think?' Suki wrote the number one and a question mark next to the apartment.

'But...' Evie started, unsure how to throw Charles back into the mix.

Suki nodded at her. 'And Alan. Don't worry. I haven't forgotten.' She sought a space to add his name, but anyone could see the whole thing was a mess. 'Maybe we should start a fresh list.' She plucked another sheet of paper off the floor and loosened a corner of the existing installation to steal a sliver of blue tack.

Once the new page was up, she began to write. Only a light grey streak came from the sharpie, with a squeak that hurt Evie's teeth.

'Bugger,' Suki said, forcing the last hint of ink out. 'Can someone get another pen?'

Not needing to be asked twice, Fiona darted to the desk. Evie guessed holding the pen would be an opportunity to be in charge again. Pebbles sensed movement and sprung up. He trotted alongside Fiona's calves, tail wagging. Evie envied him, his simple pleasures.

Fiona bent far over the desk. Evie averted her eyes as the towel failed to cover Fiona's bathing suit riding up her bum.

'While you're there, Fiona,' Dave said. 'Could you try the phone line again?'

'And try the Internet.' Charles said. 'And get some more paper.'

'Anything else, m'lords?' Fiona sneered. She slipped to the other side of the desk and lifted the phone's handset. 'What do I do, Evie?'

'Press on the green button top left. Do you hear a dial tone?'

'No. I'll wake the computer and see,' Fiona said.

'There's no point,' Charles said. 'They're connected over the same digital line.'

Evie made a mental note that Charles seemed to know more than expected about the building's telco system, while he and Fiona continued to have a testy exchange.

Her back was killing her from all the standing, and she sat down, crossing her legs. She leaned backwards onto her hands and stretched her neck sideways. A strange scratchy sound made her look over at reception again. Fiona had found her nail file and was running it over her thumb in an obvious act of stalling.

The unasked borrowing of her stuff irked Evie, but she didn't have the energy to object.

She noticed Pebbles was doing a strange dance around Fiona's feet, whimpering, tail and ears down. Perhaps he was irritated by the filing sound? Fiona nudged him away with her right leg, but he quickly returned, which seemed to aggravate her.

'For heaven's sake, Fiona,' Charles said. 'Don't be like that. Come here.'

Dave too was sitting now, legs outstretched, at an angle to Evie. They shared a grimace at the fraught tempers on display.

Fiona stomped back, nearly tripping over the perpetually enthusiastic dog. She picked Pebbles up and practically threw him into Charles's arms. 'Here. Since you desperately want someone to order around.'

Charles wrestled with Pebbles, who seemed intent on licking his face. Suki held out her hand to Fiona and asked, 'Pen?'

Fiona stamped a foot on the ground. 'Fuck. I forgot.'

Evie shot up. It was the first time she'd heard Fiona swear and worried she would pop. 'I'll get it.'

She ran to her desk, a disaster zone of strewn stationery and rubbish. Among the clutter, she pulled a few sheets of paper from the printer that sat under the table and returned with two pens, one red, one blue. Suki might appreciate the ability to colour code. Evie always felt a hint of colour added a deeper dimension to her drawings. Maybe the same would be true when they re-wrote the names of their suspects, that it might tease out additional insight.

Because she was torn. She looked at Charles, making peace with Pebbles's kisses, and Alan's name squashed in a small font into a corner of the increasingly limp white-board. Both could have motives, both could have had access, both could have chosen to set her up as the scapegoat.

Or neither.

Thanks to Suki they had four other names, with a possible motive that felt somewhat far-fetched. Would someone murder a whole bunch of people just because they liked their view?

Perhaps it was Suki's way of deflecting attention from herself. Dave continued to eye her suspiciously, waiting for that gotcha moment.

Evie handed Suki the pens. In the absence of any other firm leads, she was happy to go with it. If nothing else, it killed time while they waited for somebody to find them.

And there was the mystery of the stranger in 4B. The person nobody had met. There had to be a story there.

CHAPTER FORTY-SEVEN
Suki

Suki wished she'd gone to fetch a new marker herself. She'd been standing there waiting for Fiona like an idiot and now Evie handed her two stupid fineliners bound to tear through the paper. Not to mention way too thin to read at a distance.

She stuck them both through the top of her plait and braced for someone's inevitable chopstick comment. But she needed her hands to pick adhesive putty off the glass to stick another sheet of paper up for the final, sanitised list.

It was clear from the petty squabbles that people were getting antsy and annoyed, and she wouldn't be able to hold their attention on this exercise for much longer. If she was honest, she was starting to feel past caring herself.

Nobody would expect them to solve the mystery while confined here. The police would think it a miracle they could think straight at all, with two dead bodies in the room, and hadn't been running around screaming and pulling their hair out.

At least getting the others focused and using their brains had meant they were calm and—provided they didn't touch anything or go anywhere—feeling safe.

Behind her, Charles made a gross choking sound. She pursed her lips. He was probably making faces at his grumpy wife. Men could only ever argue verbally so long, before resorting to the physical.

But then she heard him cough and gasp. And wheeze. And Fiona shout, 'Charles!'

Suki spun round. Her arm dropped as if in slow motion upon seeing Charles clutching his throat, eyes bulging in distress.

Dave rolled to his side and manoeuvred himself up. He patted Charles on the back while Fiona looked on, aghast.

Charles pointed at his thigh and pressed two fingers to his thumb repeatedly with his other hand, like a quacking duck's beak. Suki couldn't make sense of it.

'It's his allergies,' Fiona shouted, running to him. 'Evie, get an EpiPen.' She grabbed hold of both his hands and stared him straight in the eyes as he battled for breath. 'It's all right darling. Everything will be fine in a minute. Listen to me. It's going to be all right.'

Fiona modelled deep breaths for him, and Suki found herself expanding her own chest as her pulse quickened—out, in, out, in. He hadn't touched anything, been anywhere. This shouldn't be happening.

It took Suki a moment to realise that Evie hadn't moved. Adrenaline rushed up her spin. 'Evie, what the hell? Where's the EpiPen?'

Evie just stood there with a dumb expression on her face. She shook her head and tears pooled in her eyes. Suki's stress pinched the base of her neck. 'What is it?'

'I used the EpiPen on Beatrice.'

'There's only one?' Suki asked.

Evie nodded and covered her mouth. Tears cascaded down her cheeks.

The sound of Charles's stunted breaths sliced straight through Suki. She could only watch as Dave helped lower a limp and pale Charles to the ground, his swollen red lips standing out like a mushroom on the meadow-green mat.

His wife by his side. 'Charles, Charles. Come on, you can beat this. Breathe in...out...' Fiona stared at Evie and Suki with pleading eyes. 'Help.' Her voice trembled. All of her trembled.

Charles clutched his chest.

Suki was glued to the ground. Stunned, not a clue what to do. She squeezed her fists until they numbed. She'd never felt so useless.

She heard a whisper at her side. 'You've got this.' She witnessed Evie, incredible Evie, brave Evie rush to the scene, take a huge, noisy breath and press her lips onto Charles.

CHAPTER FORTY-EIGHT

Evie

Moment later, Evie crawled away from the body, as if lost in the desert, spent and desperate for water. She rubbed her tainted lips, through the searing pain from the bruising. Her shoulders heaved with sobs. Her stomach heaved with an all-encompassing nausea.

Rising bile burned her throat. She swallowed it, but it returned with the violence of an erupting volcano. She opened her mouth and a thick stream of vomit flowed onto the green mat.

She collapsed onto her side. Next to her puddle of guilt, remnant blueberries leered at her like accusing eyeballs.

She'd failed again. For the third time today, she had failed and let somebody die. She pressed her eyes closed as flashes of her resuscitation attempts, Charles's final moment, plagued her consciousness.

With all three, she'd been aware in a strange extra-sensory kind of way of the exact moment life slipped away. An escaped wisp of invisible steam. A last, silent cry.

And she'd failed them.

Of course she had. Why had she even tried to be the hero? '*You've got this,*' she'd told herself. What a fool. She's got nothing. Two earlier failed attempts and a lifetime of mediocrity should've told her that.

And why had they left it to her? Christ, by now every-body in the room should've known CPR from exposure. They should've known she'd bomb.

Fiona, surely, should have known what to do given Charles's extensive allergies? They lived together. But she merely sat there, kneeling with her hands wrapped around his, like some sort of Mary Magdalene who thought prayer would solve the fact her man wasn't breathing.

That his heart stopped.

Because that was what happened in an anaphylactic shock. She remembered that much from the first aid training. But what good is that cardiac knowledge if you can't stop it arresting?

Evie's head pounded. The acrid smell of her expulsed breakfast made her stomach churn. She curled up like a prawn, willing this nightmare to end.

Only one EpiPen in the first aid kit and she'd used it on the wrong person. But how was she to know? When Beatrice struggled, they still thought Stephen had died of natural causes. Evie had jumped to the most logical conclusion.

No, wait, it was Charles.

Charles had pointed at Beatrice and yelled it was an allergy. He's the one who told Evie to use the EpiPen. And in doing so, he'd unknowingly sealed his own fate.

Evie shivered, remembered him gagging, gesturing, thumb plunging an imaginary syringe between his two fingers. Being cautious, always, he would never have thought he'd die this way.

They'd all been together, touched nothing but pens and paper. What killed him? Was it poison again? She couldn't bear to look at him, to see if he, too, was devel-oping blue fingers.

Whatever got to him wasn't anything she'd drawn. Did that mean she was wrong about the killer using her ideas? It certainly confirmed she'd been wrong about one thing: Charles couldn't be the murderer.

She still felt too weak to sit and turned her head to look at Fiona. Her full upper body was thrown over Charles's chest. She shook with sorrowful hiccoughs. Evie's heart ached in sympathy, but she'd also seen enough grandstanding to know Fiona was a good actress.

Dave leaned quietly against the wall, head down, hands folded in front of him like a football player during a minute's silence. Respecting the dead man he'd only earlier squabbled with.

Suki was out of range. She'd have to watch her. She'd have to watch them all, because one of them had to be guilty.

Evie sensed a furry tickle on her ankle, sensed Pebbles scuttling along her thigh, making ever-louder sniffing sounds as he neared the pool of sick.

Her lips curled in disgust. He wouldn't...

CHAPTER FORTY-NINE
Suki

'Pebbles, no.' Suki raced to catch the blasted dog before he stuck his nose into the patch of vomit.

She scooped him up just in time. His hind legs scratched her forearm as she tried to contain him. He wriggled, forcing her to press him closer to her chest.

Pebbles set his shiny black eyes on her and lifted his fluffy ears into question marks. Moisture rimmed his truffle nose. While Suki wrestled with his protesting lower half and tried to get his garish bow out of her face, she caught a whiff of his foul breath. Coupled with the sight of Evie's brown splotch on the floor, it reminded her of plates of congealed satay at the end of a busy night in the restaurant and made her want to run out the door.

But they were stuck.

Poor Evie was curled into a ball at Suki's feet, her arm flung over her eyes. She looked like she hadn't an ounce of energy left. And who could blame her? The way she'd kept at Charles. Compressions. Breaths. Unwilling to give up while the rest of them only stood by. Even Fiona, whose bloody husband it was. She should've been the one pushing, breathing life back into him through his god-awfully swollen lips.

Suki couldn't imagine how traumatised Evie would be after this. Granted, she might not be dead, but she was a victim as much as the others, scarred for life. Her gaze fell onto Evie's disfigured arm. Scarred for life, again. She wished things could have been different for her. Not only today, but before.

She tapped Evie's foot with her shoe. Evie lifted her arm a smidge and blinked at the blinding lights.

'Are you okay?' Suki asked, hoping for at least a nod, maybe even a 'yes'. Instead, Evie let her arm fall across her eyes again and pulled her feet in closer.

Pebbles squirmed. 'Calm down, boy,' she said and stroked him in the neck. This won her a smooth, pink tongue flick against her face. 'Ew.' She leaned forward and dropped him on the floor, still holding onto his collar.

She spread out her legs a little and, bent fully in two, called out to Dave. 'Some help here. If I let go of this damned dog, he'll lap Evie's sick up.'

Dave came to her side with apparent good intentions but, judging by his empty hands, no solutions.

'How about some paper towels?' Suki said.

'I'm not going into the bathroom,' Dave said. 'We can use some of the printer paper.'

'That would just smear the sick around,' Suki said. 'We need something absorbent.' She looked over her shoulder. 'Fiona, give us your towel.'

Fiona lifted her tear-streaked face from Charles's chest, her skin wrinkled like a wrung-out dish cloth. 'What?'

Dave reached for Suki's arm. 'You can't.'

'I'm sorry, Fiona,' Suki said. 'I know this is a horrible time for you. But unless you want Pebbles to eat the contents of Evie's stomach, we're going to have to clean this mess up. You've got the only towel. And it's your dog.'

'Why don't we lock Pebbles up?' Dave suggested.

For once, the shit-for-brains had a good idea. She handed him the pup and said, 'Throw him in the disabled bathroom and close the door.'

'No,' Fiona shouted. The towel slid off her as she scrambled inelegantly to her feet, avoiding disturbing Charles's body. She strode over and yanked Pebbles from Dave's hands. 'My baby stays with me.'

Dave shrugged and, to Suki's great relief, went to pick up the towel. She was happy to leave the clean-up to him. She'd already faced her own vomit that morning and had no appetite to mop up anyone else's. Dave would be fine. She bet he'd seen much worse in the service, or even as a bouncer.

She tsked and corrected herself. He wasn't a bouncer; he was the managing director of a security company. He probably had to keep fit to maintain respect among his men, and she shouldn't underestimate him. Nevertheless, he was still bound to have witnessed his share of drunken piss, bleeds and retches.

'Hey, Evie. Do you need help to get up?' Suki said. No movement at all. She was tempted to drag Evie by the legs, away from Dave sloshing the spewed breakfast around.

Suki was breathing through her mouth, still sensitive to the unwelcome smells. She left Evie to her apparent, frankly justified, voluntary paralysis and decided to check on Fiona.

They weren't friends, not by any stretch. Having got to know her a bit, she didn't think Fiona did friends, not real ones anyway. But the woman had lost her husband. Plus, if there was any hope of gaining her trust after all this, she'd have to show support.

Fiona was sitting on the ground by the magazine rack, in suitable mourning proximity to Charles. Pebbles was locked in the well between her crossed legs. He was standing on his hind feet, his front paw outstretched and resting on

Fiona's cheek. She grabbed it and blew a noisy raspberry between his toes. The dog yelped. Fiona released a slightly hysterical laugh and blew into his paw again.

Suki gave her a wry smile. It was no surprise the woman had become somewhat unhinged. Pebbles seemed to be loving it, his tail wagging furiously as Fiona made exaggerated gleeful faces. Suki imagined this might be a game they played all the time, a baby game Fiona had no other outlet for.

Fiona flapped Pebbles's ears and squished his tiny cheeks before giving him a big peck on the nose. Pebbled hopped about like a child needing a wee and licked her face.

Suki shuddered at the memory of his livery tongue against her cheek. Near her mouth, too. What was it with dog owners letting their pets lick them like that? Charles had let Pebbles loose all over his face. It was gross. The slimy saliva, the revolting breath.

Breath.

That smell.

Suki suddenly realised why satay had sprung to mind earlier. She rushed to Fiona and snatched the dog from her arms, to an indignant 'Hey'. Suki ignored her and carried Pebbles a few steps to the side.

She forced the dog's snout open, sharp teeth and black-spotted gums exposed between pointy, drool-drenched fur. She leaned in and sniffed. Intermingled with the foetid essence of carnivore was the unmistakable whiff of peanut.

CHAPTER FIFTY
Suki

'What the hell are you doing?' Fiona asked, getting to her feet. Was it Suki's imagination or had a new scarlet splotch spread across Fiona's chest?

With Evie remaining glued to the floor, Suki turned to Dave.

'Hey Dave.' Suki summoned him over with a wave. 'I need a second opinion.'

He stopped mopping and bunched the stained towel into a ball. He held it at arm's length, turning his head away. The odour hit Suki even at a distance. Remaining streaks of light-brown goo littered the green mat like slugs on a lawn.

Dave scanned the room, seemingly unsure where to put the stinky bundle.

'Throw it into the disabled toilet,' Suki said. It was the nearest closable place and, boy, did they need to seal that thing up.

He pulled the handle and chucked the towel in. It landed with a sickening splat. The automated floral spritz from the air freshener didn't stand a chance. Dave joggled his hands at his side and looked longingly at the distant sink, choosing to wipe them on his shorts instead.

Meanwhile, Fiona was tugging at Pebbles, a flush rising to her face. 'Suki, let him go. What do you want?'

Suki resisted and held on tight, despite Pebbles growling at her when she squeezed him too hard. She gripped his rear and neck with one hand slid under his belly and pushed his mouth open with the other. 'Smell.'

Fiona frowned. She caressed Pebbles's head as she bent forward and sniffed. 'It's dog breath. I don't get it. What should I be looking for?' she said, a picture of innocence.

'Nothing unusual?' Suki asked.

'No, why?'

Had Suki imagined it? She needed Dave to come quick before the evidence—if that's what it was—evaporated.

'Dave, you tell me what scent you pick up,' she said, thrusting the dog in his face.

'I'm not sure I can smell anything but sick right now.'

'Try.'

Dave closed his eyes and inhaled. 'Hmm...' He rubbed his nose against his forearm and stuck it in the crook of his elbow for a cleansing sniff. 'I don't know...There's something.' He dived back in.

'Peanut?' Suki offered.

'What?' Fiona stammered.

Dave pointed at Suki. 'Yes. That's it. I thought of a Snickers bar, and I couldn't work out why.' He held Suki's gaze as the implication dawned on his face.

'So you're with me, yes?' Suki said. 'This dog smells of peanut.'

'Yes, but how?' Dave asked.

Suki released Pebbles onto the floor. He scuttled across to Fiona, who picked him up and nuzzled his snout. She shook her head. 'It can't be. We never allow nuts near Charles.' She stared at her husband's splayed figure, confusion clouding her face. 'He was poisoned, like the others. He must've been.'

Suki sensed Evie shift position. She'd gone from lying in a rounded heap to sitting, cradling her knees tightly against her chest. She remained white as a sheet with green hues that may or may not be reflections from the floor, and still looked like she could shatter in an instant, but this was a good start. Suki predicted years of therapy ahead.

She instinctively thought '*Poor girl*' again, but if Evie was going to have to climb her way from under a shroud of victimhood, Suki could at least help her recognise the brave person she was. 'You okay, super woman?'

Evie's lips twitched in what Suki let pass for a slight smile.

Fiona had dropped Pebbles and was kneeling next to Charles. She picked up his arm and held it up to the light. She squeezed the fleshy base of his palm and examined his fingers one by one.

'Stop touching him,' Dave said. 'We need to leave everything as is, for when the police come.'

Fiona held onto the limp hand as she asked, 'How long was it before Beatrice's fingers turned blue?'

Dave gently pulled Charles loose. 'I don't know. You have to let go. I'm sorry.'

'You smelled it, Dave. Peanut,' Suki said. 'And we all know Charles was deathly allergic to everything. My God, it was the first thing I heard when I moved in.' She mimicked a posh voice, 'Here are your keys and oh by the way, we have a severely allergic man living here, so please refrain from ever eating anything ever in the public areas.' With her hand still outstretched, as if receiving her keys, she said, 'Everybody knew this. Why create some complicated mechanism to dispense poison when a nut would do?'

'But it can't be. There is no food here. That's my point,' Fiona said. She pulled herself up on the magazine rack, brushing against a cellophane-wrapped gift mascara on the front of *Grazia*.

The plastic film's scrunching sound sparked a powerful memory in Suki's mind. There *was* food here. She'd chosen not to eat it despite being famished. Her senses tingled. 'I saw a half-eaten cereal bar earlier. By the desk, on the floor.'

Evie gasped. Her legs flopped to the floor like spaghetti. She covered her mouth with both hands and her eyes shone with fear as she let out a muffled cry.

'What's wrong?' Suki asked.

'Evie?' Dave said, advancing uneasily, like a lion tamer on his first day.

'I'm sorry. I'm so sorry. Oh my God, Fiona. I'm so sorry,' she wailed.

Fiona didn't seem to understand this outburst any more than Suki, standing with a limp expression, clinging onto the magazine rack as though their gossipy pages held the answer.

Suki crouched beside Evie. She lifted her chin with her finger, flicked a loose strand of hair out of the way. 'Hey. You have nothing to be sorry about. You did all you could to save him.'

Evie jerked her chin loose and crawled crab-like away from Suki. 'The cereal bar. I didn't think... I crossed Mrs Parker and her kid this morning, screaming his head off. Straight after, I found an opened cereal bar in the lobby. That's why he was crying.' She rose and paced, mentally retracing her steps. 'I didn't want anyone to step on it. I shoved it in my pocket.' She patted her waist as though the pockets were there. Her brow crumpled in concentration. 'I was going to bin it. I got distracted and...'

As her voice trailed, Suki followed her gaze towards the windows. To Stephen's elevated body, shrouded in Evie's white-and-green jacket.

'It must've fallen from the pocket when I hung the jacket over my chair,' Evie muttered.

'And Pebbles ate it,' Suki said. She was tempted to place her hand on Evie's shoulder, but Evie had resisted her touch before.

'You bitch. You killed my husband.' Fiona launched herself at Evie. She snatched Evie by the collar and grabbed a clump of her hair in an attempt to yank her to the ground. Evie resisted, kept her balance. She slid four fingers between her collar and neck and swatted behind her with the other hand, smacking Fiona on the side.

Suki clasped Fiona's wrist and twisted it hard while trying to seize the other. Fiona let go of Evie's collar and swung wildly at Suki, striking her twice in the cheek. Suki flinched. 'Dave for fucks' sake, a little help here.'

Through the wrestling body parts, Suki saw Dave approach the three women, his arms wide like a goalie, unsure where to start, which limb to catch.

Evie bent forward with a groaning great force, propelling Fiona backwards and Suki sideways. She elbowed Fiona in the rib, but Fiona did not let go of Evie's hair.

Suki caught hold of the crossed halter straps on Fiona's bathing suit and pulled her down hard, face first. Almost with a mind of its own, Suki's knee sprung up. The crunch on contact made her stomach heave.

'Ow.' Fiona's hands shot up to her nose. Blood leaked through her fingers. She stared open-mouthed at the crimson streaks down her forearm and set her fury on Suki. She balled her fist and pulled her arm back. Before she could strike, Dave tackled her by the waist and catapulted her to the wall.

They landed at Charles's feet. Dave's bulk covered Fiona's torso in a compromising embrace, their bare and bionic legs entangled. Dave rolled to his side, arms up as though pre-empting a referee's red card.

Fiona lifted her head off the ground for a second before closing her eyes and dropping it down again with a huge sigh.

'What took you so long?' Suki shouted, panting, at Dave.

He scooted away from Fiona, who was sitting up, legs akimbo, pinching the top of her nose. 'I... I was taught not to fight women.'

Suki patted her stricken cheeks to check for soreness. 'Given the circumstances, you're welcome to dispense with the gallantry.'

CHAPTER FIFTY-ONE
Evie

Evie had never been in a physical fight before and was still a bit dazed as things calmed down.

She'd always wondered, though, what it would feel like to punch somebody. To experience the kind of rage that made you lash out. While the roots of her hair throbbed from Fiona's pulling, she sensed a little disappointment. All she'd managed to shell out was a swipe with her elbow.

She watched Fiona holding her bloodied nose, red dots spattered on her bare thighs like nascent chicken pox. Fiona whimpered, a far cry from the crazed animal she'd been when she jumped her.

It had been an extraordinary reaction by Fiona, but grief did funny things to you, didn't it? Mum had stopped eating for a week when Gran died, and never had porridge with salt again because the memories were too painful.

Besides, she couldn't blame Fiona. Evie still felt sick at the idea she had unwittingly brought a deadly weapon into the gym, completely forgetting the no-food rule. Because it wasn't food, it was waste.

With a work-mode instinct, she spotted Fiona's red stains, her own brown smears and the two dead bodies on the floor. Her lips curled downward. The mat would need an extensive disinfectant clean. They'd probably have to tear the rubber flooring out completely and bin the yellow yoga mat under Stephen.

Perhaps she should fetch a spray and paper towel from the cleaning cupboard? They'd likely have leftover hand gel from when that was mandated.

Her palms itched to scrub and sanitise the place, to get rid of the noxious smells. But they had to leave everything as was for the police, for evidence. It would be awfully suspicious of her to start cleaning, particularly as it gave an opportunity to scrub her own fingerprints. They were on everything. Although she could quite easily explain the myriad innocent traces of her, she'd confessed to bringing in the cereal bar. Her spur-of-the-moment deadly mistake. If they found her notebook and saw how the others had died, would anyone believe this was an accident?

A slow chill crept down her arms. 'What if it was dropped on purpose?' she said.

'What if what was dropped on purpose?' Suki asked, inexplicably holding onto her breasts.

Evie made sure to look her straight in the eye and said, 'The cereal bar.' She walked over to the sad string of hanging papers that represented their make-do whiteboard and lifted the sheet with the five names. 'Mrs Palmer is on this list. Could she have dropped the cereal bar intentionally, meaning for me to pick it up?'

'That's a stretch,' Suki said.

'Hear me out, though. I never see her in the mornings. Why was she coming out right at the time I came in? A time I'm not normally here but was forced to come in...'

'And what? She knows you pick things up off the floor?' Suki said, with limited credulity in her expression.

'Wouldn't you? Wouldn't we all?' Evie asked the others.

Suki tilted her head and gave her a sweet smile. 'Listen, I know you're upset. And I know you think that your weird-ass drawings are being used for inspiration by who-ever killed Stephen and Beatrice. And I'm happy to believe that too. But if they can plant things in the room to kill them, why rely on such a complex chain of things needing to go right to kill Charles?'

'How do you mean?' Dave asked.

'First, it relies on Evie picking up the cereal bar, and not leave it or it not being found by someone else. Second, it relies on Evie not throwing it in the bin before she came into the gym.'

'There is no bin on the way up,' Evie said with a petulant tone she hadn't intended.

'There's the rubbish chute on the landing, by my front door.' Suki said.

Evie sensed her case falling apart. 'True.'

Suki was pointing at her fourth finger of objections, 'Lastly, it relies on Pebbles not only finding the snack but getting his little paws on it. I don't think dogs are known for their pick-pocketing skills. Besides, I would certainly never have thought that dogs like cereal bars.'

'Or that Pebbles is a face-licker,' Evie said, shoulders sagging in a sullen admission of defeat. How foolish of her to come up with such an idea.

'But what if you do know these things?' Dave said, blinking intensely, as though forcing out a picture. He turned his gaze to Fiona and lifted his arm slowly to point like a weathervane catching a mild breeze. 'She knew.'

CHAPTER FIFTY-TWO

Suki

Suki didn't quite know what to make of the strange sound that escaped Fiona's lips. When Dave had pointed the finger at her, she'd laughed, sputtered, coughed, and snorted near simultaneously. The snort must have stung like a mother because Fiona yelled, 'Ow,' and nursed her bruised nose.

She looked a right state, to Suki's private delight. The woman had built a reputation and a following by being the glamorous face of an exclusive member's club. Confidante to the one percent, building a position of power through flirtatious gossip and mutually beneficial introductions among those that matter.

It always bothered Suki when she saw photos of Fiona in *Business Outsider* or *OK!* magazine, surrounded by the smiling, shiny bald heads of the suited men of Edinburg, that she shamelessly relied on her feminine wiles. It wasn't helping the cause. Worse still, it was no secret women had to jump extra high to join the club. God forbid she'd lose an iota of attention. Only the unarguably influential like Beatrice were welcome. Even then, Suki suspected the crafted bonhomie on display belied a lingering underground rivalry.

But fair play to her, carefully sculpting this persona with all the high-maintenance grooming and investment in wardrobe it required. But it meant never letting down your guard—or indeed your hair—like a method actor remaining in character at the end of a shoot. The alluring, formidable Fiona, queen of networking. It would have never worked had she been short and plain, or resembled a dog's breakfast like she did now.

Having recovered her decorum, to the extent that was possible in her sparkles, Fiona raised a red-stained chin and stared at Dave. 'What are you implying?'

'I'm merely considering Suki's perfectly rational points. She said this couldn't have been a planned death because all these factors would have to come together,' he said, holding up four fingers as Suki had. 'But they could easily have... if you killed your husband. You know him, you know your dog, you handed the dog to Charles.'

'No, it was an accident,' Fiona protested, eyes wide. 'I didn't know Pebbles had eaten nuts. Don't look at me like that. It's Evie's fault. She's the freak. She brought the cereal bar in knowing full well it wasn't allowed in here. That's a gross dereliction of duty. How can it be my fault that Pebbles ate it? He'll eat anything.'

A faint recollection stirred Suki's mind. 'Hold on. Does he eat plastic?'

'What? No,' Fiona said, dozily unaware of the incriminating thoughts it triggered in Suki.

'Evie, describe the state of the cereal bar when you picked it up.' Suki asked.

Evie tilted her head with a confused expression. 'It had two or three small bites taken out of it. Like a third eaten?' She shook her head. 'I don't know what you're asking.'

Suki smiled. 'If a toddler was eating it, the wrapper must have been opened quite far.'

'Yeah, it was pulled halfway down. There were crumbs on the floor, where the bar fell. I brushed them aside with my feet.'

Suki nodded at Dave, who'd clearly reached her wavelength and began walking to the desk. 'And what did you do when you put it in your pocket? Did you leave it as is, with the risk of getting crumbs in your jacket?'

'No, I folded the wrapper over,' Evie said.

'So someone had to have removed the packaging again to feed a piece to Pebbles,' Dave said. 'And that can only have been you, Fiona.'

Fiona climbed to her feet and clasped her hands to her chest. 'I see what you're doing here, you two. Colluding like this. How could you? It wasn't me. And I can't believe you're accusing me when I have just lost the love of my life.' She bit her lip and threw in a pinkie flick of a tear for good measure.

Suki wasn't falling for it. 'When I saw the cereal bar on the floor earlier, it was still fully covered. You were the only one near the desk after me, when you went to fetch new pens. And Pebbles was there right with you.' Suki ran her tongue over her teeth, trying to keep her excitement in check. It wouldn't be a good look for her to be seen to revel in this, but boy was it a coup. The mighty Fiona slammed and shamed.

'I remember because you shoved him aside at one point, which I thought was mean,' Dave said.

'He was being annoying. Maybe he got hyper because ate the cereal bar. But I didn't give it to him. He only ever gets raw food. He has a very sensitive stomach,' Fiona said, her eyes flicking between Suki and Dave.

Dave scanned the desk area and a giant grin spread across his face. He straightened his posture and crossed his arms like a bouncer guarding a portal to the truth.

'Did you find it?' Suki asked Dave, while Evie joined her side, questions lining her face.

By the wall, Fiona continued to hug herself, knees bent, as if standing on the top diving board, afraid to jump, waiting for encouragement, confirmation it was safe. But Suki had no intention of giving that to her.

'I didn't kill my husband. How dare you? Please. It was Pebbles. It was an accident. I'm telling you it's her fault,' Fiona said, pointing at Evie, eye blazing. 'She's the one who brought the peanuts in. She's pretending someone is framing her, using her drawings... but Charles knew. He kept warning you it was a double bluff. She's behind this. All of this.'

Suki could feel Evie shrink beside her. She resisted the urge to put a comforting hand on her arm, even though she could see goosebumps. 'Thing is, Fiona, you're the only one who could've unwrapped the cereal bar for Pebbles.'

'I didn't... Maybe he managed to nuzzle it from the wrapper. We've been here all morning. He might be starving. He's always getting into things. It wasn't me. I swear.' Fiona hands up in defence, though Suki saw it more as an invisible wall locking her in. 'He ate it all by himself.'

At reception, Dave took a pink post-it note and pinched something between thumb and forefinger. 'And did he also leave the empty packaging on top of the desk all by himself? Where he can't reach.'

'Clever dog,' Suki said, sarcasm dialled to eleven.

Fiona's face fell.

The game was up.

CHAPTER FIFTY-THREE

Suki

The buzz travelling through Suki's whole body was so strong, she was convinced she could stick two fingers in the socket, and it would short-circuit the whole building.

She took a deep, satisfied breath. She loved nothing more than to be right. And what was wrong with that? Anyone who pretended otherwise was a liar. It was utterly delicious.

Suki grinned in anticipation of the praise to come. She'd solved a murder. A real murder. Possibly even three. Because why not? If Fiona was capable of murdering her husband in cold blood, it stood to reason the police would charge her with all the deaths. Wouldn't that be something?

Imagine the headlines.

Elite corporate financier Suki Aksornpan outsmarts serial gym killer.

Or should that be '*gym serial killer*'? Who cares? That was for the reporters to figure out. She bet they'd have a field day making wisecracks about '*killer bodies*' and '*the strong arm of the law*'.

Her thrill subsided when she realised it would be Fiona's name in bold. She was the famous one. Fiona's photo, not hers, would front the papers, with shots of her full, sculpted body to emphasise their puns.

Would there at least be a reward? She had no idea how any of that worked. She came across enough dodgy stuff at work, which she deftly navigated around to keep her fingers clean, but this kind of crime - real, gritty, bloody, life-and-death crime - wasn't her world at all.

Dave caught her eye, his smile as wide as hers. He lifted the cereal wrapper in a celebratory toast.

'How could you kill Charles?' It was Evie's reproachful voice that cut short their gloating.

And rightly so. A tight band of shame squeezed Suki's chest. People had died. Lives had been cut short and would have a hideous impact on their families and friends. She ought to be more sensitive to that. It could've been someone she loved. It could even have been her.

'I didn't. Honestly, I didn't,' Fiona said, but her posture told another story. She'd deflated. A purple, crumpled torso over knobby legs, slipping to the ground.

'Where's my notebook?' Evie asked.

'I don't know.' Shaken by noisy sobs, Fiona leaned against the wall, arms outstretched in an almost convincing pose of seeking divine forgiveness.

Evie strode towards her, an air as sombre as November. 'How could you? How could you blame me when it was you all along? I tried to save him. I have the taste of death on my lips, and it is your fault.' She loomed over a sulky Fiona. 'I hope you rot in hell.'

Suki and Dave exchanged surprised glances. The earlier snivelling heap had grown balls, and Suki liked it.

'I've seen prison, Evie. Rest assured, you'll get your wish,' Dave said. 'The courts won't look kindly on a serial killer.'

Suki's heart skipped. He'd leapt to the only sensible conclusion, too. She was starting to think teamwork may not be such a bad thing after all. Evie, however, appeared to have lost some of her certainty, a puzzled crease in her brow.

'Serial killer?' Fiona's voice croaked. In an instant, she twisted onto her knees and upright, like a battery recharged.

'I didn't kill *them*.' Her eyes flitted between Stephen and Beatrice. Then, seemingly realising her mistake, to Charles. 'I didn't murder *anybody*. You're wrong.'

'Stop your charade, Fiona.' Dave grabbed her arm, fingers dug deep into her flesh. He pulled her along to where Charles lay, Fiona stumbling over her own legs like a baby giraffe.

He rattled her when she averted her gaze from her unsettling crime. 'Don't look away. Face it. This is on you. There's no doubt in my mind. I saw the evidence.'

Pebbles followed them as he dragged her to the middle of the mat to face the other two corpses. Dave shook his head, as though lamenting the waste of life. 'And if you've killed one, you've killed all three.'

A sliver of sunlight peeked through the clouds to fall on them like a stage light. Suki watched their silhouettes, Dorothy and Toto being manhandled by the tin man on the emerald road. To where? She couldn't begin to imagine what horrors awaited Fiona.

'I guess you're more tech-savvy than I thought,' Suki said. 'Messing with the doors and all.'

'Ah, but I've realised something,' Dave said. 'The Selkie's Lair uses the same security company. It's fair to assume it's also the same system.'

Suki couldn't help but ask, 'How do you know that?'

'My firm worked for the Lair...until she fired us,' Dave said.

'What? I don't know about this.' Fiona said.

Suki was struck by the dumb lump's inability to see the hole he was digging for himself, showing he knew much more about security systems than he'd let on. But for now, she had a bigger suspect to prod. 'Open the doors, Fiona,' she said. 'We know you can. It's time to let us go.'

Fiona flapped her arm wildly to shake Dave off. 'Are you insane? I'm not the person who locked us in. I didn't do any of this. I don't know how the system works. I don't deal with operational things.'

'Tell that to the police. I'm done. And I want out.' Dave slid his finger under one of Fiona's bathing suit traps to lug her to the door.

'But she was in the floatation tank when it all happened,' Evie said.

'See?' Fiona gestured to Evie. 'I wasn't even here when Stephen and Beatrice collapsed.'

'So how do you know they collapsed?' Dave asked, smugly.

Fiona roared and stamped her foot, which didn't quite have the intended effect on the springy mat. 'Because you fucking told me. We've been fucking cooped up together for fucking hours, going over and over how they died and who could've done it. We've even got a flip chart. A bloody flip chart.'

Ha. So much for the glamorous and composed Fiona. Suki'd always known the woman was a fraud. Nobody coos and smiles that much. Not genuinely. The veil had been lifted, and it wasn't pretty.

It must all have been new to Evie, as she stared wide-eyed at the unladylike outburst.

Suki ripped the wilted write-up of their brainstorm off the glass door. 'You were perfectly happy to agree it was a planned, remote poison attack when the suspect was someone else.' She scrunched the sheets into a ball. 'So it doesn't matter than you were in the floatation tank. In fact, I remember the door being unlocked. We were all in here, but you could've been anywhere.' Suki kicked the bundle into the corner like a football. The goal posts had moved. 'We won't be needing that anymore. It was a stupid hypothesis for a motive anyway, killing for a view.'

'It. Wasn't. Me.' Fiona spat. Dave tugged at her strap. She smacked his hand. 'Get off me.'

'I'll let go when you calm down,' Dave said, the fool not realising that only ever had the opposite effect on a woman. In a flash, Fiona had bitten his hand and kicked his prosthetic leg. He toppled to one side and managed to extend his arms in time to stop his big head from hitting the ground.

Fiona ran to the rear of the room, close to the windows, and wound herself around a multi-press, limbs snaking through the frame, dark eyes set on the others.

'Yeah, Fiona, you're doing a great job of not looking like a rabid murderer,' Suki teased, but at the same time tensed her body in case Fiona had gone feral, clinging to that metal jungle. She jutted her chin to Dave, who was working on sitting up. 'You all right?'

He nodded. 'Yeah. Bit of a sore wrist,' he said, rubbing it. He grabbed the ball of paper that lay next to him in one giant hand and threw it across the room at Fiona. In an impressive display of accuracy, it landed by her varnished toes. 'I don't care that you weren't in the room. While I'm hugely curious as to how you killed them all—though we've worked it out for Charles—what I would like to understand is why?'

Evie's voice came through as little more than a whisper. 'I know why.'

CHAPTER FIFTY-FOUR
Evie

Evie wrung her hands and took a deep breath as Dave watched her expectantly. Suki gave her an encouraging nod. It was the push she needed. She'd promised Stephen she'd keep his secret, but with both he and Charles dead—utterly unbelievably dead—it could at least be the key to getting them justice.

Fiona leered at her from behind the gym equipment, but Evie refused to be afraid. The stronger Fiona's motive for the murders, the less the focus would be on her, and whether her drawings had inspired Fiona.

'Charles and Stephen were having an affair,' she said. 'I saw them together last night, in Stephen's apartment.'

'Whoa.' Dave's eyes widened. 'I did not see that one coming.'

'Liar,' Fiona shouted. She sank onto a bench, looking crestfallen. 'He wouldn't. He loves me,' she said, clinging onto the pole like a drunk on the tram. Hugging it as though it would love her back.

Evie felt a light quiver in her stomach. Had Fiona really not known? If she didn't know, did they have it all wrong? She blinked, recalling images of how they'd worked out she was the culprit. The dog, the wrapper, she'd been last at the desk, their sneering spat. There was no other way Charles could've died and yet...

'Oh, come off it, drama queen,' Suki said. 'Nice act.'

Fiona looked up, lips parted, wet misery staining her cheeks.

'Wait, you knew about this?' Dave asked Suki.

'At first, I merely suspected. We know our kind.' Suki winked and gave him a cheeky smile. 'It was little things. Charles being overly distraught at Stephen's death for a neighbour. I actually thought he'd done it, given he'd been cycling next to Stephen at the time, but then I spotted all these stolen loving touches. A pinkie caress when Charles stood by Stephen's body, a squeeze of the knee when they cycled on the CCTV.'

'You're lying,' Fiona snivelled. Her forehead dropped into her hands.

Suki smirked. 'Sure, uhuh. Except I noticed your reaction when we watched the CCTV. You saw.'

Dave circled Charles's body, hands clasped behind his back. 'You sly dog, you,' he said.

Evie's ears pricked. His tone sounded almost complimentary. But cheating wasn't admirable. Pretending to be something you're not wasn't admirable. It was weak. And mean.

An image of her mum jumped into Evie's mind: red-rimmed eyes and a pasted-on smile, fussing and fretting over her girls. Evie could still feel the pulling sensation on the crown of her head, still remembered wriggling away and yelling at Mum to stop brushing her hair all the time. *I don't want to "always look my best".*'

She sighed. She'd been too young to understand what was going on. Until her sister, who broke the news, broke the magic. *'Dad's not really at Auntie Ruth's.'*

Thank goodness Mum had taken him back. It had been a weird few months, but the tension ebbed as the laughter flowed again. Would Mum ever think of those days? Would she still be bitter, like Mrs M?

'*It's easier to be a lover a than a husband,*' Mrs M had said, in that solemn, eyes-into-the-distance way people did when quoting others. Evie hadn't meant to pry. She'd been curious about the silver box on the shelf by the front door, with the inscription *Marjorie and Robert forever.* '*Men have a different definition of forever,*' Mrs M quipped before quickly changing the subject to '*the one good thing to come out of the good-for-nothing*': their daughter. Evie smiled. Not a day would pass that Mrs M didn't brag about her pride and joy.

And Fiona didn't even have that. Evie pursed her lips. Charles had been such an insensitive shit when Fiona mentioned their miscarriage earlier. Hideously nonchalant about an event—a being—that clearly mattered enormously to Fiona. Was it any wonder she resented him?

Her skin crawled as Evie thought of Charles always clinging onto his wife, all the displays of affection. '*Darling*' this, '*darling*' that. Who had he been trying to convince? His acts of devotion now seemed doubly evil.

She glanced painfully at Fiona. A woman who always looked her best, and where did that get her? Transformed into a heap of surrender. Evie's chest tightened. What would become of her?

'Have we not got anything to cover Charles up with?' Dave asked.

It recalled Evie's attention to the horrors before them. She shook her thoughts clean, like an etch-a-sketch. How easily she'd been drawn into Fiona's despair... when here were the real victims.

Evie might be the one forever accused of an overactive imagination, the one that comes up with monstrous means of torture in her art, but she couldn't conceive of ever inflicting true harm. No matter what someone did.

Her breath caught in her throat as a jarring image burrowed into her brain: Kaif and Martina, laughing and bumping shoulders in the pub.

CHAPTER FIFTY-FIVE

Suki

'Can you help me get a mat from under Stephen?' Dave asked Suki, walking to the rear. He pointed at Fiona with a warning look as he neared. 'You, stay put.'

Suki would have much preferred to move all the bodies out of the way, into another room if it had been up to her. There was an acrid smell hanging in the air that she kept having to convince herself wasn't corpses. Corpses didn't decompose that rapidly. And it was a gym. Gyms stank—though she had to admit this one tended to be engulfed in near-toxic levels of artificial flower scent.

She heard a clap and a dash of white ran past her. Pebbles leapt into Evie's extended arms. She hugged him tight and buried her face in his fur. A warm glow filled Suki's belly. They could all do with a hug. She hoped for Evie's sake the stupid dog would keep his tongue in check.

Suki cast a furtive glance at Beatrice's unnaturally bent elbow by the water bottle. Saliva flooded her mouth. Hers had been hardest sight to avoid all morning, the body lying pretty much in the middle of the room's open space. And though Suki would never admit it openly, there was something more moving about a dead woman than a man.

Even at this distance, Suki breathed in through her mouth. She'd held her breath when she repositioned the trousers over Beatrice's face, not wanting to catch even a hint of what was behind the blue lips.

The victims needed to be left where they fell. She knew that. That didn't make it any less eerie. They'd made a mistake with Stephen, but who could blame them? At the time, they believed he'd had a heart attack.

She went to help Dave, who was tugging dangerously at a yellow mat five layers down. With Stephen moved already, a little shoogling wouldn't matter to the evidence, though she winced at the idea of him slipping off and hitting the floor with a splat.

'Do we really need to do this?' Suki asked, crouching down the tower of mats to evaluate the physics involved in the shift.

Dave lowered his gaze. 'We should cover Charles up. It's the right thing to do.' He looked up, cringing. 'Besides, his eyes are open and it's creeping me out.'

'Me too. Can't we force Fiona to let us out?' Suki asked.

'Of course. I was so absorbed by the dead ones, I forgot about the killer.' He puffed out his chest and flared his nostrils. A stormy expression took hold. 'Right.'

Suki's heart skipped. She followed Dave's stare. Fiona's head hung limply between her legs. What would he do?

'Fiona.' Dave loomed over her. 'Get us out of here. NOW.'

She didn't respond. Was she even awake? The sky had darkened, and drizzle misted the window, casting a gloomy shade into their space. Suki stepped closer, shielding behind Dave and his tree-trunk arms. A strand of hair slid along Fiona's head, thickening the sleek curtain already in front of her face. The overhead LEDs shimmered on her expensively highlighted hair. Was she breathing?

Dave nudged her shoulder with his leg. 'Hey.'

Fiona shot up with a violent fling of the hair. Her eyes shone with an inky blackness. She bared her teeth, jaws tight. 'Don't. Touch. Me.'

Suki's pulse throbbed in her ears. Fiona's sudden revival had given her such a surprise, she was lucky to have a strong pelvic floor.

'I don't think you're in any position to be giving orders, Fiona.' Dave pulled her by the arm.

Suki squirmed. It was hard not to side with a woman who didn't want to be touched, but she reminded herself this was her pass to freedom.

Fiona planted her feet, forcefully resisting the tug as though her short rest had blown new life into her. This was the woman Suki had wanted to impress, to be pals with even. Before.

'Now come on. Let us out,' Dave said. 'I'll even let you run off. Give you a head start. Though I'm not sure you'll get very far in what you're wearing.'

The drizzle had evolved into full-on, gushing rain. The kind it didn't matter which way you held your umbrella, you'd end up drenched. Darkness crept over the edges of the thick clouds, like an army of termites. Suki shivered. A big storm was brewing.

And judging by Fiona's fuming expression, it wasn't only outside.

Fiona reclaimed her arm. 'I don't know how many times I have to tell you I'm not the one who locked us in. Do you really think I orchestrated all this to be left standing around freezing, half naked, with a shattered nose—and widowed?'

'I agree that wouldn't have been a very good plan, Fiona, but that doesn't take away from the fact that you are guilty,' Suki said.

Fiona seemed to swallow a scream. She primped her hair and smiled. 'I'm going to say this only one more time. I didn't kill anyone.' Her face lost its charm as she added, 'So leave me the hell alone.'

Evie brought the dog closer. He seemed comfortable enough in her arms not to want to jump to his owner. Suki wondered if he was more of a daddy's boy. 'We've already determined you killed Charles.'

Fiona rolled her eyes. 'Think what you like. I don't care. I'm going to stand here and wait for someone to release us.' She checked the clock. 'It's lunch time. Someone is bound to come. And as for your crazy theories, I'll make sure to explain to the police how you ganged up on me. It's terribly suspicious, don't you think?'

Evie gave Suki a puzzled look for which she feared she'd have no reply.

'Ah, screw this.' Dave grabbed Fiona by the middle and carried her under-armed against his waist, like a large duffel bag. He managed to balance her expertly, despite her wild kicking and flailing arms. Suki grimaced at the ear-piercing shrieks.

He delivered her onto the leg-press machine and held her down by the shoulders, pinned against the black leather back rest. 'Evie, give me that skipping rope.'

Evie looked around the room for a moment, and down at Pebbles, as though wishing for more arms. In the end, she foisted the dog onto Suki—who dropped him instantly, having absolutely no interest in any more of that murderous dog breath. What did pique her interest, however, was what Dave was intending to do with that rope.

'Let me go, you big brute,' Fiona yelled.

The thick twine was wound neatly around its two wooden handles. As Evie gave the rope to Dave, he said, 'Knot it around the bar right there. Make sure it's secure.' He called over his shoulder. 'Suki, come stand on this side while I hold her arms down.'

Fiona shouted in his face. 'Don't you dare. Let go of me.'
Dave had her clamped. She tried to shove him with her feet,
but he stood firm.

Suki frowned. He seemed awfully adept at this.

Dave bowed, sticking his bum out to make room between
his middle and Fiona's chest. 'Now pass the rope back and
forward to each other, nice and tight.'

Careful to avoid trapping Dave and to not squash Fiona's
boobs, Suki and Evie coiled the twine around her torso. Evie
gave Suki the last bit to take care of. 'Thread it through that
metal bar, like I did, and make a line hitch.'

'Make a what?' Suki asked.

'A line hitch. A knot,' Evie said with naïve certainty.

'Ha. Do I look like a girl guide to you?'

Dave snatched the handle from her. 'Give it here.' He
proceeded to simultaneously hold Fiona's mouth shut
and swoop the rope inside itself multiple times with a
one-handed dexterity that suggested he'd done this before.

Suki wondered what his story was. She also wondered
what the hell he was planning next.

CHAPTER FIFTY-SIX
Evie

Thunder clapped the building like a bark from the sky. Evie didn't flinch, unlike the others who'd jumped, mouth agape. The weather had always been hideous on her birthday. She watched the swirling winds mould the darkened clouds into constantly evolving shapes.

Evie sighed. Always stuck indoors. She never got to host garden parties with egg-and-spoon races and treasure hunts like her friends on the estate. Mum did her best though, with the absolute tastiest home-make cupcakes, and their dining table a giant free-for-all of furry pompoms, glue and googly eyes. She smiled at a memory of the flappy, velvet duck feet they'd paste on.

She let out a quiet, breathy laugh, as she remembered the many times she'd wished her dad had kept it in his pants that fateful Valentine's day and maybe given her a June birthday instead.

'Shut up.' Dave's booming voice drew Evie back to the scene beside her. Fiona's rage showed no signs of abating. And why would it? She sat tied to a bench, while Suki and Dave behaved like their makeshift interrogation was the most normal thing in the world. But normal it wasn't, as Evie was reminded by an accusatory squeeze deep in her belly.

'Will you listen to me?' Fiona screeched. 'For the tenth time. I am not the killer.'

Dave rubbed his face with both hands and sighed.

'You allergy-shocked your husband because he cheated on you. You poisoned his lover. And you poisoned Beatrice because poisoning her house plant with vinegar didn't give you the satisfaction you craved in bringing her down. 'Admit it.' His roar shook Evie to the core.

'Should we not give her a break?' Evie said. She'd hate to become the new target of his ire, but she couldn't stay quiet. At least she could take comfort in Dave's claim he didn't fight women.

'I know what I'm doing,' Dave growled. 'Now, Fiona, if you continue to—'

Suki placed a hand on his flexed bicep. 'Evie's right. I'm not sure this is the right way to convince Fiona to let us out.'

'I don't know how to let us out,' Fiona wailed, kicking the air. 'I didn't do this.'

Dave leaned on Fiona's thighs to bring himself nose-to-nose with her. Her eyes widened, but, incredibly, she kept her jaw tight and her chin up while Evie would no doubt have wet herself by now. Ironically, if she'd show a little more vulnerability, Evie might be willing to believe her.

'You have three avenues open to you.' Dave raised his thumb. 'One, you continue to protest your complete innocence. In which case, I don't believe you. And we keep playing this game.' He added his index finger. 'Two, you come clean. I untie you. You open the doors and run. Sounds pretty attractive.' He rubbed his chin. 'The third one requires me to believe that there are not one but two killers at work here today. That's a very tall ask, don't you agree?'

That idea had been haunting Evie, as her gut clung onto the belief that Alan was behind this, somehow. Fiona was clever. And devious. That much was clear. What if she merely took advantage of the situation? Surrounded by falling bodies, why not add one?

'I'm innocent,' Fiona said.

A flash of lightning brought a heightened intensity to Suki's fiery stare.

'Look,' Suki said. 'Dave's merely setting out the realm of possibilities here. We have to be MECE about it, as they say in consulting speak. The alternative scenarios need to be mutually exclusive and collectively exhaustive. So, if we dismiss the one where you've killed nobody, because we know better, the choices are you've killed them all, or only Charles.'

'And if you admit to killing only Charles, in a fit of jealous rage, I will leave you alone because all I care about is to get out of this hellscape.'

As if on cue, lightning struck again. Evie counted to three before thunder walloped the window panes.

Fiona juddered from the noise behind her. Finally, her shoulders slumped. 'All right. All right.' She inhaled deeply, closed her eyes, and blew out a long, thin breath. 'I knew Charles was lying to me. He got shifty. Kept avoiding eye contact. These last few weeks, I've been checking our bank accounts. I was worried he might be involved in something stupid, made a bad investment he didn't want to discuss.'

She went on, her voice unsteady. 'I didn't think about a love affair until later. He didn't seem the type. But the more I asked about his day and his whereabouts, the more affectionate he became, which told me all I needed to know. I started checking his phone. I read any message or non-work email that came in from a woman.' She swallowed hard and pinched her lips shut. She shook her head, eyes cast down.

'When I saw him and Stephen on the CCTV today, my whole insides jumped. I thought I'd throw up. I'd never considered he'd slept with a man. Instantly it all made sense. All those trips to the gym...'

Evie felt guilt stir inside. 'I'm sorry. If it's any consolation, I never noticed it either. It was only because Stephen accidentally left that parcel here that I found out.'

Fiona gave her a menacing look. 'You should've told me.'

'Ha.' Suki snorted. 'What was she meant to do? Say, "Oh good morning. Fiona. Nice to see you. Here's your towel and oh by the way, your husband is gay and sucking Stephen's dick in the steam room."' She grinned. Evie reckoned if she was expecting to trigger a giggle, she'd misread the room. The men were dead. Suki readjusted her shoulders. 'All I'm saying is it was your job to notice. Anyway, Evie got paid fifty quid to keep quiet, and she did. And I guarantee anyone with a thankless low-paid job like hers would do the same.'

'Suki.' Evie scolded. Christ, could this woman not be trusted with anything?

Dave leaned against the window, an arm bent over his head. His breath steamed the glass with intricate swirls warping the endless stretch of grey outside. 'That moving confession is all nice and well, but we're back to being locked in with not a clue who is out to get us.'

CHAPTER FIFTY-SEVEN

Evie

Evie fetched the ball of scrunched paper and went to sit by the door to the rear corridor, away from the discordant tension that was making her jittery, away from the three inescapable bumpy manifestations of death.

Suki had been so convincing about the need to follow a systematic approach to eliminating suspects, they'd all been swept into a whirl of supposition, ending up adamant these were the five names with motives and opportunity. And for what? The minute the finger pointed at Fiona after Charles's death, Suki made a giant U-turn and rubbished the whole thing. '*A stupid hypothesis,*' she'd called it.

In the absence of anything better to go on, was it not worth revisiting? Maybe from a different angle? Evie was once again drawn to Alan.

'Hey. Hey. You said you'd let me go.' Fiona rocked side to side—to the extent she could—trying to loosen the rope. Dave ignored her, maintaining his gaze on the horizon.

Suki was lying on the weight bench, her knees pulled up. Evie nearly asked her to remove those shoes from the leather, but this gym had been covered in much worse today.

The sky outside was reminiscent of the darkest grey Evie had in her pencil case, the one she'd used most recently to colour in the pigeons in her tale of possessed birds.

'Hey,' Fiona bellowed.

Suki lifted her head lazily. 'Volume...'

The screaming became louder again. 'I will not be quiet. Let me go. We had a deal.'

Evie saw Pebbles quiver and reverse under the desk, his ears and tail drooping. Poor sod must think he's in trouble, with all that shouting.

An exaggerated sigh emanated from Suki. She flipped sideways and dropped her legs on the ground, holding her hands on her thighs. One of the pens slid from her plait. Its tip planted a tiny blue dimple in the mat. 'Actually, that wasn't the deal. Dave said he would let you go if you confessed and let us out.'

'And I confessed.'

'Yeah, but only to one, not three. And we're still stuck here.' Suki said.

'You cow. You can't keep me tied up like this.'

Dave retreated from the window silently. He chose a yellow Swiss ball and began a gentle bounce while massaging his temples, eyes shut.

'Daaave.' Fiona hadn't struck Evie as the type of woman to give up on things, and so it was proving to be.

She admired her tenacity but wished Fiona could protest more quietly. Her head was starting to throb, not helped by all water being off limits.

Evie tried to keep her head down and blank out the noise, humming *Black Magic* to herself. It worked a treat until Fiona changed tack. 'Evie. Hey, Evie.'

Evie's pulse sped up. She ran her fingers over the paper in a hopefully credible display of deep concentration.

'Come on, Evie. Tell them it's not fair. Tell them to let me go. I'm cold. My arms hurt. My husband is dead...'

If she was trying to tug at Evie's heartstrings, she was failing. How could she complain about a dead husband when it was her doing?

'Fiona, will you give it a rest, please?' Suki said. 'There's no point. You have no cards to play, and we have no reason to let you stroll among us when you're obviously dangerous. And, dare I say, a little unhinged.'

Evie heard Fiona's loud, gasping intake of air and tensed up in anticipation of the barrage to come.

'What do you think this is, Suki, a negotiation? No cards to play? Don't be stupid. I have all the cards. You know who I am. I can destroy you. You'll never work in this town again.'

Suki clapped her hands. 'Ha. What a hoot. "You'll never work in this town again," says the woman who will soon be handcuffed and thrown into a cell. How do you feel about orange, Fiona? Is that your colour?'

Evie suppressed a chuckle. Suki must know prisoners only wore orange in the USA, but the fashion jibe was too delicious, with Fiona in sparkles.

Evie reckoned her inappropriate jokiness was a coping mechanism. Because there sure as hell was a lot to cope with right now.

Evie looked over at Beatrice's body and any hint of mirth fled her body. Kaif had often teased she was too serious, that she only saw the darkness. That she needed to lighten up, see the sunny side. But there was nothing remotely funny—or sunny—about today's events.

People had died. Actually died. And for two of them, she still didn't know how or why. Or if anyone was next. A shiver rocked already freezing arms. She rubbed herself, her stomach dropping slightly as the goosebumps gave way to the smoothness of her scar.

It was hard to be Pollyanna about the world when bad shit happened every day. It wouldn't spontaneously get better if she lightened up or stopped reading horror.

At least with her graphic novels you understood what to expect. You mentally prepare for the creepy experience and enjoy it knowing no real harm would come to you. Life didn't work that way. Life didn't give you any warning, no hint of the grisliness around the corner. It walloped you as you went about your day, leaving you shell-shocked and confused.

The paper in front of her wasn't giving up any answers, either. Had they been right to only list people not in this room? Could she trust this lot?

'Suki, I swear if you don't untie me, you will regret it bitterly,' Fiona said with a threatening tone that reminded Evie of her English teacher. A woman perpetually at the end of her tether, perpetually issuing deadlines for compliance, perpetually failing to follow through.

'I can live with that,' Suki replied.

'Stop it you two.' Dave huffed. 'Will you be quiet? I'm sick and tired of your bickering.'

'You could untie me, and I'll promise to be quiet,' Fiona cooed.

'No.'

Fiona wriggled, throwing her feet into the air. 'Why not?'

Dave shrugged. 'Like Suki says, there is zero incentive to let a murderer roam among us. We still have another killer to worry about.'

'Or it could all have been you, and I'm not risking it,' Suki added.

'I promise, I have no interest in murdering you.' Fiona pouted. 'Well, I do for as long as you refuse to remove this damned rope, but after that I will go sit in that corner right there and be quiet. Read a magazine. Deal?'

'No.' Dave pulled himself up to standing using the nearest bicycle handle. He turned his back demonstratively to Fiona and walked to the desk.

Fiona shouted, 'Come back here. Come here.'

Evie hoped he wouldn't touch anything he shouldn't. With the wrapper a critical piece of evidence, they couldn't run any risks. But he merely wobbled the computer mouse and looked on, dismayed, when the static browser confirmed the Internet connection was still down.

Fiona's incessant shouting was gnawing at Evie's nerves. How much longer would they be trapped here? What was the plan? The ultimate goal?

She didn't need to check the clock again to know it was past lunch time. Her belly had been telling her that for a while—ever since she donated her breakfast to the floor. An image popped into her head: Kaif, smiling, plate of pancakes in hand. Her throat tightened.

He'd asked her to call, had wanted to know when she'd be home. He had something up his sleeve for her birthday. Had been clumsy at hiding it. Tears welled in her eyes. How long would he wait before he began to worry?

Would he worry enough to come?

CHAPTER FIFTY-EIGHT
Suki

'For the love of God, woman, will you be quiet?' Suki pinched the bridge of her nose and sighed. Fiona had been screaming for over half an hour.

Suki leaned down from the bench and took off her right shoe and sock.

'What are you doing?' Fiona asked.

'What I should've done ages ago. Before you gave me this headache,' Suki replied. She flapped her turquoise running sock into the air. Tiny particles of fluff danced in the light to Fiona's continuous stream of 'Let me go. Let me go. Let me go.' She was obviously hoping to wear them down, and Suki had to admit it was working.

Suki stretched the sock out a few times, and limped, one-shoed, to Fiona. She twirled the sock like a truncheon, wishing it held a firm rubber ball to smack her with, but this would have to do.

Fiona's brow crumpled. 'Are you going to make me smell that?'

'No,' Suki said, rolling the sock into a ball. As she neared Fiona, she leaned into her face. 'Say ah.'

Fiona turned her head away and sputtered. Suki grabbed her chin and pulled her face to her, while raising the balled sock into position.

'No, Suki. No,' Fiona cried.

'Stop it,' Dave yelled from by the desk.

Suki's shoulders dropped. 'Why not? She's insufferable.'

He strode over, sharing a nod with Evie. Suki felt a small pang of betrayal. She'd made the effort to cultivate Evie's trust, was nice to her when no one else was. How come those two were pals suddenly? Or was she reading too much into it? It was impossible to think, with Fiona's incessant noise.

When Dave reached them, he tugged Suki's arm away and pulled the sock out of her hand. 'She could choke.'

Suki scoffed. 'She won't choke. It's a sock. In fact, it's high-end breathable technology developed by one of my clients.'

Dave gave her a stern look, his eyes unnerving pools of black. 'Believe me, she could choke.'

A lump formed vicariously in Suki's throat. She licked her lips. What she'd give for water... 'What are we meant to do, huh? She's driving me nuts.'

'Thank you, Dave,' Fiona said with an overly triumphant smile.

He pointed his index finger to within a hair of her nose. 'You be quiet.'

Narrowing her eyes, she screamed in a high pitch. 'Aaah.' After a big gulp of air, she went on. 'Aaah. I'm going to keep at it until you let me go, or I lose my voice. Aaah.'

A flash of lightning bathed Fiona in an astral aura before the rumbling thunder boomed and startled them all.

Dave winced and fled, hands on his ears, pacing in circles with nowhere to go. 'Stop it.' Pebbles chased him and jumped against his legs, barking, as if it were a game.

Suki's eyes readjusted to the gym's ambient lights. Outside, a wall of dusk-grey made her feel even more enclosed, even more lost in time.

Evie tried to catch the dog. 'Pebbles, come here. Shh. Calm down.'

'Do something,' Dave snapped at Suki. 'We have to get out of here.'

A spike of resentment surged up her spine. 'I was bloody doing something, but you stopped me. What will you have me do, huh?' Suki raced to the glazed front doors and banged on them. 'You've tried to open these already. What? Do you think I have some sort of door opening super-powers you don't have?'

Dave glared at her and turned to Fiona. 'Shut your stupid dog up.'

'Aaah.' Fiona refused to comply. She'd found her weapon and was going to use it until they relented.

'I can't be here,' Dave said, still covering his ears.

'Well, I'm having a ball. Party on. I'd stay here all day if I could.' Suki rolled her eyes. 'Fucks' sake Dave. Don't you think we've all had enough?' She walked over to the computer and smacked the mouse on the desk. 'See? Tried this too.'

Reaching the fire escape, she banged her shoulder into the door and rattled the release bar. All the while, Fiona was screaming, Pebbles was barking, Dave was gurning, and Evie was chasing and shushing the dog, which was only getting it more excited. Suki's shoulders ached with tension, and it wouldn't take much more to make her head explode.

'I need out,' Dave yelled, his complexion turning green. The veins in his neck sprung like coiled ropes as he clenched his jaw, rage oozing from every steroid-enhanced cell.

Suki held her arms out wide. 'I know, okay? We've tried the phones, the doors, the floor, the ceiling. We've tried everything.'

A blinding fork of lightning etched a crack along the window. Suki's heart jumped. She ignored the cacophony around her as she ran to the window and pressed her nose against the glass, bracing for the thunder that thankfully took longer to come this time. The storm may have been receding, but the sky was still eerily grim for one o'clock. In the distance, the boats bobbed wildly on the water, their masts like metronomes with a rhythm of their own.

'Strike that,' Suki said. 'There's one more thing to try.' It seemed doomed to fail, but she needed to at least be seen to exhaust all options. 'Evie, where's the light switch?'

Evie had Pebbles clutched under her arm, her other hand circling around his yapping snout as she tried to catch it without having to deal with teeth. 'Which one?'

'The one for this part of the room,' Suki replied, indicating the weights area by the window, where Fiona still screeched.

'It's there.' Evie pointed to a brushed steel three-way switch on the wall.

Suki hurried past Dave, who seemed increasingly erratic and pale. She tested the switches in sequence. Different parts of the room dimmed in turn. In one push, she turned them all off.

'What are you doing?' Evie asked.

'I have an idea,' Suki replied. She flicked the switch that triggered the lights closest to the window. Up and down, up and down. The screaming was making it difficult to concentrate, but she managed to create the pattern she was after: quick quick quick, slow slow slow, quick quick quick.

Suki saw Dave hold the sides of his head as he flickered in and out of shadow. 'Stop it,' he cried.

'It's Morse code,' Suki said. 'The boats. Maybe a fisherman or a sailor might recognise the SOS.'

She pressed the switches again. Quick quick quick, slow slow slow, quick quick quick. Quick quick quick, slow slow slow, quick quick quick.

Evie came closer to be heard over Pebbles's yelps. 'I don't think there are any people on those boats. Not in this storm.'

'You never know,' Suki replied and kept at it.

'I told you to stop it,' Dave roared and charged at Suki like a bull, knocking Evie out of the way. He grabbed Suki by the neck and pinned her to the wall in a stranglehold.

Her feet dangled in the air, and she'd lost her breath to the shock. Through the darkened room, slim streaks of cloud-bursting daylight revealed the rage in Dave's glazed eyes.

Anxiety coursed through Suki as she sipped what air she could. She pounded her fists on his shoulders and kicked him in the stomach with her knee, but he just blinked once and held firm, one hand around her neck, the other blocking her legs.

Even Fiona was struck dumb by the attack, but Suki's ears still rang from her screams. Or was it from alarm, an internal siren to wake all Suki's defences?

Cold sweat dampened Suki's forehead. Stars twinkled in her peripheral vision. Her lungs were on fire.

She slapped Dave's ears, grasped in vain at the trimmed fuzz on his head. Hair... Her heart skipped. She reached behind her, hand searching.

Contact.

She mustered her last ounce of energy, pulled the red pen from her plait and plunged it into Dave's right shoulder.

Suki fell to the ground as Dave stumbled back. She gasped for air and watched Dave yank the pen out, blood dripping onto the mat. As Suki found her feet, Dave looked at the pen and at her with a childlike, confused expression, as though waking from a dream. He opened his mouth to speak, then a dumbbell hit his skull with a harrowing thwack.

Chapter Fifty-Nine

Evie

The force of the strike travelled through Evie's arm, braking with a piercing pain at her elbow. She dropped the weight and gasped. What had she done?

Dave staggered sideways and tripped over the rowing machine's long metal tail.

'Evie, Jesus Christ,' Suki said with a raspy voice.

'I'm sorry.' Evie trembled. Her mouth had filled with saliva from the sickening sound of contact. She couldn't bear to look at the hulking shape on the ground. Was he dead?

Suki hit the lights and rushed up to her. She almost lifted her from the ground in a big hug. 'Are you kidding? You saved me. Thank you.' She squeezed Evie so hard, it was difficult to imagine Suki'd been close to passing out only seconds ago.

Evie wriggled free and faced away, not wanting Suki to see her blush. Her gaze landed on the surreal sight of Fiona still wound tightly in a rope, upright, like the spool on a sewing machine.

'Well done,' Fiona said. 'Now let me go.'

'Piss off, Fiona,' Suki said. 'Believe it or not, this isn't about you.' Suki grabbed Evie's hand and pulled her round. A small frown twitched above her eyes searching eyes. 'You okay?'

Evie wasn't sure. How could she be sure until she knew what she'd done? Oh God, what had she done? Her stomach was a swirling mess. She took a deep, steadying breath. It was time to find out.

Dave groaned. In that instant, it seemed to Evie that all the clouds had lifted. Everything in the room was touched by a benign lightness. He was alive. She hadn't killed him. She latched onto Suki as her entire body deflated in relief.

He turned on his side, face crumpled in pain, one hand on his head where she'd thumped him. Evie nearly wept in gratitude. There was no blood.

Blood did ooze slowly from the hole in his shirt, along the edge of his clavicle. They'd have to address that.

She and Suki went to kneel by his side, helped him sit up, and leaned him against the wall. His head flopped sideways. His lips parted in a droopy scowl as he seemed to lose consciousness again. Tension crept across Evie's shoulders. What horrible damage had she inflicted? Would it be permanent?

The sound of the dumbbell hitting his head returned to her. That awful bang. The pain in her elbow. The image of Dave crumbling. Evie wiped her eyes, willing the vision away, willing the guilt away.

With another deep, mindful inhalation, it worked. In floated the soothing tones of her mother's voice, 'The biggest gift you can give yourself is forgiveness.' Heat rose to Evie's neck. That was all fine and well for spilt milk and cracked teacups, but she'd broken a whole man.

Did it matter that she'd acted on instinct? A sort of self-defence, really. She'd seen him lift Suki up by the neck, not letting go, Suki unable to fight for herself. Surely it had been the right thing to do. Why else would the dumbbell have glowed the way it did, calling out to her?

'Hey, you're okay,' Suki said, carefully rolling Dave's head to a steady position. 'Dave? Can you hear me?'

Evie held his hand, his fingers cold and limp against her palm. The scarlet patch was spreading along the fabric of his shirt. She scurried around to collect what she could from the exploded content of the first aid kit. Damned Pebbles had ruined the bandage roll. Could she find another?

'Keep him still,' she said to Suki, and used the blunt medical scissors to cut a small incision in his top. She tore a few strips of tape and gave them to Suki to hold while she placed a gauze square over the hole.

'Why are you helping him?' Fiona asked. 'He tried to strangle you.'

'I'm aware of that, but I don't want Evie to live with the trauma of having killed the man,' Suki said softly.

'He's dying?' Evie said. This would be on her.

Suki folded Dave's hands on his lap and balanced his head upright again. Suki looked at Evie and gave her a rueful smile. 'I don't know.'

'But you're so smart. It's like you know everything...' Evie said, hoping Suki would magic a medical degree from her sleeve like she'd done the Morse code.

'Ha.' She smiled. 'Indeed, I am a woman of many talents.' Suki winked. 'But mostly, I'm very good at bluffing.'

CHAPTER SIXTY

Evie

'What else should we do?' Suki asked Evie a short while later, as they sat by Dave's slumped shape. 'You're the first aid lady.' She gave Evie an encouraging nod.

'Call 999,' Evie replied bitterly. 'Bandages, fair enough. But I think we've proven today I'm not the one to come to for real emergencies.'

'Rubbish,' Suki said. 'You did all you could to help the others. More than any one of us. That was brave. Stop selling yourself short.'

Evie looked down and picked at her fingernails. 'I nearly killed Dave, though.'

'Exactly. Super brave. You saved me. And I will be forever grateful.' Suki doffed an imaginary cap.

A glow warmed Evie's insides. Suki had a bewitching way of making her feel special.

'He had it coming,' Fiona added from her bench.

Suki shrugged. 'Maybe that too.'

'I'm serious,' Fiona said. 'Come closer, my throat is sore.' Evie and Suki obliged. Fiona continued in a conspiratorial whisper. 'Don't you see? He's the killer. He's the one who locked us in. Blaming me was just a clever way of deflecting attention. But look at him. Who's most likely to be the killer, huh? That violent brute or me?'

'That violent brute who knows about the security system,' Suki added. 'Let's not forget he let that slip.'

Fiona grinned eagerly. 'Right? Since we know it's him. Will you let me go?'

'Er...you killed your husband,' Evie said.

Fiona pinched her lips. 'No comment.'

'But why?' Evie asked Suki, who, unlike Fiona, wouldn't benefit from pinning it all on him. 'What possible reason could Dave have?'

Fiona tsked. 'It's not a *reason*. We need to be talking *motive*.'

They could talk all they liked, but Evie couldn't see what would send him on a murder spree. Surely Fiona sacking his firm wouldn't be it? That must happen all the time. And his name wasn't on the list they'd pulled together. He lived too high up and faced the sea.

She looked at Suki, whose mind seemed to be whirring ten to a dozen, if her brooding expression was anything to go by. Evie'd give anything to have a peek at that brain. She smiled as her own mind ran off and formed a manga picture she itched to draw: Suki, lying on a mortuary slab in her little two-piece gym outfit, hair parted down the middle as a large-eyed version of Evie herself in a lab coat sliced Suki's head open with a scalpel, grey matter bursting out and radiating like plutonium.

Dave cleared his throat. Evie jumped out of her dream and turned his way. She crept forward on her knees and watched him blink and frown, open a slit of eye, wince and close it again. Was he going to be all right? He groaned. At least he was back.

Suki slid along the mat in his direction. 'There's only one way to test for motive.' She nudged him in the shoulder. 'Hey, Dave. Wake up.'

He moaned and raised his eyebrows high, as though trying to pull open impaired eyes. A wet, pink stretch of inner lid became visible.

Suki shoved him harder. 'Come on.'

'Be careful,' Evie said.

A trickle of drool escaped Dave's mouth. He raised his arm lazily and wiped the wetness away. He smacked his lips, his eyes flickering. 'Wuh?'

'Dave, open your eyes,' Suki said. 'Say something.'

Evie's heart thumped so loudly, she worried she might miss his first words. If he spoke, that meant he'd be all right. The bruise would fade, the wound would heal, and all would eventually be forgotten.

'Whermmy?' Dave peeked at the gym, at Suki and Evie sitting by him. He caught sight of Fiona and grimaced. 'Ffck.'

'I believe, ladies, this means he's okay,' Suki said. She waved her hand in front of him. 'Welcome back. You may not be feeling fully up to it, but here's the thing. We have questions.'

It seemed passing out again was his way of avoiding them.

CHAPTER SIXTY-ONE

Suki

That bruise on Dave's head was something else. It was no wonder it was taking him such an effort to recover. It had been a good few minutes and Suki wondered when he'd wake again.

Judging by the many scars burrowed in his buzz cut, however, this didn't strike her as the first time he'd been in a fight.

She shook him gently, clutching his thick, muscular arm. What would it be like to be so strong, so big, that you could go around being feared? Owning the place. What a difference to being a five-foot-nothing Asian chick that random men in bars thought it was totally normal to lift up, purely for giggles. Of course, that hadn't happened for a while. The high heels and a perfected ability to convey a huge 'fuck you' with only a sneer had thankfully put an end to that.

Her throat hurt when she swallowed. Dave had lifted her up too, but instead of the usual rage, she'd been flooded with terror. There was no way she'd let him walk away from that. And there was no way she ever wanted to experience that again. As Dave stirred, she realised she'd have to do something.

She ran her hand over the saltire print of his shiny socket and plunged her finger over the rim by his thigh. She felt the moist skin of his stump on one side and a tacky substrate of some sort against the socket itself.

'Suki, what are you doing?' Evie asked, appalled.

'I don't think we can trust him not to become violent again.' Suki gestured to all corners of the gym. 'Can you find anything to tie him up with? Because I can't.'

Evie gave her a puzzled look but didn't seem confident enough to question. 'We used the only skipping rope on Fiona.' She got to her feet and walked around the room, inspecting everything in sight. 'We could use Dave's trousers. Knot them around his arms?'

Suki pulled a face. 'I'd rather leave Beatrice covered.'

'You could untie me,' Fiona said, grinning eagerly. Suki let out a quiet laugh and gave Fiona mental props for perseverance.

She squeezed along the edge of the socket. The squishy layer was warm and silicone-like. She tugged to gauge its resistance. 'We should pull this limb off.'

Evie's hands flew to her mouth as she gasped. 'You can't do that. That's really—'

'What? Is it rude? Offensive? Intrusive?' Suki blew a raspberry. 'Need I remind you he nearly killed me?' She waved Evie over. 'Come on, help me out. It's not going to hurt him, but it may keep him from accosting one of us. Don't you want to be safe?'

'I don't know...' Evie said.

'I do. Get your ass over here.'

Suki's tone was enough to get Evie into motion. She kneeled by Dave's feet, her balled hands held to her chest.

'He's not going to bite.' Suki wasn't enjoying touching Dave either, particularly close to his crotch.

Evie smiled nervously. 'What do I do?'

'I can't figure out if this layer here is part of the big stump cup thing or whether it's like a sock. I suspect it will take more than a strong pull. Otherwise, the whole thing would fall off when he walked, no?'

Hunched over his middle, Suki stuck her second hand over the rim and wriggled her fingers to loosen the silicone. 'Maybe if I try to roll this bit down...' She nodded to the expensive-looking grey contraption that formed his knee. '... and you pull that?'

Evie flipped position to straddle the leg and grabbed the long knee device, looking as terrified as she would holding a pipe bomb. 'Okay.'

'On a count of three. One... Two...' Suki crept her fingers further down, pinching her lips as nausea hit. The smell of sweat and balls wasn't helping. She felt the silicone loosen slightly as air snuck in. 'Three.'

Evie leaned back. Her butt must have touched his up-turned foot as she squealed and dropped to the side, right when Suki tried to scoop the socket off.

It didn't budge. But Dave's head did. It rolled forward, and with a start, jerked back up. He chewed. His eyes pressed closed, and his head fell to the left, almost taking his upper body with him. Suki caught him by the forehead and held him in place, her other hand still between his flesh and the socket.

'Come on, Evie. Don't be such a lightweight. He's wak-ing up.'

Fiona's voice pipped up. 'Try the button.'

'What button?' Suki asked.

'A black round thing on the side, low down. I noticed it earlier because it interrupted the flag pattern. It looks like a button to me. It must do something. I figure they're not likely to put a button on there for no reason.'

Suki let go of Dave's head, which dropped forward again. A low groan was followed by a gurgling sigh. The sound of waking.

Her nerves tingled. She needed to hurry. She scanned the socket and found the black dot, the size of a fifty pence coin. 'Good shout, Fiona.'

'If this works, will you let me go?' Fiona chanced again. 'I mean, you may still need to tie him up. I bet he can jump on one leg pretty well.'

'Perhaps,' Suki said, mostly to shut her up. Dave smacked his lips and opened one eye. She ran her index finger over the button, finding a thin ridge, and pressed carefully. It moved inward, and she heard a slight movement of air. 'Of course. I should've thought of that. It's held by vacuum.'

'Vacuum how?' Evie asked.

'No time for a science lesson. I'll press and, when I tell you, you pull.' Suki let the air out and after another count of three and a joint tug, Evie fell on her bum, Dave's silicone-covered stump thumped to the ground and Suki ended up with an empty socket in her hands.

She exchanged stunned glances with Evie, who grimaced, let go of the knee and scrambled away to a safe space by the window, leaving Suki holding the proverbial, very Scottish baby.

'What's he going to do when he sees what we've done?' Evie asked.

'Only one way to find out, but whatever it is, it's going to be slow.' Suki shoved the limb out of reach.

Evie's expression clouded over. 'Have some respect. He's a soldier.'

A tiny pang of guilt burst in Suki's belly. Pulling off an amputee's leg was a shitty thing to do. But who was to say he wouldn't erupt again? She, for one, had absolutely no intention of dying today.

CHAPTER SIXTY-TWO

Suki

It took a moment longer for Dave to stir. His eyes opened, and he frowned at the light. He patted his face as though making sure it was still there. It was, and it wasn't a pretty one, particularly with the bulging bruise at his temple.

Suki clicked her fingers. 'Dave. Oi. Snap out of it.' Soldier or no soldier, seeing him all dopey and vulnerable was pretty satisfying after what he'd done.

'Leavmmm'lone,' he said, lifting his elbow to push her away, but this being his wounded side, he groaned in agony. The source of the pain seemed to not quite register. He rubbed his scalp and grabbed hold of the rowing machine beside him, seemingly ready to hoist himself up.

'Where do you think you're going?' Suki said.

Dave spotted his limb lying on the mat. He looked down at his stump. Shock spread across his face. 'My knee. What the hell?'

'I'm sorry, Dave,' Evie said, hands pressed together, all innocent. 'I know it's horrible, but we had nothing to tie you up with.'

'Why do I need tying up?'

'So you don't try to strangle me again,' Suki said.

Dave recoiled. 'Wh-what?'

Suki scoffed. 'Nice try. You lifted me up against that wall by the neck and squeezed the living daylights out of me.'

He gazed at Fiona, then at Evie, who helped to jog his memory by nodding.

'I had to hit you with a dumbbell,' Evie said. 'In the head.'

He let that sink in for a moment and dropped his head in his hands. 'Oh God, I'm s-s-s-sorry. I don't remember.'

If he was acting, he was pretty good at it. Unease stirred Suki's chest. She recalled his glazed, vacant expression as her vision had blurred. Could he be telling the truth?

'What *do* you remember?' Evie asked.

'I...I...' He was still befuddled, but his sight soon set on his limb. He reached out. 'Givvv muhmy leg.'

'Sorry, no can do,' Suki said. She got up, lifted the leg, and carried it like a spear to park it against a bicycle in the middle of the room.

'All I remember,' he paused and breathed heavily, as though every syllable was an exertion. 'Fiona's screams. Noise. Bangs. Lights flashing,' Dave said. 'They triggered me.'

Suki scoffed. 'I didn't realise epileptic fits now came with strangling people.'

'I'mmm not epileptic. I s-s-sometimes... get very... angry. My senses, it's too much. I lose myself... I'm somewhere else...,' he said as he stared into that distant somewhere else, a somewhere else Suki suspected might be a place with sand and bombs. He turned to her—which caused him to twitch in pain. He frowned and spoke earnestly. 'I didn't mean to hurt you. I'm sorry.'

Suki crossed her arms. 'Hmm.' It didn't suit her for him to be all pitiful with trauma. It might cloud her judgement. The way this day was going, she needed to keep her wits about her.

'What's this?' he asked, more lucid, lifting his bandaged shoulder.

'I had to stab you with the pen I carried in my hair, so you'd let go of my throat,' Suki said.

'And I didn't realise you'd let go when I hit you in the head. I'm sorry,' Evie added.

He sighed. 'I wasn't myself.'

Evie tilted her head as she looked at Dave. 'I believe you. I don't mean to pry, but could it be PTSD?'

Dave shot her a fiery look. 'You a psychiatrist now?'

'Was it your unforeseen "not being yourself" that made you lock us up here and plan to finish us all off one by one?' Fiona said, smirking on her bench. 'Because that sounds quite premeditated to me.'

'Pot, kettle.' He sneered. 'I didn't kill anyone.'

'Not for lack of trying,' Suki pressed.

Dave let his arms flop by his sides. The impact on his shoulder made him wince. 'Why would I want to get rid of my neighbours? I hardly knew them—or you.'

'Yes, you did,' Evie said. 'I've seen you chatting with Stephen here. He's helped you with weights.'

He shrugged. 'Well yes, we chatted like any neighbour would. He was a nice guy.'

'Oh God, you were sleeping with him, too. That's it, isn't it?' Fiona asked. 'You were all secret lovers.'

'No,' Dave said. The face he pulled was one of true disgust. 'And stop projecting. We all know you killed Charles, and you have a much bigger motive to kill Stephen than probably any of us.' He pressed his hand to the mat and scooched further along the tunnel between the wall and the rowing machine. 'Leave me alone. My head hurts.' He stretched and closed his eyelids as though he couldn't focus. His chin fell to his chest.

'You know what else hurts?' Fiona said. 'My arms, my whole constricted upper body. And I'm freezing. So, forgive me for not caring about your boo-boo. Honestly, Suki,

Evie, it's him you should be tying up. This woe-is-me non-sense is all an act. He's lowering your defences, thinking up new ways to murder everyone.'

Suki laughed under her breath. If they'd been able to cap-ture the energy Fiona put into being let loose, they could've heated the whole room. She was tempted to give in, there being nowhere for Fiona to go, anyway. Besides, she'd only killed her husband, and in such an amateur way that she got caught in a nanosecond. Suki knew fine well Fiona wasn't behind the other deaths.

For all his protestations, Dave wasn't in the clear yet. There were still plenty of reasons for people to think he could be behind this convoluted locked-in death trap. It hadn't occurred to her until his attack that Dave did in fact have a reason to hate Beatrice. It was the same reason she had.

CHAPTER SIXTY-THREE

Evie

Evie hunkered by the window, knees at her chest, resting against the glass. Her back muscles numbed gradually from the cold.

This way, she kept an eye on the others: Dave struggling with consciousness huddled in his corner to her right, Suki sitting cross-legged ahead, staring into space, and Fiona on her near left. The three dead bodies she avoided with imaginary panels separating her from them, like blinders on a horse.

They'd all been sitting in silence for a while, sick of the recriminations, tired of not having any answers and desperate to go home—at least, that's how she felt. Suki and Dave were no doubt mostly zonked from their injuries.

She clutched her neck. How scary must it have been to be strangled like that? She'd had it all wrong in her drawings. The victims' eyes didn't bulge like white dotted marbles ready to pop; they lost their gloss, sunk, darkened with terror.

Fiona had crossed her ankles, one foot covering the other, presumably trying to keep warm. Her black nail varnish stood out against the blueish white toes. Zombie feet. Her head was leaned against the leather back rest, nose to the ceiling, her long neck exposed. She'd shut her eyes. Evie didn't know when that happened. A sense of dread crept over. She hadn't said anything in some time. Not made any noise. Her heart raced. Beatrice and Stephen fell abruptly, with no one near them, not a trace of a cause.

Evie bent forward and squinted, focusing intensely on Fiona's chest, her purple breasts a lone stretch of freedom between stripes of twirled twine. She saw a tiny uplift and a fall. Her own lungs followed suit with a breath of relief. Alive.

Of course she was. So foolish. Evie rubbed her temples. Was it any wonder things were getting to her?

The clock on the wall ticked softly. She'd been in here nearly five hours. How could it be that nobody had even knocked on the gym door during all this time? The conflicting messages on the building's app hadn't thrown her at first. There'd been many glitches with sensors of late. But as the doors remained closed every time they checked and the Internet connection remained down, it was clear there were never any workers due. And if people weren't coming to the gym, it was because they were told it was closed.

Except for this lot, lured to their deaths. And her. In a place she shouldn't have been. Forced by Alan to attend, made by Alan to suffer the horror of people dropping dead around her.

Her blood boiled with resentment. He'd said the scheduled girl was sick, but that could easily have been a lie. He had wanted her here, as his scapegoat. Using her drawings. Knowing the police would link it to her. Likely even planning to be the helpful person 'finding' her notebook, expressing shock at the gruesome sketches, but falling short of pointing out the similarities with the actual deaths lest it drew too much attention to himself. He'd leave that to them. And they'd see this innocent man, the poor building manager who'd have to clean up after a rogue employee... Evie.

She remembered the crumpled paper on the floor. Suki was right, that analysis of residents had been a waste of time, a nonsense hypothesis about the development. It had to be something else. As far as she was concerned, Alan had means, motive and opportunity—even if she wasn't sure how he'd managed Stephen on the bike, or how he'd planned for the others to die. They were right to stay put and not touch anything, drink anything, flush anything.

More than ever, she was certain Alan did it. He had access to the gym. He had administrator access to the security settings and the app. He knew what the residents were like, their habits.

She curled her lips in distaste. He probably watched them more than they knew. Those beady eyes lurking in the shadows, always near. She shuddered at the way he'd hovered around her, with his beastly musk, always a hair too close. Given what she'd heard about him and Tessa today, she couldn't help but think she got off lightly.

Evie massaged her stomach, trying to loosen the knots inside. Surely, they'd figure out it wasn't her? Yes, she had been in the room with the victims. And yes, if her imagination was wild enough to think she could've secretly administered poison while being seen to give mouth to mouth, chances were theirs were too. And yes, her fingerprints were everywhere, and she had truly wished them all dead at one point or another.

Yes, yes, yes, it all pointed to her. But there was one thing they'd discovered today that would have to exonerate her: the half hour blind gap in the CCTV.

She bet Alan wouldn't have expected them to find that, had been busy building an alibi all day today—and not last night. Yet she'd been in her bed with Kaif while Alan rigged the gym under the cloak of darkness.

New knots formed inside. Kaif was a super heavy sleeper. The number of times she'd had to shake him awake after he'd not heard his unreasonably loud alarm... What if he couldn't remember? Would he, under pressure, in a tiny room, blinded by interrogation lights, swear hand on heart she'd been beside him the entire night?

Her lips trembled. She was the little spoon. Wouldn't the big spoon notice a lack of pressure, a cold belly, an empty arm if the little spoon slipped from the bed?

Kaif's distinctively oval face sprang to mind, his neatly trimmed nostrils trembling and his dark flop of hair shaking as he laughed. Warmth spread across her chest as she pictured him place both hands on her cheek, soft, with a caressing flick of the thumb. His nose against hers in a loving nuzzle that often preceded a long kiss. '*I love you*,' he whispered.

A gull squawked loudly outside, shaking her from her thoughts. Evie watched it fly out to sea and pivot, beak down, for a deep dive. After fish, no doubt, or discarded crisp packets on the shore.

The sky had cleared a tad. Possessed-pigeon-feather grey gave way to three shades down in the neatly arranged rainbow in her pencil case. The aluminium tone—minus the metallic sheen, as the sun was yet to make an appearance from behind a wall of cloud. It would, eventually. It wasn't Edinburgh without seeing four seasons in a day.

She sighed. Seasons, that's how long she felt she'd been stuck here. She clasped her hands together and stretched her arms high above her head. She dropped them and slumped on a big exhale.

Her weepiness bloomed. She pressed her lips together to hold it in. Suki had told her she was brave, and she didn't want to disappoint. But dammit, it was tough. It was her birthday, and her only wish was to see Kaif, to run into his arms and stay there forever and make all of this go away.

She sighed and scanned the horizon. Where would she go after this? Who'd hire her now? Where would she feel safe?

CHAPTER SIXTY-FOUR

Evie

Evie didn't hear Suki get up or walk towards her, so she was startled when her bare feet came into view close to her own.

'Hey. You okay?' Suki peered down at her, giving her a concerned look while weirdly holding her turquoise socks in one hand.

'I'm not sure I'd call it okay, but I'll live,' Evie said.

Suki gave her a sweet smile. 'I certainly hope you will.'

Evie pulled her shoulders in and stroked her scar. '*I'll live.*' What a stupid comment to make, given everything that was going on.

'Now that you've brought that up,' Suki said. 'I think we should tie Dave up too.'

'Why? His leg's off.'

'I know, but he's very strong and I don't want to risk it,' Suki said.

'With your socks?' Unnerved by Suki looming overhead, Evie stood up.

Suki shook her head and stretched one of the socks out. 'Mine are too short. What are yours like?'

'You're kidding, right? What are you planning to do? Knot them together like Rapunzel's bedsheets?'

'No, I was going to—' Suki's eyes lit up. 'You're a genius.' She raced to her shoes. 'Get your laces. We can tie them into a long string.'

Evie had a peek at Dave, slumped and subdued by the wall, his large bruise a screaming red, the blood on his torn shirt browning, his prosthetic limb too far to grab. He didn't look much of a threat.

She watched Suki picking the laces from her shoe, occasionally tilting her head, wincing, and rubbing her neck. It made she might fear him more.

Suki returned, white laces hanging from her hand like overcooked spaghetti. 'Do one of your hitchie things.'

'What?'

She extended her arm to Evie. 'The secure knot. The hitchie thing.'

'Oh, you mean a line hitch. You really weren't a girl guide, were you?' Evie said, taking the laces from her. She paused. 'Are you sure this is necessary? I don't think he's going to do anything. He's probably had a too big a bump in the head, anyway.'

'We'll need your laces, too,' Suki said. And that seemed to be the only answer she planned to give.

'What are you girls up to?' Fiona asked.

'We're incapacitating a murderer.' Suki answered, quietly.

Fiona gave a knowing nod. She mouthed, 'I told you so.'

Evie winced. This wasn't sitting right with her. 'Hey, it's normal to be frightened,' she said to Suki. 'I can see why you might want him punished, fair enough. But for what it's worth, I reckon he's not the killer. I've been thinking and, like I've felt in my heart of hearts all along, everything points to Alan. He's the one with motive, means and opportunity.'

Suki narrowed her eyes, her lips pinched into an equally thin line. 'Dave has motive aplenty.'

'He does?' Evie asked.

'I'd like to know too,' Fiona purred from the side, with what seemed to be supernatural hearing.

Dave murmured and made a slurping sound that rattled Evie's nerves.

'Shut up, Fiona.' Suki grabbed Evie's hands, clutched them to her chest and looked her intensely in the eye. 'Help me with this and I will tell you what I know.'

CHAPTER SIXTY-FIVE

Evie

There was a nervous tension in the room that snapped and crackled around Evie's skull. Nothing was as it seemed. Dave had a motive?

'Okay,' Suki whispered. 'You take the laces and I'll distract him. You sneak behind the rowing machine and when ready, I will lift his hands up for you to grab.'

'What's all the s-s-secrecy?' Dave said in a sleepy attempt at a bellow. He placed his hand beside him on the rower's seat. It slid backward, and he rebalanced. He hoisted his bum off the ground and started bending his sound leg, looking like he planned to get up.

Suki's eyebrows twitched. 'Shit. Come on.'

'I can't,' Evie said. The wriggling laces in her hand revealed her tremble.

Dave placed his other hand, the one with the injured shoulder, against the wall. As he pushed, he released a distressed and angry groan. Evie was definitely not going to get close now.

It didn't stop Suki, though, who snatched the laces from her and rushed to him. He looked up, an awkward, grateful smile on his face.

Evie's stomach dropped. Oh God, he thought Suki was coming to help. Dave's forehead crinkled when he saw the laces.

'I need you to stay here,' Suki said. 'Get down. Give me your hand.'

'Piss off.' He tilted his body away from the pain-inducing wall, leaning on his good arm. He put his foot flat on the mat and extended his elbow to heave himself up, glaring at Suki in defiance.

Evie watched Suki smooth her hair and straighten up. Her pulse quickened. The stare-down lasted a good half a minute. An intense, transfixing confrontation to which Evie's uncontrolled imagination couldn't help but mentally add a whistling Western soundtrack.

Then, the first bullet fired. Suki kicked the rowing machine's seat Dave was using as support, sending it careening back. Dave crumbled sideways onto his hip, arm twisted, and hit the metal rail with his ribs.

'Stop it Suki,' Evie yelled, heart racing. 'This is wrong.'

'Was it right when he lifted me off the ground by the neck?' Suki asked. She placed her hands on her hips, a militant expression on her face. 'So it's okay for a man to use his bulk against a woman, but when a woman's got the physical upper hand—this one bloody once—it's not?'

Evie hugged herself. 'No, I mean... He's disabled. I don't know. Just stop.' This didn't even seem to be about Dave anymore.

Dave shifted to leaning against the wall, holding his rib, sending Suki a look that could shoot a squirrel from a tree.

Evie gestured towards him. 'Listen. He's apologised. Sometimes people lash out because they're hurt, damaged. They make mistakes.'

'I'm not damaged,' Dave sneered.

'That came out wrong, sorry, I meant—'

'It doesn't make it right,' Suki added. 'The same can be said about Fiona. She was hurt. Killed her husband in cold blood.'

'Well yes, but that's not the point...' Evie said, becoming hyper-aware she didn't know what her point was. What the point of all of this was. Why had someone locked them in like this? Was it to see them turn on each other? Because bravo, that had worked.

She snatched a glimpse at the CCTV camera. The green dot remained off. But imagine if someone had been watching... If this were all a sick social experiment. She balled her fists and took in a deep, resolved breath. She refused to participate any longer. She'd make damn sure there was nothing to see. 'Step away from Dave,' she said to Suki.

'Let me tie him up really quick, at least,' Suki said.

Dave pulled his leg in, preventing Suki from grabbing it. 'If you let her tie me up, Evie, think about it. It's only you two free, same as being alone. If I'm tied up, neither Fiona nor I could intervene if Suki went after you... So, do you trust her enough?'

'Nice try, Dave.' Suki said. 'What was it you said to me before? Ah yes. "You would say that, wouldn't you, if you were the killer."'

'He is,' Fiona shouted. 'I've said that all along.'

Had she? Evie didn't remember. The morning was all a muddle. Too many shocking, draining moments. Impossible to keep track of who was where, who said what, who blamed who. There was a list that made some sense when they built it, then not. Her gut still screamed Alan, but even the whys and wherefores of that had become a blur.

They'd even pointed the finger at her, at various times. That, she remembered. It was hard not to. And they blamed her not just because she knew her way around the building. No, the bastards all made unfair judgements about her because of her tattoos, her art. But Suki had jumped to her defence more than once. Only Suki had been kind.

'Guys. We're going round in circles.' Evie let her hands slide down her face, mouth open, dragging her skin along in a Munch-like silent scream. 'My brain can't take this. You don't know who did this any more than I do. We're not sure it's one of us or Alan, or whoever. We're not even sure the other two were poisoned. I mean, blue fingers. Who knows, right? At this point, I could even be convinced Charles's death was an accident and we're all losing it. This has been the most horrific day ever. Honestly, all I care about is staying alive and getting out of here. Everyone stay the hell put.'

A stunned vibe percolated between them. 'She's right,' Suki said. 'We should have a truce. Wait to be freed. Somebody's bound to come, eventually.'

Among Dave's grumbles and Fiona's tsks, Evie smiled at Suki. It was good to have her on side.

CHAPTER SIXTY-SIX

Suki

'Here's what's going to happen,' Evie said, hands clasped like an over-eager schoolteacher on her first day. 'Dave, you stay where you are.'

Suki'd been quite happy to help stop the squabbling but wasn't fully on board with Evie making it an opportunity to take charge like this.

Evie picked up the papers they'd problem-solved on and tore them into long shreds. 'We all get a designated area to sit.' She strode into the open area of the room, past the bicycles, and built three long lines with strips of paper on the ground. They formed a large T-shape, the top horizontal to the windows, delineating the half where Dave and Fiona were from the entrance half of the room, and the tail split the rest of the mat down the middle.

'What's she doing?' Fiona asked. Suki shrugged.

Evie walked over the line. 'Suki, this whole bit, here, with the disabled toilets on your right side, is yours.' Her gaze brushed swiftly past Charles's body, which formed an awkward, natural fourth line to Suki's new cubicle. Taking one giant step over the middle line, Evie added, 'I will sit here. I thought that might be better than having you and Dave face each other.'

'Then what?' Suki asked.

'We sit and wait,' Evie replied.

'And this collage on the floor is supposed to protect us how?'

Evie's shoulders sagged. 'It won't, obviously. But I thought if we all agreed to keep to our quadrants, we'd stop fighting and be safe.'

'Why do I have to stay tied up if you're going to trust everyone else to sit still?' Fiona asked. 'That's not fair.'

'I guess we could— Hey.' Evie lunged forward to grab Suki walking past. 'Where are you going?'

Suki pulled her wrist from Evie's admittedly gentle grip. 'I'll sit where you want, but I didn't sign up for the whole trust bit.'

She collected the prosthetic leg from against the bicycle. By the rowing machine, Dave stretched out his arm. 'Give me that.'

Without acknowledging him, Suki carried it to her space. She sat down and crossed her legs, keeping the limb tucked by her side. You never knew when a big stick with a chunky end could come in handy.

Evie's face clouded with uncertainty. 'Oh, umm...'

'You can sit down in your space, Evie,' Suki said, hiding a satisfied smirk. Nobody told her what to do.

'What about me?' Fiona asked, wriggling the fingers of her constrained hand in a small wave.

Evie searched Suki's eyes, which she rolled exaggeratedly in response. Suki turned to Fiona. 'For the love of all that is good, will you give it a rest?'

'But—' Fiona pipped.

Suki held up her hand. 'How about this? If you can be quiet for a whole fifteen minutes, we'll release you. Deal?'

'Deal.'

'Meaning one-thirty-five?' Evie said, looking at the clock.

'One-thirty-four,' Fiona haggled.

Suki rolled her eyes again. 'Fine. You win.'

Fiona's eyes shone with achievement.

She hadn't won, of course. She wasn't even playing at the same table as far as Suki was concerned. Suki had merely thrown her a chip, a gesture of goodwill she could cash in later. Technically, there was nothing to stop Suki from changing the rules afterwards but at least this would offer them all a moment's respite.

Besides, Fiona was no threat. Suki shifted to sit diagonally inside her box. A good vantage point from which to watch Fiona, currently staring at the clock and Dave, ahead, busy scratching his shorts. Good thing they were far apart.

'You're always making deals, aren't you?' Evie sat down, angling herself in her box within chatting distance to Suki. So much for quiet time.

'You'd be surprised how often it's useful to apply negotiation skills outside of work,' Suki replied.

Evie wrapped her arms around her knees. 'I wish I could do that.'

'You're doing all right. We're all obediently sitting where you told us to.' Suki smiled, but it elicited only the slightest of upturned lip from Evie. 'You wanna hear the secret?'

Evie's raised eyebrow was all the encouragement Suki needed. Why not share some wisdom while wasting time? 'The most important thing is to keep a clear head. People get emotional, their pride or ego gets in the way. They want revenge, even when it's destructive to themselves. It clouds their decision-making, and that's when you swoop in.'

Evie rested her chin on her knees. 'I got shafted by the insurance company.'

Seeing Evie's scars for the first time earlier had already been a shock, but looking at them up close, their pink mounds and white valleys told a story of horrendous suffering. Suki's chest tightened. No matter how many distracting tattoos Evie had placed around them, they were hard to miss.

'I'm sorry about that. Insurance companies are the worst. I bet you want to burn them to the ground.' Alarm rang in Suki's ears as she heard herself speak. 'Oh God, I'm sorry.'

Evie graciously waved her awful faux pas away. 'Don't worry.'

'But that's the instinct I was telling you about, the vengeful rage to tame. Take Fiona. Made a rookie mistake.'

'How so?' Evie lifted her head, eyes wide with intrigue, like a kid being told a ghost story.

Suki inched closer and spoke in a soft voice. 'Imagine. Proud, successful woman. Big reputation to protect. She comes in here today, finds out her husband cheated—with a man, no less. She's raging. Hurt. Probably disgusted. All the emotions. She'd been suspecting something was up, but still, it's a shock. So what does she do? She takes advantage of people dying mysteriously to get her revenge. Punish him for ruining her life.' Suki sighs and shakes her head. 'Except she did that to herself. She acted rashly in a moment of passion, made a mistake and got caught. When she should've waited. She had leverage. Could've done much better.'

'Leverage?'

'It means you hold power. An ace up your sleeve. Something you can influence the other party with. Fiona might easily have figured out a way to destroy Charles and keep all their money. Also redeemed her sense of self by, I don't know, taking a toy boy. But she acted on emotion and now she's screwed.'

Evie snuck a discreet, compassionate glance at Fiona. 'Yeah.'

'The golden rules. Listen up. First, you protect yourself—*numero uno*—and your loved ones. Because that's what matters most in life. Then, you find and use leverage to get what you want. And only afterwards, only when you've achieved that, should you even start thinking about revenge.'

Was the girl even listening? This was valuable stuff. It seemed like Suki had been giving a lecture to herself as Evie stayed hung up on Fiona.

'You don't think she's behind the other deaths?' Evie asked.

'Ha. No. I saw how she turned rigid when she spotted Charles and Stephen's subtle stroking on the CCTV. This was news, and Stephen was already dead.'

Evie's eyes drifted and Suki followed her gaze to Dave. For an instant, she panicked. He was slumped. His eyes were shut. Was he dead? It was the merest of snores that allowed her to breathe again.

'Was it Dave?' Evie asked. 'You said he had a motive. What is it?'

A hard lump trudged through Suki's stomach. She'd failed her own test; told Evie this when she was wired from Dave's attack. Forgot to protect number one. She tightened the elastic band at the bottom of her plait to stall, but not answering the question could break the ally relationship she'd sought to build.

She should have never mentioned Dave's motive, as it might incriminate her too. Suki's mind whirred. Could she benefit from confessing to Evie that Beatrice had nearly caused her dad's death? Perhaps she'd feel for her and not give it too much further thought. She seemed convinced this Alan dude was behind the lock-in, anyway. At this stage, would Evie ever think the murderer was her?

As she felt the girl's inquisitive laser-eyes burning a hole in her chest, she debated whether to come clean or not. She settled on not.

CHAPTER SIXTY-SEVEN
Suki

Suki picked at the loose tongue of the shoe by her side and scanned the room. Fiona was fixated on the clock's ticking hands. It showed they had six minutes before she'd be freed.

Making sure to be out of earshot, Suki spoke quietly to Evie, 'I know I said motive, but it may not be enough. Plus, it's only to do with Beatrice. Part of me thinks Dave is guilty, but then again...' Suki let that linger. She didn't need to prove anything categorically. She only needed to keep suspicion off her.

'Why don't we let the police decide?' Evie asked.

The word 'police' didn't fill Suki with confidence she hadn't made a big mistake, but it was too late. 'Okay, here goes. Remember I said earlier that Dave's company was financially unstable? And he hated that I knew? I understand his anger because he nearly lost it all, recently. And Beatrice was to blame.'

Evie was all ears, so Suki went on. 'NatClyde bank had found themselves with a big black hole and to address that, her department started putting the squeeze on the businesses they'd lent money to. They particularly preyed on the ones that maybe had missed one payment, or asked for an extension, and walloped them with penalties and fees. It was hell for the business owners. Proper despair. These weren't resilient companies with lots of cash. They were small, everyday hustling firms. Plumbers, caterers, Mom and Pop shops.'

Her own 'Mom and Pop' sprung to mind, their ordeal etched into her memory with a wounding knife. Mum hiding from Dad in the small office behind the restaurant's kitchen, crying. She wouldn't have wanted him to see that. Suki could still hear the harrowing sniffs as her mum wiped away the tears when Suki walked in. She'd never seen her mother cry before. Mum was happy, Mum was bright, always a smile. Not just for the customers. Mum was life. And mischief personified. She'd hold up fingers as marks out of ten behind the back of any date Suki brough to the Fragrant Orchid. Put the pressure on by rocking an invisible baby in her arms with a big fat wink.

But Mum had been broken. Besieged by the intimidating letters with big red stamps on them. '*Why didn't you tell me?*' They'd been too proud to come to their daughter when the demands piled up.

Suki felt the guilt gnaw a hole in her heart, even today. She could've done something. She should've known they were in trouble. The whole point of them scrimping and saving for her to have the best educations was for her to bloody know what to do with a bullying bank. What else was the point if you couldn't save your own family? Instead, Dad worried himself into a heart attack as the restaurant faced ruin. Suki pressed her eyes shut when the vision of the paramedics working on him hit her again. The ambulance's flashing lights. The fear.

'Suki?' Evie asked, with a concerned tone.

'Sorry.' She smiled. 'The bastard bank basically forced a lot of these firms into bankruptcy, plundering their cash and buying the assets at knock-down prices to sell them at a profit. Some of the affected businesses survived, though it will take them ages to return on a solid footing. Including

Dave. Which is why I have this idea for a merger. Anyway, this all happened on Beatrice's watch, at her direction really. You can see why he hates her.'

She peeked over at Dave. Da Vinci himself couldn't have been painted a better portrait of victimhood: bashed, bruised, robbed—although she was to blame for that part. A dull weight of shame pressed in her chest. She slid the prosthetic limb an arm's length away.

Pebbles came trotting in from nowhere. He jumped at the socket playfully, tartan bow bouncing and ears flapping with every leap. Suki pulled the limb in, but that made Pebbles wag his tail even harder. He danced around, then stuck his entire head inside the socket. 'No, get out. That's Dave's.' She pulled the dog from the hidey-hole before tossing him out of the way.

She took the limb and rose, needing no further reminder this didn't belong with her. Pebbles dashed around her legs like a slaloming skier as she walked to Dave and placed the leg on the mat within reach, with a knowing nod.

'Now leave me alone, you dressed-up weasel,' she shouted at Pebbles. Whether the fluff ball was scared or offended, Suki didn't care. It did the trick, and he retreated.

Evie watched her sit back down in her space. 'He must be sick of being in here, too,' she said. 'I wonder when it will dawn on him that his owner's gone?'

Trust Evie to have a bleeding heart about the dog. That was exactly the type of soft clap-trap Suki had tried to educate her about. So that she could stand her ground. Like the companies with the bank. 'By the way, the companies I was telling you about formed a club. They exchanged private information, which allowed them to prove a pattern and sue the bank. It's worth a shot, but I think their odds are terrible. The big institutions are the hardest to beat. You throw a stream of lawyers at it until you can no longer afford your own. Well, you know that, with your insurance.'

Evie lowered her eyes and brought in her shoulders. Suki'd obviously poked a sore point, but she didn't regret mentioning it, because this time she might be able to help hit the financial institutions where it hurt.

'I suspect you've exhausted your avenues with that claim,' Suki said. 'But if you play your cards right, you could cash in after today.'

Evie's brow furrowed. 'What do you mean?'

'Unlike the rest of us here, you're at work. A terrible thing has happened to you. Not physically, but you can claim compensation for trauma and distress.' Suki saw Evie squirm. 'Listen. This is what employer liability insurance is for. I'll help you find the right solicitor. And I'll tell you what. You'll be able to demand an even higher amount if it's Alan that did this. Because they knew he's a wrong'un yet still protected him. And while he should be tortured with hot pokers for the rest of time for what he did to that poor woman before me, it also makes them complicit.'

'It's time,' Fiona squealed.

CHAPTER SIXTY-EIGHT
Evie

Fiona kicked her legs high into the air. 'It's one-thirty-four.' She was the most animated thing in sight, what with the uninspiring backdrop of a listless grey sky. She was probably working on her circulation, but given her gleeful expression, Evie reckoned that if Fiona could've bounced, she would have.

Evie scrambled to her feet. 'I'll untie the skipping rope. She won't do anything stupid now and the police can deal with her once we're out.'

'Fine,' Suki said. 'But think about what I said.'

She did, all the way to Fiona, but it made her feel dirty. She shuddered at the thought of profiteering from people's deaths. Besides, she didn't have it in her to have that kind of fight again. After many months, her hopes had been dashed enough. It was up to her alone to improve her prospects.

Fiona smiled, seeing her on her way. 'Hurry.'

Evie heard Suki say, 'No, I don't want it.' She turned around to see Pebbles standing over his offering at Suki's feet, the tip of his teeny pink tongue flapping. He'd brought Fiona's earphones. Evie smiled. Long and striped, a black-and-yellow adder with two heads, it made sense he mistook it for a toy.

That this marked the start of a game of fetch was clearly lost on Suki, who chucked the thing in Dave's direction.

Evie untangled her knots by weaving the wooden handles in and out of the ropes, while watching Pebbles chase after the rubber contraption.

'Ouch,' Fiona said.

'Sorry, I'm trying,' Evie replied. The ropes had rubbed fiery red welts on Fiona's skin. She didn't remember making it this tight, but they'd all been stressed out at the time.

When she looked up again, Dave had the earphones. He dangled them high above Pebbles, a big grin on his face. The dog yelped and hopped in delight.

'Go get it,' he said as he threw it far away. It landed with a flop on Beatrice's outstretched forearm. Evie's stomach churned at the unwelcome reminder that things were far from cheery.

'Baby, come.' Fiona patted her knees as Evie pulled the last of the rope from her.

Pebbles gnawed disturbingly close to Beatrice's greying flesh to pick the toy up. The mythical snake wriggled like a live one in the pup's jaws as he ran to his mistress. The two heads bobbed, beady-eyed as they approached at speed. Evie tensed up, visualising their mouths opening wide, revealing long, poisonous, pointy fangs. Ready to bite. Pebbles unwittingly bringing death to Fiona, like he'd done to Charles.

Heat shot up Evie's neck. She fanned herself. What nonsense. It would be fine. They were earphones. Nobody'd tampered with them to make them deadly, although both Suki and Dave had handled them seconds ago.

Fiona picked Pebbles up and snuggled him. The dreaded snake fell with a lifeless thud onto the green mat.

Evie exhaled. See? Harmless earphones. She had to stop letting her imagination run away with itself, seeing the horror in everything. It wasn't doing her any good to be paranoid. There was nothing to fear. Fiona'd had them on earlier, anyway, in the floatation tank.

The remnant notion of a murderous Pebbles mingled with the mental image of Fiona in the tank. Evie trembled as a troubling thought seized her: it was like how Fiona died in her drawings. Pebbles drowning Fiona. Another similarity to her work she couldn't shake. But if the killer was copying her ideas, her locations, Fiona would've died in the tank today. Yet she didn't. Why?

The earphones' yellow stripes reflected the overhead light, flashing the answer to Evie with its mere existence. Fiona used her new swimmer's headset, and not the foam ear plugs that had been laid out for her.

Her heart raced. She'd been the one to hand the towel and ear plugs to Fiona. Poisoned ear plugs her prints would be all over. Again.

Why would someone do this to her?

CHAPTER SIXTY-NINE

Evie

Evie wound the skipping rope neatly around itself and placed it on the bench to cover a moist smirch, the last evidence of Fiona's imprisonment.

She bypassed a very much alive and free Fiona canoodling Pebbles and headed, shaken, back to her spot. A spot she had no intention of leaving again until this whole thing blew over.

'Hey,' she said to Suki, as she plonked down behind the white paper lines. She itched to tell her about the ear-plug theory, if nothing else, to make sure she wasn't nuts. What if Suki laughed?

'They seem happy,' Suki said.

'Yeah. They've only got each other now. Not that I think Pebbles has a clue.'

Up ahead, Fiona stood and reached her arms up high, her boulder of a diamond ring glinting under the lights. She bent fully double and showed off her limberness by placing both hands flat on the floor. She rose, unfolding her spine vertebrae by vertebrae and stretched her arms out sideways.

'What do you think will happen next?' Evie asked.

Suki cocked her head. 'When they find us, and the police come? I'm not sure.' She picked up a piece of paper and began tearing bits off it. 'I guess they'll interview us. They'll want to know what happened. Ask us who we think is behind it. The usual stuff you see on TV shows, I'd expect.'

'No, I mean after. What will happen to us all?'

After a long exhale, Suki replied. 'I don't think it's good news for Fiona, if that's what you mean. But you shouldn't worry. You—you and I—are going to be fine.'

Evie pulled a sceptical face. Unlike her, Suki wasn't the one who'd have a lot of explaining to do. 'You, maybe.'

'You will too. Trust me. I know you don't think it, but you have a lot going for you,' Suki said.

'Yeah, right.'

'I'm serious. You see things differently. You're creative. Content is king.' Suki waved her hand over Evie's tattooed arm. 'And look at this. You're very talented. You need to leverage your gift.'

'There's that word again,' Evie quipped to hide her blush.

'Leverage is everything.' Suki grinned, putting up a finger like a lecturer. 'I'm saying you need to find a way to make this your profession. Did you know the creative industries contribute over one-hundred-and-ten million pounds to the UK economy? Do you know what that means?'

Evie shook her head. 'No, what?'

'It means I'm very good at memorising big-ass numbers that nobody knows what to do with, just to mark my point.' Suki spurted with laughter.

As Evie giggled, Dave's bellow made her jump. 'Where the hell are you going?' She soon saw the target of his ire. Fiona was walking out of her spot in the direction of the changing room at the rear.

'Not that it's any of your business, Dave, but I am bursting for a wee,' Fiona said.

'Again?' Evie said.

Fiona sneered. 'Talk to me when you're my age.'

Suki jumped up and bounded towards Fiona, sticking an arm and a leg in her way. 'Hey. No. You can't go anywhere alone.'

Fiona huffed. 'Who's coming with me, then?'

'Not me,' Dave said, who'd reclaimed his limb and escaped his quadrant. 'For all I know, you're hiding a stack of lethal cereal bars in there.'

'You're a cock, Dave,' Fiona said.

Evie noticed Suki shake slightly, her lips pressed together, forging small dimples in her cheeks. If Evie's talent was art, hers was the ability to shrug off all the ghastliness and see the funny side. Had none of this affected her?

'I don't want *her* to come with me,' Fiona said.

'That's convenient. Because I don't want to come with you,' Suki replied.

Evie braced for what would undoubtedly follow.

'Evie?' Fiona pleaded, crossing her legs. 'Desperate, here.'

She'd resolved not to leave her spot, but there was also another issue at play. 'I don't think leaving Dave and Suki alone is a good idea, do you?'

'You can go in here, where we can see you,' Suki said, gesturing to the disabled toilet door on their right.

All Evie's senses skipped. 'She can't go in there. It could be dangerous.' She felt everyone's eyes on her, as well as a little foolish for the somewhat extreme warning. But what if she was right? What if a killer had borrowed ideas from her notebook? The disabled toilet would guaranteed be a death trap.

'Okay, that's a no,' Suki said. 'We should give Evie the benefit of the doubt.'

Fiona bent through her tangled knees and held her hands to her crotch. 'I really need to gooo.'

Suki chewed her lip. 'Here's the deal. You don't touch anything. Nothing at all. You hover, not sit, you don't wipe, you don't flush, you don't wash your hands.'

Fiona grimaced and stuck her fingers in her ears. 'Too much info. I get it. No touching.' She began walking to the door.

'And the door stays open,' Suki added.

Evie heard Dave snicker. A flash of annoyance passed through her. This wasn't about torturing Fiona. This was deadly serious. At least Dave had stayed somewhat close to his patch, standing as he was by the chest-pull machine.

'Absolutely not,' Fiona said, clutching the strap of her bathing costume.

Suki shrugged. 'Sorry, but that's the deal. And frankly, I think you should be grateful we've untied you at all, given what you've done.'

Muttering under her breath, Fiona nodded and grabbed the door handle. Before stepping inside, she said, in a bossy tone directed straight at Suki, 'Don't look.'

'Don't worry, that's not my thing.'

Evie averted her eyes, even though she was at the wrong angle to see past the half-opened door, anyway.

'Oh no you don't,' Evie heard Suki say. She turned to see Suki pulling at the nearly shut toilet door.

Suki managed to get it to three-quarters open only for Fiona to jerk it back. Deal broken, Suki wasn't having it. Evie stared in disbelief as the tug of war waged on, the women's grunts punctuating the to-and-fro as if it were the final at Wimbledon.

Pebbles barked. Dave laughed loudly. 'You are all insane.'

'For fucks' sake. Fine,' Fiona shouted. Suki stumbled backwards and fell to the floor as the door flung half-open.

On the mat, Suki rubbed her shoulder. Evie and Dave exchanged awkward glances, and both turned away from the scene. No point robbing Fiona of her dignity.

They waited in silence. The expected tinkle didn't materialise. Instead, Evie heard a solid thud, the unmistakable sound of a body collapsing.

Martina:
It's time to fetch Evie

Kaif:
I know. I'll get in touch with Mrs M

Martina:
OK. I have one more quick job to do

CHAPTER SEVENTY

Evie

'Shit,' Suki said. 'Shit shit shit, what happened?'

As Suki opened the door further, Evie saw Fiona sprawled out, face first on the lino, feet on either side of the bowl she didn't get to use. A small puddle of blood pooled above her lip from where she probably hit her previously injured nose.

Stunned, Evie went rigid. The pervasive scent of toilet-flowers clashed with the horror of the sight. Her knees buckled. This couldn't be...

'What did you do?' Dave asked, as he strode towards them like an enforcer. He cupped Evie's elbow and helped her up. Together, they advanced on Suki.

She spun round, eyes as wide as saucers. 'I swear I didn't do anything. I wasn't even looking. She walked in there and just... collapsed.'

'Is she breathing?' Dave asked.

'How the hell should I know?' Suki said, neither of them opting to cross the threshold.

He jutted his chin to the cubicle. 'Well, check.'

'I'm not going in there,' Suki said. 'I don't know what she touched.' She stamped her foot. 'Goddammit, she wasn't supposed to touch anything.'

Evie felt light-headed, the sickly smell stirring a swirl of nausea inside. She clasped her hands to her chest for balance. A shiver ran through the entire length of her; an eerie sensation of things falling into place, a last piece of the puzzle.

'We have to help her,' Dave said. 'Evie?'

'Do it yourself, you big clod,' Suki said, slapping him on the chest. 'It's not like we haven't had three first aid demonstrations from her already.'

Dave threw his hands in the air. 'No way. Whatever knocked Fiona out is still in there.' He squinted into the space, keeping the rest of his body at a fair distance. 'Can you see anything? What do you think it is?'

'Evie's the one who said it was dangerous. Ask her,' Suki said.

Evie twitched. Way to be thrown under the bus when she'd been proven right. She told them to stay out and looked at Fiona, a heap of pale flesh sprinkled with aerosol petals.

Her heart jumped. The scene came into greater focus, as though illuminated by the light bulb that had switched on in her mind. 'It's the air freshener,' she whispered.

'What?' Suki asked, scrunching her nose.

'Every time you open and close the doors in any of the changing rooms or toilets, the air freshener spritzes.' She held her nose and stepped far back. 'Get away from there.'

'God, she and I must've triggered that thing ten times.' Suki said, astonished. 'Fuck me, that's a sneaky place to put your poison. I'm not being funny, because this is a horrible, horrible thing, but hats off to whoever came up with that, if that's what did it.'

Suki used her knuckles to nudge the door and fled to the reception desk. She picked up the phone and pressed some buttons, looking as if listening intently, then shook her head.

'We can't do nothing,' Dave said, his crossed oversized arms and shoulder-width, solid stance on the mat, suggesting that was precisely the amount he would do.

'Perhaps that's what she wanted.' Suki said.

Evie tilted her head. 'What?'

'I mean, think about it,' Suki said. 'Perhaps she knew damn well what would happen, because this whole thing was her set-up all along. And given the sentence she was facing for Charles—and if the police figured out she killed them all—this could well have been intentional. Her way out?'

Dave smirked. 'Or she didn't want to wet herself in front of us, and you used the opportunity to guide her in there or slip her something.'

Pebbles appeared from under the desk and trotted, oblivious, to his dead mistress. Suki lunged and scooped him up before he could enter. 'You're an ass, Dave. Besides, would I orphan this little guy?' She tickled the fur between Pebbles's eyes.

'You hate that dog,' Evie said.

'Hate is a big word. I'm *not a big fan of* this dog, or most dogs.' She carried Pebbles to Evie. 'That doesn't make me a bad person.'

Evie took a few steps back, her hands splayed in front of her, but Suki stayed the course, intent on handing over the dog. An icy panic flooded Evie's veins. She tingled with heightened awareness. Nobody had watched Suki watch Fiona. What if she had slipped her something, like Dave said? What if she still had it on her?

Flashes of the day flickered through Evie's mind like a video montage, her heart palpitating in sync. Where Suki'd been standing. Her filling her water bottle. The others' accusations. Suki being alone with Beatrice, being alone with

Fiona. Hadn't she been by Stephen's bike before he hopped on? Didn't she say she'd seen the cereal bar before Fiona?

Suki surveyed her with an air of puzzled amusement. 'Evie, what's wrong? It's just a pup.' Her smile triggered a tussle of conflicting feelings. This was the woman who'd defended her, who believed her—believed *in* her. And yet...

Heat flushed across Evie's neck and temples. She sought the coolness of the wall, its comforting solidity as her certitude wavered.

Evie kept her eyes glued to Suki, bracing against her bonkers unpredictability. She continued to slide backwards, her hands searching the air behind her until she touched metal. Unexpected. The fire exit. She lay her palms flat on the door and pressed her entire length against its cold surface.

Her bum hit the handle, and with a deafening, improbable clink, it opened. Evie's throat thickened as sparks of memory flew and the magnitude of Suki's deception dawned on her. All day, it had only ever been Suki who'd tested this door.

CHAPTER SEVENTY-ONE

Evie

'You.' Evie's voice trembled, as much as the rest of her. She didn't wait for an answer and flipped round the door.

On the landing, she secured the exit with the tips of her trainers wedged underneath and hands pressed up top. She stood like this for a few seconds to steady her breath. But she couldn't stay here.

Two sets of stone stairs branched off on either side of her square her patch of concrete, leading in opposite directions. White walls like a tunnel to salvation. Twelve stories down to outside, freedom, air, or one up to safety.

Up it would be and, as she made that choice, she spotted a short scaffolding bar lying across the first step down that she could easily have tripped over. Good call.

She ran up the stairs, skipping every other step, ears pricked for any action behind her, straining to filter out the thumping of her pulse. Should she have blocked the door with the steel bar? Would that have put Dave at risk? Would Suki come after her? Questions demanded her attention, but her attention was fully directed at one thing: saving herself.

Footsteps echoed in the stairwell, going down.

The fire exit sign at the top loomed large. With two more leaps, she reached the heavy door to the thirteenth-floor corridor and swung it wide open. There, not ten feet from her, walked Mrs M, greying curls brushing against her shoulders as she leaned cautiously on her walking stick.

'Mrs M.' Evie panted, a stitch in her side. Her friend turned, and it felt like sunshine.

'Evie. I was coming to look for you.' She opened her arms in welcome, a vision in beige knit inside the plush, red-carpeted hall. She shuffled forward. 'Kaif called. I don't understand. It's your birthday. You're not supposed to be here.'

'We need to go.' Evie skipped to her and grabbed her by the elbow to swivel her round. Mrs M's sensible shoes collided in the pivot. Man, she was slow. 'Give me your keys. I need to call the police. Four people have been murdered.'

Mrs M's face fell. 'What? What people?' She fumbled nervously inside the pocket of her long cardigan. 'What's going on?'

The keys jangled as Evie snatched them and sprinted away. 'Sorry. I'll meet you there.' Guilt crashed her conscience like a comet as she left Mrs M behind. But it would be fine. Suki hadn't followed.

'Go, go. I'm coming,' Mrs M said, shooing her away.

The leather key holder was decorated with an enamel coin sporting a top hat circled by a garland of white lilies. Evie tried the first bronze yale key, which slid into the lock but wouldn't turn. 'Crap.' She'd only ever rang the bell before. It was the third key that did the trick and Evie felt a burst of relief as she entered the apartment, embraced by its familiar old-person smell.

She left the door ajar for the straggler and headed straight for the phone, which she knew was on the side table by the large, green sofa. Many times, Evie had sat by Mrs M's feet, instructed not to make a noise with a finger to the lips, while Mrs M picked up her handset with a polished 'Yes?' and went on to hold very serious conversations while admirably suppressing stoned giggles.

For a moment, the floor-to-ceiling view caused a disorienting wobble in her step. This was the same view she'd faced for hours, longed to escape from. The same view that contoured the day's atrocities. She sucked air deep into her lungs as she clutched onto the fringed standing lamp.

The phone lay where she'd expected to find it. She pressed the giant green square and dialled the simplest of numbers on the simplest of geriatric, large-buttoned interfaces.

'Emergency services, how can I direct your call?'

'Police, ambulance... I don't know. They're all dead.'

CHAPTER SEVENTY-TWO

Evie

'Yes, that's correct. Four dead bodies,' Evie said to the police despatch woman who'd taken over the call. 'Three survivors.' Her throat thickened. She hoped it was three.

Despite the apartment's radiators set perpetually on scorching, she shivered. What if she'd abandoned Dave to his death? Could he have escaped with Suki gone? Her chest tightened. He wouldn't have managed those stairs.

From the corner of her eye, she noticed Mrs M come in. Tension fell from her shoulders. Thank heavens she was all right.

Mrs M put her walking stick down absent-mindedly, seeming to concentrate on listening to the call. The stick fell across the door, triggering in Evie a frightful sensation of being locked in again. But that was stupid. She was safe. The police was on its way.

'Please stay where you are,' the woman on the line said.

'Yes. I'm not going anywhere. It's the thirteenth floor. Bell says Macaulay. Please hurry.'

She hung up and looked round to find Mrs M gone.

An instant later, Mrs M appeared from the kitchen, a tall glass of water in hand. 'I thought you might need this.'

'I'm to stay here,' Evie said, accepting the drink.

Mrs M placed her arm over Evie's shoulder and guided her to the sofa to sit. 'I think that's wise. You've had such a shock. Drink up.'

She seemed fretful, picking lint from the wool of her skirt. Who could blame her? Evie barged into her apartment with a completely surreal story of murder. She must be terrified.

Evie stared at the glass, at the ripples disturbing the clear liquid, at the flattened fingerprints on her deformed white fingers. She pressed her lips tight and scanned every inch of the room to remind herself where she was. Not the gym.

She took in the threadbare rug by the entrance, the Chesterfield cabinet, the large mirror with the multi-coloured glass mosaic surround, the fringed lamp that needed a good dusting, the wooden frame that held the travel souvenirs and, nearer by, the coffee table, covered in magazines, business correspondence and an order confirmation from a brand that seemed out of place.

'Evie?' Mrs M tucked a strand of Evie's hair behind her ear.

'It's nothing.' Evie smiled meekly and took a sip. 'It's... We all thought the water was poisoned. Suki even slyly drank from her bottle to prove she was innocent.'

Mrs M stiffened. 'Suki? Who's Suki? Why was she there?'

It seemed a strange question, but Evie replied, 'She came to the gym, like the others. She's a recent new resident. You'll have seen her. Tiny. Wears huge heels. Always on the phone. Asian.'

Mrs M's brow twitched. 'And you're saying she killed these people?'

Refreshed—almost fortified—by the water, Evie said, 'I never once believed it was her until that last moment, w hen... I can't fully explain it, but it all fell into place. You know? Like the universe giving me a huge sign.'

'Oh?'

'She had it all planned out so well, too,' Evie added, annoyed at the unintended hint of admiration in her tone. 'The evil bitch.'

Mrs M flinched, brought the blanket onto her lap. 'Why would this Suki person do this?'

'I don't know. After Stephen and Beatrice died, just like that...' Evie clicked her fingers. 'And we found out we were locked in. It was crazy. Everyone was blaming everyone. Even me. The cow made it look like I'd done it.' Tears welled in her eyes. 'She made me trust her and then... But I still don't know why.' She cleaned the trail of snot from her nose and rubbed her finger on her trousers.

A checked cotton handkerchief materialised as if from nowhere, crumpled. Probably from one of Mrs M's many pockets.

'Thanks.' Evie sniffed. 'We had this whole big theory that it was to do with the development next door, triggered by last night's meeting. Because all the victims had voted in favour. We even went through a list of all the people who might not want their view ruined.' She let out a scornful laugh and wrung the handkerchief as she would Suki's neck. 'It seems stupid now. It had been Suki's idea. She'd called it a hypothesis to test, when in fact it was a complete misdirection.'

'How awfully conniving,' Mrs M said.

Evie shifted to face her, eyes wide. 'This woman is super smart... You won't believe what she did. It's genius.'

'What?' A flash of excitement crossed Mrs M's face. It unsettled Evie for a split second. It felt disrespectful, wrong. But to be fair, Mrs M hadn't been in the room. She'd not experienced how hideous it was, seen the bodies. And she was used to Evie regaling her with horror stories... Except those were fiction. Not this.

'She poisoned the air freshener in the disabled toilet. So that when it squished, it suffocated you...literally and instantly. I mean, this stuff must be poison-dart-frog strong.'

Mrs M blew out a long breath. 'Wow, that *is* genius.' She shook her head. 'Poor Dave.'

Evie's stomach lunged. 'Dave?'

The colour drained from Mrs M's face. 'Did you not say Dave?'

'No. Did you know he was an amputee?'

Her brow creased into a deep frown. 'An amputee? No. Goodness. It was a guess.' She flashed Evie a smile, blinked a few too many times. 'You're always complaining about him going in there. That's why.' She grinned again, her eyes roaming. Evie noticed her stiffen before starting, without rhyme nor reason, to casually rearrange the papers on the coffee table. 'Was it not him?'

As she slid one stack of letters over another, Evie caught sight of the purple logo that had puzzled her earlier, a pretentious athletic brand an old lady would never wear. She leaned forward and grabbed the papers.

Mrs M gasped and brought her hands to her chest as though she'd touched burning coals. Her eyes shone with fear.

Evie up the order confirmation. Nausea flooded her stomach. The room spun. It was addressed to Stephen.

'I can explain,' Mrs M said, lips twisting into a nervous smile.

Evie bent forward, breathing hard, eyes pressed shut, her mind racing until it stopped with a violent burned-rubber skid of a halt. Her whole body plunged into a state of alarm as she straightened up and zeroed in on the wall. 'Where's the vial?'

'What vial, dear?' The 'dear' and singsongy voice was fooling no one. Evie jumped to her feet and pointed at the frame with little wooden cubbyholes that held Mrs M's travel knickknacks. One square was empty. 'The one from the Amazon. You called it the flask to eradicate evil men. It belongs here. Where is it?'

Mrs M's shoulders slumped. She tutted, rose, and smoothed her skirt. 'You always did notice the little things.' She grimaced at Evie and shook her head with the despondent what-am-I-going-to do-with-you look Evie knew all too well from her teachers.

Evie steadied herself against the tropical wallpaper. 'Oh my God, it was you?'

'How I wish you hadn't figured it out.' She sighed and folded the panels of her cardigan around her.

Evie massaged her temples and with every revolution came a sense of clarity. Mrs M had been walking *away* from her, not to. The steel pipe *had* blocked the door... and she must've just removed it. Why? Why now? But that wasn't the biggest question screaming inside her head, flowing to her lips on a searing wave of rage. 'How could you do this to me?'

Her expression softened. 'I'm so sorry, Evie. You weren't supposed to be here. It's your birthday,' she said, with a ridiculous celebratory tone. Her smile faltered. 'The app was supposed to keep you and everyone else out, saying the gym was closed.'

'No, I mean, how could you frame me like this?'

'Frame you?'

Her puzzlement seemed genuine. Evie's nerves tingled. Could she have got it wrong? The similarities were maybe not as strong as she'd made them out to be. But the inexplicable smiting down of the residents, the locations where they fell...

'All the deaths are like my drawings. You said it yourself. Dave in the disabled toilet... Even though it was Fiona who died there in the end.'

'Not the floatation tank? Huh.'

Evie seethed. 'You used me. Used my drawings to make it look like I did this.'

'No, no. You have it all wrong. Yes, I used your drawings and our chats for inspiration. Where else was I going to get ideas? But nobody is going to think it was you. Nobody is going to put the same two and two together that you did.'

Hot tears streamed down Evie's cheeks. 'They will, they will. My notebook is missing. I worried the killer would use it against me, point the police to me. I was scared. My fingerprints are on everything. I had to tell them. I told everyone the deaths were like my drawings, so they would believe it wasn't me.'

'Ah.'

On seeing Mrs M chew her lip, Evie sank into a puddle, hands over her face. Giant sobs hiccoughed through her. 'Why did you frame me? I thought we were friends.'

Mrs M crouched down beside her and gently stroked her arm. 'It's going to be all right, Evie. Trust me. I didn't frame you, silly girl. I framed Alan.'

CHAPTER SEVENTY-THREE
Evie

Evie shuddered as Mrs M's treasonous hand slithered down her back and elbowed her away. 'Get off me.' She crawled to nearer the door, eyed the handle, hesitating. The police had told her to stay put. It seemed crazy now. She should run, take the lift, meet the police downstairs, tell them everything. But something kept her here: the bombshell her friend—former friend?—had dropped.

'Alan? Alan, Alan?' Evie asked. She gazed blankly ahead of her, sifting through her memories, her strains of thought back into the order they'd been, returning to that spooky sense of knowing, despite all other signs. 'I thought it was him. Many times. He had access to the system, access to the building, access to the toiletries... Everything pointed to him...'

Mrs M's chests swelled with a sickening air of pride. 'That was deliberate. I made sure he was the one responsible for all the poisoned items in the room. That he'd be on call during the night, when I slipped in and put them all in place—wearing gloves, of course.'

'But I didn't wear gloves,' Evie said, holding her ten guilty fingers up. 'I touched everything. I'm the one who arranges the toiletry samples, the drinks, replaces the air freshener, hands over towels and ear plugs...' Mrs M nodded almost imperceptibly in time with Evie's list. '...puts out the tampons.'

'Tampons?' she asked, eyes wide.

'There was a box on my chair when I came in. I reckoned Alan had listened to you. You'd said you were going to see him, would add it to the list to discuss. And when there was one missing and Beatrice had collapsed, I thought that's what killed her.' Evie gave a light shake of the head. 'But we realised it must've been the shampoo.'

'You seem to have figured out a lot of things. Brava. Though heavens, Evie... a poisoned tampon? What do you take me for?' When Evie's mouth dropped open, Mrs M gave an understanding nod. 'Okay, don't answer that. I'd hoped it would take the police longer to figure all the causes out. Who else knows?'

A forceful chill rattled Evie. 'There's hardly anyone left.' She slowly rose, her back still against the wall, eyeing the walking stick that was within reach.

Mrs M paced, wringing her hands, deep in thought. 'Right. Only Dave and Suki, am I right?'

'Yes.'

'Good.'

The little of what remained in Evie's stomach curdled. Good? That four people had died? 'You're a monster.'

'Hey, my priority in this moment is helping *you*,' Mrs M scolded. She tapped her lips with two fingers. 'You didn't guess Stephen, did you? No, I expect no one will ever figure out how he died. But we might need to help the police along with that to get you off the hook.'

Evie blurted out, 'How did he die?' and immediately felt awful and dirty and morbid for letting her curiosity get the better of her.

'I accepted his delivery, as I returned from a walk. It was new athletic gear, and I got the idea. I put a few drops of poison on the branded label inside his shorts, let it sink into the fabric and covered it with a thin film that dissolves when wet. You always said how sweaty he was…it was only a matter of time.' She raised her eyebrows and paused. Waiting for what? Evie's congratulations? When none came, her cheeks sunk. 'Oh lassie, don't look at me that way. You're the one with the rich imagination. Look how you inspired me.'

Evie pushed her chin out. 'I have nothing to do with this.'

'Well, yes, that was my point,' Mrs M said, mouth pinched. 'I brought the box to the meeting and waited to see if I needed to activate my plan. Turns out I did. I pretended I lost sight of Stephen when people were leaving and asked Alan to bring it down to his apartment. So, you see? With a little hint about shorts, it'll all point to Alan. And you're fine.'

An angry walrus of a scoff escaped Evie. She clutched at her hair and shouted, 'Oh my God, I'm a million miles from fine. You're insane. How could you think I'd be okay just because I'm not the prime suspect in a homicidal rampage?' Her pulse thumped in her ears. She was near breathless with disbelief. 'Aside from the fact that it was me—me—who brought the box to Stephen. And so I am still very much in the frame, thank you bloody kindly. I've spent half a day locked up in a room with people dropping dead around me. Trying to save them, touching them with my lips. Not knowing if I'd be next.' Tears welled in her eyes as she relived her powerlessness, her failure. 'And you're all "it's okay, they'll think it's Alan and we'll move on". I mean, Christ. What the hell have you got against Alan? And if you hate him that much, surely—surely—there would've been a better way to punish him? One that didn't involve murdering innocent residents. Maybe kill *him*? There's an idea.'

Mrs M approached, her hand outstretched, but as Evie shot daggers at her, she brought it back in. She sighed deeply and rested the rejected arm on the side cabinet, her charm bracelet tinkling against the glass top. Her eyes flicked to the walking stick across the door, making Evie tense up and grab it.

Mrs M held her hands up in defence. 'Listen. I'm sorry. I truly am. You weren't supposed to be here. It's your birthday.'

'I know it's my sodding birthday,' Evie hissed, clutching the stick firmly. But Mrs M was staying put. Calm. Almost casually so, ankles crossed and leaning on the cabinet, the only thing missing from this cocktail-party stance was a bloody Martini. How could she be calm? What kind of freak was she?

'And this hasn't got anything to do with Alan. I merely needed a scapegoat. Who better to frame than a disgusting man who got away with rape?' Her curls fanned her shoulders as she shuddered, her stare darkening. 'He had it coming. He had to have *something* coming. Poor Tessa will never recover.'

Evie held the walking stick to her chest, clutching onto it for dear life, this buoy that would keep her from drifting deeper into this ocean of crazy. 'Then why?'

On Mrs M's face, the bud of a smirk. 'It's funny. Suki was very close. It is related to the building, but nothing to do with the view.' She turned and walked to the tall window on the garden side, beckoning Evie with a wave. 'Come.'

'No.' Evie's thigh muscled tensed with a mind of their own. Now. Now was the time to leg it.

'Suit yourself,' Mrs M said, looking out the window and down. 'I couldn't allow people to dig up the tree.'

Like the sunbeam that pierced through the clouds outside, a clear, bright vision reached Evie. The bench. A sudden chill expanded in her core. 'You killed all these people for your dog?'

Mrs M sniffed. She stepped back, and wiped the condensation from her cheek, eyes downcast.

'Are you serious?' Evie said. 'What? Is Bobby buried by the tree? You planned all this—all these murders—so that nobody would disrupt your dog's grave?'

She'd heard enough and grabbed the doorknob, still facing Mrs M for fear of turning her back to an obvious lunatic, poised to slip around the door in an instant. Escape would be easy. Mrs M was way over there, and slow.

'Bobby isn't a dog.'

CHAPTER SEVENTY-FOUR

Evie

Evie's hand slipped off the brass knob from surprise. She sloped sideways, on course to bang her shoulder on the nearby shelf. She steadied rapidly, the silver trinkets saved from a fall.

One caught her eye: the square box that had intrigued her so, her gut telling her all along there was more to the story. The engraved box Mrs M would only speak of venomously. *Robert and Marjorie forever.*

Her heart palpitations were so strong, Evie wasn't even sure Mrs M heard her when she said, 'Your husband? Bobby is Robert?'

Mrs M nodded solemnly.

'What did you do?' It came out a whisper, as if Evie's voice didn't want anything more shaken loose, as if the usual decibels would make it seem all too real. The harrowing truth spoken. Mrs M had killed before.

'You have to understand, Evie. He was abusive. Not only to me... I had to protect Anna. She was still small.' Mrs M hugged herself, a liquid shine in her eye. She ran her hand over the fabric of an armchair. 'I bought an apartment when I left him, in the stone mid-rise at the rear of the courtyard, over there.' She pointed. 'It was with my own money, made with my own business. I was terribly proud. It looks ancient compared to the modern ones that have sprung up around it, but it's not really. At the time, it hadn't even been completed.' She smiled ruefully. 'I moved in as soon as it was legally permissible, but the place was still in many ways a construction site. One night he came looking for us. Had seen an article about me that stupidly said where I lived.' She winced. 'I should've never let him in.'

'What happened?'

Picking imaginary fluff off the armchair, Mrs M inhaled. 'He wanted money. I was already successful, whereas he was drifting all across the country, working odd jobs. When I refused, he became violent. I begged him to stop, to at least be quiet. Anna was in her bedroom.' She looked Evie square on. 'But he was very strong. In the end, I did what any mother would.'

A bloom of compassionate warmth travelled along Evie's limbs. Imagine the despair of the situation. Thinking you were free only to be caught in another's evil clutch. Nowhere to go. You'd lash out, wouldn't you? You'd hide the body. Of course you would. But as Evie's defences began to melt, an icy sensation took hold, Mrs M's actions understandable, perhaps even acceptable, only up to a sickening point. 'Why did you have a plaque made for the bench?'

'When they started work on Platinum Peak, I needed a reason for them to leave that spot in what was thankfully remaining a garden alone,' Mrs M said. 'I ordered a tree that I insisted had to go in the middle, making up a sob story about my beloved dead doggie and how I wanted to honour him. I bought the expensive penthouse practically sight unseen and became their anchor resident, so the developers were more than happy to oblige.' She laughed mirthlessly and shook her head. 'Would you believe they're the ones who put the bench there, with the plaque. As a gift.'

'Oh, no.'

'Indeed. But actually, it's been good, in a way. Because I sit there and tell him all the good things that happen to me, and to Anna. How well we've done without him. What do they say? Living well is the best revenge.'

Evie shocked herself by laughing along. Her chest tightened, shame and anger vying for space. Mrs M had deftly drawn her into her story, lured Evie to her side, tugged at her emotions. And she almost fell for it. None of this forgave what she'd done then—and definitely not today.

Where was the police? Why hadn't they rung the bell yet? She patted the door, trying to find the knob again, keeping her eye on Mrs M with a placating smile on her face. Let her think she'd argued her side while Evie fumbled behind her for escape.

'Where are you going?' Mrs M's stern voice pierced Evie like an icicle. 'We have to get our story straight before the police arrive.'

Evie tried to disguise her tremble as she said, 'Our story? There is no *our* story. You can't expect me to cover for you when you've killed four people today.'

She expected her to appeal to their friendship, which, truthfully, was what had kept Evie in the flat thus far. A disconcerting sense of loyalty mixed with a pathetic need to know, to understand. She braced for the pleas to keep quiet to protect Anna—who didn't deserve to be told her mother was a murderer—in favour of letting the blame fall on Alan, who admittedly did deserve to be punished.

But Mrs M deployed none of that. Instead, her tone dripped with the poison she'd used on others. 'Wasn't that you?'

Evie's blood ran cold. 'What?'

Mrs M advanced, striding with disturbing confidence. Evie froze, her back to the door, peeking left and right into the corridors that would not bring her to safety any more than jumping out the windows. They didn't open.

'Well, there's nothing to tie me to any of this,' she said. 'But you, you were in the room when they died. You told everyone about your notebook, in which you sketched out multiple gruesome murders of exactly these people ... and your fingerprints are on all the poisoned items. If an officer were to piece that together, somehow—either through pure skill or perhaps with a little help—they'd reach the right conclusion. I'd be shocked, of course, unable to believe that such a nice girl would do these things. Then again, she's a bit of an oddball, you know. Look at those creepy tattoos.'

'You wouldn't...?'

She arched an eyebrow. 'Want to find out?'

Acid rose in Evie's throat. She sucked in cold air to douse the burn, to bide her time and not take the bait. 'It would never stick... I'd... I'd send them straight back to you, to the garden.'

'You're right, it might stick better when they discover your lovely friend Martina was behind the hack of the building's systems and app.'

The acid burned anew, a thick, blazing extra dollop of betrayal. 'Martina? Why would she do that?'

'Don't you know? She performs coding jobs for people on the dark web to earn extra cash. She showed me when she was here. Fascinating. My guess is she won't have a clue it's this building some random stranger paid her a handsome sum to reprogramme. She doesn't seem to ask many questions. It would be most unfortunate if there was an investigation into her activities...' Mrs M wrung her hands, a sly satisfied smirk on her face. 'I didn't realise her being your friend would come in this handy.'

'She's not my friend.' It came out so quickly, Evie didn't even fully consider it. But it was out. Did she mean it? A snapshot of Martina and Kaif laughing in the pub flashed through her mind, stirring the simmering jealousy she'd felt when she first walked in, that she always felt. Martina had given her the Uzumaki book, beautifully gift-wrapped, such joy on her face... Could it all be an act? A way to ingratiate herself with Kaif and steal him away?

'I don't think that's how she feels.'

Evie gave as best a faux shrug as she could, bristling with curiosity underneath. But none of that mattered. She was in danger, had to focus on saving herself. *Numero uno*, as Suki had said. She couldn't let Mrs M chip away at her resolve. 'Whatever.'

'You're right. Screw her,' Mrs M said, throwing her hands in the air. 'Serves her right for doing illegal things, right? Why would you care if she gets hurt? No, not to her...'

A creeping unease engulfed Evie. Where was this headed? Her hand was on the knob, the door was ajar, the hallway a skip away and yet, and yet, she couldn't run... Who would get hurt?

'The police might also be very interested in Kaif's drug dealing.'

'It's not dealing. He only does that for you. You told us you were ill.'

Mrs M pulled up her shoulders. 'I'm dying soon. What do I care if I get caught with some weed? But Kaif. This wouldn't look good on his CV.'

That threat punched the air right out of Evie. Her chest heaved; eyes popped. Who was this person? She heard Mrs M's charm bracelet rattle as she fixed her hair. Many carats of expensive gems ensconced in gold. The fruits of a successful businesswoman who knew how to strike a bargain.

A woman who'd stop at nothing to protect the one she loved... The same way Evie now had to.

Evie leaned against the door, battered by waves of nausea. How could she live with herself, letting Mrs M get away with it? Framing an innocent—no, strike that. Alan could rot in hell.

She breathed in, lengthened her spine, held her head high. 'Fine. It was Alan.'

'Wise move.'

White heat of resentment flushed her skin. But she refused to feel bad because you know what? She did what she had to do to protect herself, and Kaif, and even Martina, though that could hardly be considered a driving factor. She dared anyone to do differently.

Mrs M might get off scot-free and live happily ever after, but there was some consolation in knowing that wouldn't be for long.

Still, watching Mrs M leisurely pick up her handbag in preparation for leaving confirmed to Evie just what a bum end of the deal she'd been left with. What a shit negotiator she was.

The buzzer rang.

Evie's gaze met Mrs M's narrowed eyes. '*Go on*,' they seemed to say.

Deflated and resigned, Evie opened the door. But as she caught a glimpse of a scarlet dress on a Vettriano print along the corridor, she was reminded of Suki's red soles, of the night she helped her release her expensive stiletto while Suki shredded someone to pieces on the phone. No way Suki would be leaving empty-handed.

Evie pushed the door to a close. 'Actually, Marjorie. Before I agree to do this. There is one thing I'll need from you.'

CHAPTER SEVENTY-FIVE

Evie

Mrs M conceded instantly. So quickly that Evie cursed herself for not asking for more. But she didn't want more blood on her hands. It was bad enough as it was, having to keep a secret that she knew would eat at her forever.

As they stepped out into the corridor, Evie turned left, to the stars of the fire escape.

'This way,' Mrs M said.

'But the doors—'

'Not anymore. When Kaif called and told me you were in there, I immediately signalled to Martina to turn everything on again. Kaif's on his way.'

At this piece of news, Evie's heart skipped. She fidgeted with the seam of her top the whole interminably slow walk to the lift and waiting for it to arrive. Time could not move fast enough, as could the lift—which seemed to have decided to need to be many other places before finally hitting the top floor.

Inside, she stood behind Mrs M, intent on not giving the woman's smug victory an audience, intent on keeping some level of threat going by standing slightly too close to her back, only the smell of Dior and moth balls between them.

The lift pinged and opened onto a bustling scene, uniformed officers milling, the white checks of their caps forming a flashing line like the lights in a tunnel. Mrs M extended her walking stick to part the crowd. They hardly looked up, engrossed in their shoulder-worn radios.

The doors to the gym were open. From the landing, you could not yet see the bodies. Evie's knees wobbled. For a minute, she counted her breaths and stood motionless, forcing the flow of people to go round, like a boulder in a river. Other than a mess on her desk, the gym looked normal. If she stayed there, she could pretend none of this ever happened.

A young man of Evie's age registered their presence. 'This area is off limits, I'm afraid,' he said with a friendly scrunch of his freckled nose. No way had he seen inside the gym, with such an unaffected air.

It seemed none of the officers were breaching the threshold to the green mat, either. Would Dave still be there?

'This young lady is the gym receptionist,' Mrs M said in a tone that made it clear she wasn't used to being fobbed off. 'She's the one who escaped the carnage and called you.'

'Oh. Wait a minute. Please stay here,' the chap said and hopped over to what Evie assumed was a superior: a woman in a dark blue trouser suit, her brown hair in a low bun. He tapped her cautiously on the shoulder and retracted his finger like a startled tortoise when she turned, looking annoyed.

He leaned in and whispered in her ear. Her eyes widened and focused on Evie so hard she might as well have directed a red laser at her chest.

Evie caught a glimpse of a paramedic's green trousers to the right of the big doors that she noticed, with a flicker of irrational possessiveness, they'd propped open with her chair.

The paramedic would be closest to where Charles lay. Much too late to be of any use. How many ambulances would they have sent? How many people were in there? Weren't they worried about contaminating the place?

The woman with the bun strode towards her, emanating the kind of authority that reassured Evie they knew what they were doing. It was in hand... and Evie could wash hers. No more would she be expected to save the day—not that she'd managed that very well. She could state her peace and leave. Never to return.

'My name is Detective Inspector Ansford.' She said, in an unexpected English accent. 'I understand you're one of the victims.' That last word making Evie flinch. 'And you are?' Ansford asked Mrs M.

'Marjorie Macaulay. I live upstairs. Evie came to me when she escaped. Told me what happened.'

'Am I correct in saying you don't have any first-hand experience of what went on in there?' the DI said to Mrs M.

'No, but I—'

Evie gasped at DI's audacious dismissal of the old woman with nothing more than the shake of the head and a finger pointing to the lift.

Mrs M's nails dug into Evie's upper arm as she gave it a hard squeeze. A silent warning contrasting with her loud, offended tut as she left.

Her dramatic exit became all the more uncomfortable by the delay between her pressing the button and the metal doors sliding open.

Evie shifted to block her from sight, a weight lifting from her shoulders as she did.

The DI clicked her pen and flipped to a new page in her spiral-bound jotter. Rapid, efficient movements. 'What's your name?'

Evie's stomach flipped as she heard Kaif's voice shout, 'Mrs M.' She watched him step out, a stupefied expression on his face as he took in the crowd.

'I'm Evie Stirling. I'm the receptionist.' Evie replied, with one eye on Kaif. 'Kaif, here,' Evie shouted. She came back to the DI. 'I'm sorry. This is my boyfriend. Please let him stay.'

Ansford frowned and scanned her, oozing the unsettling suspicion of airport security with a glove on.

Kaif snaked his way to Evie and swallowed her up in a giant hug, a gift-wrapped parcel squeezed flat against her shoulder. 'What the hell is going on? Are you all right?'

He released her, slipped the gift between his knees, and held Evie by her shoulders at arms' length for a proper inspection.

'Four people died,' Evie said.

'Holy shit.' He dropped his arms, one hand headed for his pocket. 'I have to call Martina.'

All the warm comfort Evie'd felt dissipated from her in a steamy rage. Why would he think of her at this moment? 'Don't let me get in the way,' Evie said with a giant dose of snark, feeling slightly less powerful when she caught Ansford's sour gaze.

Kaif stepped towards her, dropping the gift on the floor. 'No, it's not like that. I have to tell her to cancel your surprise party.'

One hundred powdery butterfly wings fluttered in Evie's belly. 'You planned a party for me?'

The DI's testy tone put the lid firmly back on the bell jar. 'Look I hate to interrupt the reunion, but in case you missed it, this is a murder scene and I have an investigation to run.' She cocked her head in the direction of the stairs leading up, wordlessly instructing Evie to meet her there.

Evie sensed a void at her side as she began to walk. Kaif stayed behind. She watched him picking up the gift, the blue bow unravelled. It must have got trampled.

Her chest tightened at the sight of him, crestfallen as he tried to repair the torn paper. As she observed his efforts, her stomach fell. Through a ridged, white triangle where the panels of paper no longer met, she saw the unmistakable lines of one of the drawings from her notebook.

'Miss Stirling. I appreciate you will be in shock after to-day's events. I'm quite happy to let you go home with your boyfriend to recover...'

The snap of her closing her jotter made Evie jump.

'Huh?' Evie hadn't been able to take her eyes off the drawing—definitely hers. Her skin itched from uncapped nerve endings.

'Evie. Do you need a paramedic to look you over?' Ansford asked.

'What? No. I'm fine. I'm just...' Just what? Could she admit to being comprehensively confused? To fearing everything she knew to be true wasn't? Why had Kaif called Mrs M? Why did he have her drawings?

The DI's pruned expression softened to plum. 'Listen. Come to the station tomorrow. We'll take your statement. But can I ask you one thing?'

'Uhuh.'

'Do you have any idea who killed all these people?'

'No,' Evie lied.

And if pressed, she would lie again.

EPILOGUE

Standing by the window, Evie cupped her warm mug and basked in the very welcome spring sunlight. She watched people pass by, letting her mind wander after two hours' concentrated work.

It was easy to tell the tourists from the locals. Having walked an interminable stretch of roadworks since the last bus stop, their shoulders would be slumped, arm nearly screwed off from the rattling of their rolling luggage, faces sporting a disillusioned '*is this it?*' expression as the tiny stretch of historical buildings came into view along a curve of water.

The rest of Leith's old harbour area was merely a collection of modern high-rises, not snazzy enough to be a New-York-style attraction, but too upmarket to be affordable to the likes of her. Though all that could change after today.

A couple with young children walked by, the mother herding her offspring to safety as hipsters on electric scooters whizzed by. At least she'd get the satisfaction of an excellent, though overpriced, artisanal coffee at one of the innumerable cafés in the area. One of them belonged to Tessa. It's where Evie chose to get hers, out of an odd sense of sisterhood she couldn't quite explain. Victims of Platinum Peak.

'Hey, Evie?' Rona called from the white wooden doorway leading to the main shop. 'I have a lady on the line about her husband who's died. Sixty-eight. Retired academic. Service is in two weeks. Can you fit one more in or are you full up?'

She put her mug down on the windowsill, disrupting the shadow created by the logo etched on the glass. A top hat surrounded by a lily garland.

Evie fished her mobile phone from her pocket. 'Let me check,' she said, swiping her screen to call up her calendar. 'Only if she can meet this Sunday to tell me about his life. And she has to have notes ready.'

'No worries. I'll get that sorted.' Rona slipped to her desk silently, a skill befitting the atmosphere the funeral director liked to maintain.

Evie took a sip of her tea. It was way too strong, but she didn't have the heart to tell Rona. Evie was the last person who'd want to be a cow to the receptionist.

She consulted her diary some more. In her experience, she needed at least five hours to gather enough interesting titbits to feed her artwork. She would have to sacrifice the planned shopping trip. Martina would be disappointed. She'd been sending her pictures of dresses all week on WhatsApp.

The tea was truly undrinkable today and, having also lost its warmth, it served no further purpose. She chucked it in the flowerpot and returned to work.

This project hadn't needed as much background from the family. She'd heard the stories first hand. She picked up a paintbrush and dipped it into the green.

As she twisted the tip of the brush to make little clumps of leaves on the tree, her phone pinged. She wiped the brush on her apron and checked.

A text from Suki.

On my way - little late

Evie smiled as she imagined Suki walking with the highly raised knees of a tiptoeing mime to prevent her stilettos sticking between the cobblestones on her way here.

Their first meeting—after—had been as awkward as the word itself. Exceptionally so. Evie nearly cancelled a few times in the run up, but she didn't know who else to turn to, Suki being the only financier she'd ever met.

She remembered walking the plush yellow carpet of Madainn Finance, sensing all suited-and-booted eyes on her as a friendly Aussie chap directed her to Suki's office.

'So, Evie, we meet again,' she said from her large leather chair, stroking an imaginary cat. Then she cackled and rose with extended hand, promptly dispersing the panic that had struck Evie as she recognised the Bond reference for what it was: the greeting of an arch enemy.

Suki's forgiveness was swift in coming. 'I was flattered, in a way, you thought I'd masterminded it all and had the strength to keep the pretence going all day.'

They settled into business at the oversized oak table. Evie explained her vision and strategy. She shared her progress to date, which Suki quickly pointed out represented 0.0013% of the nation's creative industries. A stunning display of mental arithmetic, until Evie double checked with a calculator when she was writing her business plan. Pure bluff. It merely confirmed why Evie wanted her on side.

'It's awesome. The venture capitalists won't ever have seen anything like this before,' Suki said, before telling Evie about the ways of the 'vulture capitalists' and the three golden rules in dealing with them.

Texting not to worry, Evie smiled at the memory. It seemed Suki had multiple sets of golden rules. One for every occasion.

It had been the first golden rules, imparted when locked in, that got Evie her start. Suki had gone on about the power of leverage and, in that awful moment when Evie had given into Mrs M's extortion, Evie realised she hadn't used hers: the location of the husband's body.

Mrs M's eyes had narrowed when Evie said she wanted one more thing before they were to go downstairs. 'What is it? Money?'

Typical of the rich to think cold hard cash solved everything.

Evie dipped a thicker brush into the dark brown and traced three horizontal lines one over the other, a thin slit in between. Fine hairs on the brush sprung sideways, indicating it needed replacing. And these were expensive.

Money would have been nice, but Evie would never take it from Mrs M. She was complicit enough, having kept her silence—something she'd never shared with anyone and still tried to banish from her mind. But sometimes, while slipping into slumber at night, or hearing about the investigation on the radio, she'd find herself propelled back in that instant, her stomach a heaving, corrosive mass of conflict.

No, no money exchanged hands. All she'd asked for was an introduction to the director of the funeral business. She alone negotiated the partnership. She alone obtained a start-up grant from the city. And now that trade was booming, Suki would help her expand and hire new artists across the UK.

New colours were needed. Dark brown mixed with a hint of mossy green was perfect for the tree trunk. She stepped back and looked at the relative dimensions on the cream background. The whole was coming together nicely, a pleasantly distributed collection of a life's meaningful vignettes.

She searched for a scrap of paper. This needed writing down. It would make a great statement for the funding presentation. Suki'd said it would be a tough sell and to describe it in a positive light. Thankfully, she had a full order book, a good 'proof of market.' Yet another new term to master.

'*We'll make a mogul out of you yet*,' Suki had teased when Evie hadn't the first clue what a balance sheet was.

To Evie, this proposition was a no-brainer. A similar idea had come to her last year, but it had taken being surrounded by dead bodies—for an eternity—for it to percolate to the surface in its current form.

If millions of people around the world immersed themselves in graphic stories about other characters, why wouldn't they want them about themselves? Difference being, of course, they were no longer here to read them. It was for the benefit of their family and friends.

She noticed an imbalance in the depiction of the all-important tree and went to work on fixing the leaves. Not much more to go.

With every order, she got faster. This one took only two days. Not bad if you considered that each coffin was decorated from head to toe, plus all sides, with—what was it again?—*a collection of a life's meaningful vignettes*. Or, as listed less elegantly on her website: up to thirty drawings of important moments or personal items with which to remember your loved one.

She cocked her head and admired her work. Definitely nicer than a boring wooden casket, no matter how much brass you tacked onto it. The scene with the ships, the little boy and his penny was her favourite. She'd captured his joy perfectly.

Many hours of experimenting had been required to change her natural dark style to something lighter, more loving-memory-inducing. Often, after work, she'd have to exorcise the sickly sweetness of it all by setting her pencils to work on some truly gruesome sketches. These were kept under lock and key nowadays. For her eyes only.

Her chest tightened. Poor Kaif. His birthday gift to her had been relegated to safe storage, too.

She was reminded of the rocking of the taxi driving them home that day, his comforting arm around her. Torn parcel by his side. Her nerves had prickled. It wasn't really something you did, was it? Ask for your present when people had died in front of you mere minutes ago. But she had a burning need to get answers.

'Is it a book?' she'd asked sheepishly.

'Huh?' She snuggled into him. He squeezed her in return. 'Oh, this. Well, yes. But... er...' A suitable hesitation in the face of likely tastelessness. He winced as he handed it over, as if the parcel were a ticking bomb. 'Happy birthday?'

It was heavy, corners sturdy. A hardback. She could still hear the sharp tearing sound as she pulled at the golden paper to reveal a proper book cover that made her head spin. *Illustrations from the awesome mind of Evie Stirling.*

'You took my notebook?'

His face crumpled. 'Yes. Was that bad? I'm sorry. I took it from you bag last night so that I could have your best drawings scanned and hard bound at the printers today. Martina made the cover. Oh God. I'm sorry. I'm awful at gifts...'

'No, no you're not.' she pecked him on the cheek. 'I love it. It's very thoughtful. I was just worried.' More worried than she'd ever let on.

That was the comforting moment she fast forwarded to, whenever her trauma caught up with her, whenever harrowing flashes of that day came out to torture her. It was the moment she'd made peace with her decision to save herself, save Kaif, save Martina. A semblance of peace, anyway, with all the fluidity of a Middle Eastern accord.

The worry, however, ended up been a permanent presence slithering under her skin for weeks. The police asked to see her drawings, probably tipped off by Dave, sharing her theory of similarity. It made sense for it to be him, cooperating fully, no doubt wanting to earn brownie points with the police force. Could come in handy as the owner of a bouncer agency. Or part-owner. Suki recently mentioned she'd completed his merger, and he was going on an extended holiday. To where, he didn't say, other than there would be no sand.

Evie patted her pocket, hearing the reassuring jangle of her keys, including the one for the drawer where she placed her notebook when the investigation lost interest in it, and, by extension, her.

Though Evie had never pointed the finger at Alan—that was a step too far—they'd learned enough about him to make him a strong suspect. They also discovered a small vial of incredibly potent poison in his office. A small detail of planning Mrs M omitted to mention when she'd made it sound as if Evie would for sure go down for the murders.

Even with the poison in his office, the police couldn't make the murder charges stick. Instead of being at home, on call, where Mrs M had presumably made sure he'd be, he'd gone off to the casino with a bunch of pals. The papers had a field day reporting how the CCTV gave him an alibi for the period the one in the gym had gone blank. The real explosive headline came when they nailed him for child pornography instead. Hundreds of images on his PC. While Evie would never be certain they were his, and not planted there like the poison, it gave her a conscience a good cleansing.

On the bus here she'd seen the Selkie's Laird was still closed. Nobody had picked up the reins at the private club since Fiona died. Too tainted, given the police seemed to have latched onto the idea Fiona committed a multi-murder-suicide. It probably helped them work reduce their bulging case load. There was hee-haw they could do to verify their theory or prosecute her now.

Evie stepped to the tail end of the coffin. The vial was there, subtly placed between a colourful range of cleaning products to denote Mrs M's hygiene services.

Anna had insisted all her mother's companies be represented, having been proud of each of them. The other thing Anna had insisted on, Evie refused: payment. She hadn't taken money then, nor would she now. Anna had thanked her profusely for what she'd considered a parting gift to her family. If only she knew what Evie's true gift to her had been.

'Hey hey, tycoon, are you ready?' Suki tapped a drumroll on her briefcase as she walked into the room. 'Lovely day to raise some cash.' Her eyes grew wide as she took in Mrs M's coffin. 'Oh wow. You're almost finished. Will you go to the funeral?'

Evie shook her head. She'd never explained why they were no longer friends, though Suki was perceptive enough to notice. *'Ha. Friends, schmends.'* Suki'd shrugged.

'I've got the presentation on my laptop and the handouts. What else do we need?' Evie asked. She took off her apron and pulled out a baby wipe with which to clean her hands. She picked up her engagement ring and slid it on. It still felt weird. She reckoned it would be a few years before she'd have that telltale permanent groove at the base of her finger that married people get. She ran her thumb along the curvature of the platinum dragon's tail and the bumps of its diamond eyes. Kaif had chosen well.

Suki examined the doodles. 'What a life, eh?' A moment later, she pointed at a tableau of a group of men in patterned jumpers sitting around a table with Mrs M, various bottles of booze on their side. 'What's this little thing on the side of the table leg?'

'That's Olle, the Swedish skiing mouse.'

'Each to their own,' Suki said, pulling a face. She came round to Evie's side and checked out the scene she'd been working on. 'Ha. Is that her dog, Bobby? He looks like Pebbles. What a coincidence.'

'Right?' Evie said, with an unstoppable curl of the lip.

'I still can't believe Dave took Pebbles in when no one else would have him,' Suki said.

As she headed to the door, Evie stayed behind. 'Wait a second, I forgot something.'

'I'll wait outside. See if there are any nice-looking women in this forsaken part of town.'

Evie chuckled. She picked up a brush and swirled it in a blob of silvery grey. The setting with the tree, the bench and dog looked incomplete, and she'd figured out why.

It was intended as an illustration of Mrs M's darkest side, a side known only to Evie that she couldn't disregard. A secret Mrs M would now take to the grave, and Evie to hers.

But having had to sprinkle positivity on so many designs, it had come out too forgiving. And she wasn't ready for that. Far from it.

With an assured, final stroke, she painted a spade leaned against the tree.

Did you like this?

Check out Heleen's other books

ACKNOWLEDGEMENTS

My hatred of all things exercise—well known to friends and family—appears to have slipped into my creative consciousness unintentionally: Grace, the main character of 'In Servitude' is a personal trainer (I give her a hard time); there's a distressing scene in the gym in 'Stay Mad, Sweetheart'; only Radha of 'What I Hid From You' appears to have escaped the gym curse (because she's juggling too much already!). And now this.

I'm grateful to editor Sara Cox for brainstorming solutions to knotty plot problems, for her strict challenge and unwavering loyalty. I value my agent Annette Crossland for her efforts in championing me in this over-saturated market.

Thank you to my generous beta readers for their enthusiasm and insights—Nic P, Ally O'C, Tania A-M, Sharon B. Also to Chris S for location research during lockdown, and to my sister Martijn for her eagle-eyed finding of mistakes.

Writing is a very solitary activity, and being alone is not really my bag. So I'm extremely happy that I have found the most amazing author friends who keep me going and help celebrate my achievements. A loving shout out to Rob Parker, Awais Khan, Claire Duffy and Sarah Moorhead, only ever one WhatsApp away.

The bloggers, librarians and readers who have read, reviewed and shouted about my books are the best, as are the lovelies that have given little old me a platform: Jacky Collins, Vic Watson and Simon Bewick. I hope I'll continue to deserve your support.

Lastly, to the first reader of every manuscript, my husband Grant, for making me feel like I'm the most talented woman in the world.

ABOUT THE AUTHOR

Heleen Kist is a Dutch, formerly globetrotting career woman who fell in love with a Scotsman and his country, and now writes about its (sometimes scary) people from her garden office in Glasgow. 'Killer Bodies' is her fourth suspense novel, inspired by her hatred of exercise.

She was chosen as an up-and-coming new author at Bloody Scotland 2018. Her previous titles have been finalists in a number of awards, and she longs to one day be the bride.

Heleen hopes you enjoy her writing and would love to hear from you on twitter (@hkist), Faceboook (@heleenkistauthor) or Goodreads. You can also sign up to her newsletter on www.heleenkist.com.